DAUNTLESS

DAUNTLESS

ELISA A. BONNIN

SWOON READS
NEW YORK

A Swoon Reads Book
An imprint of Feiwel and Friends and Macmillan Publishing Group, LLC
120 Broadway, New York, NY 10271 • fiercereads.com
Copyright © 2022 by Elisa A. Bonnin. All rights reserved.

Our books may be purchased in bulk for promotional, educational, or business
use. Please contact your local bookseller or the Macmillan Corporate and
Premium Sales Department at (800) 221-7945 ext. 5442 or by email at
MacmillanSpecialMarkets@macmillan.com.

Library of Congress Cataloging-in-Publication Data is available.

First edition, 2022

Book design by Mallory Grigg
Feiwel and Friends logo designed by Filomena Tuosto
Printed in the United States of America
ISBN 978-1-250-79561-8 (hardcover)

10 9 8 7 6 5 4 3 2 1

To Isa. Be dauntless.

CHAPTER 1

❦

The valiant who met Seri at the entrance to the command hall was a woman. She was on the short side, energetic, with close-cropped black hair. Her name was Raya, and her armor—heavy, dark-colored, and decorated with several menacing spikes—seemed entirely at odds with her cheerful personality. There was a mark on her face just below her right eye, the symbol for courage in the face of danger. She eyed Seri with no small amount of skepticism as Seri stammered out an explanation for why she was there.

"Yes," she said, when Seri finished. "Captain Turi said something like that in his reports. You're the new aide."

Seri nodded slowly. She clutched the wooden chit the captain had given her in one hand, feeling the edges press into the skin of her palm. She had no idea what she had done during the journey to make the captain think she was worthy of this role. All she'd done was keep an inventory of their supplies, and she had a feeling they'd only assigned her that task to keep her out of the way.

"Turi had good things to say about your work." Raya watched as Seri shifted uncomfortably on the platform outside the door, still dressed in the damp, mud-spattered clothes that had seen her through five days in the rainforest. "Come in. The commander's office is this way."

The headquarters was simple as far as buildings went, but

after five days in the wild, it seemed an unimaginable luxury. Seri's mind was spinning, trying to make sense of rooms and structure and not the chaotic tangle of trees, roots, and vines that made up the world below. She was sure she was staring and quickened her step, not wanting Raya to think she was dawdling. If Raya had noticed Seri's lapse of attention, she didn't show it, opening the door to a room at the end of a hall and stepping back to let Seri peer inside.

The room smelled strongly of ink and the oil the valor used to tend to their armor. Inside it, Seri could see a low writing desk with a well-worn cushion placed in front of it. A cot rested in the corner of the room under swathes of insect netting, neatly folded and put away.

Seeing Seri's gaze drawn to it, Raya spoke up.

"The commander's using the office as her quarters at the moment. We haven't gotten around to building the barracks yet, and the valor wouldn't hear of her sleeping outside. Don't worry, though. With as little time as she spends in here, you're not likely to bump heads."

"Um . . . ," Seri said. Her mouth was dry—she wondered if she should have stopped to get a drink of water before racing all the way up here. "What *exactly* am I supposed to do?"

"Turi didn't explain?"

Seri shook her head. "He said that Commander Eshai"—even saying the name out loud did not help any of this feel real—"that the commander needed a personal assistant. And he thought that I would be a good fit."

Raya frowned in thought, cupping her chin. "Hmm. Well, you're to help the commander keep herself organized and on schedule and help her with anything else she requires." She inclined her head toward the writing desk. "The commander should have a list of things that need doing somewhere in that mess."

"Where is she right now?"

"On patrol. She should return soon. I'll leave you to it, but I'll be outside if you need anything."

With a nod, she left, Seri lingering in the doorframe. Seri took a deep breath to steady herself before walking forward, feeling the gentle give and sway of new flooring beneath her feet. She dropped her pack and knelt beside the cushion, not wanting to dirty it with her traveling clothes. The desk was made of new wood, like everything in the settlement. She could still smell the resin and sap.

Less than a week ago, she had been a nobody in her home village, just another face in the crowd when Captain Turi and a few other valiants had come through. It was the last stop on their tour of the border villages, looking for volunteers willing to settle a new spreading tree. Now, she was sitting in front of Eshai Unbroken's desk. Eshai Unbroken, the youngest person in history to command an entire valor. A whole company of valiants, sworn to protect the People. The girl who had slain a legend.

Seri pinched herself, but when the world failed to dissolve, she realized she wasn't dreaming. Feeling oddly disrespectful, she reached out, sorting through the scraps of rough-pressed paper and the wooden chips the valor favored for their expeditions, before finally pulling out a string of small boards, each one with writing on them. They were tasks, as Raya had promised. A few looked simple enough—"Set up platforms for the settlers," "Name the settlement," "Arrange patrols." Others looked a little more complicated—"Found provisional govern-ment," for one. Another was simply labeled "Turi???" Some of them had been scratched through with what looked like the point of a knife, in a vicious way that suggested satisfaction. Many of them—most of them—looked untouched.

She was still sorting through them, letting unfinished tasks dangle from her fingers, when she heard someone clear her throat from the doorway. Seri startled and dropped the boards, letting them clatter onto the desktop.

A girl stood at the door. She was young, somewhere in her late teens, and taller than Raya. Seri wouldn't have immediately called her pretty, although she was striking in her own way. If Seri had seen her out on the street, she might have marked her for a valiant, but not for a hero. That was, of course, if Seri hadn't seen the pale, milky white of her armor, the marks that snaked their way up what was visible of her arms, marks of excellence and leadership and resourcefulness in battle that stood out sharply against her brown skin.

She wore her hair long, which was a vanity Seri wouldn't have expected. Black as night and straighter than Seri could ever hope to get hers. It fell to the small of her back, cutting through the white of her armor.

She realized she was staring and scrambled to her feet, thrusting her hands behind her. The valiant tilted her head to the side, unamused.

"So, you're the one Raya and Turi decided to foist on me. What was your name?"

"S-Seri, Commander."

The valiant sighed, stepping into the room. She loosened the ties on her gloves, slipping the armor off her hands. The name-mark on the back of her right hand read 'star.'

"There's no need to call me 'Commander.' You aren't part of my valor. I'm Eshai. But from the way you're acting, you've figured that much out already."

Seri nodded, her heart thudding. She hoped her nerves didn't show on her face. Eshai put her gloves down on the desk, flexing her fingers and gently rotating her right wrist. Seri wondered if something was bothering her. An injury?

Noticing her gaze, Eshai gave her a chagrined smile.

"Hurt it in a training session. Most of the valor fight well enough to keep me on my toes. I hope that doesn't disappoint you *too* much."

"N-Not at all." Seri looked away. "I didn't mean to stare."

Eshai sighed. "It's fine. If we're going to work together, you can stop being so skittish. I don't bite."

"Yes, Com—" She caught herself, her face warming. "Er, ma'am."

Eshai rolled her eyes, but the gesture was almost fond. She slid her gloves back on without looking at them. "Well, come on. I'll give you a tour of the settlement. If you're going to assist me, you should know what we're up against."

The settlement—Seri's new home—was in rough shape. The spaces where the settlers were supposed to make their homes were nothing more than naked platforms suspended among branches in the spreading tree, the bridges rickety, makeshift things that swayed alarmingly when Seri walked on them. Eshai didn't even notice, leading her across the bridges as if they walked on solid earth, but Seri held on to the rope railings with a death grip. The town hall, a large structure in the central square, had four walls and a roof but was otherwise bare on the inside except for a serviceable kitchen. For all the comforts they had, they might as well be camping out in the rainforest.

But the air was cleaner and cooler up here. And if the civilian architecture was roughshod, anything belonging to the valor was solid. The barracks hadn't been built yet, but a platform had been designated for the purpose, and there were tarps spread over it to keep off the rain. Although there weren't many buildings, there were ballistae, great huge bows that fired arrows as large as spears, mounted so that at least two of them could be trained on any enemy that approached the village at any time.

It was necessary, Eshai explained when Seri stopped to stare. They were in the borderlands, and while the innermost parts of the known world had mostly been cleared of any beast *too* dangerous, the same couldn't be said for this place. A lone beast wouldn't be too much of a challenge, but they tended to hunt in packs. In that case, winning a battle became a question of speed.

"You may think you understand beasts, but the beasts of the known world are tame compared to what's out here," Eshai said, her expression growing distant as she looked out at the endless expanse of green. "There are beasts here straight out of children's stories, beasts with power no one in the known world has ever seen. If you want to survive out here, you need to remember that."

Seri nodded, her stomach churning at the mention of strange beasts. She knew all too well how true that was.

Eshai looked at her, and might have been about to say something more, but a valiant who Seri didn't recognize leapt from one of the nearby branches with inhuman agility, landing on their platform. Seri stumbled, nearly falling over from the impact. Eshai barely moved, turning her head toward him.

"Commander," the valiant said, not sparing Seri a second glance. "Zani and I found something while on patrol. Something that we think you should see."

"Danger?" Eshai asked, one hand already reaching for the long spear strapped across her back.

"Not at the moment. It's just odd. And closer to the settlement than we'd like."

Eshai's fingers still hesitated over the shaft of her spear, but as Seri watched, she relaxed them, letting her hand fall back to her side. "Is it on the ground?"

"Yes, Commander."

"All right," Eshai said. "Lead the way." To Seri she added, "You might as well come along. This could be educational."

There was something in the way she said *educational*, something wry and sarcastic that had Seri's stomach twisting itself into knots all over again. But she nodded, trailing along behind Eshai as the valiant led them both away.

The thing in the woods was a carcass. Not a beast carcass— Seri wasn't sure she could have handled seeing that—but a monkey. It was curled around itself, its throat torn out. It looked like it had been there for a few days at least, and it stank. Seri coughed, turning her face away as she felt her gorge rise. Eshai spared her only a glance before walking toward the animal, her other two valiants close behind. They looked troubled, casting the trees around them a dark look. Seri didn't understand why they were so bothered by a dead animal, but their unease was catching. She knew valiants were used to fighting beasts on the ground, but she wasn't a valiant. Valiants had armor to protect them, armor that made them incredibly powerful in close combat. Seri had the clothes on her back and no weapon.

She stayed close to Eshai, keeping one hand over her nose and mouth.

Eshai used the shaft of her spear to turn the animal over, letting off a wave of noxious gas that made Seri's eyes water. The wound was infested with maggots. She looked away, unable to watch. The ground squelched as Eshai bent down.

"A natural predator?" Seri heard her ask.

One of the valiants, the one that had approached Eshai, shook his head. "Predator would've eaten it, Commander."

"Only a beast kills like this," the second valiant said. He was an older man, his black hair streaked through with gray. Seri assumed he must be Zani.

"Monkeys usually manage to get away," Eshai said. "Could this one have been slow? Or injured?"

Zani shook his head. "Blood on the branches. It was killed in the trees. And fell."

Eshai's gaze shifted from the creature to the trees, and with a sudden terrible certainty, Seri understood what the problem was. Beasts didn't climb. They couldn't. Shouldn't. That was why the spreading trees were safe. The teachings echoed in her head.

The beasts roam the forest paths. Be cautious, child of the People.

"Double up patrols for the next three days," Eshai said, her voice carrying the clear tone of command as she looked back at the other two. "Search for any evidence of this beast. Work in pairs—no one leaves the settlement alone. Inform the settlers of the extra precautions. If we're lucky, it's already decided to pass us by, but I'm not taking any chances."

"Yes, Commander," the valiants said, touching their hands to their hearts in salute.

On the way back to the settlement, Seri kept her eyes on the trees, unable to shake the feeling that they were being watched. Eshai kept her gaze fixed ahead of her as she walked, calm and confident. Seri didn't know how Eshai could be so calm. The tension coiled inside her so tightly she thought she might burst. When she couldn't take it any longer, she opened her mouth.

"There couldn't possibly be a beast in the trees. Could there?"

"I've seen a lot of things that shouldn't be possible out here," Eshai said. "And beasts *do* occasionally get into the spreading trees. Sometimes they get desperate. They're poor climbers and any valiant worth their armor would shoot them down before they made it halfway, but . . ." She shrugged, as if to say, *things happen*, but Seri wondered if a clumsy, desperate beast would have been able to kill something as nimble as a monkey.

She shivered, thinking back to the settlement, to the platforms open to the air, no walls yet, nothing but tarps to keep off the rain. "The settlement—"

"If you're afraid, you can sleep in the command hall tonight. I'm probably going to work late, so I might need you."

Relief flooded her, relief she immediately hated herself for. How could she feel relief at being able to rest within the safety of four walls when the other settlers would brave the open air? And yet, she couldn't bring herself to turn Eshai's offer down.

"We'll have the other settlers stay inside the town hall for the next few nights," Eshai said, as if reading her mind. "There will be guards on watch until we're sure it's safe. Take note of that in case I forget."

"I—yes, ma'am," Seri said, her fingers itching for something to write on. She made up her mind never to report to work without a writing board again. "I'll remember."

"Good," said Eshai. "Ivai and Zani should be relaying my orders as we speak. I'll address the valor during the evening muster. And you and I have work to do."

She changed direction quickly, making Seri stumble to keep up.

"Work, ma'am?"

Eshai nodded. "I'll be teaching you how to operate the ballistae. If you're going to be at my side, you should know how to defend the village. What would you say to noon tomorrow? We should train when the light is best."

The ballistae. Seri's mind flashed back to those killing machines. And, as always, she thought of blood. Blood, on the grass, on her body. On Ithim.

Her stomach lurched, but she nodded.

"Yes, ma'am."

CHAPTER 2

✤

"**W**ake up, sprout. We've got work to do."

Seri groaned, rising from a dream of running through the rainforest. She could still feel soft earth beneath her hands, smell rain on the air. Another one of *those* dreams. They had been coming to her more often since leaving the village. She shoved the thoughts away, rolling over onto her back. The floor was hard beneath her. At some point, she must have rolled off the pallet she had made up in the corner. She blinked up at the unfamiliar ceiling above her, momentarily confused, and then she remembered.

The settlement. They'd arrived. She was in Commander Eshai's office.

Seri sat up, eyes wide, but Eshai was gone. Her cot was still there, tucked into a corner, but there was no sign of her. Instead, the same valiant who had met her yesterday stood before her—Raya, Seri remembered. Raya cocked her head to the side as Seri stared at her.

"Come on," Raya said. "Up, up. You're helping me fetch water."

Seri rose, her legs a little unsteady. After five days of hard travel, her muscles were stiff and sore. She bent down to rub some life back into her limbs while Raya watched impatiently.

"I—I think I'm supposed to be helping Commander Eshai."

Raya grinned. "The commander's busy. And if you're going to stay with the valor, you've got to work. Everyone does."

Before she smiled, Seri would have said she had a face like a doll, heart-shaped and perfectly framed by short hair, a darker shade of brown than her skin. Adorable. When she smiled, Seri quickly revised that concept. Raya's smile was like a panther baring its teeth.

"Don't worry, sprout," Raya said. "I'll put you to work."

Raya led her down one of the ladders fixed to the trunk of the spreading tree, then down to the water. The lake that fed their settlement's tree was small but deep, the water crystal clear and blue as the sky. Good water, Raya told her as they walked. That was what a border settlement needed to be successful. Good water, and a capable valor.

Seri had been born in the borderlands, and her own village had been the closest to the unknown world before this settlement was founded. She didn't need Raya to tell her what she already knew, but she held her tongue.

It was early in the morning, but the settlers were already about their business, scurrying like ants across the open ground at the base of the spreading tree. Many of them were heading to the water themselves, carrying jars slung across their backs or waterskins over their shoulders. A few were heading out to the farms. Seri was surprised to recognize some of the settling party that had come with her from Elaya. She had thought they would still be resting from the long journey, but maybe Elaya had more settler spirit than she'd believed.

The sight of them made her feel uneasy. She recalled Eshai's words about a climbing beast. She wanted to tell them to head indoors, but what were they supposed to do? They were in no more danger on the ground than they had always been, and there was work to be done.

Something red hurtled through the air toward them, resolving itself as a valiant in red armor only when he whistled sharply at Raya. Seri drew up short, startled, as he landed on the ground in a crouch. She was surprised to find she recognized him. Tarim, who had always had an easy smile and a friendly word for the settlers. He had been one of the valiants that had guarded them during the march.

Tarim paused to give Seri a grin.

"I see she's put you to work already." He spoke to Seri, but she had the distinct sense the comment had been meant for Raya.

Raya sniffed. "Everyone needs to work. And the commander said I could have Seri help me with the water."

"Is that what she told you?" Tarim cupped his hand over his mouth and said to Seri in a stage whisper, "Raya won't do her chores unless she bullies someone else into doing them with her."

"At least I do my chores at all, Tarim," Raya said. "Unless hopping around for the settlers' amusement is on the duty roster now."

"I'm *patrolling*. The commander doubled the patrols, or haven't you heard?"

"If you're patrolling, then get moving. It's not like a beast is going to fall on us here. Seri and I have work to do."

Before Seri could say anything, Raya grabbed her by the arm, maneuvering her around Tarim. Fully armored as she was, her grip was like iron. Raya hardly noticed when Seri stumbled before catching up.

Seri looked up at Raya's face, expecting to see her angry, but Raya was smiling. No, not just smiling. Chuckling, as softly as possible to keep the sound from reaching Tarim.

"Fates, he can be an idiot sometimes."

"You two are friends?"

"We trained as valiants together. I don't know if that makes us friends." She snorted, waving dismissively, but Seri wasn't convinced. Raya released Seri's arm quickly, as if she were surprised to find that she was still holding it. "Oh! Sorry about that. Now, about the water . . ."

Grass faded to silt at the lake's edge, the smooth surface of the water reflecting the sky. Seri stood a little apart from Raya, watching as the valiant dropped the buckets she had been carrying to the ground. There were four, each tied to one end of two poles Raya had slung over her shoulders. She had brought them from headquarters, but while a valiant's strength meant carrying them filled would be easy, *Seri* wasn't a valiant. She didn't think she could lift one of them full, let alone climb with it, and she had no idea how Raya would manage to carry both by herself. Strength aside, Raya wasn't very *big*, and four full buckets of water took up space.

Raya stretched her arms up over her head, rubbing at a knot in the small of her back. She grinned at Seri.

"Now," she said, picking up one of the poles and handing it to Seri. "Here's how we're going to do this. You're going to fill these buckets for me."

"I am?"

Raya nodded. "Yes. And while I run this set back, you're going to fill the other. If we keep going like this, we can fill up water stores for the entire settlement. We could go faster if Tarim would help, but—" She shrugged.

Seri looked at the buckets skeptically. "You're going to drop these off . . . and come back?" she repeated. "Are you sure we shouldn't just get a cart?"

Raya grinned, a flash of teeth. "*Never* underestimate a valiant. Now, if you don't mind, the water?"

Seri was still uncertain, but she nodded, taking the buckets from Raya. She stripped off her shoes and rolled her trousers up past her knees, wading into the lake. The lake's sandy bottom squelched between her toes.

Filling buckets for someone else to carry was a child's job, and every child of the People knew the best water was farther out from the shore. In the eyes of the People, Seri was an adult, but she hadn't been an adult very long. She still remembered going down to the water with—

—with Ithim. With her mother.

No. Don't think about that.

The buckets sliced through the surface of the water as she dipped them in, first one and then the other. Raya didn't wait for her to return to shore, instead wading in after her to take the pole. She hoisted it over her shoulders with one hand, raising her other hand in a mock salute before kicking up a spray of water and leaping into the air. By the time the water settled, Raya was almost to the spreading tree, faster than Seri would have thought possible. Although she'd lived in a border village, she hadn't really seen valiants *move* until now. Elaya had been a quiet, sedate place. Maybe there *was* a lot Seri still didn't know about the world.

She blinked water out of her eyes and started filling the second set of buckets.

It was done quickly, which left her time to stand there, waist-deep in the water, and think. Time to look down at the surface of the lake, at the sky reflected in it, and at her own face staring back at her.

It always surprised her to see her own face. She had some vague image of herself as a child, all wide eyes and bare feet and messy hair. There weren't too many opportunities for her to sit by the water and look at herself, and each time she found herself wondering if the creature looking back at her could truly have the same body as the one she inhabited.

Eyes too big for her face, brown skin. Brown hair that refused to lie flat no matter what she did to it, cut roughly so it fell just past her chin. Unremarkable brown eyes. She looked like a child wearing her mother's clothes, pretending to be an adult.

What was she doing out here?

She'd walked away from Elaya and now, six days later, she was play-acting at being a settler, an aide to *Eshai Unbroken*. It felt as if everything she'd done since Ithim had been a dream, like the world had ceased being real when Turi arrived in Elaya asking for settlers to come with him to a new spreading tree and Seri had picked up her bag and walked off without looking back.

"We made good time," Raya said later, as she and Seri made their way back to the spreading tree.

Despite her best efforts at drying off when she got out of the water, Seri's shoes were soaked. She grimaced at the unpleasant squeaking sound they made with each step. Raya was dry as a bone—she supposed valiant armor did get wet, but it didn't stay wet for long. *Raya* wasn't punctuating every step with something that sounded like a dying bird.

The valiant was in a good mood, but Seri didn't share the sentiment. She wished Raya hadn't left her in the water alone. It had been the most time she'd had alone in days. Too much time to think—and she never wanted to think again.

She said something agreeable in response—she wasn't even sure what it was. It didn't matter. Raya seemed perfectly capable of holding a conversation without her.

"Don't look so glum, sprout. You'll be back to your duties soon enough. And the next thing you know, you'll have a house and a farm, and we'll be moving on, so you can try your luck assisting the next valor commander. And—oh."

Raya stopped, and Seri did, too, the sudden movement cutting through the drone in her mind. They had come back into the shadow of the spreading tree. Although their ladder was still far off, they could see the platform that would eventually become the town square.

It was packed with people. Valiants stood along the branches, watching the crowd, but the group huddled in the center were entirely settlers. Even from this distance, Seri had no problem recognizing the figure in gleaming white standing in front of them. Eshai. She had her helm tucked under her arm and was gesturing with one hand as she spoke, and though Seri couldn't hear her voice, she could see the way the crowd shifted uncertainly with her words.

She knew what Eshai was saying. From the grim look on Raya's face, Raya did, too.

"Is she . . . telling them about the climbing beast?"

"Looks like it," she said. Then, with a pat on Seri's shoulder, she added, "You're going to be busy."

She started to walk, leaving Seri to catch up.

❦

Raya's prediction came true—Seri *was* busy.

She spent her days following Eshai around, staining her fingers with charcoal as she scribbled notes onto the wooden chits she carried with her. She watched as Eshai organized the valor, securing the settlement and patrolling the outskirts. In the early afternoons, when the day was hottest, she sat with Eshai in the sweltering heat of the command hall and listened while Eshai explained how to write correspondence in her name and how to draft official reports to the council in Vethaya. In the midafternoons, Eshai took her out to the village boundaries, where the ballistae waited. Seri joined the group of valiants and volunteers who were being trained to operate them, learning how to load, wind, and fire bolts at wooden targets the valor placed in increasingly difficult locations. It was hard work, and her arms burned with the effort, but Seri's arrows usually hit their marks, and once she learned the trick of it, she found herself hitting even the most well-hidden targets.

At night she ate her evening meal in the command hall with the valor and fell asleep on a pallet near the back wall of Eshai's office. Often, she would fall asleep, exhausted, while Eshai was still awake, the sound of the commander's soft tones or the hiss of a brush on parchment following her into slumber. The exhaustion was good for one thing—it stopped her from having too many dreams.

The settling operation continued at a rapid pace. Makeshift buildings rose faster than Seri could believe, houses appearing where naked platforms once stood. Settlers were assigned to trades, and land was tilled for farms. Industry was everywhere. Seri's own chosen platform remained bare. There wasn't enough *time* to think about her house. Her work with the valor occupied all her thoughts, leaving no room for anything else.

The members of the valor, for their part, took this as the natural order of things. Though Seri wore no armor and carried no spear, they accepted her as one of their own, letting her sit with them at the tables and carrying food to her and Eshai when they worked late at night. Her work often left her isolated from the other settlers, so the fact that the valor went out of its way to include her was touching.

It also disturbed her. She felt the weight of her secret grow heavier in her chest every moment she spent with them, for every name she learned and every time she felt her fondness for them deepening.

It was as if for every moment she spent at the valor's table, enduring their good-natured teasing and smiling as they bantered, she felt the distance between herself and them widen more and more. Here they were, the finest of the People, the ones that had earned the pieces of their armor through blood, sweat, and tears. And here she was.

There were words for what she was, words she heard in the back of her mind as she sat there in the company of heroes.

Fraud. Impostor.

Ithim's face flashed through her mind, stained in blood.
Murderer.

❧

Eshai was the best of them all.

It took Seri a few days to stop seeing the commander as a figure out of legend and start seeing her for what she really was, which only made her more admirable. Eshai was the type of person to address each of her valiants by name, to pick the hardest duties for herself so even though the entire valor was working extra shifts, they could see their commander working alongside them. She had a temper, which surprised Seri, but once Seri noticed it, she saw how much Eshai worked to keep it in line, to stop herself from lashing out at others in frustration. She was disorganized, and often spent too much time on one task, neglecting the others, but she never gave Seri any grief when she reminded her that there were other things to be done, and eventually Seri stopped being afraid of telling Eshai that she had to let something go and move on.

She wasn't perfect, but she did her best. The valor saw that, too, and respected her for it, not as a hero, but as a leader.

"I served with the commander when she took the settlement," Raya said one night when Eshai had asked to be alone.

Seri perked up. "So, you were there when she fought the serpent?"

All around the table, valiants chuckled, making Seri flush. She sat in the command hall's lounge with Raya and some of the others, a plate of fried fruit on the table between them. Many of the valiants drank karan, a bitter concoction that Seri knew was a stimulant of some sort, keeping them awake through the long night ahead.

Raya grinned at her. "Most of us were there, sprout. She wasn't a hero when we left Vethaya. She was barely commander. She was so young, and it was our first expedition. When that thing showed up, I thought we were all going to die."

"What was it like?" Seri asked. "I mean, I know what the stories say, but did it really dissolve valiants' armor?"

"It did more than that," Raya said, her hand brushing against the exterior of her own armor, a dark, deep shade of red. "The ones that got hit by it, they lost their memories for a while. They said it was like something in their minds, eating away at them from the inside. When it hit them, they couldn't move. Some of them got their memories back, but . . ."

"You only get one shot at armor," Tarim said, breaking in. He sat at the far end of the table, tracing patterns into the wood-work with the tips of his gloved fingers as he sipped at his flask of karan. "Armor usually only crumbles when a valiant dies, but if it happens when you're alive, you'll never be able to bond with armor again. You can kill all the beasts you like, but it just won't take."

"So, what did they do?" Seri asked. One of the valiants pushed a plate of fried plantains nearer to her. Seri took one and ate, but she barely tasted it. Her eyes were on Raya, her thoughts drifting through memory.

Raya shrugged. "They went back to their villages. Or they moved to other settlements. I didn't keep track."

"They would have died if it wasn't for the commander," Tarim said. "For a second, back then, I thought we were done. But the commander's armor didn't break. It started to, and I thought she was going to go down, but then it turned white and came back. She killed the thing in the end."

"She told me it was because of her past," Raya added. "When the commander was a kid, she got really sick—a blood fever. It left her with a gap in her memories. She said she could feel the snake in her head, but when it reached the gap, it ran out of memories to steal. That confused it long enough for her to kill it. So, she got lucky, more than anything. But that's usually how it is, when you become a hero." Raya shrugged, taking a sip of karan. "The commander's never put herself above us. She'll be the first to tell you she got lucky."

"That was back when Lavit was with us, too," said Tarim. "I miss having him around."

"Lavit?" It was the first time Seri had heard the name.

Tarim nodded. "He was second-in-command of the valor when we started out. A childhood friend of Eshai. We had a betting pool about whether they'd get together. Still do."

Raya scowled at him. "Seri doesn't need to hear your gossip."

Tarim snorted. "Please. Like you don't still have a bet out. Besides, it was practically true. The two of them came from the same village. Went and became valiants together. Ask Turi, he knows more about it than I do."

"*Don't* ask Turi," Raya said, shooting Tarim a look that could have stripped paint. "The last thing he wants is to be reminded of *that*."

Seri couldn't stop herself. "Reminded of what?"

She knew she had asked the wrong question by the silence that fell over the room. Tarim looked down at his flask as if it had soured, and Raya's expression darkened. Sitting there, she wished she could take it back, but words, once spoken, could not be unspoken. She was about to tell them not to answer when Tarim spoke.

"Naumea," he said, the word sounding like a curse. He took another swig from his flask, grimacing as if he wished it contained something other than karan.

"A massacre." Raya ran her fingers contemplatively over the spikes protruding from her armored gloves. "It was when the commander was just another sprout like you, serving in Commander Ushi's valor. Most of the valiants who went out to Naumea that day died. They got the settlement in the end, but it was hard won. Turi, Eshai, and Lavit—they all survived, but they were the lucky ones. That spreading tree is watered by valiant blood."

There was a look of deep sadness in Raya's eyes. Seri wasn't sure what possessed her to ask the question, but it slipped out before she could force it back. "Were you there, Raya?"

"No. I wasn't there. My brother, on the other hand . . ." She shook her head, turning her acidic glare back onto Tarim. "I don't want to talk about it. And if *I* don't want to talk about it, Turi *certainly* won't."

Tarim pressed his lips tightly together but nodded, chastised. A heavy mood hung over the group for a few long moments before Tarim looked up. The smile on his face looked forced.

"So I hear you're a fair shot with the ballistae. Is that true?"

Seri blushed, thinking about the last target she had struck. They had tried to hide that one in the shadows of the tree line. "It's nothing special. The commander has me practicing a lot, that's all."

"Come on, don't be so modest," Tarim said. "You might have a talent for this."

A talent.

Seri knew that Tarim was only trying to cheer her up, only trying to lighten the mood. Because of that, she laughed and brushed it off, stayed to finish off the plate of fruit before excusing herself to see if Eshai was in a better mood. But the words followed her into the night and well into the next day.

She had a talent for this.

A talent for killing.

❧

"Steady!" Eshai's voice was close to her ear. Seri jumped, releasing the bolt. It went wide, slamming into the soft earth several yards away from the target. Looking at it, she felt a pang of shame, one that only intensified when she saw the troubled look on Eshai's face.

"What's wrong with you today?" Eshai asked. "That shot should have been no challenge at all."

She'd allowed herself to get distracted thinking about what Tarim had said. But she couldn't tell Eshai that, not when the commander already seemed burdened by so much.

"Nothing." She waved her hand absently. "The heat."

It was a particularly muggy day, the air so thick even in the spreading tree that she felt she could almost drink it. The sort of heat that spoke of a coming storm. Eshai's expression softened in sympathy, and that only made Seri feel worse.

"I forget you aren't one of my valiants sometimes. But you need to learn to focus even with the heat. Beasts don't wait to attack at a convenient time."

"You really think it's going to happen? We're going to be attacked by tree-climbing beasts?"

Eshai's expression grew distant, fixed on the tops of the nearest trees. Seri wondered if she was remembering Naumea. "I think it's wise to be prepared. I think an attack will happen eventually. Whether they come in number, or one at a time, we're too tempting a target out here. And we're far from rescue. When they attack, you and the settlers will be our last line of defense. I can't be everywhere at once."

Seri shivered. "I don't think I can—"

"Don't think. When the moment comes, you'll know what to do. You're the kind of person who can do what she has to."

Seri wondered if her guilt was so obvious. If it was a stain on her, like the mark of her name, something she could never erase. Would she go to her grave burdened by Ithim's blood?

"How do you do it?" she asked Eshai. "How can you be so brave? I'm terrified."

Eshai rubbed at the skin of her right arm, where the survivor's mark peeked out from under her white gloves. It was only given to those who lived when they should have died. Seri had never seen her uncertain before. It startled her. She'd forgotten Eshai could falter, could feel things like fear. "I won't pretend to have an answer. I'm still looking for those answers myself. But . . ."

"But . . . ?"

"You look at a situation, and you ask yourself what you can control. Most of the time, the *outcome* will be out of your control. But there are usually things you *can* change. Something that can buy you more time, give you the possibility of success, even if it's small. And when you realize what that is, you ask yourself one question: What would you rather live with? Would you rather live with the knowledge that you tried and failed, or the knowledge that you might have been able to do something, but you were too afraid to try at all?"

"What if you make the wrong choice?" Seri asked, feeling as though something was squeezing her throat. "What if you break something that can never be fixed? What then?"

Eshai looked back at her, and Seri got the sense that Eshai was *truly* looking at her, *truly* seeing her for the first time. It was hard not to look away.

"I don't have all the answers. I guess you think about what you did. What you could have done. What you would have done, had you known what you know now. You carry that memory with you, and maybe, if you're ever in the same position again, you'll do better that time."

"Is that what you learned from Naumea?"

Eshai's expression darkened, and Seri wished she could take it back. But before she could stammer out an apology, Eshai brought her hand down on the ballista with a crack.

"Hit that target. Then I'll answer your question."

Seri swallowed, but nodded, walking back over to the ballista. She loaded one of the heavy bolts back into its slot, muscles straining as she wound the crank that fed the bolt into the machine. When it snapped into place, she released the crank, grasping the handles with both hands. Her hands shook, but she breathed deep, forcing them into steadiness as she wheeled the machine around to face her target. She fixed the target in her sights, leaning forward to get a better look.

Her mind was filled with Ithim, but she needed this answer.

She needed to know.

She inhaled, and then on the exhale, released the lock holding the bolt in place. The whole contraption shuddered as the bolt came free from its housing. It slammed into the target dead-on, the wood splintering and bowing back beneath the weight.

Seri breathed in, releasing her hands. She stepped back from the ballista, looking over at Eshai. The commander eyed the target, frowning.

"A good shot. Did you ever train with the bow?"

Seri shook her head. "I never used a weapon. I didn't have any interest. That was always . . ." Ithim. ". . . other children."

Eshai nodded slowly. She drew in a breath, her shoulders moving with the motion. "You asked about Naumea. There was nothing I could have done to save those who died. I was on my first expedition, and I barely knew what I was doing. The beasts came upon us in numbers we weren't expecting. It was all I could do to stay alive. But I still see it when I close my eyes. And I still wonder if there was something I could have done. Some way I could have changed things. But if Naumea happened now, I think it would turn out the same way."

Eshai looked over at Seri. "There's a *reason* you volunteered to come out here, isn't there?"

She had repeated the lie so many times over the weeks, she almost believed it. "I'm here because there was nowhere else for me. I'm a caretaker's ward, and—"

Eshai shook her head. "Others might believe that. I won't. I was a caretaker's ward, too."

That surprised Seri into silence. The stories about Eshai, the songs—they didn't mention *that*.

"I know what it's like to have nothing of your own and nowhere to belong. It drives a person to do a lot of things, but it doesn't drive them to leave the safety of their village practically as soon as they're named an adult. *Other* things do that, Seri, but not this."

"I . . ." Another lie came to mind, but her mouth wouldn't form the words. She couldn't lie to Eshai. But could she tell the truth?

It almost felt like she could. Here at the edge of the world, she could tell Eshai anything.

The sound of a horn cut her off—three quick blasts in succession. Eshai turned away, her expression hard, her gaze fixed on the distance. The call rang out again, and Seri felt it shake her down to her bones. It was the first signal the settlers learned when they arrived.

Beasts sighted. Valor to positions.

Eshai's expression was grave as she pulled her spear from its bindings, taking it in both hands. "Go back to headquarters and wait for instructions. We'll finish this later."

Seri nodded, and Eshai bent her knees, leaping to the ground with enough force to shake the platform behind her. Seri kept her eyes on Eshai until she was out of sight, then turned, racing over bridges and across platforms as she ran toward the command hall.

The other volunteers were waiting when she arrived, a group of frightened villagers huddled in the hall while Raya watched over them. The valiant had her spear out, a wicked red blade that matched the rest of her armor. She held it loosely in one hand, watching the world outside from the doorway. She would tell them when they were needed at the ballistae and where to go. *If* they were needed.

After a few minutes of tense silence, another horn rang. Two long blasts, followed by a single short one. Seri's heart jumped into her throat for a moment before she understood their meaning. *All clear.* She sagged in relief.

The tension in the room evaporated in an instant, the settlers who had been recruited to man the ballistae letting out relieved sighs. A few of them even laughed, but the mood was somber. Raya returned her spear to her back wordlessly, her expression grave. Seri thought she almost looked disappointed.

"You can leave if you want," she told the volunteers. "It doesn't look like you'll be needed today."

The command hall emptied quickly after that, most of the volunteers leaving the room. A few lingered to hear what had happened, and Raya didn't stop them.

The valiants returned in pairs and groups of three, sweaty from the exertion but otherwise unbloodied. Seri joined Raya in passing out cups of water, which they all drank grate-fully. As she moved through the group, she listened to their conversations.

"They were definitely there," she heard Tarim say to Raya, who listened to his report with a face like stone. "They didn't pick a fight, but they were *there*, all right."

Seri's relief at the all-clear vanished instantly. It was the look on Raya's face, the same look the other valiants wore. None of them seemed relieved. The settlers acted as though they had escaped, but looking at the valor, Seri realized the truth.

They hadn't escaped anything. All they had done was delay the battle.

Eshai arrived last, looking as tired as the rest of the valor and just as frustrated. She picked up a cup of water from the tray, downing it without saying anything. Seri, who had some experience with the commander's dark moods now, kept her distance as Eshai made her way back to her office. When she stopped at the door, though, Seri held her breath.

"Seri," Eshai said, jerking her head into the room behind her. "With me."

Seri nodded quickly, coming to join Eshai.

"What happened?" she asked, shutting the door behind her.

"We found signs of the beasts' passing," Eshai said, removing her helm and shaking out her long fall of dark hair. "Beasts. More than one. A few of us even caught glimpses of them, but they vanished before we could engage. You understand what that means?"

"They'll be back."

Eshai nodded grimly, and Seri wished, with a sinking feeling, that she hadn't been right.

CHAPTER 3

⍦

The close encounter with the beasts had lit a fire under the valor. Before, extra patrols and duties had been taken with a sort of grim resignation, a few of the valiants grumbling under their breath. Now, there was no complaining, only disciplined ferocity. Seri wasn't surprised. To become a valiant in the first place, one had to prove a natural willingness to hunt beasts, killing five of them to gather the pieces that formed a valiant's armor. A person could stumble into killing a beast once, perhaps even twice. But to do so five times and to then make the pilgrimage to Vethaya to present oneself to the Council of Valor? That took a drive few among the People could match.

Watching them prepare for battle, Seri could see that drive. She saw it in the way they worked to fortify the village, the discipline in their patrols, and even in the way they trained together. She could see it now as Eshai led them through a spear training exercise in the open ground at the foot of the spreading tree. The commander stood in the center of the circle in her white armor, her spear flicking through the air as she turned aside her valiants' advancements. She fought three of them—Tarim, Zani, and an older valiant named Perai—and although it was clear she was straining with the effort, they hadn't yet managed to overwhelm her.

Eshai stepped through the motions like she was dancing,

bringing up the shaft of her spear to catch Tarim's and knock it aside, then flipping the spear end over end to bring the blade down on Perai. Perai blocked her blow just as Eshai stepped nimbly to the side, sliding out of the way of Zani's thrust. Seri had barely seen what Zani had done wrong before Eshai was advancing on him, the flat of her blade knocking him down to the ground and, according to the rules of this engagement, out of the fight.

"He overstepped," Raya said from beside her, watching the fight with a sort of hunger. Seri hadn't asked for commentary, but Raya had been steadily providing it anyway, apparently convinced that Seri needed to know the finer details of what was happening. "He overcommitted to an attack. Any beast would have taken him down."

"But why do it like this?" Seri asked, as Eshai turned to square off against Tarim and Perai, who had now launched into a coordinated attack with deadly precision, filling the gap for their fallen comrade as if he had never been there. "What's the point of having one against three? It seems like it's unfairly hard on the commander, and easier on everyone else."

"It's meant to train both sides," Raya said. "The commander takes the part of a lone valiant against a beast, a beast perhaps as strong, or as fast, as three valiants together. The valiants act as a group facing down a single enemy, one they've separated from the pack. They have to keep coordinated, and have to avoid running into each other, or they'll be more hindrance than help." She smiled, baring her teeth. "When we can help it, we don't fight alone."

Seri found herself eyeing Raya's armor with some apprehension. Armor made from beastskin grew with the valiant it was bonded to, granted them abilities beyond an ordinary human, and changed appearance according to what was in the valiant's heart. Eshai's white armor, strong, steadfast, and clean, spoke of her abilities as a leader. Turi's dark green armor, nigh invisible when he was in the trees, spoke of his preference to remain hidden until the right moment to strike. She didn't like thinking about what Raya's distinctive spiked armor said about her.

She was drawn away from her thoughts by a shout from the assembly. Eshai had just disarmed Tarim with a hard whack to the wrists, forcing him to drop his spear before kicking him aside. Tarim stumbled over to where Zani waited, rubbing at his wrists and wincing. Raya clicked her tongue in annoyance.

"He's always been impatient. When he sees the fight isn't going his way, he charges in instead of taking a moment to think about his position. Hopefully, his wrists ache long enough to burn that lesson into his head, the idiot."

Seri didn't comment. The insult was laced with fondness, and Seri wasn't sure Raya was aware of the look on her face. She didn't ask about the relationship between Raya and Tarim and didn't really need to—she'd learned early on that relationships among valiants could sometimes be a nebulous thing, brought about by necessity and proximity. Sometimes they weren't. Sometimes they were more permanent. But she didn't know Raya well enough to feel comfortable asking which sort this was.

Tarim came to join them, his hand brushing Raya's arm as he did. Raya didn't shake him off, but she did feign disinterest, moving to the side to give him more space. Seri pretended not to notice. As she turned to watch the battle, Tarim drew up next to her.

"How's it going, sprout?" he asked with a teasing grin. "Is Raya boring you to death? Blink twice if you need me to rescue you."

Raya shoved him in the arm. Tarim laughed, stepping to the side with the blow. He looked up at the fight and let out a low whistle.

It had come down to two people, Eshai and Perai. They had stopped fighting, and eyed each other warily, spears held at their sides.

"Now we'll really see a challenge," Raya said. "Both of our prowling beasts facing each other. Keep your eyes peeled, sprout—this isn't a battle to miss."

Seri thought she could go her whole life missing battles, but she didn't say so to Raya, unsettled by the eager look in her eye. Instead, she watched as the two warriors lifted their spears, coming together and springing apart.

The artistry in their movements took Seri's breath away, despite her reservations. The two of them clashed, wood clacking as they turned aside each other's spears, armor rattling against armor as they tried to find openings in each other's defenses. Perai moved with all the confidence of years of experience, Eshai with the tenacity of youth. Seri didn't see what happened, but one moment Perai was charging in with an apparent powerful blow, and the next there was the loud crack of wood against armor, and Perai was on the ground.

The crowd of valiants erupted into applause. Seri turned toward Raya in surprise.

"What happened?" she asked. "Did Perai overstretch herself, too?"

Raya shook her head. "Perai?" she asked. "Never, not that one.

You don't get to be her age in this business without being as cautious as a cat. But she was too cautious, and our commander took advantage of that. You didn't see the decisive blow?"

Seri shook her head. Even to her sharp eyes, it had all been a blur.

Raya grinned. "Pay closer attention next time. Real fights aren't like the plays they put on for children in the villages. If you want to win, you'll have to train your eye."

Seri bit back the retort that she wasn't interested in winning battles. Raya wasn't paying attention to her anyway. She was already turning toward the crowd of valiants, looking to see who would be chosen next to fight, angling herself to be more visible to whoever was doing the choosing. She got her wish, stepping forward with a pair of valiants to battle against Turi. Eshai, meanwhile, slipped off to the sidelines, tugging her helm off. Her breaths came in heavy pants, sweat-soaked dark hair clinging to her face.

Tarim made himself scarce before Eshai could reach her, and Seri wondered if he was trying to avoid discussing his performance in the spar. She fetched Eshai a flask of water. Eshai drank gratefully, pouring the rest over her head and handing the empty flask back to Seri when she was done.

"She almost had me," Eshai said, nodding at Perai, who had been enfolded into a group of younger valiants on the other side of the circle. "I got lucky."

"It didn't look like luck. I don't think the songs do you justice."

Eshai snorted, shaking her head. "I don't care about the songs."

"Do you hate it?" Seri asked. "The attention, I mean?"

Eshai frowned and didn't respond for several long moments.

"No. I don't hate it, not exactly. But . . . it's not what I wanted for myself."

Seri wanted to ask Eshai exactly *what* she had wanted for herself, but the commander was no longer paying attention to her. She watched the unfolding battle closely, her gaze on Raya. Raya fought with the same controlled grace Seri had noticed in the others, but there was a gleam in her eyes that concerned Seri. She wondered if Eshai noticed it, too, if that was why she was looking at Raya so carefully.

Before Seri could ask about it, Eshai turned to her. "What about you? Have you ever thought of learning the spear? It's not as if you have to be a valiant to learn, and it might be a good idea to know the basics, especially out here."

Seri shook her head, fighting down a wave of revulsion. "It wouldn't be proper. And I don't think I'd be much good at it."

Eshai was watching her curiously again, and Seri worried they were going to have a repeat of their conversation by the ballistae, that Eshai was going to push her for her secret. Eshai, however, only nodded.

"Fine," she said. "I'm sorry for prying. Your secrets are your own, and as long as they don't endanger this settlement, you should keep them. But I do think you should at least learn the bow. You have a talent for it, and if you're going to be a settler, you should study a weapon."

Seri tried to picture herself with a bow. It was easier than seeing herself with a spear. Much less personal.

"If that's what you think."

"It's not what I think. It's the offer I'm making. I could teach you how to shoot, if you wanted."

Seri thought about it. It would be easy to tell Eshai no, but she had a feeling that wouldn't be the end of this conversation. And it would be stupid of her. Eshai was right—they were in the borderlands. Seri couldn't expect someone to be around to protect her all the time, and she had a known hero offering to teach her how to defend herself. No matter her reservations, that was a hard offer to refuse.

"Fine." She let out a breath, shoulders slumping in resignation. "You can teach me."

Their lessons took place in the evenings, after work. Seri found the bow was much more personal than the ballista, although just as difficult. Her arrows went wide of their target for the first few days until she found her rhythm, and while she was still far from striking the painted center of the target with any regularity, her arrows hit the board most of the time. Eshai was impressed, and her pride made something inside Seri twist with guilt. She wanted to put the bow away, to never pick it up again.

They were still in the borderlands, though, and the beasts could attack at any time. She kept at it.

When the call to arms rang again, Seri was already in the command hall, helping Eshai with administrative duties. The horn call rang through the command center, and Eshai jumped up from her desk, nearly knocking over a cup of water. Seri steadied it with one hand as Eshai pulled the discarded pieces of her armor back on with practiced ease, bundling up her hair to tuck beneath her helm.

"Stay inside until you hear the signal," Eshai said, running out the door. Seri felt the platform rattle as she leapt into the air.

It wasn't like the last time, with a long moment of tension broken only by the sound of the all-clear. This time, Seri heard the roar of beasts almost instantly, followed by the roar of the valor's war cries.

The battle had begun.

Seri sat there until she could sit no longer, her eyes moving from the desk in front of her to the bow and quiver set aside against the wall. She stood and walked over to the quiver.

It had a leather strap attached to it, meant to fit over the archer's shoulder. Seri picked it up by the strap, feeling its comforting weight. From outside, she heard a cry of pain, immediately drowned out by angry shouting. She couldn't pick out any single voice in the strain. They were all indistinguishable to her, less people she knew and more a singular force of nature.

The leather was soft beneath her fingertips. Seri wet her dry lips with her tongue, swallowing hard. She slung the quiver over her shoulder, bending to pick up the archer's glove that had fallen to the floor. This, too, was leather, old and worn from the years of being passed around the training field, but well-maintained, nonetheless.

She could stop here.

Eshai wouldn't blame her if she hid. Nobody would. She wasn't a valiant, she wasn't a hunter, she was barely even old enough to be a settler. She could bolt the door and sit curled up in the corner of Eshai's office with her hands over her ears. She could blot out the sound and pretend no one was fighting, and if they died, she could pretend she'd never heard them. That it was not her fault, that there was nothing she could do. And maybe, when she tried to sleep at night, she could force herself to believe it. That she had had no other choice, just like she'd had no other choice with Ithim.

The glove was smooth on her skin as she slid it over her left hand.

Fates, she was so *tired* of guilt.

Her eyes drifted to the locked chest in the corner of the room she had borrowed for herself, the only belongings she had brought with her from Elaya. Seri stared at the chest for a long moment before she swallowed, turning away. She fastened the glove into place and picked the bow up off the floor, then made her way out of the office into the reception hall.

The battle was louder here. The valiants hadn't closed the front door in their haste to leave. It swung wide open in the breeze, the curtain of insect netting hanging over it the only thing that separated her from the outside world. Seri fit an arrow to the string, feeling the tautness of it between her two fingers. Then she crept over to the door and peered out.

A spreading tree was always surrounded by open ground—its sheer size made it so very few other trees could grow in its shadow. This battle had been joined at the edge of the tree line separating spreading tree from rainforest. The beasts were all the same breed—shambling, dark-furred creatures. Their faces resembled hornless goats, but they walked like predators, mouths full of sharp teeth, and they had long, slender tails. They were a breed she recognized from the stories—*abensit*. Shadow walkers. Crystals jutted from their fur, glittering stones in bright red or blue or green. Her heart leapt into her throat as she saw them, making a quick count. So many—there had to be at least twenty.

The valor was on the ground trying to stop the charge, but Seri had learned enough from listening in on their conversations to know this was not a good battlefield for them. Valiants preferred close combat—it let them make the most of the abilities granted by their armor—but they worked best on a battlefield where they could use the trees to their advantage.

The beasts advanced on them from outside the tree line, pushing them into the swath of empty ground in the spreading tree's shadow. That was a good thing for archers and people on the ballistae, but the valiants and their spears were the fastest way to stop a charge. And if beasts were allowed to surround a spreading tree, the situation could easily become a siege.

Settlements died in sieges. They relied too much on supplies—food, water, and medicine—that could only be acquired on the ground.

Eshai's valor, though, had prepared for this. They moved in groups of two or three to a beast, one shoring up the hole when another fell, targeting their opponents with steady fury. Seri caught sight of Raya in her distinctive spiked armor, charging at one of the *abensit* as it turned to deal with another valiant. Eshai flew from battle to battle, her spear flashing as she darted in where she was needed. She stayed only long enough to turn the tide of a fight—maybe distract a beast's attention away from an injured valiant, maybe step in to fill a gap until another could be found, and then she was off again.

Two of the beasts already lay felled farther away from the charge, their blood staining the thick grass. Three armored figures lay on the ground as well, the sight of them making Seri's vision waver. Her fingers tightened on the bow string, tugging it back before letting it go slack again.

She didn't have a shot. The battle was too far away. As Seri stood there, she felt trapped between two voices arguing in her head. The first voice said she had done enough. She'd come out, she'd seen the battle, she'd proved she was willing to fight. She could stand aside with a clear conscience. The valor had trained for this all their lives. What else could she do but wait for the horn call?

The second voice said, in a quiet whisper, *What if?*

What if they didn't win the day? What if this became bloody? What if this battle took something from them, leaving its scars even if they won?

What if this became another Naumea? Would Seri be the one that hid?

The running dream was in her mind. She remembered the way the soft earth felt beneath her claws, the scent of blood in the air. She'd always hated the running dreams, but in that moment, she felt possessed by them. The creature in those dreams didn't run, didn't hide. It was stronger and braver than she was.

The air was difficult to breathe, as if someone had tied a cloth around her nose and mouth. She thought she could taste her heartbeat. On the battlefield, a beast charged forward with a roar of rage, shaking off the two valiants that had pinned it down. It raised one powerful claw, swatting a valiant in bright blue armor aside—Tarim. Tarim hit the ground in a sprawl of limbs and didn't immediately get back up.

Seri sucked in a breath, ignoring the chill inside her as she ran out the door.

❦

Battle was messy, bloody work. Eshai sucked in a breath as the *abensit*'s jaws snapped shut on empty air, clamping down on the area where her chest had been a moment ago. She swung her spear around, the blade catching the beast just under its forearm. Summoning up all her strength, Eshai bent her legs, crouching down and turning her hips to the side. She thought she felt her armor creak with the motion and let out a loud battle cry as she flung the beast away from her, sending it crashing to the ground. Vesui and Beri, the two valiants she had come to aid, quickly moved forward for the kill. They didn't even look at her, their attention on the beast. This gave Eshai a moment to catch her breath, to gulp down hot, humid air as her vision swam.

Two breaths, no more. Enough to chase away the stars appearing before her eyes. Eshai gave herself that long before she tightened her grip on her spear, turning in search of someone else to aid.

It was loud, her ears ringing with the sound. The valiants' helms enhanced their senses, good when tracking a lone beast through the forest, but troublesome in the heat of battle. Learning to manage the influx of sensory information was one of the most important parts of the novice valiant's training. Remembering what her teachers had taught her, Eshai searched for that still, cool place inside her. She went back, as she always did, to when she and Lavit had gone to Lanatha together.

Alone in that lake, the water embracing her and bearing her aloft, her eyes turned toward the sky. She let everything unnecessary fade away as she held herself in that image, her gaze settling on Zani and Arkil, both of them standing guard over a wounded Perai as a beast charged at them. Willing energy into her tired legs, Eshai crossed the distance toward them.

The valiants' armored boots allowed them to run faster, to

jump higher than any human could unaided, but they did nothing to stop them from getting tired. She could feel the strain in her legs, the burn in her muscles as she forced herself to cross the distance, but she didn't falter. She leapt into the air as the beast bore down on Zani and Arkil, angling her spear point for the delicate vertebrae at the base of its neck.

The spear slid home with a satisfying *thunk*, sending a shot of impact up her arms. Her gloves gave her strength, allowing her to direct the power of the armored spear, but she could already feel the strain. She held fast, bearing the beast down to the ground. It thrashed as it went—it often took these creatures a while to realize they were dead—but eventually it fell, and Eshai was able to stand on its back, pulling her spear free.

She stumbled as she swung her legs over the side, a motion not lost on Zani. He looked at her, his eyes widening in concern from behind the bluish gray of his helm.

"Commander."

"I'm fine," Eshai barked. "Get Perai out of here and split up. Vesui and Beri need a third. Zani, you go. Arkil, find somewhere else you're needed."

Zani looked as though he might argue, but the two of them touched their hearts in salute, running back to carry Perai away from the front lines. Eshai swept her spear out to the side, shaking off the gore that had accumulated on the edge, and turned her head to survey the rest of the battle.

Turi had the western front contained. Eshai didn't think he needed her support, or her meddling. He was a survivor of Naumea as much as she was. He knew what they fought to avoid. The eastern front, though, was undermanned. And, Eshai realized with a jolt of alarm as she turned her head in that direction, the beasts had noticed. They were gathering, about to press against the eastern side of the spreading tree with renewed force.

Eshai let out a shrill whistle, causing the valiants in her vicinity to turn their heads toward her. She whirled, pointing her spear at the nearest three clusters, those whose battles were almost done.

"You, you, and you, with me!" she cried, running for the eastern front. They saw what she had seen and followed without hesitation. She heard Turi's voice from behind her, barking out orders to fill the gaps those valiants had left.

Something was wrong. This wasn't normal. It almost seemed as though the beasts hadn't wanted her to notice their new charge, as though they had meant to keep the valiants' attention fixed on the western side of the settlement, distracting them while they moved in from the east.

But that didn't make any sense. That was tactics, strategy.

Tactics and strategy were the domain of man, not beasts.

She thought about it for only a moment before stopping her run, her valiants moving past her to plunge into the fray. Eshai fumbled at her hip for the horn she carried, raising it to her lips. Two long blasts, to signal the volunteers to their stations, three short to identify the eastern edge of the settlement. They would need all the help they could get.

She was summoning the breath to repeat the order when she saw the creature move out of the corner of her eye, one of the *abensit*, but larger and faster than the others. It was bearing down on her, too fast for her to react. Eshai gritted her teeth, bracing for impact.

The creature struck her like a bolt of lightning. She felt the weight of its body crashing into her, knocking her off her feet and ripping the spear from her hand. The impact rippled through her vest, and she felt something crack as the beast's bulk bore her down to the ground. She could smell its hot breath as its jaws snapped at her face.

Eshai raised her arm up to protect herself, but the creature's jaws closed around her gloved forearm. Its fangs didn't cut through the beastskin of her glove, but she felt the power behind the bite, a crushing force. She thrashed, trying to break free, but something dug painfully into her side, sapping her strength. Eshai tilted her head back and saw the valiants fighting in the distance, felt a surge of panic run through her. They hadn't been watching her, they hadn't seen—she didn't have the breath to call for help. She struck at the beast with her other fist, trying to push it off her, but it was relentless. Her vision was darkening—she was going to die. Fates, she was going to die.

A ballista bolt came out of nowhere, slamming into the beast's flank and knocking it off her. Eshai sat up sharply, breathing in gulps of sweet, sweet air. She placed a hand at her side and it came away bloody—her armor had cracked, piercing the skin beneath. She whipped her head around toward the beast to see it thrashing in pain, pinned to the ground by the bolt. She watched as it slumped to the ground and died.

Eshai looked over her shoulder with wide eyes, turning her gaze back to the spreading tree. It was impossible. There was no way a volunteer could be on the platforms yet. It was impossible, but . . .

Seri lifted her head from the ballista platform, looking back at her.

❦

A precarious series of rope bridges and platforms encircled the spreading tree, referred to by settlers as the Belt. It was rarely used, because it was impractical for getting from one makeshift building to the other, since most of the buildings were clustered around the center of the tree. But it connected the twelve ballista platforms protecting the settlement, and it was easily accessible from headquarters.

Seri ran along the Belt, her quiver smacking into her back with each motion. She was alone. The valor hadn't yet sounded the request for aid, so none of the other volunteers were out, and all the villagers had retreated into their shelters. Her heart pounded with each step, loud and jarring in her chest, and she wondered what *she* was doing out here. It was madness to be out in the open like this.

And yet, she couldn't bring herself to turn back.

She paused on one platform to take stock of the battle, her eyes scanning the carnage from left to right. Most of the beasts were concentrated to her left, on the northwestern front of the village, but there were a handful of battles occurring to her right. Those looked mostly in hand. If she wanted to be the most use, she should turn and get to one of the northwestern ballistae. Except . . .

A sensation of wrongness, of uncertainty, made her lift her head again, looking over at the right side of the battle—the northeastern side. Her eyes caught a glimpse of something prowling in the forest. Many somethings, coming around to the side where the village was undefended.

A trap.

From her vantage point, she could see everything that was

happening, but the valiants on the ground below had no way of knowing. And she had no way of signaling them.

Seri groped at her belt and cursed—she hadn't thought to grab one of the horns from the command hall on the way out. She took off at a run, the wooden platforms rattling beneath her feet as she made her way across them toward the northeastern ballistae. Everything else faded as she reached one, picking up a bolt that had been stacked nearby and slamming it home. She knelt to turn the crank, ignoring the burning in her shoulders as she moved as fast as she could, then bent down to grab the handles that turned the mechanism.

She could feel her heart racing as she scanned the battlefield below, looking for a target. Everything looked so small, so fast. This was nothing like practice.

Her mouth went dry, her heart pounding. What was she doing? Her shot was going to go wild, and she was going to draw a beast onto her. Worse, she was going to hit a valiant. She was going to kill someone again.

Her throat closed as she thought of Ithim. Her fingers slackened on the handlebars.

A figure in white darted across the open ground of the battlefield. The movement jolted Seri out of her trance. Eshai.

The commander was saying something, ordering groups of valiants over to the other side. Eshai had seen it, too. Seri watched as she slowed to a stop, as the valiants moved past her. And Seri saw the beast prowling in the shadows behind her, drawing close for the kill.

Seri's mouth opened in a cry, but it was no use. From this distance, there was no way Eshai could hear her.

Her grip tightened on the handles in alarm, and before she knew what she was doing, she was swinging the ballista around to aim at the beast. Her heart was still pounding too fast. She told herself to breathe, slow and deep.

She felt her heart settle, her breathing slow. And then the beast leapt onto Eshai, pinning her to the ground, and Seri felt her heartbeat skyrocket again. There was no one around to help her. If Seri didn't take the shot, Eshai would—

Eshai would die.

She swallowed hard, tightening her grip.

Seri pulled the trigger.

The machine beneath her reared, the impact moving through her like a battering ram. She gritted her teeth and held on, braced against the force. The bolt soared through the air, knocking the beast off Eshai and pinning it to the ground.

For a moment, all was silent. And then Eshai turned, her gaze moving from the dead beast to the ballistae. She was wearing her helm, so Seri knew even at this distance, Eshai could tell that it was her.

Eshai's gaze locked onto Seri for a moment. And then she brought the horn back to her lips and blew. Seri reached for another bolt without hesitation, feeding it into place as the call for volunteers rang through the air.

The valor rallied quickly after the horn call.

Eshai snapped her spear up beside her, gesturing at the tree line as the beasts concealed there abandoned stealth, charging full tilt into the fray. From there, it became a numbers game.

Calling the valiants over to bolster their defenses meant there were enough valiants clustered around the eastern front to halt the charge, but not enough to make it easy. Seri's ballista fired twice more, neither of her bolts finding their mark, but managing to drive beasts away from congested areas. Eshai's spear had better luck. It found targets, and Eshai could feel the snap of resistance as her spear carved through flesh and bone.

Her awareness faded. Blood flew, but none of it was her own, so she kept fighting. Impacts jarred her to the left and right, attacks caught on the hardened leather of her armor, but none pierced the armored vest's layer of protection, so she kept moving, swaying under the press of the melee. It became hard to shout orders amidst the chaos, but the beasts were still coming, so she kept shouting despite the rawness in her throat.

Her mind was somewhere else entirely, another slaughter, another spreading tree. The taste of blood thick on her tongue, the cries of the dying in the air.

Somehow, the thought that she herself wouldn't survive never occurred to her, not even when her grip faltered on her spear, not even when a beast's paw caught her in the torso and sent her reeling back, her vision blurring as her cracked armor dug into her side.

She had made a habit of surviving where smarter people would have died.

The volunteers arrived, and the air filled with soaring bolts, slamming into the ground between the beasts and the valor. The charge halted. Eshai glanced behind her to see every ballista station staffed, even the ones that faced Turi's battle. And then, out of the corner of her eye, she saw something glorious.

She saw Turi, still alive, his mottled green armor coated in blood. He was running at her, yelling a battle cry, and all the valiants that had fought with him were behind him, running as well. Eshai roared back as Turi reached her, their forces charging into the wall of beasts with renewed energy. The wall broke beneath their assault, those few beasts that were left turning tail and running away.

The other valiants cheered. Eshai did not. She kept her eyes on the fleeing beasts, feeling the twinge of pain in her side with every hard-won breath, and braced herself. Because she knew when she turned around what she was going to find.

It was always the same, after every battle like this. Every battle that ended with valiant blood on the grass. She wanted to be wrong, had wanted to be wrong so many times before, but she could count on the fingers of one hand the number of times she had been.

She and Turi had trained them as well as they could, and many of them were older and stronger than she was, but she had tasted the battle and taken its measure. She knew that this was a fight that brought death.

When she heard the first wail, Eshai knew she was right.

CHAPTER 4

⚘

Water was sacred to the People.

It was the greatest necessity for a spreading tree. None of the great trees that housed their civilization had ever been found away from a large lake, a body of water from which the tree could draw strength. Water birthed their homes, their safety. It cleansed them and housed their souls when they died, keeping them safe while they waited to return.

Water was their beginning. And earth was their end.

Eshai floated, naked aside from her bandages, in the lake that fed the settlement's spreading tree. Even after the battle, the water was cool and unspoiled—a lake that fed a spreading tree somehow always was. The wound in her side where her armor had cracked stung, but in the water, she barely felt it. She let that coolness wash over her, looking up at the stars, and thought about the people she had lost.

A chime sounded, ringing the hour bell. Eshai ducked beneath the water's surface one last time and let her feet sink to the sandy bottom of the lake. She rose, water streaming down her skin and her hair hanging heavy across her shoulders as she walked back to shore. The sky was mostly dark, only a sliver of orange and violet left on the horizon.

Seri waited solemnly on the lakeshore, holding a towel for her. As Eshai stepped out of the water, Seri draped it over her shoulders, careful not to touch her even by accident. Eshai brought her hand up to catch the towel before it could fall, walking toward the place where Seri had laid out her armor. As Eshai left, Seri moved to the water, unfastening the simple dress that she was wearing. She handed it wordlessly to Raya, who waited to attend her.

Eshai stopped walking, looking over her shoulder. Seri's back was to her, unmarked except for the collection of lines across her shoulders, just under the dark fall of her hair. They proclaimed her a woman grown, able to wed and travel and lift the spear and stand for the dead.

She didn't know what made her speak, some observance of the girl's youth, perhaps, or the fact that Seri had stopped at the edge of the water.

"Think about the dead," Eshai said. "This isn't the time to worry about the living. I usually—"

"I know how to stand a funeral watch, ma'am."

Strong words. The mark on Seri's back looked fresh, barely a year old. She wanted to ask whose vigil Seri could possibly have stood, but she knew from the way the girl's shoulders bowed that the question wouldn't be welcome. She nodded stiffly, turning to go. And paused again.

"You earned a piece today. With that kill. It was well done. You'll have to decide what you want. I suggest you don't choose the spear. Young hunters always choose the spear, but it's useless without the gloves. You don't have to make a decision right a—"

"I want the vest."

Eshai stopped talking. "Right. The vest."

She hesitated, glancing at Raya. Behind her, she heard Seri step into the water.

She should follow her own advice. The cares of the living could wait. This was a night for the dead.

Eshai made her way forward, toward her armor, which Seri had laid out for her on the ground. She dried herself off with the towel and pulled on the clean underclothes resting there, then started the familiar ritual of armoring herself. Despite the battle she had been in earlier, her armor was unstained. Dirt and blood slid right off beastskin armor in water, and Seri had washed hers in the lake, the task of the watcher's attendant. Already, she could see Raya moving off with the bundle of Seri's impure clothes. She would return with a simple gray shift, the traditional attire of a watcher who was not of the valor. The cycle would continue for every hour throughout the night, until the last hour before sunrise, when Eshai, who had been first, would wash the armor and attend to the needs of the last watcher.

At sunrise, they would bury their dead.

Eshai tugged her gloves back into place, doing up the laces with a practiced hand. Then she picked up her spear, walking away from the lake to the roots of the spreading tree.

There was no one there, but torches had been placed around the site to light the way for the watchers. Already, the torches had attracted small swarms of insects, but the air close to the bodies was thick with a strong citrus smell. Inevitably, some insects would find their way to the dead before the sun rose, but it wasn't the watcher's job to prevent that. The incense smell burned in Eshai's nose as she picked her way carefully over the roots, looking for a spot where she could watch and wait.

It was said among the People that the soul lingered for a night before passing back into the water. It was during that night when the soul was the most vulnerable, untethered from their flesh. The watchers would ensure none disturbed the bodies or did anything to impede the soul's passage into the next life. They would wait and see, in case the soul decided to impart one last message, a word of wisdom or a request to a dear friend. It was an important tradition, the standing of watch, one Eshai felt she had done too many times to count.

She'd never done it for her parents, though. She could barely remember their faces, but she knew they had died in the wilderness, alone. She thought of them always, even when she couldn't remember them. She couldn't help but think of them whenever she watched for the dead.

Four figures were laid on cloth sheets among the roots, their armor stained black. Valiant armor died with the valiant that wore it, and theirs had almost crumbled away. Eshai stood on one of the roots and waited, looking out over the four. She listed their names in her head. Urai, Bassi, Wila, Tarim.

Only four, when there could have been so many. But they were *her* four. She was supposed to keep them alive.

Eshai squeezed her eyes shut, letting her head tip back so it rested against the trunk of the tree. Her eyes stung behind her eyelids, but she held the tears back, trying to keep her breathing even. She didn't know if the stories were true, didn't know if the soul really lingered, or if it passed on immediately, or if there was even a soul to begin with. But she knew one thing.

Her valor trusted her. Even though she was young, even

though she didn't know what she was doing half the time, even though there were days when she thought about turning the command over to Turi and running as far as she could in any direction. Her valor *trusted* her.

And if her four were still around, in any fashion, Eshai wasn't going to let them see her cry.

The morning after the dead had been interred beneath the roots of the tree, Eshai called the valor together into the command hall. Seri had been invited as well, ostensibly to take notes. She leaned against the back wall, fighting off exhaustion, her heart still heavy from the vigil.

She hadn't known Urai, or Bassi, or Wila that well. She had only known their names. But she had known Tarim. He'd been kind to her. It ached to see the empty space he had left behind.

The valiants, those able to stand, filled the room. She caught sight of Raya by the entryway, her expression a dark cloud, her armor a shade darker than it had been yesterday. She looked as if she hadn't slept, even after her watch. Eshai glanced at her once before addressing the room.

"I've been thinking about yesterday's battle. The way those beasts acted was not normal. Do you agree?"

A murmur passed through the crowd. Seri stopped writing, listening close. She'd heard the strategy employed by the beasts had been unusual, but didn't quite understand why.

Turi spoke up. "It was odd, Commander. Some beasts are pack hunters, but I've never seen any move like that. If I didn't know better, I would say they were being guided."

Seri's eyes widened. *Guided?* It was an impossible thought, and from the way the valiants murmured at that suggestion, they agreed. Eshai, however, didn't find it as impossible as she should have. She nodded.

"I think so, too. Regardless of what caused it, the council needs to know. I will travel to Vethaya to report to them. While I'm there, I'll ask for reinforcements and aid. Turi will be in charge while I'm gone."

"So, you're running away?" Raya asked, her tone almost casual.

Seri froze, charcoal resting against the writing board. Heads turned, facing Raya. She stood in the back of the room, a look of fury on her face.

"Is that it, Commander? You're running away?"

Eshai met Raya's gaze coolly, appearing almost unaffected. Almost.

"If you think the council will listen to anyone else in this room, you're welcome to nominate them to go instead." Silence fell, and Eshai waited it out, her gaze flicking from Raya to the valiants on either side of her. "No one? Then it's settled. It has to be me." Her gaze slid to Turi. "Any objections, Captain?"

"None, Commander."

Eshai nodded. "I'll leave as soon as possible. If any of you have any letters or word that you want me to carry to your loved ones in Vethaya, let me know. Seri. Raya. I want to see you both in my office. Separately."

Seri tensed, but found she couldn't truly worry about her own fate. Her mind was on the storm brewing in Raya's eyes as she brushed past her, following Eshai in.

It was maddening, standing outside the commander's office and waiting for Eshai and Raya to finish. The walls were thin enough that Seri could hear a heated discussion happening inside, but not thin enough to make out the words. Her fingers curled tightly around the writing board she held in both hands, smudging the charcoal. She had to remind herself not to hold her breath.

The door opened and Raya stalked out. Her footfalls were heavy on the floorboards as she stormed away, barely shooting Seri a passing glance. Seri pressed herself back against the wall, wanting to escape Raya's attention as much as possible. It was only when Raya had turned the corner that she heard Eshai sigh.

"You might as well come in, Seri."

Seri stepped into the room. Eshai was leaning against the wall, pinching the bridge of her nose with one hand. There were dark circles under her eyes, standing out against the warm brown of her skin. She let out a long sigh before letting her hand fall away.

"Um," Seri began, shutting the door behind her. "Is everything all right?"

"Four of my valiants are dead, and one seems determined to drive herself into the ground," Eshai snapped, bitterness coloring her tone. "No. Everything is *not* all right. Raya will be accompanying us to Vethaya."

Seri's face colored at the rebuke, but any embarrassment she might have felt faded as the rest of Eshai's words sank in. "*Us,* ma'am?"

Eshai nodded. "You're my aide. So, you'll be coming with us to Vethaya. I plan on leaving first thing in the morning."

A thousand questions raced through Seri's mind, competing for space. She settled on the most pressing.

"Why?"

"Because of what you did," Eshai said, holding Seri's gaze. "You saved my life yesterday, and likely the lives of many other valiants. There aren't many people who could do what you have done."

Seri shifted, feeling uncomfortable. She lowered her eyes to the ground. "I just—"

"Did what you had to?"

Seri's mouth snapped shut. Eshai continued.

"You've earned your first piece of armor. Whether you like it or not, you're on the path to becoming a valiant. Personally, I think you would make a good one, but it's not my place to decide that. You, however, may have to face that decision someday, and it *is* my place to give you the tools to *make* that choice. You'll come with us to Vethaya, the City of Valor, and see for yourself how we conduct our affairs. Do you have any complaints?"

Vethaya, the First City of the People. She had never been there, hadn't even come close. Vethaya was much farther from the border than Elaya, farther inland. It was one of the People's largest cities—a place of safety.

But it was also a place where someone might know her.

Seri fought down the panic, reminding herself it was unlikely anyone in Vethaya would even know where Elaya was. She nodded.

"I understand."

Eshai nodded again. "I'll give you the rest of the day off," she said. "Go make your preparations. I'd prefer to be alone right now."

"Yes, ma'am."

❧

The settlement worked fast, and by the next morning, Seri's beastskin vest was ready. It fit oddly and was the ordinary brown of new leather, but Seri could already feel it changing in shape and size as she slipped it on over her shoulders. She had spent the entirety of the previous day lugging around an irregularly shaped lump of pink crystal—the beast-heart, carved from the flesh of the beast she had slain. Now, shards from that crystal were studded across the leather vest, almost like decoration. According to the valiants, the beast-heart was now attuned to her, and eventually the vest would fit like a second skin, so light she would forget it was there. The crystals would sink into the armor and fade, and the transformation into true armor would be complete. It would heal when it cracked, like a living thing, and would change color and shape, becoming something that reflected her inner heart. If she acquired other pieces in the future, they would match, looking as though they were part of the same set.

"You should expect it to change a lot in the first few years," Eshai said, tugging on the straps of Seri's vest to check the fit. "It takes a while for armor to settle. My old commander used to say it takes about as long as it takes the wearer to understand who they truly are."

Raya, standing with her pack slung over her shoulder, said

nothing. Seri looked between the two of them, struck by the differences in their own armor. Eshai's regal and gleaming, Raya's sharp and menacing. She ran her fingers over the new leather of her vest and tried to feel like it was part of her. It still felt like something *other*.

"Wear it the entire time we're traveling," Eshai said, stepping away from her. "Take it off only to wash. Armor's only good if it's on you—the vest most of all. You never know when you might need it."

Seri nodded to show that she understood, but fussed with the straps again after Eshai stepped away. Somehow the vest felt loose, even though the straps were snug against her skin. The leather itched, her skin crawling where it brushed against it. It was all in her mind, but still, Seri couldn't stop herself from shuddering. She wanted to take it off and hide it somewhere, but Eshai was watching her, so she tugged the straps tighter and tried to ignore it.

They set off eastward, back into the known world and onto the roads that would lead them to Vethaya. For the first two days, they were a somber party. Raya walked at the head of the group, her expression dark and her eyes fixed straight ahead of her. She didn't say anything to Seri, and pointedly ignored Eshai. Eshai, meanwhile, had very little to say. She would answer questions if Seri asked them, but her answers were distracted, and it was clear her mind was elsewhere. More than once, Seri caught her watching Raya with concern when she thought Raya wasn't looking.

It was damp, miserable travel, although they saved one day by rafting down a nearby river. The rains came in the early afternoon, soaking everything and churning the ground to mud. At night, they strung their camp up in the trees, using makeshift platforms to keep them off the ground. They also changed into their dry clothes, and at Eshai and Raya's insistence, Seri made sure her feet were completely dry before sleeping. The vest, at the very least, seemed to dry quickly on its own.

In the evenings after making camp, Seri was left to her own devices. She used the time to practice archery. It wasn't that she was particularly dedicated to the bow, but it felt good to have something to do. The bow was reassuring in her hands, and the act of pulling back the string, sighting on a target, and letting the arrow fly calmed her. The more she practiced, the more comfortable she felt, her shots grouping closer and closer to the center of her target.

"You're getting better," Eshai remarked on their second evening, looking up to watch Seri as she crossed the ground to reclaim her arrows. "You have a knack for this. Doesn't she, Raya?"

Raya scowled at the question, but she looked Seri's target over anyway.

"You should have gotten the gloves. If you want to make it as an archer, you'll need them."

Seri pretended not to hear her, carefully working the arrows free from her target. Raya didn't say anything more, getting up to patrol the perimeter.

"I'm worried about her," Eshai said to Seri the next day, when they took a break for lunch. Raya had taken to the trees immediately after they stopped, claiming she wasn't hungry. Seri could hear her moving through the foliage, the steady thump of her boots hitting branches as she leapt from tree to tree.

"About Raya?"

Eshai nodded. She took a slow sip from her water flask, then gestured at Seri's vest. Even after three days, it had already begun to conform to her body, so much so that Seri barely noticed she was wearing it now. Its color had begun to change, patches of violet appearing around the edges.

"Armor matches your heart. Have you ever wondered how Raya's turned out that way?"

Seri thought about Raya's dark red armor, about the look on her face during training matches. "She likes to fight."

"Many valiants do. Before even joining the valor, an aspirant has to hunt and kill five beasts. The people who do it when they're young are usually those who enjoy the hunt."

"Were you like that?" Eshai couldn't have been much older than Seri when she joined the valor. She might have even been younger if she was valor commander at the age of nineteen.

Eshai shook her head. "No. I'm one of the odd ones out. I joined the valor for another reason. Raya is different."

"What's the harm in it? She likes to fight beasts. Fighting beasts is her duty."

"It's more than that," said Eshai. "Raya doesn't just like to fight beasts. She likes to *kill* them. She hates them more than anything, and that hate is eating her alive."

"Because of Tarim?" She still felt a pang of regret when she thought of the other valiant. She hadn't found the words to talk to Raya about him yet, to express how sorry she was.

Eshai shook her head. "It's not just Tarim. Raya's had an unlucky few years. But armor like that is a bad sign, Seri. You might not realize it, but armor that warped is a step away from breaking."

"I thought armor only broke when a valiant died?"

"That's how it usually works. But armor reflects a valiant's heart, and a strong heart requires more than just life. If a valiant's spirit decays to the point where their armor crumbles, it's almost as if they've died. They'll never be a valiant again."

Seri wanted to ask more, but the warning glance Eshai shot her stopped her. Raya returned a second later, landing with a squelch as her boots sank into the soft mud. Eshai said no more, but Seri found herself thinking over Eshai's words late into the night, her fingers splayed against the changing surface of her own beastskin armor. Seri remembered Raya before the attack, before Tarim's death. Raya had spoken of the commander with obvious respect. She wondered how that respect had turned to anger overnight, and realized it wasn't *Eshai* Raya was truly angry with.

She wondered if Eshai had noticed, too.

The next day, they started training again. To her chagrin, Eshai took Seri aside and insisted on teaching her how to fight hand-to-hand. It wasn't something Seri had ever been interested in learning, but Eshai reminded her that she never knew when it would be useful. Having armor made her able to move her body in new and interesting ways, and it would be a shame to not know how to use that.

So, Seri went with her and started to learn, suffering through lessons where Eshai insisted she know how to kick and punch, and gritting her teeth when Eshai decided to teach her how to take a fall. The armor did a lot to blunt the impact when Eshai grabbed her by the straps of her vest and flung her over her shoulder, but she still felt jarred by it. She realized as she got up, rolling to her feet the way Eshai had taught her, that Eshai no longer saw her as a civilian. She'd slain a beast. As far as Eshai was concerned, she was no longer an aide, but an aspirant, someone on their way to becoming a valiant. The thought made her feel uncomfortable, and it was that discomfort more than anything that made her refuse when Eshai offered again to teach her the spear.

"It's not for me," Seri said. "I'm better with the bow."

Eshai looked disappointed, but went off to practice on her own. Seri sighed, rubbing at her sore shoulders as she walked back to camp. She sat down next to their supplies, wondering if Eshai would scold her for taking her armor off just so she could rub at that one *knot* that had formed between her shoulder blades.

"She always does that, doesn't she?" Raya asked, emerging from the trees with an armful of firewood.

Seri jumped. She hadn't expected the valiant to be there. Although Raya's armor *seemed* heavy, Seri hadn't heard her approach.

"Um . . ."

"The commander." Raya inclined her head in the direction Eshai had gone, letting the bundle of firewood fall to the ground. "She acts like she knows best. She wants to turn you into a valiant, and she wants to turn *me* into a penitent at Lanatha. Do you know why?"

"Er . . . I've slain a beast? And your armor . . ."

Raya snorted. "She wants to do both those things because it's what *she* did," she said, beginning to arrange the wood into a pile. "She wants to send me to Lanatha because that's what her commander did when her armor got like mine."

Seri frowned, fighting down her unease. "The commander's armor was like yours?"

Raya shrugged. "After Naumea. She was hard after that—brutal. She kept finding excuses to get back in the fight. Old Ushi said enough was enough and sent her off to Lanatha."

"I've heard you talk about Lanatha before," Seri said. "What is that?"

Raya's look was incredulous. "You don't know? Who taught you your songs?"

Seri flushed, feeling the heat rise to her face. Raya let out a slow breath.

"Sorry. Caretaker's ward—I forgot. Lanatha's . . . a special place. They call it the Mother of Waters. It's a spreading tree in the middle of a lake, just . . ." She spread her hands wide to indicate breadth. "Cleanest water you'll ever find in the known world. They say it's where the First Valor went for shelter, after they founded Vethaya. It's sacred."

"And people just *go* there?"

"Valiants and civilians—they're called penitents when they're there. They go to be 'cleansed' from whatever ails them up here." She tapped her head. "In practice, it's a lot of swimming and sleeping and meditating. And talking about your feelings. But the commander doesn't get that some people don't need to be cured. And some people don't want to forget. Some people want to *remember*."

"Is that why you won't go? Because *you* want to remember?"

Raya was silent for a while, brow furrowed in thought. And then she stretched out her arm. Not a lot, but enough for Seri to see the marks that crept over her skin, a story of courage and strength and battle.

"They mark us up for everything," she said. "When we're born, when we come of age, when we marry, when we have kids. When we create something or win a fight or get acknowledged by the elders. We get marked up for all our gains, but no one ever marks us for our losses. And those are the ones that sting the most."

Raya shrugged, letting her arm fall back to her side. "Maybe this armor is my way of marking up my losses. Because Tarim was *here*, damn it, and my brother was *here*, and I'm not going to close my eyes and pretend they didn't exist."

She held up the flint in her hand, studying it carefully. "Life's like fire sometimes, sprout. You can't just ignore the burned parts of you."

"But don't you sometimes have to put the fire *out*?" Seri asked. "Before *all* of you burns up?"

Raya stared at her, blinking, and Seri got the sense that she'd startled her. But then Raya looked straight at her and said, "I guess you'd know, wouldn't you?"

Seri looked down at her hand, at the name-mark that stood out in sharp relief over her skin. *Seri.* Little fire. She felt something inside her twist uncomfortably, her mind taking her back to that time in the rainforest with Ithim. Her mother must have known, when she named her that, how much of the world Seri would burn.

Raya held the flint in front of her nose and Seri jumped, startled.

"Look, enough moping," Raya said. "Let's get *this* fire started, or we won't have any dinner tonight. Why don't you try to start it this time? You've seen me do it enough."

Seri swallowed but nodded, taking the flint from Raya. It

hadn't seemed that hard. She just had to strike the flint the right way—to make a spark.

Dry leaves caught and smoldered at Seri's hands, the fire spreading to cover the tinder. It was only beginning to grow when Raya jerked her head around, her eyes wide. Through the trees, Seri saw Eshai do the same, snapping to attention.

Raya kicked at the flames, extinguishing them before they could grow. Seri leapt back, surprised.

"What—?"

"Shh!" Raya hissed, holding a hand up toward her. She turned to Eshai. "Two of them, small ones. Maybe humans. Maybe beasts. I can't tell. Can you?"

Eshai shook her head.

"Orders?"

Eshai gave her a sharp look, and Seri realized she must have been able to hear *everything* they were saying. Raya would have known that—she would have been intimately familiar with a valiant's hearing. But instead of reprimanding them, Eshai jerked her head toward the trees.

"Take north and east, I'll go south and west. Three leaps' distance around the camp. If you don't find anything, come back."

Raya nodded, disappearing into the canopy. Seri turned to Eshai, alarmed.

"What is it? What's going on?"

"We heard something in the forest." Eshai's expression was grim. "Something's been watching us. I'm going to put you up in that tree. Keep an arrow on your string and an eye on camp for me."

Something's been watching us...

Those words echoed in Seri's mind as she sat crouched in the tree, her back pressed against the trunk and her feet wedged awkwardly into the space between two branches. She kept an arrow to her string, her stomach tight as she watched the camp. The thick foliage surrounding her suddenly didn't seem like enough cover, the drop to the ground more dangerous than it should have been.

Seri had lived her whole life in the trees, but to be in one with no platform and no railing was another thing entirely. She wasn't a valiant; she didn't have the boots that would give her the agility to leap from branch to branch. If an attacker came across her sitting here, she would be exposed, worse than useless. She told herself her vest would offer her some protection, but it was hard to be confident in something that rested so easily on her shoulders, something she forgot she was wearing.

Her fingers were shaking on the string. She reminded herself to breathe, in and out, waiting.

It went on forever. Seri's legs started to cramp, sweat trickling down the back of her neck and into the space beneath her armor. She felt a prickling sensation up her back and prayed to the fates Eshai hadn't chosen to put her in a tree with an insect nest. But she hadn't heard the all-clear, didn't trust in her ability to get down from this tree by herself. She waited. Her mind played tricks on her, conjuring scenes where Eshai and Raya had been killed and she was the only one left alive. Where she would have to stay in this tree until nightfall, or else climb down from it and try to find her way to Vethaya on her own.

Where she would wander lost and starving in the rainforest until she finally died.

When Eshai landed on the branch next to hers with a thump, Seri screamed and nearly dropped her bow. Eshai blinked.

"Sorry for startling you. I'm going to let you down now."

Eshai wrapped an arm around her waist, leaping from the treetop. Seri's stomach lurched with free fall, and she clamped her lips tightly together, not wanting to scream again. When she landed on the ground, her feet threatened to buckle underneath her. She shook out her legs, massaging away the stiffness as Eshai stepped away, rubbing at the healing crack on her armor.

Raya materialized out of the shadows of the forest, walking over to them. Her spear was drawn, a dark scowl on her face.

"Anything?" Eshai asked.

"No," Raya said, flicking her spear blade out to the side before replacing it in its harness across her back. "Nothing. I thought I saw something moving in the trees, but whatever it was got away."

There was silence, and Seri realized after a moment that Eshai was looking at her. She shook her head.

"It was quiet. I didn't see or hear anything."

"You don't have a helm," Raya pointed out. "They could have been right behind you, and you wouldn't have known."

Eshai glared at Raya. "There's no point in scaring her. Whatever it was got away. We have a bit of daylight left. Pack up the camp. We'll find somewhere else to sleep tonight."

Raya frowned, but the truce that crisis had brokered apparently still stood, because she nodded, leaping into the trees to unfasten their platform. Seri gathered up their cooking things, wincing as her stiff muscles protested the movement. It was while they were packing that Raya spoke, her voice so soft and quiet that Seri wasn't convinced she meant for any of them to hear her, or that she was aware of speaking out loud at all.

"It was so small . . . ," Raya said. "It looked almost human . . ."

CHAPTER 5

꙯

They encountered no one else on the road to Vethaya.
The day after the incident, they started sleeping in
outposts. They were deep enough in the known world
that villages weren't hard to find, but far enough from the interior that most of the villages they came across still had their
own valors. Seri was so relieved to be sleeping indoors, with
real food to eat each night, that she forgot all about the incident
with the strangers in the woods. It had probably been nothing.
They were all on edge. There was no point in continuing to
worry.

On the fifteenth day after they left the settlement, Vethaya
came into view.

When Seri saw the City of Valor for the first time, she froze.
Up until then, her new settlement's spreading tree had been the
biggest she had seen, but even that was dwarfed by the monster
that housed Vethaya. From where she stood, she could barely
see the top of the tree, and at this distance, it was hard to make
out the curve of the trunk. The city rose up like a wall, blocking
out the sun and dominating the skyline.

Eshai noticed her reaction and turned to look at her, a spark
of amusement in her dark brown eyes.

"Welcome to Vethaya. Stay close. It's easy to get lost."

The nearest ladders were placed along the outer ring of
branches, near valor outposts. They used one of them, climbing

up onto a well-used platform. The valiants on duty drew themselves up taller to salute as Eshai and company passed by, but Seri caught them exchanging looks of unease.

Unease was a common theme in the city. She could feel it in the air as they walked through the afternoon crowd, people turning their heads to look at them from where they were clustered outside taverns and beside streets. Seeing so many people after living with the same hundred-odd souls for months was startling, but seeing the way those same people watched them, expressions darkening before they returned to their whispers, disturbed her.

Eshai and Raya noticed, too. They exchanged a glance, their feud forgotten, before Eshai turned to grab the arm of a valiant heading in the other direction. The valiant, a young man in dark blue armor, turned to look at her with wide eyes, his gaze continually flicking from her face to her armor's signature white.

"C-Commander Eshai—I—"

"Don't worry about it," Eshai said, holding up a hand to forestall his apologies. "What's going on? Why is everyone so tense?"

"It's—well—" The young man looked out of the corner of his eye toward his friends, another pair of valiants, but they had already stepped away, looking anywhere but at Eshai's face. He drew in a breath, squaring his shoulders. "It's Anaya Settlement, Commander. You know the one?"

"The newest southern settlement, yes," Eshai said, nodding. "It's been settled for a few years now, hasn't it?"

"Well, yes. It has, but . . ." He looked again to his friends, then looked back at Eshai, wetting his lips with his tongue.

"C-Captain Besai, from the Anaya contingent, just came in a few days ago. He said the village's been attacked. A group of beasts. Over seventy dead, most of the settlement devastated. The council just sent someone out there for aid."

Eshai frowned, releasing the valiant's arm. Seri felt a chill run through her.

"When?" Eshai asked.

"Two nights after the water moon."

Raya's face darkened. Seri understood. Two nights after the water moon would have been about eighteen days ago. Assuming the valiant wasn't mistaken, that was the same day they had been attacked.

"Thank you," Eshai said. "You can go."

The valiant scrambled off, rejoining his friends. All three of them escaped into the crowd, not looking back.

Eshai turned to face Raya and Seri, the passing crowd giving them a wide berth as they streamed around them. "Raya, do you remember where my apartment is?"

"Spearwork Branch, right? What about it?"

"Do me a favor and walk Seri there. I might be a while. Show her where the market is on the way." Eshai reached into her pouch, drawing out a wooden cylinder attached to a leather strap. A series of notches had been cut into the cylinder. Seri recognized it as a key, although she couldn't remember the last time she had seen one in person. She had never lived in a city large enough to need them.

Eshai handed the key and a painted blue chip bearing her name-mark to Seri, who took the items with both hands.

"The key will let you into the apartment," she said. "Air it out, then head down to the market and buy enough supplies to last a few days. I don't think we'll be staying long. I'm going to speak to the council immediately."

Seri thought Raya was going to argue, but she only watched as Eshai turned to leave, her expression thoughtful.

"You think they'll listen to you?" she asked, before Eshai could get too far away.

Eshai looked back over her shoulder, giving Raya a wry smile. "I can only try," she said. "Take the evening off when you're done. I'm sure there are people you want to see. We'll meet up again at the second bell tomorrow."

Raya nodded, motioning to Seri. "Come on," she said. "We've got a ways to go."

When Seri and Raya were gone, Eshai turned back to the main thoroughfare that cut through the city, ending at the towering structure that cradled the trunk of the spreading tree. She started walking, aware of the way the crowd parted to either side of her, the weight of their gazes on her armor. They knew who she was by that, even if they didn't know her face. She knew the rumors would soon be spreading. Eshai Unbroken, just returned from their newest and farthest settlement. On the heels of another officer come to report misfortune. It could mean nothing good.

Eshai wished they wouldn't give her this much credit. She wished her armor were less distinctive, wished she could move through the crowds in peace. But more than that, she wished they weren't so right.

The valiants on duty outside headquarters let her through

without a word, although Eshai noticed them exchanging glances as she passed. A brief chat with the receptionist told her the council was in session today, which was fortunate. She removed her helm—it was only polite inside of headquarters—and tucked it under her arm as she made her way toward the council chambers.

The Vethaya headquarters was an odd structure, built around the trunk of the spreading tree. Each floor was circular, with a winding staircase that climbed the trunk, occasionally making room for larger branches to extend outward. The council chambers were at the top. It was a climb that would be exhausting for anyone not wearing full armor. For a valiant, it was merely tedious and annoying.

In theory, the council's meetings were open to any valiant who wished to sit in, and any officer could address the council at any time. Because of this, Eshai had no doubt the tedium was intentional. It made sure no valiant would bother the council except in great need. And it also drove home just how the council saw itself.

A group sitting on top of the world.

The stairs finally leveled off, stopping just outside the curtained archway that led into the council's chambers. She could hear conversation inside. There were two valiants on duty, neither of whom she recognized. They recognized her, of course, their eyes moving over her armor. They held the curtain for her as she walked past, admitting her into the council chamber.

Conversation stilled as she walked through the door.

Eshai paused to look around, taking note of the people that sat on cushions on the polished wooden floor, arranged in a circle. The councilmembers were all aged valiants who had proven their worth and who were still valued for their wisdom, although their spear-bearing days were behind them. They wore their armor still, rested their spears on the ground beside their cushions. Twelve spears, pointing inward toward the center. All around them were raised benches where any valiant could sit if they wished to listen in on the council's discussion.

Eshai's gaze swept the benches, and she was surprised to find her old commander sitting there, his arms folded over his chest. Ushi's gaze met hers, his expression solemn. He nodded to her, and she nodded back.

She didn't head for the benches, which was what, she thought, the council had hoped for. Instead, she walked straight into the circle of spears. There, Eshai dropped to a knee, pulling her helm to herself with one hand and pressing her fist to the floor.

"I come to address the council."

The room was built to carry sound. Although she didn't shout, it felt as though she did, her own voice echoing back at her. She didn't dare look up, but wondered in the silence that followed if the councilmembers were exchanging the same troubled glances she had seen from the valiants.

A woman spoke first, a withered, gray-haired woman in blue armor flecked through with white. Anai of the Dancing Waters. Her legend had been old when Eshai had first taken up the spear.

"Speak then, Commander Eshai."

"I come with a report from the settlement project. Eighteen nights ago, we were attacked by beasts. I understand that at this time, the settlement of Anaya was also attacked." She paused, waiting for a contradiction, but none came. "The invaders were repelled, but at cost. Four valiants were returned to the earth.

No settlers were killed. We are fortunate to have been spared the fate of Anaya."

There was a release of tension in the room. To their mind, the situation wasn't as bad as they had feared. Eshai felt that and recognized that a dismissal was close at hand. Stubbornly, she went on.

"It was only good fortune that saved us, but I am concerned about the actions of the beasts. When they attacked us, they showed strategy and foresight. We believe that were it not for the actions of the settlers—" Of Seri, really. Stubborn, innocent Seri. Eshai kept herself from saying her name. Seri likely wouldn't thank her for bringing her to the council's attention. "—we would have suffered severe losses inside the settlement itself."

She fell silent, waiting to be addressed. As she waited, she could feel a new tension in the air, replacing the one she had dispersed a moment ago. It was a while before someone spoke, this time a man wearing bright gold armor. Sukuna of the Sun.

"What would you request of the council, Commander Eshai?"

"Reinforcements, Councilman," Eshai said, launching into the speech she had been preparing since they left the spreading tree. "Our settlement is almost a day away from the nearest village, even for a valiant. Another attack could be disastrous. We cannot entrust our future to luck. The temporary addition of a second valor would greatly strengthen our position."

Silence fell. Eshai had a sense they were watching her, taking her measure. She was meant to be a valor commander and a hero, but she hadn't been either for very long. It was a feeling that still unnerved her. She forced herself to remain still, to keep her eyes on the ground. As the silence dragged, she felt her discomfort intensify. It hadn't been a difficult request. Surely, they would have an answer for her by now.

Someone spoke from her left, a man's voice, even older than Sukuna's. She thought this was Emrei the Wise but didn't look to be sure. "We have already sent reinforcements to Anaya. It sounds to me, Commander, as though you still have most of your valor and that the major threat has been repelled. The threat in Anaya has not been. Our focus must be there for the meantime."

Eshai looked up before she could stop herself, raising her gaze to the council. "Councilman—did you not hear what I said?"

"Don't be impertinent, Commander," Anai said, her voice cutting. "The council has heard you. We believe your valor to be sufficient."

"We have some trainees that have not yet been assigned to a valor," Sukuna said. "You may have your pick from them to replace the four you lost. You may also have any supplies you require, and your choice of medics and support staff. This council would be willing to assign up to twenty more valiants to your command, in recognition of this perceived threat. But we can do no more."

"Twenty-four?" Eshai repeated. It was barely a third of the full valor she had requested. And many of those twenty-four would be recruits, fresh from the training grounds. "With all due respect, Councilman Sukuna, twenty-four more valiants will hardly matter in the face of another coordinated attack."

"You use the words 'coordinated attack,'" a woman in deep pink armor said from Eshai's left—Namari of the Blossoms.

"What evidence do you have that this attack was truly coordinated?"

"While one group of beasts occupied our forces, another group moved to attack from an undefended side," Eshai said, struggling to master her temper.

"That hardly suggests coordination," Namari said. "Beasts are creatures of opportunity. We know this. Perhaps a second group of beasts merely chanced upon the opportunity granted them by finding an unprotected side of the settlement."

"And this all happened on the same day the beasts attacked Anaya?"

A tense silence followed, and Eshai knew she had disturbed them. The members of the council exchanged glances with each other.

"That is troubling, I'll admit," Sukuna said. "But hardly evidence of coordination. Rest assured, however, that this coincidence will be investigated fully."

"Investigated," Eshai said. "And meanwhile, I have to return to my settlement and inform my settlers that their council is leaving them unprotected? We need more *help*, Councilman."

"Settlers understand the risk when they volunteer to settle, Commander," said Anai. "They understand no reward can be claimed without risk. This council has heard you, but we have other business to attend to. We cannot simply commit valors to the will of a first-year commander, regardless of her reputation. You are dismissed."

"My people trust the Council of Valor to help them. If the settlement falls, their blood will be on *your* heads!"

Anai's gaze was as cool as the waters she was named for. "You are *dismissed*, Commander."

Eshai stared at Anai for a long moment, seething. Then she drew in a breath and grabbed her spear from the floor, getting to her feet. She bowed low toward the councilmembers, leaving the chamber before she could say something stupid.

Ushi followed her out. Eshai barely noticed until his shadow crossed her. He was a large man, bearded and built like a boar, and his figure blocked out the sun from the window. She looked over her shoulder to see him with his arms folded, watching her.

"Making waves as usual, aren't you, young star?"

"They think I was exaggerating. You know me, Commander. I do *not* exaggerate."

Ushi nodded. "I know you, Eshai, and I know you've never been one to ask for help unless it was needful. Even then."

"Then speak for me to the council. We need reinforcements. I have people—"

"We *all* have people to protect. I could speak for you, but it wouldn't help. The council is concerned not just with the fate of one settlement, but with the fate of the entire known world."

The frustration was so sharp it burned. Eshai felt heat behind her eyes and fought it back, because she would *not* cry in front of Ushi. "Then what? My settlement has to be sacrificed before they admit there's a problem?"

"You might not believe it, but the council believes there is a problem. That is why they will investigate. But they will be unwilling to commit resources until the full scale of that problem is understood. It will be slow, but any creature that must protect a domain as large as the council's often is." Ushi's gaze shifted to the curtained doorway. The valiants on guard duty were doing their best to pretend Eshai and Ushi were invisible.

"This is the burden of command. We must understand the council will not always help, nor will it always listen. And we must do the best we can with the resources we have. My valor has grown since you left it. I will petition the council to allow me to transfer five of my best to your valor."

Eshai let out a breath. It wasn't what she had hoped, but she recognized the significance of Ushi's offer. She bowed her head, touching a hand to her heart.

"Thank you, Commander."

"I assume you'll be along to inspect the recruits tomorrow," Ushi said. "You should rest tonight. There are a lot of people in Vethaya who would be happy to see you."

His smile suggested that he counted himself among that number. Eshai nodded in thanks and tried not to think about how she would break the news to Raya and Seri.

Spearmaid's Market was a whirlwind to Seri. An open-air market, it was situated on a platform strung at the junction between two different branches, Spearwork Branch and Maiden's Turn. Raya had showed her to Eshai's apartment, staying just long enough to help her air out the place, then had brought her here and left to find a stiff drink. Seri had tried not to panic when Raya walked away. It was mostly a straight path from the market to Eshai's apartment building, so she wasn't too worried about getting lost, but navigating the market was another thing entirely.

There were too many things to see. Seri told herself she was only here for food, just a few household necessities to tide her and Eshai over for a few days, but it was hard not to glance to the left or right, to look with envy at the flowing, brightly colored dresses or the jewelry glittering on racks. Even ordinary supplies were different here, and she spent some time marveling at the price of rice in Vethaya before purchasing some. It was hard to believe this wasn't even the city's main market. The central market was said to be grander.

The armor surprised her as well. She thought she would have been out of place in her vest and even debated leaving it at the apartment, but there were people in armor all around her. Many of them were valiants, with the full set, but many weren't. She bought meat from a butcher with a set of armored gloves and no other pieces of armor, fruit from a scrawny older woman who had somehow earned a pair of boots. No one even looked at her twice. What would have drawn notice in a small village like Elaya was just everyday life here.

It wasn't all grand and beautiful. There were beggars clustered at the entrances to the market, ragged people with hands outstretched. She had heard of them but had never seen their like before. Such things had never happened in a village like Elaya, where there were too few people to let anyone fall through the cracks.

Her work with Eshai earned her a small stipend, so she handed a few chits to an old woman trailed by several of her grandchildren, then used a few more to purchase a skewer of bananas fried in syrup. Seri ate as she walked, carrying her purchases in one hand. A troupe of dancers was performing on the platform, two men and two women. The men were crouched on the ground, each holding the ends of two bamboo poles, which they pounded on the ground and clacked together in a stark rhythm. The women danced nimbly between the poles as they moved, narrowly avoiding getting their ankles caught in the space between them as they danced. Seri slowed as she passed, unable to stop herself from watching the spectacle.

She didn't see the girl heading the other way until she practically crashed into her.

With her vest, Seri barely felt anything, just the slightest push to tell her she had bumped into someone. The other girl, however, jerked alarmingly to the side. Seri reached out and grabbed her by the arm to steady her, eyes wide in alarm. The girl was on the small side, shorter than Seri but still somehow taller than Raya. She looked to be roughly Seri's age. Her hair was long and brown, falling down her back in soft waves, and she wore a thin blue cloak fastened at the shoulder. Her eyes, when she turned to look at Seri, were a shade of brown touched with gold, like sunlight warming the earth.

Unbidden, Seri's eyes drifted to her right hand, where her name-mark would be. It was covered by a glove, though not an armored one.

"I'm so sorry!" she said. "I wasn't watching where I was going."

The girl stared at her for a long moment, looking, Seri realized, at her vest. Its color had settled into a pale violet threaded through with patches of blue, the color of the sky at twilight. She'd almost forgotten she was wearing it. The vest had softened the blow for Seri, making it difficult to gauge just how hard she had hit her.

"Are you hurt at all?" Seri asked, drawing the girl's attention back to her. The girl shook her head.

"Fine," she said. Her tone was clipped, and there was something odd about the way she spoke, a strange lilt to her words that Seri couldn't place. "Watch where you're going next time."

She glanced pointedly at Seri's hand, which still held tight to her forearm. Seri flushed and let go. The girl turned away, and Seri spoke before she could stop herself.

"Wait!"

She stopped, looking over her shoulder. Seri felt her flush deepen and wished she hadn't spoken at all. But she *had* to say something now. The girl was watching her expectantly.

"Erm . . . I really do feel bad. Can I buy you a fruit juice?"

The girl's brows arched, but she didn't say no.

Seri bought two cups of mango juice from the nearest stall and settled on a bench with the strange girl to watch the dance. Her name, Seri learned, was Tsana, which was not a name she had ever heard before. She couldn't place its meaning immediately, but she liked its sound.

"My name is Seri," she said, holding up her own right hand to show Tsana her name-mark, a glyph stylized into the small flame of a candle fire. They watched the dancers in silence while Seri worked up the nerve to speak. "Are you from Vethaya?"

"No. I'm only visiting. I arrived here a few days ago."

"What brought you here?"

Tsana's eyes were on the dancers. They had switched places now, the women clacking the bamboo sticks while the men leapt in and out of the space where they met, the rhythm growing faster and faster.

"Curiosity."

It was impossible to read Tsana's tone. "Do you . . . like it?"

"It's . . . different from what I expected."

Seri laughed nervously, wincing inwardly at the sound. "It is, isn't it? There's so much of it. I don't even know where to look."

"You aren't from Vethaya?" Tsana sounded surprised. She turned toward Seri for the first time. Seri found herself staring into her eyes, and it took her a moment to answer.

"Um . . . no. I'm visiting, just like you."

Tsana's gaze drifted to her vest again, and Seri realized Tsana had probably marked her as an aspirant. It was a notion she would have been quick to correct in anyone else. This time, she didn't bother. A part of her *wanted* Tsana to think she was an aspirant—someone to be admired.

"Can I ask you a question?" Tsana asked.

Seri nodded. "Sure. Anything."

"How did you get that armor?"

Seri raised a hand to the vest she was wearing, her fingers brushing against the feel of the leather. She remembered the weight of the bolt in her hands, the recoil of the ballista as she fired it at the beast attacking Eshai. "An attack on my settlement. It wasn't anything special. I got lucky."

Something flashed in Tsana's eyes, something strange, yet familiar. Seri couldn't place it just then, but it bothered her. It felt important she understand that look.

She opened her mouth to ask if something was wrong, but the sound of her name, shouted across the marketplace, stopped her. Seri looked up sharply to see Eshai walking toward her, her helm tucked under her arm. She leapt up from her seat, embarrassed.

"Eshai!" she said, as the commander reached her. "I was just—" Seri looked behind her, meaning to gesture at Tsana, but the other girl was gone.

❧

She and Eshai finished up the last of their purchases and walked back to the apartment together. Seri relaxed somewhat when she realized the commander's anger wasn't directed at her, but rather at whatever had transpired in the council chambers. It still didn't feel good being around Eshai when she was angry, but her anger faded as they left the market, stepping onto Spearwork Branch.

"Who was that girl you were talking to?" Eshai asked. "A friend of yours?"

Seri shook her head. "I just met her today. Her name was Tsana."

"Sena? Like 'vine'?"

"Maybe. I didn't get a good look at her name-mark." Seri suddenly wished she had asked Tsana where she was staying. In a city as large as Vethaya, she doubted she would find her again. "But it sounded like she pronounced it differently, so I'm not sure."

"Hmm. Do you know what she's doing here?"

"I didn't get that far. She was asking me about my armor. Maybe she's interested in valiants?"

"It's possible," said Eshai. A lot of people came to Vethaya to get a glimpse of the valiants at work. Aspirants weren't hard to come across, although technically one wasn't supposed to make the pilgrimage to Vethaya until one was ready to join the valor in full.

But it didn't fit somehow. The look in Tsana's eye, when she had asked Seri about her armor, hadn't been admiration, or even jealousy. It had been something else. Something darker.

Anger, Seri thought. Or rage.

Or *fear.*

Eshai stopped dead in her tracks, and Seri almost crashed into her back. She managed to stop herself just in time, jerking to the side to avoid walking into the commander.

"Eshai, what—?"

Eshai didn't answer. Her gaze was trained on someone standing at the front of her apartment building, holding a cloth-wrapped bundle in one hand. A valiant, a young man. His skin was the same shade of brown as Seri's, lighter than Eshai's by a degree, and his armor was blue as the sky. Unlike Eshai, he wore his helm. He looked awkward standing there, shifting his weight from foot to foot, and then he caught sight of Eshai and turned to face them.

His eyes were something. A brown so dark they were almost black, glittering like jewels in the slender lines of his face. They reminded Seri of flower petals in their shape. Between the eyes and the armor, she thought this was the sort of person who had people throwing themselves at him left and right, the sort of person the young girls in her village might have gossiped about if he passed by. But then she saw the surprised, somewhat awkward smile that appeared on his face when he saw Eshai, and Seri understood that it didn't matter, because whoever this person was, he was almost assuredly taken.

"Eshai." He coughed, sounding embarrassed. "I—er, heard you were in town, so I brought some food. I didn't know you would have company."

Eshai jerked back into motion. "I didn't know you were here, or I would have sent word. This is Seri, one of the settlers from my assignment. Apparently, the valor thought I needed an aide. Seri, this is my former wardmate, Lavit. Commander Lavit now."

"Somehow," Lavit said. He turned toward Seri and seemed to instantly grow more confident. "It's nice to meet you. Should we go inside? You can tell me more about what Eshai's been up to. I'm sure there are a lot of things she won't tell me."

CHAPTER 6

⚘

Eshai was oddly subdued as they entered the apartment, leaving Seri to unlock and open the door. Seri shot her a cautious glance, worried she had upset the commander somehow, but Eshai wasn't meeting her gaze, instead looking off to the side and down at the ground. The expression softened her features, making her look so much younger. It was easy to forget that Eshai wasn't more than a few years older than Seri, barely an adult herself in the eyes of the People. Seri never thought she would see Eshai *nervous*, and she chanced a glance at Lavit to see if he had noticed.

He hadn't, because he wasn't looking at her, either.

From there, it was two flights of stairs before they reached the apartment itself. The stairs were still a novelty to Seri. In her own village, there hadn't been a single building with more than one floor, the elders still afraid that the platforms would not be able to bear any more weight. But Vethaya's platforms were not the simple platforms that made up her own village or their new settlement. They had been built up over the course of centuries and were almost as stable as solid ground.

The building was made of bamboo and thatch, which served to cool it, and Eshai's apartment was on the top floor, on the side of the building that faced away from the spreading tree. Because it was in the upper branches of Vethaya, the air here was cool and sweet, with fewer insects and none of the stench of waste plaguing the lower branches. It was still a small apartment, and the furniture was not necessarily fine, but Eshai, Seri thought, didn't seem opposed to drawing on the advantages of her rank and fame.

Seri was grateful for that, though. It was quiet here, and after the whirlwind of the market, she needed that.

Although, she mused—watching Eshai and Lavit dance around each other—she doubted she was about to get much rest.

Lavit followed Seri in, placing the food on a low wooden table. He unpacked the dinner he had brought while Eshai locked the door behind them. Beneath the cloth wrapping was a pair of parcels wrapped tightly in banana leaves. One contained garlic rice, the other, skewers of grilled chicken. The smell of the sauce wafting up from the skewers made Seri's mouth water, despite the snacks she had eaten at the market.

"If I knew you had company, I would have brought more food," Lavit said, looking apologetic. "I can send for more."

Seri breathed deep, feeling the tension in the air. Occasionally, one or the other would glance at her, as though Seri's presence was the only thing stopping them from saying what was on their minds. She took that as her cue to leave.

"Don't worry about me. I was hoping to explore a little more. I've never been to a city as big as Vethaya."

Eshai looked concerned. "You won't get lost?"

"Spearwork Branch isn't that hard to find. And I'm sure I can ask for directions."

For a moment, Eshai looked like she might protest. But she glanced once at Lavit and reached into her pouch instead, coming up with a handful of wooden chits. "Here," she said, handing the money to Seri. "For dinner. Stay out of the Lower West, or anywhere that isn't brightly lit and guarded. And if anyone gives you trouble, you remember the hold I taught you?" On their trip over, Eshai had taught Seri a particularly nasty joint lock, meant to be applied against a grab to the shoulder or the wrist.

Seri nodded. "Don't worry. I remember."

"You should go to Sarani's, in Central," Lavit said. "The owner's a friend. Tell her I sent you."

Seri smiled faintly. "Thanks for the tip."

❦

Silence fell after Seri left the apartment. Eshai sat beside Lavit on the couch, her eyes on the door. Neither of them spoke. It was Lavit who broke the spell first, as the last of Seri's footsteps faded away.

"Well," he said. "I get the feeling she has the wrong idea."

"Just watch," Eshai said, rolling her eyes as she leaned back against the cushions. "Both our valors will be gossiping about us for weeks."

"What else is new?" Lavit asked, picking up one of the skewers. "You should have seen the look my second gave me when I left work today." He handed another skewer to her. Eshai glanced at it. Leg and thigh, the parts Lavit knew she preferred. She sat up, taking the skewer from him and tearing out a strip of meat with her fingers.

"How long have you been stationed out here?" The last she heard, Lavit's valor had been sent south and east, to secure some of the newer settlements.

"Since solstice. A moon or so. Things were pretty slow at our post, so the council recalled us, told us to sit tight in Vethaya for a little bit. We've been on rotation as the city guard. It's been a good break so far. We've taken on a few greenleaves that could use the extra training before we head out again, which is starting to look like it might happen sooner rather than later. I've heard word that we're going out to reinforce Anaya." He took a bite from his own skewer and washed it down with a handful of garlic rice, before looking sidelong at Eshai. "Is it too much to hope that you're here because you have *good* news?"

Eshai frowned, looking down at her meal. Thinking about the council's response made the food lose its savor. If she didn't stop herself from thinking about it, she could still see them, four of her valor nestled in the roots of the spreading tree. There was also the looming threat of whatever beast had stalked the trees. All the beasts in the attack had walked the earth just as they should have, but Eshai didn't think the threat had passed just yet.

"We were attacked. I asked the council for reinforcements. A second valor. They offered me two dozen valiants instead, four greenleaves and twenty extras. Ushi offered to send some of his own people along, but still."

Lavit snorted, taking another bite of food. The suggestion went unspoken—here was a veteran valor, housed in Vethaya, doing nothing but keeping the peace. It was a valor the settlement could actually use. And, Eshai had to admit, she wouldn't have complained about Lavit's valor being seconded to her command. She was happy for him—she knew his own command was something he had always wanted. But it always drew him so far away.

"How badly did you make out?" he asked.

"We lost four. It could have been a lot worse."

"Anyone I know?"

Eshai remembered the days when he had been her second instead of Turi, and although she felt guilty for it, she found herself wishing she could go back to them. Things had been simpler then. "Urai and Tarim. The other two joined on after you left."

"Damn. I liked Tarim. Didn't know Urai very well, but . . . it's a shame."

"It is."

They ate even as the silence stretched on around them. They had both developed valiants' habits over the years, including the ability to eat no matter the situation. In Vethaya, scarcity was seldom a concern, but in the unknown world, food wasn't always a sure thing.

Lavit set down his skewer, picked clean to the bones, and looked over at her. "I wish I could go with you. But my hands are tied, Eshai."

"It's enough to know you believe me. We'll make do somehow. In the meantime, you should watch Anaya. This doesn't feel right, Lavit. Something's happening here."

Lavit nodded, his expression solemn. He watched her as she sat up, setting her own skewer aside.

"We'll make it through this, or no one will," he said.

She saw an echo of the confident boy he had been, the one who always said he would be a hero worthy of the songs. Despite everything, it still made her smile.

"Right."

❧

Seri walked aimlessly along the branches of Vethaya, trying to understand the heaviness in her heart. She wasn't sure why she felt this way, surrounded by wonders she thought she'd never see. Seeing Lavit and Eshai together, seeing the easy confidence they shared, made something inside her churn.

She remembered what it had been like, to have someone that close. To have someone she could trust. If she closed her eyes, she could still see Ithim's open, honest face, hear his laugh as they played among the roots of Elaya. They would play until his mother called him back, and Seri would feel that same twisting feeling. That quick stabbing pain as Ithim's mother called him from the lower platform, there and gone.

She'd been a jealous child even then, and she'd always hated that. When she saw Ithim's mother, she remembered her own. And she remembered how it felt to sit there, beside her mother's bed, and hold her hand as she left her behind. The light of her eyes fleeing and fading away, down and down into the dark.

She knew she would never have family again. But if things hadn't ended the way they did, would she have what Eshai and Lavit had? Would Ithim be beside her still, laughing and joking as if they were children?

No. Probably not. She'd ended that herself, the day she'd raged at him for having a mother.

Her whole life, she had only ever been a poison. She had been named wrong. She wasn't a small flame, but a ravaging fire.

The restaurant Lavit had recommended was in the Central District, close to the trunk of the spreading tree. As Seri walked along the path, the lights of the city brightened, the glare hurting her eyes until they adjusted. Laughter rang out in the streets, people packed in shoulder to shoulder. The middle level of the Central District was Vethaya's most populous, and it never slept. It was the beating heart of the city, fed by a constant stream of Vethaya's young, adventurous, and foolish. Seri got directions to Sarani's from a group of youths her age, all of them wearing at least one piece of armor. She followed the path they indicated and then stopped when it opened out into a square.

She realized she was going to do something foolish.

Tsana was standing in the square, still wearing the same blue cloak. She had positioned herself off to the side, where she could watch the crowds without being seen by them. Seri might not have noticed her, either, but her eyes had picked out Tsana's cloak, a spot of shadow in a riot of color.

She took a step forward, then hesitated, her fists clenched at her side. Her feet scraped against the platform as she shifted her weight. Would Tsana think it strange if Seri approached her? They were only acquaintances. The last thing Seri wanted was to make her uncomfortable.

There was something in the air that galvanized her, stopping her from moving back. A feel to the city, to this place that thrummed with a life all its own.

Tonight was a night for being reckless.

She started crossing the square. Halfway across, she realized Tsana had spotted her. The girl's eyes went from watching the crowd to focusing on her. They caught the light like jewels, gleaming in the dark. Tsana didn't move, didn't say anything as Seri approached, but she held Seri's gaze the entire time.

Seri said, "I didn't expect to see you here."

Tsana's response was to incline her head toward the square, a massive platform positioned directly outside the ring around the trunk that marked the Central District. "This is where people usually gather at night, isn't it?"

"I'm not sure," Seri said. "I'm new here."

"Eshai Unbroken isn't with you?"

"Not this time. She had another engagement. I'm just out looking for dinner. Are you waiting for someone?"

A pause, and then, "No. I'm just watching the crowd."

Seri swallowed. Now or never. The words left her mouth, but she could have sworn a different person had spoken them. Someone smarter and braver than she. "Then do you want to get dinner with me?"

Tsana looked up, and Seri saw the surprise in her eyes. They rounded and widened, softening her face. There was a long, stretched-out moment before she answered.

"Yes. Yes, I'd like that."

Sarani's was a small, crowded eatery nestled in the shadow of the trunk. Seri despaired of ever finding seating, but at the mention of Lavit's name to the hostess, she and Tsana were immediately pulled into the crowd and settled at a table by the corner. The press of people inside the building was overwhelming— Seri was certain she had never been anywhere so cramped in her life—but Tsana didn't seem to notice. When the group next to them erupted into loud, boisterous laughter, she even smiled a little. It made Seri smile, too.

They ate a simple meal of rice and chicken stewed in a dark vinegary sauce, and Seri endured the waitresses' pointed questions about Commander Lavit and when he would be back and whether he was attached and whether the rumors about him and Eshai Unbroken were true with a strained smile and reassurances to mention her to the commander the next time she saw him. When Seri wasn't being badgered about Lavit's private life, she and Tsana talked. They talked about every topic under the sun. Tsana was interested in everything Seri had to say, about the settlement, about Eshai, about what it was like to be attached to a valor without being one of them. She said very little about her own life, but Seri got the sense from a few of Tsana's half answers that her past had not been very good. That sense only deepened when they were finishing their meal and Tsana said, so quietly Seri almost couldn't hear her over the crowd, "I've never been anywhere like this before."

"They didn't have a tavern at your spreading tree?" Seri asked. "Not even a town hall or a mess or a festival?"

"No," Tsana said, lowering her eyes to her plate. "They had those things. But they never wanted me in them."

They ate dessert—mango slices and sticky rice cakes covered in sugar—and when the bill came, Tsana reached for her coinpurse. Seri reached out and grabbed her wrist, gently pushing her hand away. Eshai had given her only enough to pay for one meal, but Seri had her own money. She paid for both and tucked her empty coinpurse away before Tsana could see.

The two of them stepped out into the night air, wandering aimlessly along the branches of the spreading tree. Seri was full and couldn't imagine eating another bite, but she found herself grasping for reasons to prolong the encounter. She didn't want to go home just yet.

The street was packed with revelers, filtering in and out of the bars and taverns clinging to the spreading tree's trunk. Seri was an adult in the eyes of the People and could have technically gone into any of those establishments, but the noise, the music, and the crowds intimidated her. She thought about leading Tsana somewhere quieter, one of the platforms on the outer branches maybe, but Tsana stopped walking. They had reached a portion of the street where the sky shone through the gaps in the canopy, the moonlight a bright silver contrast to the warm light of the lanterns. Up until that moment, Seri thought Tsana had been relaxed. They'd been talking about music— neither she nor Tsana could recall ever having heard anything like what was filtering out from the taverns—but all conversation stilled as Tsana tilted her head up to look at the moon. A tension ran through her, a guardedness even more notable because of its previous absence.

"It's late," she said, not looking back at Seri. "I have to go."

"Right now?"

Tsana sighed, her shoulders slumping in resignation. "I don't want to. I had fun tonight. But my—my traveling companions will be expecting me."

Seri spoke before she could think better of the words. "Can we—would you like to meet again?"

Tsana's eyes widened, and something came back into them. A little spark of light, a glimmer in the dark. She said nothing for a long moment, and then when she spoke, she sounded breathless, as if she, too, were trying to get the words out before she could stop herself. "Tomorrow?"

Seri nodded quickly, and it only occurred to her later she would have to check to see if Eshai needed her. "That works. Tomorrow afternoon? We can meet at the market."

Tsana nodded. "I can be there after the third bell. We can meet at the entrance."

"Then . . . tomorrow?"

For a moment, Seri thought she saw Tsana smile. It was only a moment, and Tsana ducked her head quickly as if embarrassed. "Yes. Tomorrow."

CHAPTER 7

☙

Tomorrow turned into the next day and the day after that, and before Seri knew it, she and Tsana had spent three days together. She would have felt guilty about abandoning Eshai, but as it turned out, Eshai didn't need her much at all. She spent her days tangled up in endless council meetings or inspecting the settlement's new recruits. The few tasks that Seri could still help her with were quickly snapped up by Lavit, who stepped into the role of aide so smoothly it was almost as if the job had always been his. Seri might have felt a little put out by that, if it wasn't for the fact that it gave her more time to spend with Tsana.

It wasn't that she and Tsana were *doing* anything, really—certainly not anything for Eshai to tease her about or to send her heart racing every time it was mentioned. They were just seeing the city together—and there was so much of Vethaya to see. They didn't have much pocket money, and they saved what they did have for food—but Seri never felt the lack, because while they couldn't do much shopping, they were always talking. Tsana's smiles became more frequent, and Seri's nervousness eased, until one moment where she was surprised to hear herself laughing and more surprised to hear Tsana laughing along.

For those three days, Seri forgot the world. She forgot what had brought them to Vethaya, forgot the troubled settlement, even forgot what had happened in Elaya. She couldn't remember being this *happy* to be with someone again. It felt as if nothing else mattered. When Tsana asked her about her father one day, as they were sitting on the shore by the lake watching Vethaya's children splash in the water, Seri answered with barely a twinge of self-consciousness or discomfort.

"I don't know," she said, rubbing absently at her name-mark with the thumb of her other hand. "My mother said he was a traveler. He died before I was born. A beast killed him."

"And your mother?"

"She's dead, too . . . ," Seri admitted, and *this* stung. It was a reminder that she was still someone with a past, that she would always be Seri of Elaya. She tried to smile, to lighten the mood, but it must have seemed forced as she told Tsana, "I don't have any family anymore."

Tsana didn't press her on that, didn't ask her for details the way others might have. She just held Seri's gaze for a long time and said solemnly, "Neither do I."

Every day, they stayed together until the valor bells rang, calling the night shift to duty, and when they parted, they parted reluctantly, as if they were both worried they would never meet again. There was nothing inherently romantic about their meetings. They didn't hug, they didn't kiss, they barely touched, but to Seri there was always a *promise* of something in those interactions. A potential and a possibility—something that thrilled her as much as it terrified her. She couldn't bring herself to ask Tsana if she had noticed it, too, but in the night, as she lay awake on the couch in the living room of Eshai's apartment and stared up at the wooden ceiling, she found herself dreaming fanciful things. Things like abandoning her settlers' claim and going back with Tsana to whatever village she was from. Things like telling Tsana that since neither of them had anyone in this world, they might as well go off somewhere together.

The only dark spot in those days were the running dreams. They came on with more intensity, so she sometimes woke confused, unsure whether she was the girl or the thing running through the forest. But not even the running dreams could spoil the warmth in her heart.

If Seri had had the choice, she would have stayed in those days forever, never leaving Vethaya. She knew, because Eshai looked troubled whenever Seri saw her, that there were troubling things happening in the city, but for once, she felt divorced from the misfortunes of the world.

Until one morning on the fourth day, when Seri had made plans to meet Tsana at a park and Tsana never showed up.

She didn't think anything of it at first. Maybe Tsana was late. But the longer she waited, sitting on a bench in the corner of the park platform, the more she began to worry. The sun rose high in the sky, crowds of people passing her by as they enjoyed the day. Occasionally, she caught sight of a flash of wavy, dark hair, heard a laugh that reminded her of Tsana, saw a silhouette out of the corner of her eye. Each time, she jumped and looked, and each time, she was disappointed.

By noon, she was thirsty and hot, and had paced the park enough times that she was sure she could identify every leaf, every flower, every buzzing insect in her immediate area. Her stomach was growling, and her heart was heavy in her chest, and she finally allowed herself to admit that Tsana wasn't coming.

Her first thought was fearful—what if something had happened to her? She walked the length of the city, visiting all the places she and Tsana had gone, all the places they had wanted to return to, but even though she walked until her feet ached, she knew she had only searched a fraction of Vethaya. And in that fraction, Tsana was nowhere to be found.

She was just . . . gone.

Seri's feet ached and her legs burned from walking, but she couldn't bring herself to return to Eshai's apartment. Eshai would know the moment she saw her that something had happened, and Seri didn't want to explain. She went somewhere else instead. A platform on the outer branches where she could look out into the forest and think, where she could be alone.

Seri looked down at the dark world below. The rainforest looked like it always did, anywhere in the world. She could have been looking out at the view from her settlement, or the view from Elaya. It was always the same, a constant overpowering presence. Watching. Waiting.

She didn't know how long she stood there until she saw the light. Hours, maybe. Minutes. But when she saw it, she stirred, looking more closely.

It was faint, a glimmer in the darkness, but it was bright enough to catch her eye. It winked out almost instantly, making her think she had imagined it.

And then she saw it again.

It took her a moment to understand what she was seeing. The light was moving through the trees in the world below. It didn't have the flickering quality of a torch or the steady orange glow of lantern light. There was something cold about it, something eerie.

It was strange, and her time in the settlement had given her little taste for strangeness.

The light gleamed through the trees once more before disappearing beneath the cover of branches. It reappeared again a moment later, slightly ahead of its original position. Seri frowned in frustration. Her fingers itched to reach for a weapon, and she thought about running back to Eshai's apartment for her bow. But no, there was no time. The light was still moving. If she left now, she doubted she would find it again.

Making her decision, Seri squinted at the light, fixing its position in her memory. Then she ran back along the branch. On the outermost branches, there were ladders everywhere, and it didn't take her long to find one. She scrambled down it quickly enough to turn the palms of her hands raw and tender.

Above her, the great expanse of the city spread out, but on the forest floor, she was alone. Even in the heart of the known world, even so close to the City of Valor, people still felt odd about being on the ground at night. Seri felt a rush of fear, but her travels from Elaya to the settlement and then to Vethaya had steadied her. She gave the ladder one last look, making sure she remembered its placement, then ran off after the light.

The rainforest was quiet, the only sound the chittering of nocturnal insects and far-off animal calls. She made her way along a well-worn track that led to the city's fields, moving slowly. She tried her best to stay quiet, not wanting to draw attention to herself or to scare the light away.

She didn't see the light again for some time, long enough that she wondered if she had dreamed it. Just as she was about to give up and head back to the city, she saw something glittering ahead. Now that she was on the same level as the light, she could see it more clearly. It was a steady, cold light, white tinged with blue. She had never seen anything like it before, and the sight rooted her in place.

A ghost?

No, of course not. Ghosts were tales for children. Ithim would laugh if he had heard she even thought that. There had to be some other explanation, something *more rational*.

Seri crept forward, trying to make as little noise as possible as she edged toward the light's source.

It had stopped moving. As Seri drew closer, she realized why. There was a small clearing ahead, where a tree had fallen after being struck by lightning. Two people stood in the clearing next to the hollowed-out husk of that tree, and one of them held the light. Seri scrambled up the roots of one of the bordering trees and pulled close to its trunk, peering around to get a better look at them.

The one holding the light was a man. He was older, his skin leathery and hair gray, but he carried himself with an air of command. He wore a thin cloak over what looked to be a simple tunic and trousers; she saw no evidence of armor. His belts were fastened with buckles that gleamed coldly in the pale glow—Seri wondered if they were fashioned out of stone. He held the light itself in his hand. It was coming from some sort of blue crystal, one that filled Seri with a sense of unease. It took her a moment to understand why. The crystal looked a lot like the kind that grew out of beasts.

He was talking to someone, a smaller figure with her back to Seri. They were talking softly, but Seri recognized the low, urgent tones of an argument. The girl had her back to her, so Seri couldn't see her face, but the cloak she was wearing and her style of dress told Seri that it could be no one else.

It was Tsana.

She said something in an urgent voice that Seri couldn't make out. When the man responded similarly, Seri realized what was happening. It wasn't that she wasn't close enough to make out the words, it was that she *couldn't understand the words at all.* The man and Tsana were speaking, and their words seemed to have meaning to them, but they were not words she knew. It was like she was in a daze and could no longer understand human speech.

It was as fascinating as it was unsettling, and Seri found herself leaning closer, trying to hear them better. There was only one word she could understand, one they spoke with enough frequency to give Seri chills.

Vethaya.

Even without understanding them, she recognized their tone. Whatever the man was saying, Tsana wasn't pleased. She was defensive, her shoulders raised and her hands clenched into fists. It was a posture intimately familiar to Seri. She'd seen it in other people her age, people who had just barely passed the test to call themselves adults. People who bristled at older adults treating them like children.

Who was the man to Tsana? Where had he come from? Why were they speaking like that?

Seri pressed herself flat against the tree, trying to shift around so she could get a better look. That was when she heard it, a sound that pricked all the hair up on the back of her neck and made her fight not to run. A beast's growl.

Something padded its way out into the clearing, coming to stand behind the man. An *abensit*, eyes gleaming in the light. Seri opened her mouth to cry out a warning, but the man did not seem scared. Impossibly, he reached his hand back, and the beast pushed its head into the touch. The man's fingers crept up the beast's head, scratching it behind the ears almost lazily, and the beast let out a pleased, guttural sound.

Seri stared, watching as the beast closed its eyes in pleasure, rubbing its head into the man's hand. A thought occurred to her, although it made no sense. It was like telling her the sky was red instead of blue, or rain fell upward.

The beast *listened* to him. Like a pet.

Keeping his hand on the beast's head, the man fixed his eyes on Tsana. He said something curt, and even though Seri didn't understand the words, she knew the tone. *End of conversation. You'll do as you're told.*

Tsana tensed, and Seri thought she would protest more. But then her shoulders slumped in defeat and she bowed her head, muttering something sullen under her breath. She didn't seem to care about the beast at all.

Other beasts padded out of the darkness toward the pair, standing in a semicircle around them. Two of them were *abensit*, the other two smaller, lizardlike creatures that Seri didn't have a name for. How many more were lurking just out of sight? The beasts she could see were all standing around the man, watching him closely.

Beasts, organized into ranks, waiting for orders like a valor before an engagement.

This wasn't just an argument, Seri realized. This was a *council of war*.

She had to get back. She had to get to Eshai and warn her about what was happening before the beasts descended on Vethaya.

Seri edged around the tree, her heart pounding in her chest as she tried to slip away. The ground fell away beneath her as she slipped on a layer of moss coating the tree roots. She cried out as she tumbled, crashing to the ground.

The sound echoed in the stillness. All conversation behind her stopped. Seri looked over her shoulder and saw them both looking at her, stunned.

The man raised his arm, pointing it at her. He snarled a word. Seri ran.

The beasts pursued her as she plunged into the rainforest. There were many of them, but she was light and fast, and in the thick of the trees, she could slip through gaps they couldn't. That was the only thing that saved her as she ran, pure animal terror propelling her toward the lights of the city. But Seri knew the trees wouldn't save her for long. If she was going to get to the city, she was first going to have to run through the clearing, the yards of open space between the trees and Vethaya. She couldn't hope to outrun the beasts *there*.

She put on a burst of speed, leaping over roots and around small trees as she pushed her way through the undergrowth, trying to put as much distance between herself and her pursuers as possible. Seri had always been able to see well, even in the dark. It was her oldest secret, the thing she had never told anyone, not even Caretaker Nasai. Not even Ithim. It had been her mother's last, solemn charge to her, to never tell anyone what she could do. Even without the helm, she could see uncommonly far during the day, and well enough to move even in blackest night.

She used that ability to its fullest now, hoping the beasts couldn't see as well as she could. Even as she thought it, she knew there was no chance. From what she understood, she could see almost as well as a valiant wearing an armored helm, and the armor drew its power from the beasts.

But maybe it would be enough to let her get away. Distance was all she needed.

She burst out of the trees and into the clearing, her heart racing as she looked around for the closest ladder. She wouldn't make it to the city proper, but a watchtower had been built on the fringes, just under the city's canopy. Compared to the bulk of Vethaya's spreading tree, it was a flimsy-looking structure, a hut resting on a platform built on bamboo stilts, only about three or four stories off the ground. If she could make it there, or if she could draw the attention of the valiants on watch, she might be saved. Seri ran toward it, beasts charging at her out of the undergrowth. There was no way the valiants wouldn't have noticed the beasts, wouldn't have heard the sound they were making, but Seri screamed anyway, waving her arms frantically at the tower.

Nothing happened. No valiants burst out of the watchtower to rescue her, no alarm bells rang. There were lights burning inside the watchtower, but it was otherwise still.

Why was no one coming? They must have seen her by now. Unless . . . unless there was no one there to see.

The watchtower was still her only hope. Seri ran for the ladder, lungs burning as she raced toward it. Behind her, she heard a snarl and felt something slam hard into her back, claws raking her armor. The impact shoved her forward, sending a shock of pain from her right shoulder to her hip, but the vest dispersed the force, keeping her upright. The beast stumbled—it had clearly been expecting to take her down. Seri jerked to the side, managing to slip out from under it.

She kept running. The other beasts were spreading out, moving to flank her. She was getting tired, and there was now a persistent ache in her back, just below her shoulder. She was slowing down.

The ladder was twenty feet away. Ten. Five. Three.

Seri closed the last few feet in a leap, fingers outstretched to grab onto its rungs. As soon as her fingers closed around bamboo, she started to climb, nearly catching her feet on the rungs as she pulled herself up. The ladder jerked alarmingly as the swarm of beasts reached the bottom, but she kept climbing, fighting the lurch of her stomach as she pulled herself up.

A sharp crack sounded, close to her ear. Seri glanced to the side and saw the bamboo splitting, revealing the hollow interior. Below her, beasts were pulling on the ladder, trying to rip it free. Seri climbed faster.

The ladder came free with a snap, beginning to fall into the swarm of beasts on the ground. Seri leapt from it and grabbed the platform, pulling herself up breathlessly onto its surface. She peered over the edge, breathing hard, to see the beasts trampling over the broken remnants of the ladder.

There was no other way down, and the watchtower wasn't connected to the main body of Vethaya. She was trapped.

Seri tried to stand and nearly slipped in blood. She looked around, a scream freezing in her throat.

The tower platform was littered with the corpses of valiants—three of them. They had only recently been killed—their armor was still crumbling away. Their throats were torn out, their spears lying uselessly at their sides. Two looked as if they hadn't even seen their attackers. The third had his spear out, but the edge was unbloodied. It had been too late.

Seri fought her gorge rising, aware suddenly of how exposed she was on that platform. The watchtower creaked and swayed, and Seri's heart nearly stopped. She looked down, peering into the dark, to see something she would have considered impossible: The beasts she had fled were scaling the stilts that supported the structure, their claws holding fast as they pulled themselves up the side of the watchtower.

The sight was so wrong that Seri recoiled from it, unable to understand what she was seeing. Two thoughts came to her at once. The first, that this looked nothing like the clumsy, uncoordinated climbing that Eshai had described, and the second, that some of them had clearly dealt with the valiants early on.

The valiants who were supposed to alert the city in case of any threat.

The thought came to her like lightning, terrifying in its ferocity. There was *no one* to alert the city!

The watchtower was one of four, built high off the ground, so the watchers could see the open space in every direction. There was a small hut at the center of the platform, for storage and to keep the watchers dry when it rained. It wasn't shelter, but it was something at least.

Seri scrambled to her feet, nearly tripping over the dead as she ran through the door. She closed it behind her, looking around.

The only light came from the lanterns strung along the outside of the building. The smell of lamp oil and blood stung her nose. She caught sight of a shattered lamp on the floor next to a single valiant. The valiant clutched a piece of flint in one hand. He hadn't had a chance to light the lamp. His chest rose, and he let out a wet-sounding breath, blood bubbling from his lips. He was still alive.

His spear was at his side. She picked it up. As a weapon, it was useless—she wasn't nearly strong enough to wield it comfortably without the armored gloves—but valiant spears were nigh unbreakable. She shoved the hut door shut and threaded the spear through its handles, forming a temporary barricade. That done, Seri ran toward the valiant, crouching beside him and placing her hand on his chest.

"Hey," Seri said, "can you hear me? Hey!"

The valiant's eyes fluttered from behind closed lids, but they didn't open. She wasn't sure if he even knew she was there. She felt around for injuries. His heartbeat was there, but it was slow, and his chest felt *wrong*. Broken somehow, beneath his armor. She recoiled, feeling sick. His color was off, ashen, and blood pooled beneath him. He wouldn't last long. She tried to think of something she could do for him, but all she knew was basic first aid. He needed a real medic, or a miracle. He needed *help*.

Seri tore her eyes from him toward the rope he had been reaching for, the rope that connected the watchtower to the alarm bells in the city. She ran for it, grabbing on to the rope with both hands. As the tower shook and trembled underneath her, Seri pulled on the rope with all her might, once, twice, a third time.

A single bell tolled in the distance. It rang three times, and in the moment of silence that followed, Seri thought her heart would stop. But then a cacophony of sound rose up—the alarm bells across the city. The valor would be coming. All Seri had to do was hold out until then. The beasts were on the platform now, and she could hear them throwing themselves against the door, trying to break in. The spear held, though. Mercifully.

She returned to the valiant's side, trying to staunch the bleeding, but it was too late.

"Come on," Seri said. "You have to stay alive. Help is coming . . . come on . . ."

The valiant on the floor let out one last rattling breath and fell still. Seri cursed, groping for his wrist. She couldn't find a pulse, and his chest didn't rise again. A spot of black appeared in the center of his armor. She gritted her teeth, feeling tears prick her eyes. And then a more urgent thought came to her.

Her head snapped up, eyes fixing on the spear.

Armor crumbled when the valiant it was bonded to died.

And the spear, her only defense against the beasts that tried to get in, was beginning to turn black.

CHAPTER 8

Alarm bells rang throughout the city, a distinct, discordant sound. Eshai jumped to her feet, nearly knocking over the remnants of the drink Lavit had brought over to share. The wine hummed in her blood, but she had only had a glass before the alarm bells began. Fear and alertness took over, chasing the soft edges away from the world and bringing it back into sharp focus.

Lavit was already moving. He ran for the door, picking up both their spears. He tossed hers to her as she turned around, and Eshai caught it by the shaft, feeling its reassuring weight in her hand as Lavit brushed aside the insect netting to lean out the window.

"Where is it?" she asked, reaching for the pieces of her own armor.

"Western watchtower. Do you know where Seri is?"

Eshai shook her head, fighting her own fear as she armored herself. "She hasn't come back before midnight the past few days. But if she's smart, she'll hear the alarms and run for shelter. We should hurry."

It was chaos in the streets of Vethaya, the platforms and bridges clogged with people scrambling to move closer to the trunk of the spreading tree. Neither Eshai nor Lavit moved through the streets. They leapt from rooftop to rooftop, crossing little-used branches and making their own way toward the western edge of the city.

They didn't speak, each of them following each other without words. Despite the direness of the situation, there was comfort in this, in hunting with Lavit again. But Eshai didn't allow her thoughts to stray very far down that path. She needed to be focused.

It was when they reached the western fringe of Vethaya that they heard the first screams. Eshai quickly looked down. There shouldn't have been anyone out that late—even the farmers returned to Vethaya after dusk—but a group of boys were on the ground, running for the ladder. Aspirants, she realized with frustration. They'd gone out seeking a beast for a piece of armor and had found more than they'd bargained for. They were being pursued by a mixed group of beasts—the goatlike *abensit*, being led by a pair of larger, apelike creatures. *Varrenai.* The thunderers.

Blood stained the grass a few feet away. Eshai saw a limp form out of the corner of her eye. One of their number hadn't made it.

Lavit moved before she could, leaping from the tree branch. He held his spear up over his head, skewering one of the *abensit* and pinning it to the ground in a smooth, powerful motion. As a second *abensit* lunged for him, he pulled the spear out of the earth with both hands, twisting it around and knocking the roaring creature out of the way.

Eshai leapt to follow him, landing hard on the earth. She ducked underneath a *varrenai*'s upraised arms, drawing the blade of her spear across its chest. Before the arms could fall, she leapt back, slitting its throat with her spear. She swept the spear through the air to clear it of blood, bringing it down on the head of an approaching beast. Lavit moved to give her space as she advanced, the two of them coming to stand with their backs to each other.

The beasts changed direction, moving around Eshai and Lavit as if they were stones in a river. Eshai looked over her shoulder to see that the group of boys were nearing a rope ladder, the first already climbing. Lavit's eyes met hers, the briefest question in them. Eshai kicked off the ground in answer, rushing at the beasts on one end of the formation. She didn't need to look behind her to know Lavit had done the same thing, closing in from the other side. She could hear his spear cutting its way through their ranks and focused on doing the same, her own spear moving through the air like lightning as she faced the incoming beasts.

Adrenaline set her heart pounding, bringing with it a mingled sensation of fear and exhilaration. She had almost forgotten what it was like to fight alongside someone who knew her so completely, who could understand her intent without words.

Eshai ducked under the lunge of the second *varrenai*, stabbing her spear-point through its throat. She looked over her shoulder again to see that the boys had all begun the climb, the slowest of them already halfway up the ladder. A glance in Lavit's direction showed him standing alone, surrounded by a ring of *abensit* corpses, his spear bloodied and shoulders heaving from the effort. He looked back at her, catching her eye. She jerked her head upward into the trees. Lavit nodded, and Eshai leapt, launching herself into the air. She landed on one of the slender, lower branches, the branch shaking with the strain. It shook further as Lavit landed beside her.

The ground beneath them was swarming with beasts, dotted here and there with clumps of battle as Vethaya's valor charged to meet its foes. It was hard to make out individual valiants in the snarl below.

Lavit's hand on her arm made her look up. His eyes were on the western watchtower, its ladder lying broken on the ground. Its bell rang steadily, repeatedly, in defiance of the beasts scaling the side of the structure.

She looked behind her and saw the beasts around Vethaya doing the same. They had stopped their pursuit and started to climb, claws digging into the trunk of the spreading tree. And although they moved slowly, Eshai knew they would soon reach the top.

No one else had noticed them. No one else had bothered to look. Eshai had feared this for months but seeing the proof of it outright made something deep inside her recoil. If they weren't safe in the trees, they weren't safe anywhere.

Fear tugged at her reason. She forced it away. They were valiants. They had a job to do. The rest could wait.

Lavit jerked his head toward the watchtower, and Eshai reached for the horn at her side. As Lavit leapt, she blew on the horn, a loud, clear call. Three short bursts, followed by a fourth longer one. It was a call most valiants learned to fear, although it was only heard in smaller spreading trees, ones lower to the ground. Never in Vethaya. Never, before today.

Beasts in the trees. To arms.

She followed Lavit to the watchtower as the call rang up around her, spreading like fire in the city.

Seri rang the bell.

She rang it out of a sort of stubborn desperation, more because she didn't know what else to do rather than out of bravery. From outside, the beast continued to try to claw its way in—she didn't dare look over her shoulder to see how far the spear had crumbled. Instead, she rang the bell, with hands that were starting to feel numb from the strain, a growing sense of despair with each peal.

It was hopeless.

It didn't matter how many times she rang the damn thing. No one would come for her, not when there were beasts attacking Vethaya. Eshai didn't even know she was *here*, and Seri had no way to signal her. The only weapon she had was holding the door closed—and it was already disintegrating. And even if she did have her bow, what could she do? An arrow wouldn't stop that beast, not even if she could loose it before the beast killed her.

If she survived this, she was going to learn the spear. She was going to stop being such a fool and take Eshai up on her offer to teach her.

Except, it was becoming increasingly clear that Seri wasn't going to survive.

I'm going to die here, she thought, looking down at the stained floor at her feet, breathing in the reek of lantern oil and blood. The fumes were starting to make her dizzy, and her shoulders burned from ringing the bell. The realization sank into her bones, bringing with it a deep weariness.

This derelict watchtower, surrounded by foulness and death, was going to be her grave.

Ithim's face burst into her mind, twice over. She saw him as he had been, young and bright and smiling, all the promise of the future in his eyes. And again, looking up at her from her lap, all that light and promise fleeing down and down into the dark. He had seemed almost at peace then, like he had simply gone to sleep.

She was going to die here. And if she was more fortunate than she deserved, she would meet Ithim in the water, when her soul returned there.

Her eyes blurred with tears as she looked down, her fingers slackening on the rope. It was fitting. She was finally getting what she deserved, what she should have gotten a year ago. When Ithim died, and Seri walked away, whole and alive. Rewarded even, for killing her best friend.

She wondered if Ithim had it in his heart to forgive her.

She wondered if she would have done so, had their roles been reversed.

The bell rattled weakly as the beast charged the door again, hinges creaking under the strain. At this rate, the door would cave in before the spear did. Seri looked over her shoulder to find the spear almost completely black. It would crumble, and then, one way or another, this would be over.

At least she had done something with her death. She had warned Vethaya. People would survive because of her. She had saved *lives*.

That was good enough, wasn't it? Her debt canceled out? What better way was there to die?

She'd done her best. No one could expect anything more of her. She wasn't a hero, wasn't anyone special. She wasn't *Eshai.*

The smart thing to do would be to give up and stop fighting. Except . . .

Except no matter how much Seri tried to put it in those terms, the fact remained that she didn't *want* to. She didn't *want* to die. It might have been a selfish thought, but she wasn't ready—to face Ithim, to own up to her past. She wasn't ready to be finished with living.

The sound of a horn ringing—three short blasts and one long—echoed through the air, and Seri's head jerked up, head turning toward the window. She knew that call—Eshai had made sure she learned it after everything they had seen at the settlement. Beasts in the trees. The valor would be fighting in earnest now, trying to drive back the beasts from their home. The scale of destruction would be unprecedented—no beast had ever gotten into Vethaya.

And she was the only one who would know *why*. The only one who had seen the strange old man.

For that reason, and for that reason alone, she *couldn't afford to die.*

The thought galvanized her, spurring her into action. Seri cast her gaze around the room, looking for something, *anything* that could save her. The crates that surrounded her had been shattered, their contents spread across the ground. First-aid supplies, rations for the valiants on duty, and oil for the lamps.

Oil for the lamps.

She glanced down at the back of her hand; the name-mark inscribed there.

Little fire.

It would be dangerous. It might kill her anyway. But maybe, just maybe . . .

Seri raced for the crates, pulling the lids off and throwing them aside. There was no time for finesse, no time to think twice. Eshai's words drifted through her mind. She had to look for the things she could change. If she didn't act, she was doomed.

She reached for the bottles of lamp oil, uncapping them and tossing the cork away with a casual flick of her wrist. In the last few moments before the spear gave in, she doused the tower room with lamp oil, throwing it over everything she could reach. She upended a bottle over the crates in the corner, the ones she couldn't reach in time.

And then she bent down, searching the dead valiant's pockets.

She found what she was looking for in a pouch belted to his trousers—part of a standard kit. Her fingers closed over the flint as she glanced at the door. The spear had mostly crumbled away at the edges, and what was left had already cracked. She ran a hand over the fastenings of her vest, checking to make sure they were secure, then backed over to the window.

She would have one chance to do this. Only one. Seri looked over her shoulder, gauging the distance of the drop. It seemed dizzyingly, impossibly high, and she felt a flicker of doubt. But she didn't have time to worry about things like that. Even if the door held, there were already beasts coming around the back of the watchtower. The window was small, barely big enough for a person to fit through, but if they tried to get in through there—

The spear broke, the door caving in with a crash. A beast rushed in, fangs bared, ready to strike.

Seri raised the flint in her hand and struck it against stone. Once, twice, the way Raya had taught her.

A single spark blossomed at her fingertips, falling onto the oil-soaked ground.

Light and heat blazed into existence too fast to believe, the force of it stealing the breath from her lungs. Seri closed her eyes tight against the onslaught. Her stomach was twisted in knots. She had never been so afraid, but events set into motion couldn't be undone. She opened her eyes and launched herself through the insect netting that covered the window.

Open air greeted her on the other side. For one brief moment, it felt like she was flying, carried by her own momentum. And then she started to fall, her stomach lurching so strongly that she couldn't even scream.

Above her, she saw the tower burn.

There was a sound like a rush of air, and then the watchtower burst into flames. Eshai heard a beast roaring in pain from inside the tower, but the beast was hardly her concern. Her eyes were fixed on a figure falling from the tower window—one clad in a beastskin vest of violet threaded through with blue. Eshai wasn't close enough to reach her. But Lavit was farther ahead.

"Lavit!"

Lavit dove off the side of the branch, leaping toward the falling girl. There was a terrible, frozen moment when Eshai thought he wasn't going to make it, where she braced herself for the girl's moment of impact. But then, just before she landed, Lavit grabbed her by the arm, pulling her close to his chest. The two of them hit the ground. She saw Lavit twist aside at the last instant, taking the brunt of the fall in a way that made her heart stop. Eshai leapt down to join them and didn't let out the breath she was holding until she saw they were all right.

The girl was Seri, her skin flushed red from the heat of the fires, the edges of her hair singed. She coughed, staring dazedly up at the sky. Her expression was panicked, but it sharpened as she caught sight of Eshai.

"Eshai—" Seri said.

"Hush," said Eshai, fighting down her astonishment. Seri, here? Her eyes drifted to the top of the tower, and Eshai understood. Seri had rung the bell. "You're all right. You're all right."

Seri shook her head, struggling to sit up. Lavit obligingly slid out from under her and used his arm to support her upper back, helping her.

"I saw him. The man commanding the beasts. He killed the men in the watchtower."

Lavit shot Seri a surprised look, then immediately turned to face Eshai. There was a question in his gaze, and Eshai found herself grateful that he waited to confirm with her, rather than challenging Seri on his own. She looked down at the girl, seeing the certainty in her eyes, and felt troubled.

This fit with everything she had been saying to the council. If someone was commanding the beasts, that would explain their behavior. But it also had far more disturbing implications. Who among the People would ever ally themselves with the beasts?

How?

The sound of a growl in the distance, followed by a valiant's war cry, brought her back to the present. She could worry about those things later. For now, there was work to be done.

"Where did you see him?"

Seri pointed off into the distance. "There. Southwest of the city, in a clearing. The beasts came from there. You should be able to find it easily."

"Was he alone?" she asked.

Seri inhaled sharply. It was a soft sound, and if Eshai hadn't been wearing her helm, she might not have heard it.

"Seri . . . ," Eshai said, repeating each word slowly, "was he alone?"

Seri shuddered like she was coming up from underwater. She looked up at Eshai, her eyes wide, and said, "I—there was someone with him. I couldn't see them clearly."

The words sounded like a lie, but there wasn't any time to get to the bottom of this. She looked back at Lavit, about to tell him to take Seri off the battlefield, but he was already helping her to her feet, an arm around her waist to steady her. He inclined his head toward the branch above them. Eshai nodded.

"Look for a medic and have those burns seen to. Stay out of the way of any battles. I'll look for you when I return. If you do have to leave the medic's tent for any reason, I'll meet you at the apartment. Do you understand?"

Seri nodded.

"When this is over," Eshai said, "I want the full story from you."

She saw the hesitation in Seri's gaze, but it faded quickly. Seri nodded again, her expression stronger this time. Eshai glanced at Lavit, who leapt into the air, bringing Seri into the spreading tree.

❧

"Do you believe her?" Lavit asked later, as they raced away from the battlefield, following the wide swath of churned ground the beasts had left in their wake. The creatures had not been subtle, leaving a trail Eshai was sure she could follow with her eyes closed.

Seri's story seemed impossible, but as she considered Lavit's question, she found she couldn't think of any other answer.

"I do. Seri has no reason to lie."

Lavit frowned, and she lost him for a moment as he kicked off one of the young trees, propelling himself ahead of her until she caught up. Beneath his helm, his brow was furrowed in thought.

"Brave of her. What she did back there."

Eshai thought of the flames engulfing the watchtower, thought of Seri falling to the ground. Lavit wasn't wrong. It had been brave of her. But what was Seri doing there in the first place, and how did she come across this man?

Those were all questions that could be answered later. All questions that *would* be answered later. For now—

The trail stopped abruptly in a clearing, just as Seri described. Here, the grass was flattened, the moss that clung to trees and nearby rocks scraped away. It was clear the beasts had come through here, but there were no people around anymore, any trace of them lost in the muddle.

She wasn't optimistic that they would find anything, but she searched anyway. As Lavit disappeared into the trees, Eshai scanned the clearing, her spear at her side just in case. The beasts had torn up the ground so thoroughly it was hard to imagine how the space had looked before. But one thing was clear—the beasts had all come from one direction. And the ground on the other side of the clearing hadn't been marked quite as clearly as this space. They had gathered here calmly. Waiting.

Lavit returned a few moments later, tense.

"Found marks on the trees," he said. "And droppings. The things were here for a long time. And on the other side of the clearing, I found this."

He tossed something to her, underhand. Eshai caught it without thinking. It was a stone of some sort, although Eshai had never seen a stone like it before. It was small and round, with a loop carved into the other side, and it was surprisingly light. The front of it had been engraved. The pattern was unfamiliar to her, but it was clear that this hadn't been left by any beast. A human *had* been here.

Movement out of the corner of her eye made Eshai turn, nearly dropping the stone. Something small was moving through the trees, rushing away from them at high speed. Eshai hadn't had more than a moment to catch a glimpse of it, but she thought she had seen a girl.

She tossed the stone back to Lavit and leapt forward, chasing after her. Branches whipped at her face, but Eshai barely bothered to push them out of the way, spurring herself on faster and faster. The rainforest passed her by in a blur, but as she kicked off a tree and launched herself into the branches at the base of the canopy, she looked down and saw her clearly.

It *was* a girl, clinging to the back of a beast—a grayish-blue lizard moving through the forest faster than anything its size should have moved. The girl didn't look up, but Eshai was surprised to find she recognized her.

It was the same girl she had seen with Seri.

The moment of recognition, of hesitation, cost her. The girl and beast jerked to the side, disappearing into the rainforest in a rumble of scurrying feet. Eshai banked, pushing herself off a tree as she tried to change her trajectory, but by the time she burst out of the trees, the girl and the beast were gone.

CHAPTER 9

Tsana ran for a few more minutes after losing Eshai Unbroken, her heart pounding in her ears as she lowered her body closer to the *makwai*'s racing form. She hadn't heard any sign of pursuers, and Asai's messages, sent to her at a frantic pace from far away, showed the valiant retreating, but Tsana kept running. It might have been a trick. The safest thing to do was to get away as fast as possible.

The *makwai*'s scales were rough beneath her fingers. Tsana made sure to grip its sides tightly with her knees, knowing that if she fell off, the beast would keep running without her. She had never truly mastered the skill of communicating with any beast other than Asai.

She shouldn't have gone back. She knew that even as she cut a path through the rainforest, changing direction several times to throw off any valiant that might be on their trail. She should have left reconnaissance to Asai and taken shelter in the hideout like her master had instructed her.

But she couldn't help herself. She'd seen the fear in Seri's eyes as she ran, had seen the ferocity with which the beasts pursued her.

She hadn't expected to find Seri alive. But somehow, Seri had survived.

The scene was burned into her mind. The watchtower burning,

a single figure falling from the window before being caught by a valiant.

Tsana was surprised at her own relief.

Seri was alive.

She kneed the *makwai* in the sides, bringing the beast to a halt. The *makwai* stopped reluctantly, already locked into the frenzy of its run, but all her master's beasts were well trained. Tsana dismounted, landing on the rainforest floor with shaky legs, and placed one hand on the *makwai*'s scales so she could look it in the eye.

One of its eyes fixed her, bright and golden, and Tsana thought she could see herself reflected in it. She wondered if her master was watching her now, and if so, what sort of welcome she could expect when she returned.

There was no acknowledgment, none of the understanding she shared with Asai. Unlike her master, she would only ever have one bond. She barked out a word of command, and the *makwai* turned, darting off into the rainforest. Tsana wasn't worried about the beast. A *makwai*, rider-less, would only be found if it wanted to be found.

When it was gone, it left her alone. Tsana drew in a breath, feeling suffocated by the weight of the sheer amount of *life* pressing in on her on all sides. *Anything* could be waiting in the trees and bushes that surrounded her. Any predator, any poisonous insect, any disease. Any valiant.

She shook her head, telling herself she was being foolish, and searched for Asai.

She felt the beast's answering call, though it was faint. Asai had lingered by Vethaya to watch the aftermath. She was waiting, camouflaged, on the trunk of one of the smaller trees that lived just on the edge of Vethaya's shadow. Through Asai's eyes, she saw Eshai Unbroken and her companion returning to the city, saw that the attack had slowed, the valor's defenses pushing the beasts back. Vethaya would be bloodied today, but not by enough. It was hardly the decisive blow her master had been hoping for. The heart of the city would be safe, and Tsana's stomach churned with mingled anxiety and relief.

It was all because of Seri, because Seri had seen them.

Seri had raised the alarm, and Seri had survived. All because Tsana had wasted time campaigning for Seri's life.

There would be consequences for that. But there were always consequences. That was just life.

She drew in a deep breath, willing herself to be ready for those consequences. And then she opened her eyes, because now was not the time to linger. She sent a response to Asai, instructing her gentle beast to keep watching, to send her reports every thirty heartbeats until the battle was done, then started off on the long road back to the meeting place.

The hideout wasn't a true cavern, merely the hollowed-out shell of what might once have been a fledgling spreading tree. But it was the closest thing to a cavern they could find in this soft land, even though the wrongness of living aboveground made Tsana's skin crawl.

Her master was waiting in the center of the hideaway, by the cool, blue light of their navira lamp. After so long away from home, the navir crystals were starting to dim, and the unsteady light made his shadow seem longer and more imposing than it otherwise would have been. His back was to her, but she could already sense his anger. She hesitated at the entrance.

"Were you seen?"

There was no point in lying. He would have the answer soon enough, from any of the beasts that survived the raid. He was the seventh *enkana*, after all. There was very little he wouldn't know.

She bowed her head in contrition. "Yes, master."

"By whom?"

"Eshai Unbroken."

She expected the blow, but not the speed with which it was delivered, the startling efficiency. One moment, she was standing at the entrance to their hideout, her head bowed. The next, there was a sound like a thunderclap, and she was lying on the ground, the side of her face smarting. Tsana tasted blood in her mouth but willed herself not to whimper, raising one hand to her cheek as she propped herself up with her other arm. Srayan was not looking at her.

When he spoke next, his voice was tightly controlled, anger brimming just below the surface. "Report, Tsana of Astira."

There would be no more punishment. Srayan's anger was swift and immediate, but it did not linger. All the same, Tsana would rather not try his patience. She rose, smoothing out the fall of her cloak as she faced him, back straight and hands clasped behind her.

"The valor suffered losses, and the beasts successfully invaded the western edge of the city's lower branches." She hesitated. "This area is a densely packed residential zone. The confusion slowed the valiants' ability to repel our forces."

"But also slowed our force's ability to advance. So, rather than storming Vethaya and leaving the valor without a capable command structure, all we've done is fought a prolonged battle in some worthless corner of the city."

There was no point in denying it. "Yes, master."

"It was that girl that did this? The one you spoke to me of?"

Tsana remembered a figure falling from a burning watchtower, the sound of alarm bells echoing behind her. She lowered her head.

"Yes, master."

"Hmm."

Srayan turned away, and relief eased some of the tension across Tsana's back and shoulders. He would not hit her again.

"Remind me, Tsana. How many years do you have?"

"Seventeen, master."

"You're still a child, then, despite what the law might say. With a child's reckoning of the world." He looked at her. "I can't blame you for your regard of the girl. It's only natural that you would want to spare her."

Tsana swallowed. She was fully aware that her fate, that Seri's fate, might hinge upon what she said next. And so, she chose to hold her tongue, to say nothing. Srayan looked back at her, a gleam in his eyes that she had only seen when he discussed the enemy. A hatred so deep it scared her.

"I saw the girl. She has our eyes. Given time and training, she might have been one of the bonded. But I also saw what she was wearing. The desecration our enemy calls armor."

"Master." Tsana's voice was tight. "With all due respect, she wouldn't know better."

"No. She wouldn't. But do you truly believe, after everything you've seen, that you could convince her?"

"She's one of us."

It was the same argument Tsana had been repeating since their meeting in the forest. It sounded tired to her ears, exactly what Srayan had accused her of. The words of a child. She looked away, ashamed of herself.

"By law, possibly," Srayan said. "But the girl serves the Unbroken. The same Unbroken you were foolish enough to be seen by. They will be on their guard now."

Tsana said nothing, her fists clenched tight at her side.

"You have a request," Srayan said, sounding annoyed. "Make it."

It was things like this that made Tsana wonder if Srayan could read minds. She thought about saying nothing and decided against it just as quickly. Ignoring a direct command would only incite further punishment, and her face still burned. She looked up.

"I would like one more chance. Seri doesn't know. Let me talk to her, tell her the truth. Give me one more chance to convince her to come with me."

"No," Srayan said, his voice flat. Tsana caught her rebuttal in her throat before it could escape. Srayan's eyes were on her, as if daring her to say anything more. "No. You can tell her about her history, you can tell her what you suspect, but you *cannot* tell her why we are here. If the girl refuses you, the first thing she'll do is tell Eshai Unbroken everything you've told her. And you will tell her *nothing* about our plans. Do you understand?"

Tsana stared at him, feeling, unbelievably, the first touch of hope.

"Does that mean—?"

"One chance," Srayan said. "If the girl refuses to join us—and she *will* refuse—I will hear no more of this from you. If you are seen—"

"I won't be." She had made the mistake of underestimating the Unbroken before. She would not do so again. Already, she was reaching for Asai in her mind, reaching along the bond that connected them for the power Asai shared with her. She'd let herself be distracted by Seri's survival, and it was that distraction that had allowed Eshai Unbroken to see her.

She would not be distracted now.

Asai's power was seeping toward her across the bond, dripping over her skin like water, painting her in all the colors of the world around her until she was invisible, but Srayan never cared when she vanished before his eyes. It was as if reacting to such a thing would be beneath him.

"See to it that you are not" was all he said. "Go."

There was no point in bowing, not when he could no longer see her. Instead, she darted out of their hideaway before he could change his mind, heading back toward Vethaya.

CHAPTER 10

꙰

A medic's tent had been set up on the fringes of Vethaya, near the lower branches where the fighting had been worst. Seri sat on a covered barrel that served as a stool, trying to hold still as the medic, a no-nonsense old woman whose scars spoke of years in the valor's service, applied a cool poultice to the burns on the side of her face. She couldn't help but twitch as the gel hit her skin, causing the medic to tut and grab her arm tightly.

"Hold *still*, girl!" She tilted Seri's head to the side to examine the injury. "Lucky. Very little scarring. You might get an interesting mark out of this for your trouble, but you'll still be pretty." The old woman cackled to herself, but Seri felt her stomach twist. Remaining 'pretty' was the last thing on her mind. "You'll have the armor to thank for that. Good thing you didn't take the spear like every other young whip your age, eh?"

The armor. Seri's eyes drifted over to the vest sitting in the corner of the tent. It had been slightly, but only slightly, singed by the flames, and even now, the marks from the fire were fading away, leaving it as whole as it had ever been. Without the armor, she would have been in much worse shape.

She closed her hand into a fist, drawing in a deep breath.

Maybe it was time to stop telling lies.

A commotion from outside the tent made Seri look up, earning her another harsh tug and a scolding from the medic. She had caught enough of a glimpse to see two figures in armor making their way through the clamoring crowd, one in white armor, the other in blue. Eshai and Lavit.

They came to her, not stopping to answer any questions. Eshai's face was a storm. She held something in her hand, something that she let tumble to the ground at Seri's feet.

Seri glanced down—with her eyes only, saving her another of the medic's reprimands. A black stone, stained with ash and blood, but gleaming with its own inner light. A beast's heart.

"Yours," Eshai said, when Seri raised her eyes toward her. "We found the corpse in the watchtower. I trust you set the fire."

Seri nodded, her mouth dry. "I was trapped. It was the only thing I could think of doing."

"Smart," said Eshai. "And stupid. What were you going to do if Lavit wasn't there to catch you? Alone in the middle of a battlefield and disoriented from the fall?"

"I didn't think about that. I just wanted to survive a little longer."

Lavit chuckled. "I like this one."

Eshai scowled at him, a look laden with unspoken meaning, then turned back to Seri. "You should be familiar with the process. Keep that close to yourself until it bonds to you, and then turn it over to one of the smiths for processing. I think you should get the gloves next. You're too good at archery to let your skills go to waste, and we could move you up to a more powerful bow."

Seri felt it again, that cold twisting in her gut, like she had eaten something that was still alive. In the back of her mind, she could see Ithim, falling. She could see Tsana in the rainforest, arguing with that man, and felt a rush of guilt and anger and shame.

She had to stop telling lies.

"That . . . won't be necessary, ma'am."

Eshai's brows rose from beneath her helm. Seri looked away.

"I already have the gloves. I think I'll get the boots next. And, although I wouldn't mind a stronger bow, I was also hoping you could teach me the spear. If I'm not being too presumptuous."

A long silence followed. Seri felt the medic's fingers still against her skin, slowly pulling away. She looked up to see Eshai watching her, her face an unreadable mask. Lavit was doing everything in his power to look elsewhere.

Eshai held her gaze for a long moment, then sighed. "There's a story here."

Seri nodded. "A long one."

"Tell me later." Eshai glanced off to the side, toward the path that led up to the trunk of Vethaya. "I have another battle to fight right now." She held the key to her apartment out to Seri, who took it, then nodded in respect at the medic. "When you finish here, head back to the apartment. Get whatever sleep you can. I have a feeling we'll be leaving soon."

Eshai left Seri behind, walking through brokenness. She and Lavit walked in silence. He knew better than to speak to her at a time like this.

The beasts had been stopped before they could get too far into Vethaya, but not without taking a toll on the city and its people. Everywhere Eshai looked, she saw evidence of destruction and death. Houses crushed beneath the weight of battle, platforms broken, half of their load fallen to the earth below. Vethaya's poorer citizens in rags, sitting by the side of the road with their hands wrapped around their knees, shaking, wailing for lost loved ones, or wandering the streets like ghosts, faces blank and distant.

Eshai understood. She had been a ghost once, a long time ago.

Here and there, the corpses of beasts littered the tree branches, and—too many times for Eshai's taste—the bodies of the valiants who had fought them, sad, broken figures in crumbling armor who had defended Vethaya with their lives. Some of them had already been gathered by their comrades. Others remained where they lay—Vethaya's valor was still occupied with the concerns of the living.

There would be a lot of funeral watches tonight. If Eshai were especially unlucky, she might find herself standing one of them.

Every sight she saw hardened her resolve. Every step she took made her stronger.

"Commander!"

Eshai lifted her head to see Raya coming toward her, beast blood spattering her dark armor. She had her spear in hand, but she brought it up sharply as she approached Eshai, so she avoided even the appearance of pointing it toward her commander. The light of the battle high gleamed in her eyes, but it had simmered into rage, the steady, ever-present anger that had burned behind Raya's eyes since her brother's death at Naumea.

Eshai offered Raya a curt nod. "You survived."

Raya nodded, and for once, she had no flippant comment to give. She breathed out. "I was at a bar in Central. With some of my friends from training. When we heard the alarm, we went back for our armor. I met up with some of them when we made it to the battlefield."

"How did they fare?" Eshai asked.

Raya's expression darkened, her lip curling as she looked out at the nearest beast carcass. "Not well. I made it to the bar late. They were halfway to drunk by the time I arrived."

Eshai took note of Raya's posture, the way she held on to her spear, the warped shape of her armor. A mark for her losses, she had told Seri, that night on the way to Vethaya.

"Take the night. See to your friends. It's unlikely any decisions will be made by morning."

"No," Raya said. "With all due respect, Commander, no." At Eshai's raised brow, she went on. "You're going to talk to the council, aren't you?"

Eshai glanced to the left, at the towering bulk of Vethaya's trunk, dominating the skyline. She nodded stiffly. There was no point in hiding it.

"Then I'm coming with you."

A responsible commander would have sent Raya back, despite her wishes. Ushi would have, in her place. But Eshai was not Ushi. She could never be anyone else but herself.

"Do what you want."

Raya fell into step beside Lavit, who adjusted his position so he was walking behind Eshai rather than in front of her. Eshai didn't realize just how they looked until they had gone a few paces. Raya and Lavit walking behind her, in full armor, spears in hand. Eshai walking at their head, a figure in white.

The two of them looked like her honor guard.

They didn't need to enter headquarters. Word of their coming must have spread, because Ushi was waiting for her when she arrived, and he wasn't alone. There were three councilmembers waiting with him—Anai of the Dancing Waters, Sukuna of the Sun, and Emrei the Wise. The three councilmembers were arrayed behind Ushi like statues, their eyes on her.

Eshai didn't bow. She didn't lower her head. A part of her knew that that was what protocol demanded, but she remembered the destruction she had seen, the death, and her spine refused to bend. She kept her gaze on them, aware of her impertinence and ready, more than ready, for the punishment to come.

She looked over at the council, meeting their eyes in turn.

"Well?" she asked. "Do you believe me now?"

Seri awoke from a dreamless, uneasy sleep to the sound of voices in the hallway outside. She rolled over and opened her eyes, disoriented for a moment, and then remembered she was lying on the couch in Eshai's apartment, covered in a thin blanket with her new beast-heart waiting on the ground at her feet. She lifted her head just as the door opened, letting in a square of lantern light. A moment later, Eshai stepped in, still dressed in her armor. She paused in the middle of removing her boots, looking up to see Seri watching her.

"Go back to sleep. We won't be doing anything more tonight."

Seri wanted to, but she let the blanket slide from her shoulders instead, getting up to help Eshai with her armor. Seri took her vest and helm from her, setting them into the rack by the door.

"I had some water brought," she said, inclining her head toward the washroom. "There should still be enough for you."

Eshai nodded, looking equal parts grateful and relieved. "Thank you."

She brushed past Seri, who remained there for a moment, lost in thought. Then, as she heard the door to the washroom close, she drew in a deep breath and went about putting the apartment in order, bolting the door, lighting a lamp, and setting out a plate of fruit. She folded up her blanket, resting it on the arm of the couch.

Eshai emerged from the washroom a surprisingly short amount of time later, her hair dripping. She wore a thin shift that clung to her still-damp body. Seri politely averted her gaze as Eshai sat cross-legged on the floor, picking up one of the fruit pieces. She frowned down at it as if it had personally offended her.

"Is there karan?"

"You need your sleep."

Eshai scowled but didn't argue, taking a bite of the fruit. Seri waited as she ate, hands folded neatly in her lap, trying not to worry at the fabric of her own clothes. After a moment, Eshai wiped the fruit juice off her fingers, looking up at Seri.

"How are your wounds?"

Seri raised a hand to the bandages that covered the side of her face, snaking down to her shoulder and neck. "They might scar. But I'll live."

"Hurts?"

"Not right now. The medic gave me something for that. And a salve. I'm to apply it twice a day until the skin heals."

Eshai reached for another piece of fruit. "You should be proud of what you did. People are alive because of you."

Seri thought about Ithim again, thought about her decision in the watchtower to survive. She thought about Tsana and felt her stomach twist in shame. To hide it, she bent down, picking up the beast-heart and placing the heavy stone in her lap. "Thank you."

"Things are only going to get more complicated from here," Eshai said. "We're being deployed. I'm leading an expedition to the unknown world, to track down whatever led the attack. Raya's going back to the settlement in a few days, with fresh valiants and instructions to keep things together until my return." She paused, looking Seri in the eye. "You can go back with her. I won't need an aide in the unknown world."

"But you'd let me come with you?" Seri asked, surprised that she was even given the option. Her hands moved over the smooth surface of the stone in her lap. Eshai's gaze tracked down to it, then back up at Seri again.

"You've proven your mettle. If you want to come with me, I won't stop you. But I need to know, Seri. What were you doing out there tonight? How did you get the gloves, and why didn't you tell me you already had a piece of armor? I'm not taking you with me until I know."

Seri swallowed, trying to work past the knot in her throat. She'd been expecting this, and despite the dread that she felt in her soul, she knew she couldn't keep avoiding the subject.

"I was trying to meet with Tsana . . ." The morning, so bright and full of promise, seemed like an age ago. The girl she had been when she left the apartment had been an entirely different person. Now all she felt was numb, tired down to her bones. "We were supposed to meet at a square, but she didn't come. I . . . I looked for her."

"All day?"

"All day . . ." Her voice caught on the words and she bit her lip, trying to pull herself back into numb detachment. That was the only way she could tell this story. Any of these stories. "Toward the evening, I . . . I ended up on one of the viewing platforms. That's when I saw someone moving into the rainforest, carrying a light. It looked suspicious, so I followed them."

"You could see someone moving at that distance?" Eshai asked. "In the dark? Without a helm?"

Seri nodded, looking down at the ground. She felt a shudder move through her, even though she had already resolved to tell Eshai everything. She was at her mother's bedside again, holding her hand and watching the light leave her eyes, vanishing down dark wells. "I've always been able to see in the dark, see far away, all of that. My mother said if anyone knew, they would say I was cursed." She swallowed hard, but it did nothing to dislodge the knot in her throat. "When she was dying, she told me to never tell anyone what I could do. So, I didn't."

Eshai nodded slowly, and Seri could see in her eyes the feelings she dreaded. Skepticism, unease, maybe even fear. She never wanted anyone to be afraid of her.

"That's why you're such a natural at archery."

Seri nodded. Eshai breathed, in and then out.

"All right," she said. "We'll set that aside for now. You saw someone walking into the forest in the middle of the night. You followed. Why?"

"I wanted to see what they were doing," Seri said. "I didn't have time to find anyone. I didn't want to lose them."

"What did you see? Tell me exactly."

She'd been prepared to tell this story, but the words stuck in her throat. Because Tsana had been out there, in the forest, talking to that man. Seri knew exactly what that implied, and she didn't know if she wanted to discuss it. To believe it.

"Seri," Eshai prompted.

"Tsana was there," Seri said, looking up. "She was talking to someone. The person with the light. It was a man, the one I described to you. I couldn't understand what they were saying. They were having an argument, but the words they were using . . . they didn't make any sense."

"They were using different words?"

Seri nodded, feeling like an idiot. The explanation sounded clumsy even to her, but she couldn't think of how else to describe it. "The words were different. The—the sounds were different. Sometimes they said something I understood, something like 'Vethaya'. Sometimes I didn't even recognize them as words. They made noises like . . ."

"Like . . . ?"

"Like beasts." Seri shuddered. "Sometimes they sounded like they were imitating beasts."

"What else do you remember about them? Other than the fact that they were arguing."

Seri searched her memory. It was oddly fragmented—after the beasts attacked, everything else came all at once, but she remembered looking out from behind a tree at Tsana and the man, remembered meeting the man's eyes. She had a clear picture of *that* exactly.

"They wore different clothes. I noticed this with Tsana, too, but it was more obvious with the man. They wore something on their clothes, an ornament, I think, except I'm not sure what the material was. It looked like a kind of stone, but it reflected light. The light they were carrying."

Eshai didn't seem as skeptical as Seri might have expected. She nodded slowly, considering.

"Tell me about the light."

"It came from these crystals, like the crystals around a beast-heart. But the light somehow seemed . . . cold." She shivered at the memory, at the gleam in the man's eye, so very like the strange stones that adorned his garments. "I didn't like it."

"They controlled the beasts."

Seri nodded. She was sure of that now.

"They did."

Eshai paused to think. Seri let her, grateful for the lull in the questioning. There were things she was going to have to speak about soon, things she had never spoken about to anyone.

"A human will behind the beasts explains their behavior," Eshai said. Seri looked up, but Eshai was no longer looking at her. When she spoke, she seemed to be talking to herself. "Another People in the unknown world? Unharmed by beasts?"

"A-Another People?"

Seri heard the words as Eshai said them, but they didn't make any sense. The People were all there were, born out of the rainforest, given shelter by the trees and harried by the beasts.

Eshai looked back at her. "There have been . . . theories," she said. "Valiants that go out into the unknown world have seen things. Things that were clearly made by human hands, but farther out than any of us have ever ranged. Some people think that there was a civilization—an older People that died out before we founded Vethaya. Maybe they haven't died. The forest is large enough to hide them."

It didn't make sense to Seri. It felt as though someone had taken the sum of everything she had ever known and struck at it with a mallet as if it were one of Vethaya's alarm bells. But Eshai's tone never changed, remaining as solid and matter-of-fact as it had been when she started this conversation. Seri clung to that, taking refuge in it. If Eshai said there were other people in the unknown world, that was clearly true.

"Why would they attack us?"

"That's what I don't understand," Eshai said. "But the council believes that another People is responsible for this. That's why we're leading this expedition, to go out into the unknown world and find them."

Find them. Find this other People, and . . . find Tsana. It all came together in a rush, a hundred connections Seri should have made from the beginning. Eshai's expedition was going out to find Tsana. And when they found her, they would kill her.

She couldn't let that happen. Not without hearing the truth from Tsana first. She *couldn't*.

Seri swallowed, meeting Eshai's eyes. "I want to come."

Eshai held her gaze for a long moment, and Seri felt distrust there, a distrust she wanted to flinch away from. She wondered what Eshai saw in her eyes.

"The truth first. Tell me about the gloves."

Seri felt the old resistance build up inside her, saw Ithim's face in the back of her mind, his eyes sightless, staring. She could hear her mother's voice. She had to tell Eshai. She couldn't keep lying. She opened her mouth but found she couldn't form the words. She had kept this secret inside herself for so long that now, even wanting to tell the truth, she didn't know how to begin.

She stood up instead, walking to her pack. Eshai didn't stop her, but Seri could feel the valiant's eyes on her as she knelt beside her things, digging for the sack at the bottom. She hadn't wanted to bring them, but leaving them behind at the settlement, where anyone could have found them—that would have been worse.

Her fingers closed around the sack and again, she hesitated. She had spent so much time pretending they didn't exist, carrying them around anyway. Her curse.

She fought back the uncertainty and the fear, grabbing hold of the sack with both hands and lifting it out of her pack. Before she could change her mind, she walked over to Eshai, taking its contents out carefully. She hadn't seen them in months, but she wasn't surprised to see that they had changed, taking on the same violet color as her vest.

Eshai's eyes drifted to the gloves as Seri returned to her seat on the couch, setting the gloves down on the table between them. When she spoke, she didn't speak to Eshai, her gaze fixed somewhere in the middle of the table. The words came easier now, as if she were telling a story that had happened to someone else.

"Our village is a new settlement, and I was part of the first generation born there. There weren't many other children around when I was young, and most of them didn't want anything to do with me. My father was dead, my mother was always sick, and then after she died, I was the caretaker's ward. I only had one friend when I was younger, a boy. His name was Ithim."

Her voice broke on the name. She was unprepared for the strength of the memory that gripped her. Not Ithim dying, but Ithim as he had been, when they were children together. Ithim as a boy when all the light was in his eyes, and he was telling her excitedly about the future. When she was just a girl and everything was bright and beautiful and she first learned that it was possible to love someone so deeply without being in love.

"Go on," Eshai said.

Seri looked down at her hands and realized they were shaking. She gripped them tighter.

"We grew up together, Ithim and I. We were like siblings. But when we were older—" She hated this part of herself. The words were like bamboo shards in her throat, sharp and cutting. She wouldn't have said anything, but Eshai had been a caretaker's ward. Maybe Eshai understood. "I was always . . . jealous. Ithim had everything I wanted. He had family. He had other friends. Everyone loved him. So, we fought one day, something stupid." His mother. The fight had been about her. About how Ithim would never know how Seri felt because she was alive, and he had her. "I said horrible things."

She fell silent. Eshai waited before prompting her.

"And then what happened?"

"I apologized the next day. We talked. He apologized, too." She had to pause, to think before continuing. "He invited me to come out and check the snares with him. We were in the rainforest that day, just the two of us. There was a beast." Seri's eyes moved over the gloves, taking them in. "It was heading for the village."

"You killed it?"

Ithim. Ithim dying.

"Eventually," Seri said, her voice hushed. "But not at that moment. We saw it heading for the village. Ithim had a spear with him, a normal one—not armored. He told me he was going to draw its attention, hold it off. He sent me back to the village to get help."

"He must have been brave."

"He was," said Seri. She remembered that day, how heroic Ithim had looked. How afraid she had been. Her stomach twisted with shame as she continued the story. "I did it. I left him. But I didn't get very far."

"The beast?"

Seri nodded. "I was running through the forest, heading for Elaya. But then I heard a crash. I heard Ithim scream. I went back. And in the clearing, I saw . . ." Her hands started shaking, visibly now. Seri closed them into fists to try to calm them, but the shaking wouldn't stop. Eshai reached across the table and calmly placed her own hands over Seri's. They were warm and calloused, the hands of a valiant. She met Seri's eyes.

"Tell me."

Seri drew in a breath. Another. "You won't believe me."

"You'll be surprised what I'll believe," said Eshai. Her grip tightened on Seri's hands. "Tell me."

One breath and then another. In and then out. "I saw Ithim. But he wasn't dead. He was wounded, but he was standing. He was like . . . like an animal. The beast was there, but it wasn't like any beast we've ever seen. It was small. Weak looking. It was controlling him."

"*Controlling* him?"

"He wasn't himself. I looked in his eyes and . . ." Terror. Pain. Bloodlust and rage. ". . . I didn't see anything of him in there.

He attacked me. I picked up his spear. I tried to fend him off, to call out to him, but he didn't respond. It's like he didn't know where he was. He was stronger than me. He pushed me up against one of the trees, and I . . . I had the spear . . ."

Eshai cursed under her breath, looking away. Her grip on Seri's hands loosened. Seri wanted to stop speaking but found that she couldn't. In her mind, she was there again, her back against the tree, the spear in her hands. The air filled with the smell of blood.

The spear had taken Ithim through the chest. She hadn't meant to kill him. It had just been instinct. But he had rushed at her with no regard for his own safety, and she had raised the spear. It broke his spine. He went limp, his eyes on hers.

"I killed him," she said, speaking softly into the hush that had settled over the apartment. She felt tears leave wet tracks down her cheeks. Seri swallowed, fighting past the knot in her throat. "I didn't mean to do it. But I killed him. It was so easy. He just . . . fell to the ground . . .

"I was holding him when he died."

On the ground with Ithim, his broken body gathered into her arms. His eyes on hers, and as the light faded from them it felt like she had been in this moment before, with her mother, watching the people she loved leave down those darkening wells, vanishing somewhere she couldn't follow. His body gave one last convulsive twitch before falling still. Had it been her imagination, or had he looked almost like himself in the end? Almost grateful. He had been moving his hand. To attack her, or to reach for hers? She still didn't know.

The memory made her cold. She shivered.

"The beast just . . . sat there. It didn't attack. I forgot about it for a little while, but when I remembered . . ."

When she remembered . . .

There were no words for the anger that had run through her then, the scream that tore itself from her throat. It was an animal rage, red-hot and blazing. She remembered the weight of the spear in her hand as she lifted it from Ithim's flesh.

"It tried to stop me. But not . . . not physically. I walked toward it, and I could *feel* it in my mind, like, like it was trying to invade it. It didn't work. I was too angry." She pulled her hands out from under Eshai's and drew her feet up onto the couch, pulling her knees close to her chest.

"I stabbed it again and again and again."

Silence. Eshai hadn't spoken. Seri almost wished she would.

"When I came back to myself, I was standing in the clearing. The beast was dead. Ithim was dead. And I was alone, covered in blood. I didn't know what to do, so I went back to the village. I told them a beast had killed Ithim, and then I killed the beast. They gave me the beast-heart and made me choose what piece of armor I wanted. I chose the gloves. No particular reason. I just wanted them all to go away."

"And then you left Elaya?"

Seri bit her lip, nodding. "Ithim . . . they—before the vigil, they washed him. There was talk that he was killed by a spear wound. They couldn't be sure, but people knew we had had a fight. They never said anything outright, but they always suspected . . . they thought . . ." It still made her sick. She swallowed, pushed through it anyway. "They thought I went out into the forest with him to kill him. I couldn't tell them the truth. A beast that steals minds? No one would believe me. I don't even know if *you* believe me. You probably think I'm a murderer, too."

"I believe you, Seri," Eshai said firmly. She pulled her hands back, getting to her feet. Seri watched her as she went to stand by the window, the moonlight illuminating her profile.

"Why?"

"Because I've seen you. You aren't a murderer. Just a haunted girl. And . . . I've seen beasts do strange things." One of her hands went up to her arm, her fingers tracing lightly over an old scar. "Not a beast that stole minds, but a beast that stole memory."

"The serpent? The one that made you Eshai Unbroken?"

Eshai nodded, her lips pressed into a tight line. She shook herself out of memory like she was rising up from underwater. "What do you want to do now?"

Seri hesitated, looking down at the gloves. She reached out, almost afraid, before letting her fingers rest fully on one of them. She felt no sting—Seri wondered why she had always imagined they would burn. She tried to imagine herself putting them on, these hateful things that had been born out of the beast that killed Ithim.

Then she thought of Tsana, and the beasts that had attacked Vethaya. Thought of the destruction in the lower branches and the wailing of the dead. So many other people, who had walked away from this as shells of themselves. So many people who had lost their Ithims.

Her fingers closed around the glove, pulling it to herself. She slid her other hand into it, flexing her fingers. The leather felt stiff, but familiar, as if eventually it would become as comfortable as her own skin. It didn't burn.

She looked up at Eshai and didn't falter when she spoke. "I want to come with you. Teach me the spear."

Eshai smiled, and her eyes warmed with something. It took Seri a moment to recognize it as pride—she had never seen that look directed at her. It made something inside her warm—a hunger she didn't even know she had. "We'll start training tomorrow. Get some rest. It's going to be very busy in the next few days."

CHAPTER 11

✤

The arrow slammed into the target they had set up for her, a flimsy piece of wood hanging from a vine in one of the trees across from the eastern watchtower. An appreciative hum rang out from the watching crowd, a few people murmuring darkly as money changed hands. She knew, because Raya had told her, that helmed valiants sometimes had trouble making that shot.

Seri let out a breath and lowered her bow, feeling the strain in her arm from the recoil even through the strength granted by her gloves. Her bow had been replaced with a valiant's longbow, a weapon crafted from the branches of a spreading tree and beast sinew and impossible to draw without the gloves' enhanced strength. With them, and the helm as a guide, a valiant could shoot farther and more accurately than any other archer.

"Go ahead and set up the next one," Seri told one of the gamblers, a young valiant from Lavit's valor named Navai. "I'll wait."

He grinned at her, the platform shaking as he kicked off it and bounded into the trees. Seri waited, resisting the urge to fidget. She wished they wouldn't stare. It still made her uncomfortable, wearing these gloves so openly, and their attention didn't help. It also bothered her that they apparently held her talents in high regard. She'd heard from Raya that many from Lavit's valor were discussing her *promise*.

What promise? she thought, watching Navai cross the gap

between the watchtower and the forest with effortless ease. *If they saw how stupid I looked trying to move in these boots, they wouldn't be talking about any promise at all.*

She shifted her weight from foot to foot, afraid to do any more than that lest she accidentally send herself flying. It had been two days since the attack on Vethaya, and she had only gotten the boots the day before. Her first training session with them, one Eshai had mercifully decided to hold out in the rainforest where nobody would see her, had been an unmitigated disaster. Seri had spent the rest of the afternoon in the river, trying to get all the termites out of her hair, and she'd been bitten by a leech for her efforts. She had no idea how Navai and the other valiants managed to do it, making it look as easy as walking.

But she would have to learn soon. The expedition would be leaving in two days, under Eshai and Lavit's joint command. And when they left, she couldn't afford to lag behind.

Navai returned a moment later, crossing the open ground in three quick leaps and then launching himself the rest of the way to the observation platform. He caught the lip of the platform's railing with one hand, pulling himself over to the side to land beside her. He offered her a deep bow, his eyes bright.

"If you can hit this one, you have First Valiant's own skill at archery," he said, leaning against the railing. "If you can even see it to begin with."

Seri *could* see it, although she understood why Navai thought she wouldn't. The valiant had tried to conceal the board in the foliage, but he hadn't accounted for Seri's keen sight. She debated missing the board, just to keep her secret a little while longer.

It would have been the smart thing to do. But as she drew the string back to her ear, Seri realized she was done hiding. So what if they thought she was a witch? She was through pretending she couldn't do what she could do.

She drew in a deep breath, fixed the target in her mind, and released. The arrow struck the board and tore it straight off its vine, sending it clattering to the ground.

"Well, they looked spooked," Raya said sometime later, as Seri hoisted herself onto one of the lower branches. The other valiants had arrived ahead of her, leaping clean off the ground rather than bothering with the ladders, but Seri thought it best not to embarrass herself after that display. Raya offered her a hand and she took it, letting the other girl pull her to her feet. "What did you do to them?"

"Nothing," Seri said. "I was just practicing archery."

"Ah, is that all it was?" Raya asked, looking at the valiants' retreating backs. She shook her head, a grin on her face. Raya was one of the few valiants that hadn't reacted at all to Seri's preternatural skill with a bow. She found herself oddly grateful for that.

Raya looked back at her. "I was looking for you."

"For me?" Seri glanced at the position of the sun in the sky. She wasn't due to meet Eshai for a few more hours yet. "Why?"

"We're heading back to the settlement. Thought you might want to come say goodbye."

The valiants that had been chosen to reinforce the settlement didn't look much older than Seri herself, although they wore full armor. She was ashamed to find that their age alone made her doubt their skill. They seemed an eager group as they clustered around the cart of supplies they were bringing back, one they would take turns pulling during the long journey.

Eshai was there, which Seri had expected. Lavit was there as well, and that surprised her a little. The two of them turned toward Raya when she approached them, so Seri waited a respectful distance away. She'd been there only a moment before Lavit caught sight of her and waved her over, stepping to the side to give her room to join the circle. Seri went, feeling self-conscious, horribly aware of the fact that the new recruits were watching her speak to their commanders so casually.

"You came," Lavit said, a gleam of mischief in his dark eyes. "Finished terrifying my valor? They're starting to think you're some sort of demon."

Seri managed a nervous smile. Her earlier confidence, that strong feeling she had had about not hiding, had vanished in the midday heat. Eshai, who knew the truth about her sight, gave Lavit a sharp look.

"I keep trying to find places to practice in private. They find me every time."

"I'll try to keep them off your back during the expedition," Lavit said. His smile was warm despite Eshai's glare. Seri returned it.

"With any luck, they'll have better things to do than bother Seri on the expedition," Eshai said. She looked over at Raya. "You have everything you need?"

Raya nodded, sullen. Eshai's expression was hard, and Seri

realized she was seeing the aftermath of an argument she had missed. She thought she knew what it had been about, and that thought was confirmed when Raya spoke next.

"I wish I could go with you. I'd give those beast-loving bastards hell."

"Someone needs to reinforce the settlement and report what happened here," Eshai said, sounding tired. "It can't be me."

"I guess not," Raya said. She brightened a little, looking over at Seri. "And our little firebrand certainly isn't making it back to the settlement alone. So, fine. I'll take the recruits back, tell Turi what happened, and make sure all the settlers are nice and safe. But promise me something, Commander?"

Eshai's voice was tight. "That depends on what it is."

"If it looks like there'll be fighting," said Raya, "if it looks like you'll need reinforcements, send for me. Don't make me sit in the settlement alone if there's fighting to be done."

Eshai hesitated, and Seri saw her eyes lingering over the shape of Raya's armor. She nodded slowly. "I'll send a message to Turi. He can decide what to do from there."

Raya let out a little bark of a laugh. "Good enough."

Eshai looked out over the assembled group of valiants again. "We have to head out," she said, sounding reluctant. "Another meeting with the council. You'll be—"

"Yes," Raya said, interrupting her. "We'll be *fine*. Now, go on, go shout the council down or whatever it is you two are going to do."

Eshai rolled her eyes and seemed on the verge of making a comment, but she shook her head instead, turning and walking back toward the center of the spreading tree. Lavit sighed, giving Raya and Seri an apologetic smile, before hurrying to catch up with Eshai. She moved to the side almost without thinking as he drew up next to her, giving him space to walk beside her.

It was funny, watching the two of them. Lavit was a head taller than her at least, but in her white armor, Eshai was the more striking of the pair. Lavit, however, didn't seem to care. He walked beside her, the two of them falling into easy conversation as they made their way down the street. As if they were walking down the branches of their own home spreading tree, and weren't two valiants in full armor, each of them commanders in their own right.

"What are you thinking?" Raya asked, noticing her inattention.

She had been thinking about loneliness and Tsana and all her complicated feelings about Ithim and his death, but instead she said, "Lavit's eyes are wasted on a man."

Raya let out a burst of surprised laughter, slinging an arm around Seri's shoulders.

"So that's how it is. Poor Navai."

Seri flushed, pulling her head out of Raya's hold. She took a step back and stumbled as her boots carried her farther than she intended, managing just barely to keep from falling on her rear.

Raya grinned at her, turning to watch Eshai and Lavit. There was an odd expression on her face, and for a moment, Seri wondered if Raya's thoughts were moving along similar lines.

"Don't worry," Raya said. "Lavit's eyes are wasted on him regardless. There's only one star he'll ever fix them on."

❧

Seri stayed long enough to watch Raya leave, the procession of valiants and their cart making their way across the forest floor until they vanished into the trees. When they were gone so far that not even she could see them, she sighed, turning around. She eyed the branch above her, her toes curling in her boots as she considered the jump. Better not. She was more than likely going to end up banging her head against the bottom of the branch, and if anyone happened to see it, Lavit's valor was never going to let her live it down.

Best to find the nearest ladder, even if it *was* two branches away and in the complete opposite direction from where she wanted to go. Seri swore to herself that she was going to get the hang of these boots eventually.

Something stopped her just as she started to walk, a light flashing out of the corner of her eye. Seri looked toward it. It was deep in the rainforest, so deep that no Vethayan scout would be able to see it without a helm. Without knowing what they were looking for.

A clear blue light, the same kind that had drawn her from Vethaya in the night. It flashed, once, twice, a third time, as if someone was covering it with their hand.

As soon as she noticed it, it winked out of existence entirely.

Seri felt a chill. She looked up at the city above her, mouth dry. If she hurried, she could find Eshai or a valiant, any valiant, and take them out into the rainforest. They might even be able to find the source of that light. She knew that it had to be one of them—those other people. Maybe it was the old man she had seen, the one that commanded the beasts. But maybe it was Tsana.

That light flashed again. Just once, but lingering longer than all the other flashes, as if in reproach. Or invitation.

She should have turned around, should have gone back, except—

—Except if it was Tsana, she *wanted* to see her again.

Seri pressed her lips together tightly and started to walk toward it. The light flashed a few more times as she made her way through the rainforest, each time only when she was about to stray from the path. Seri saw no one watching her through the trees and wondered how they were keeping an eye on her. There was no way the person on the other side of the light could see her unless they wore a helm or had the same keen eyesight she did. The thought disturbed her, but she kept walking, keeping an arrow to her bowstring, just in case.

The light flashed one last time, leading Seri to a place where the earth sloped downward, an outcropping of rock jutting outward from it. A tree grew on the outcropping, its great roots wrapped tight around the striated black earth. And Tsana was waiting, her back to the rock wall, a glowing stone cupped in her left hand.

Seri waited by the trees, not coming closer. For a moment, the two of them simply looked at each other. Tsana's eyes moved over Seri, taking in the two new armor pieces—the gloves and the boots, now the same twilight color as her vest. And Seri looked at Tsana, taking in everything that had changed. The strange, gleaming stones that now adorned her clothes, more visibly than before. The weapon she wore belted to her waist, some sort of long knife resting in a sheath of leather. The look in her eye, half-wariness, half-regret. Slowly, Tsana raised her hands, showing them empty.

Seri hesitated, then just as slowly returned her arrow to its quiver. She felt like a fool, but she supposed if this were a trap, she could at least stumble-leap her way in the direction of Vethaya. She slung her bow over her shoulder.

There were a thousand words in her mind, but what came out was: "I looked for you. I spent the whole day looking."

Tsana flinched, and Seri saw something cross her eyes. Doubt or pain or fear, Seri wasn't sure. "I know. I'm sorry."

"What are you doing here? If Eshai finds you—"

"I wanted to talk to you," Tsana said, interrupting her. "That's all. Just talk. I wanted to . . . see you again."

Seri breathed slowly, in and then out. She should run, she knew that. But she couldn't help herself when Tsana looked at her like that. She met Tsana's eyes. "Do you know how many people died because of you?"

Tsana looked away. Her eyes were shadowed, and Seri felt something inside her drop. She realized that all this time, she had been thinking, *hoping*, that Tsana hadn't had anything to do with the attack. That she was mistaken, that she had seen something else, that Tsana was just in the wrong place at the wrong time. But the guilt on Tsana's face was all the confirmation she needed.

There was only a little space between them. But Seri felt like Tsana was sliding farther and farther away.

"I'm going," Seri said, and her voice sounded flat even to herself. "You should run, before someone finds you. I can't—"

"*I tried!*"

The words came out just as Seri started walking away, and

the anguish in them made her stop in her tracks. She looked back to see Tsana staring at her, face scrunched up and tears in her eyes. Her hands were clenched into fists at her sides.

"I tried to make him stop! To—to delay, but he wouldn't. I tried to convince him to spare you! But I—he wouldn't— agh—this speech . . . you don't have the words." She drew in a breath, running a hand through her hair, and looked up at Seri. Her eyes were wide, desperate. "Do you even know what you *are*?"

A wave of cold ran through Seri. She remembered Lavit's words, said casually. *They think you're some kind of demon.*

"What do you mean?"

In response, Tsana held up a light in her hand, the glowing stone. She waved it between them like a talisman, as if it could turn back time, make everything that had happened fall away. "I suspected, but when you followed me that night, I knew. You wear their armor, but none of them would have been able to see me from so far away. Not without help."

Seri felt like she was neck-deep in frigid water, just trying to stay afloat. Her mother's words were ringing in her head, the words she'd repeated over and over again until sickness took her. Don't tell anyone what you can do. Don't tell anyone who you are. Tsana's voice was a ripple on the water, but her mother's voice was inside her, a mark on her soul.

"I don't understand what you're saying."

"You're like me. Like us. You don't even know what you might be able to do."

She raised her other hand, holding it out between them. Seri was captivated by slender fingers, the warm brown of her skin. She realized suddenly that Tsana was not wearing gloves, that for the first time, she could see that there was no mark on the back of her right hand. No name. The smooth expanse of the back of her hand was mesmerizing, something Seri had never seen before.

Then, as if Tsana was dipping her hand in paint the color of the world, it vanished. Before Seri's eyes, starting with her fingertips and dripping down to her wrist, until it seemed like there was only an empty space at the end of her arm. The boundary between air and skin shimmered and rippled like water.

Seri stared, and Tsana said, "Let's sit down and talk. Please?"

The two of them stood with their backs to the rock wall, a cautious distance between them. Seri looked away from Tsana and wondered if Tsana also felt like her world had come apart at the seams. She scanned the tree line in front of her, picking out individual leaves in the rainforest canopy, while Tsana plucked blades of grass from the ground and held them in her—perfectly solid, perfectly visible—hand.

"I was born like this," she heard herself saying, pointing at her eyes. "I didn't even know it was strange until my mother told me."

Tsana nodded. "I think you might have gotten that from your father. He must have been one of us."

"I can't do what you can do."

"I wouldn't expect you to be able to. The only people who can camouflage themselves the way I can are the ones that bond with a *coratal*. A . . . lizard beast, you might say. The larger beasts hunt them, so they don't live this far away from the caves. You wouldn't have them here."

"What do you mean 'bond with a beast'?" Seri asked, shaking her head. "What does any of this mean? My father—my father was just a traveler—"

"I don't think he was just a traveler, or your mother wouldn't have told you to hide who you are. I don't know how he ended up so far into this land, or why he took up with your mother. But your eyes tell the story, Seri, they're *our* eyes. *Our* People. We can *all* see far away, and we can all see in the dark. When I first arrived in Vethaya, it surprised me that your People couldn't."

Seri swallowed. She wanted to say something, to voice a denial, but her mind was empty of words. Tsana's explanation *fit*. It made so many of the things she had always wondered make sense, but it also gave her a thousand questions more.

"I've been thinking about it, and I think your father might have come from Vima. It's one of our—one of our settlements, you might call it, except we live underground instead of in the trees. I've looked at your People's maps and it's the closest one to your village of Elaya. My master is from Vima. If you come back with us, he might know something about your father. He knows a lot of people . . ."

But Seri had stopped listening. She turned toward Tsana, incredulous. "Come *back* with you? I *can't*!"

"Why not?"

"I have to—" Seri stopped. If Tsana didn't know about Eshai's expedition, she wasn't going to tell her. The thought came, somewhere underneath all that cold-water-numbness she was feeling, that Tsana had basically admitted they were here for war.

"Is this master that man you were talking to?" she asked instead. "The one who attacked Vethaya?"

Tsana flinched, but nodded. Seri thought back to the destruction of the lower branches, to the valiant with the crumbling armor, lying on the floor of the watchtower. She felt something building up inside her, fighting through the layer of cold that had settled over her. A steady, burning anger.

"Do you know how many people you killed?"

Tsana flinched again, and Seri saw her quickly look away. "It was necessary—"

"Necessary? You attacked a city full of innocent people. *Children* died—"

"Because you kill the beasts!" There was anger in Tsana's voice now as well, cold and terrible. Her eyes gleamed like the strange ornaments she wore. "You murder them, and you wear their skin. Do you have any *idea* what you are doing?"

"*They* kill us. Are we supposed to roll over and die without defending ourselves?"

"Is *that* why your valiants go out into the rainforest? To *defend yourselves?*"

"Why do you care so much about the beasts?"

"Because they are *us*, Seri!" Tsana said, placing her hand over her heart. "They bond with *us*, with *our* People. It's a bond that connects our *souls*. They learn our reason and we learn their skills and that's how we *survive*. That's how it's *always been*. Your People only take, and take, and take. You wouldn't understand. All you care about is settling your spreading trees."

Seri froze, conflicted. The second charge of valor echoed in her mind. She had seen it before, written on a scroll in the command hall of her nameless settlement.

Go forth and make the unknown world known, for in you is the future of the People.

How could she even begin to explain that? How could any-one not already understand?

Tsana looked at her and seemed to think from Seri's silence that she had won. "I can show you more if you come with us. You don't know what you might be capable of doing."

"I don't want to see any more." Seri filled her mind with the images from the attack. Of death, in Vethaya. Of four bodies resting in the roots of a spreading tree. "You kill my People, Tsana. Say whatever you want about it. That doesn't make it right."

Tsana opened her mouth as if to say something more, then closed it, her eyes flashing as she looked over at Seri. Anger or regret, Seri wasn't sure, but wrapped up in her own anger, she didn't care.

"Then we have nothing more to say to each other," Tsana said.

"It looks that way."

Something behind Tsana's expression broke, but she left before Seri could see any more of her face. Seri waited until she could no longer see Tsana, until she was sure she was gone. Then she turned, heading back to Vethaya.

When she was out of earshot, Seri threw back her head and screamed. It was raw and visceral and tore at her throat, but it didn't make her feel better, and it didn't make anything right.

CHAPTER 12

⚚

The branch filled her vision, faster than Seri was ready for. She grabbed it with her gloved hand, dispersing the force through the leather and swinging up onto it. She paused for breath, relieved that she hadn't crashed again.

"Keep going!" Eshai barked from the ground below her. "Finish the course!"

Seri bit back a sigh, kicking off the branch. She braced herself for the lurch of her stomach as her footing fell away, launching her into the narrow gap between two trees. She used the canopy to adjust her direction, pushing lightly off one branch and launching herself toward the next. Below her, Eshai continued to bark orders, as if Seri were one of her valiants. Sweat pooled beneath her vest, and the air tasted like rain.

The course was hard and unforgiving. It demanded all her attention. Seri tried to keep her thoughts from drifting, to focus on each leap, but her mind was still on her last conversation with Tsana. Tsana walking away, Tsana leaving. Tsana telling her she was—what? Not really of the People?

The next tree came up faster than Seri had been expecting. She caught it with all fours, cringing as the force of impact dissipated through her gloves. Seri pushed herself off the trunk, hoping she had only imagined Eshai's shout of dismay. The angle was all wrong, and Seri knew if she didn't correct it, she was going to miss the final branch entirely. Rather than

fall, which would end the course and result in a failure—
again—she reached out and gripped a smaller branch with
her gloved hand, using that and her momentum to swing
herself toward it.

The last branch filled her vision, but she was going too fast.
Her eyes picked out the colored cloth a valiant had tied around
the branch. As she flew past, Seri reached out, snagging it with
two fingers. It came free of its knot, and Seri gripped it tightly
in her hand as the ground rose up beneath her. She bent her
knees for impact, but ended up rolling to a stop anyway, coming to a rest in the roots of a tree.

She shook her head to clear it, pushing herself up and brushing the mud from her armor. A millipede had found its way
onto her vest. Seri brushed it off as well, careful not to kill it.
She was looking down at the cloth in her hand when Eshai
arrived, landing on the ground with all the grace and power
Seri hadn't been able to manage.

"Clumsy. But you *did* finish. Good job."

Seri nodded, too tired to protest. She balled the cloth up into
her hand. In the two days since they had left Vethaya, Eshai
had been a terror, much to the amusement of the valiants they
traveled with. As tired as she was, though, Seri had to admit it
was having an effect. She never would have been able to run
that course in the beginning.

Eshai's expression softened as she looked her over. "How are
you feeling?"

"All right," Seri said, rolling her shoulder. She winced as it
twinged in protest. "Better than before. I still need more practice."

"We all do," Eshai said. "But not with the boots for now. Head
back to camp and get some water. You can rest while we're on

patrol. After patrol, we'll work on the spear. We'll do movement drills to help you use the boots, gloves, and spear together."

Seri managed not to groan out loud. She *had* promised to learn the spear, but spear work was harder on Seri than archery. And Eshai was a harsh teacher when they were on an expedition. Eshai's lip quirked in an amused smile.

"Lavit's volunteered to teach you tonight. He's a fantastic spearman. You could learn a few things from him."

And Lavit, at least, wasn't as hard on her as Eshai. Seri tried not to look *too* relieved as she nodded in acknowledgment. Eshai dismissed her with a wave of her hand, and Seri turned to return to camp. With a sigh, she realized it would take too long to walk back from here. No doubt Eshai had planned it that way. A slow, steady race back to camp. Nothing difficult, just a handful of jumps. Inelegant, but the valor could make fun of her all she wanted when she got there.

She tried not to look too dejected as she bent her knees, launching herself into the trees. As she leapt into the air, she caught sight of a figure in blue armor crossing the tree line below her, moving in long, steady strides from tree to tree.

Lavit, off to patrol with Eshai. Seri wondered if the two of them were aware that the whole valor spent Eshai and Lavit's patrols gossiping about them.

She landed on a branch a little too hard, wincing at the way the impact jarred her knees. Seri rested a hand on the tree trunk for support, pausing as she considered the best way to get to the nearest tree. On her right, a bird with brilliant red and yellow plumage chirped angrily at her for disturbing it, fluttering around her ear. She tried to tune it out, focusing on the steady flow of her breath.

The past few days had been exhausting, more than she would have ever thought possible. Unlike the trip from Elaya, Lavit's valor kept up a punishing pace, only barely slowing to accommodate her. When they did stop to rest, Eshai filled their evenings with training. She was excused from most of the camp chores to train, likely because the sooner she could move like a valiant, the faster they would get where they were going, but that didn't make her any less tired.

And yet, as she stood on that branch with exhaustion buzzing through her system, she realized she still had more to give. Somehow, impossibly, she didn't feel like she had reached her limit yet. She could climb higher from here, get faster, grow stronger.

And strangely enough, she *wanted to*.

Despite everything she had learned about herself—no, *because* of that—she wanted to keep moving. To follow Eshai into the unknown world, where Tsana and her people lived. To find out if Tsana was telling the truth about her father. To find Tsana again and . . .

And what?

You murder them and wear their skin . . .

She raised a hand to the vest she was wearing, tugging at a strap.

Find Tsana, and do what? She wasn't sure, but she knew the unknown world was a place of possibility. If she never made it there, she wouldn't be able to do anything at all.

She kicked off the branch, choosing an angle that propelled her to the next tree and back in the direction of camp.

❧

Eshai watched as Seri started off toward camp, tearing through the canopy in her wake. She shook her head, listening to the howls of a group of distressed monkeys Seri had dispersed. Right now, she had about as much finesse as a falling boulder, but there was room to grow. They really would have to teach her to be quieter, though. The way she was, she would alert every beast in the unknown world to their presence, and their enemies would be able to hear them from miles away.

Enemies.

It was odd to think of having enemies—human enemies. But she couldn't deny what she had seen. She rested the butt of her spear on the ground, flexing her fingers on the shaft. The spear was a familiar weight in her hand, but she had never, not once, turned its blade on a human.

Could she do it? Even when she thought about the death in Vethaya, she had her doubts. It was one thing to fight beasts. Beasts were just another of the innumerable dangers in the rainforest, like disease or insects or predators or venomous snakes. Valiants—no, the *People* fought beasts because that was the only way they could survive. When looked at from that perspective, it was a very impersonal thing. In the rainforest, predators killed prey and even beasts fought each other over territory. If Eshai didn't want to become prey, she was going to have to be a predator.

But humans were something else entirely.

There were valiants that had turned their spears on each other, rather than on the beasts. There were valiants who were murderers, just as there had always been murderers in the history of every settlement of the People. Some people became valiants *because* they craved power, because they wanted to hold power over others, make people fear them and what they could do. Eshai was not so naïve as to pretend she didn't know that.

But that didn't make it right. That wasn't why *she* had become a valiant.

She became a valiant because she *believed* in something. She *believed* in the charges as they had been written, believed if she were a valiant, she could do something to help the People. To protect them. The life of a valiant was hard and painful, and she'd lost so much of what she loved to that life. But even at its worst, at its hardest and bloodiest, she *believed*.

Believed what she was doing was right. Believed in valor.

Now . . .

Well, things were different. And when it came time to cross spears, she didn't know what she would do.

Lavit appeared a moment later, cutting through the canopy with barely a ripple in the leaves. He landed lightly on the ground beside her, knees bent to distribute his weight, and straightened up. He was smiling, as if he had just heard a good joke and wanted to share it with her.

"I saw our little landslide making her way back to camp. She hasn't fallen over yet."

"How many leaps do you think it will take her?" Eshai asked.

"I got out here in ten," Lavit said. "Given the angle she was using, I'd say twenty or twenty-five."

"That high in the air?"

"She'll have a bird's-eye view to report. Assuming her stomach holds out that long."

Eshai thought about what Seri had told her, about her ability to see farther than anyone else could. It bothered her. It was a loose thread on a garment, something she couldn't help but tug on every time she wore it. Even though she knew the act might cause the fabric itself to unravel.

She looked away, but that didn't go unnoticed by Lavit.

"What is it?" he asked. "You're doing it again."

"I have no idea what you mean."

"Whenever we talk about Seri, you start to pull away. What did she tell you?"

"It's not my place to discuss it," Eshai said, although she wanted to. Seri's secrets bubbled up inside her, and Lavit would be an easy person to talk this through with. He would keep it to himself if she asked him. But Seri's secrets were hers to tell, and trust went both ways. "You'll have to ask Seri."

"Whatever it is, it's bothering you." The two of them started walking, making a quick circuit of the area. They would take to the air shortly, but it was easier to talk on foot, when her words weren't being drowned out by the wind. "Does it have to do with that girl you saw?"

Eshai shook her head. "No. That's something else." Something she *could* talk about, she hoped. "Although I'm not sure how Seri is dealing with that, either."

"You said you saw them together in Vethaya?"

"I saw them at the market. Seri said that was the first time they met. But they spent basically every day together since."

"What do you think she was doing in the city?"

"Probably the same thing we're doing. Reconnaissance." Walking into the home of the enemy to see their defenses before they attacked. If she thought about it, it didn't seem that different from circling a beast den while they slept.

It was so strange to think of it that way.

"How does Seri feel about that?"

"I'm not sure. She won't talk to me about it. They were only together for a few days, but they were quite close." Eshai hesitated before she added, "She's always struck me as a bit of a loner—Seri, I mean. She's polite and friendly enough but even at the settlement, I never saw her making friends. When she was spending time with Tsana, she was . . . happy. They didn't know each other very long, but . . ."

Lavit shrugged. "Sometimes when you meet someone, something just fits. It didn't take *you* very long to start following me everywhere."

Eshai laughed. "That's not how I remember it. The way I remember it, *you* were constantly hovering around *me*."

"Because I found you half-dead in the rainforest," Lavit said. "Or don't you remember that?"

She did. She remembered it in a haze of fever, the way she remembered everything from those early years. The fever that had struck her had taken away her memories of her family, of her home village, of everything that had happened to her before the age of nine, but she *remembered* Lavit. Remembered the scrawny boy with his armored boots and his hunter's bow, looking down at her like he was surprised to find she was still alive.

She dismissed Lavit's comment with a flippant wave of her hand.

"So *you* say. But Yana never said anything one way or another."

"Please, Yana told you the full story. You just never believed it, because you don't want to admit that I had my boots before you had yours."

"Now why would I be that petty?"

"Maybe because *I* earned my boots joining a hunting party like a proper aspirant, and *you* got lucky hiding in the corner of Yana's workshop with a knife."

"I almost *died*. That's not something to laugh about."

"No, it isn't," Lavit agreed. "And for the second time in as many weeks. No wonder Yana always said someone needed to keep an eye on you."

Eshai reached back with one arm and shoved him. Lavit stumbled back, although she knew he could have ignored the shove if he wanted to. He laughed, and she realized she was laughing as well.

It felt good to laugh, to be children together again. To think about how Yana would scold them when they returned to his house after another day spent too long in the forest. But they weren't children, and this wasn't a hunting trip outside the village. The reminder of where they were, what they were doing, sobered her almost instantly. She stepped away from him.

They walked in silence after, Lavit giving her the space to sort through her thoughts.

"Seri was a caretaker's ward, you know," Eshai said. "Like us."

Lavit said nothing for a long moment, the only sounds coming from the vibrant world around them. When she looked back, she saw he had his arms folded, a thoughtful expression on his face.

"Is that why you're so attached to her? She reminds you of yourself?"

Eshai shook her head. "Seri couldn't be further from who I was." Sixteen hadn't been that long ago, but it was strange how far it seemed in her mind. She'd been so different then. Just a girl chasing after Lavit, not knowing that Lavit was, in his own way, chasing her. "But you have to admit, there is something about her."

Lavit nodded. "She has potential, and the valor likes her. We need someone like her. A protector, not a hunter."

Eshai caught the look on his face. She remembered the boy Lavit had been, so full of anger and rage against the beasts that had taken his parents from him. She still saw that boy in him now, but it was muted, tempered with an adult's knowledge of the world. Hearing him say that startled her.

"What?" she asked. "Having second thoughts? I thought hunting beasts was what you lived for."

"It was. But these aren't beasts." Lavit's expression was grim. He had told her what happened to his family once, when they were children talking in the night to ward off nightmares. He had never spoken of it again. "How can they control them, Eshai? Why don't the beasts tear them apart?"

"I don't know," she said, trying to gentle her own voice as she responded. "I honestly don't know, Lavit. I've never heard of anything like this."

Lavit shook his head, and the uncertainty faded, replaced by the confidence Eshai knew. The confidence that was a mask, meant to protect him from the world.

"We'll end this ourselves," he said, "however they're doing it. What happened in Vethaya won't happen again."

The lower branches, filled with the dead and the dying. The memory flashed through her mind. Her heart was a flame, and the memories fed it, giving her the will to push herself forward. Inch by inch, day by day.

"It won't. I'd swear my spear on it. My name."

"Careful about that," Lavit said. "We can't lose Eshai Unbroken, can we?"

Eshai rolled her eyes. "I told you never to call me that. Come on. We've wasted enough time. Let's finish this patrol."

She launched herself into the air with an easy kick, springing off the branches of the nearest tree. Lavit caught up quickly, bounding through the air beside her.

"I wonder if you should tell Seri you've had your boots since you were nine," Lavit said, as he drew up next to her. He had to raise his voice to be heard. "It might make her feel better."

Eshai looked back in the direction of camp, thinking about Seri's clumsy strides. So much progress, in a relatively short amount of time. She remembered the number of bruises she'd had when she was practicing with her own boots, the number of times Lavit had to rescue her from the tops of high trees. She grinned, shaking her head.

"Let's not. It's probably best she doesn't know."

"Right. Would detract from the legend."

Eshai kicked off a trunk, letting the extra momentum carry her into a graceful backflip before she landed on a branch ahead of Lavit. Lavit put on a burst of speed to match her, passing just over her left shoulder like an arrow clad in blue.

"Race you to the marker," he said.

She grinned, putting on a burst of speed to match him.

Srayan pushed them hard after Tsana returned empty-handed from Vethaya. She came back to their hideout to find it already packed, Srayan gently handling a pair of *makwai* with one of his hands on each of the beasts' heads. He looked at her, and he didn't look at all surprised to see her alone. When his brows arched and she shook her head, defeated, he inclined his head toward one of the *makwai*, mounting the other. Tsana followed.

They moved with single-minded intensity, barely stopping to rest. Tsana knew, because of the reports she continued to get from Asai, that the valor was still trailing them. When she mentioned this to Srayan, he grunted, but did not change their course.

One night, while they were sitting around a fire near the meager shelter they had built up to keep them off the ground and out of the ever-present wet, Tsana dared to ask a question.

"Where are we going, master?" she asked, picking up a skewer of meat. She bit into it and ate slowly, not looking at Srayan's face in case her question angered him.

It hadn't. He only looked thoughtful, tapping one of the empty skewers against his knee. His reply, when it came, wasn't an answer but another question.

"Is the valor still moving in the same direction?"

Tsana checked with Asai. Her bondmate presented her with an image of the valor bedded down in the trees for a night, followed by a series of images and sensations that showed their forward progress. She nodded.

"Yes, master."

"Then we press on. I have a plan."

The certainty in his voice chilled her. Tsana looked away, remembering the futility of their previous arguments.

"Something troubles you," Srayan said. "What is it?"

"I . . ." She hesitated, then gathered her courage. "Master—isn't it time that we reported back? We have already fulfilled our mission to the Conclave."

"The Conclave will trust my judgment in this matter," Srayan said, which was the same thing he had said the last time Tsana had brought it up. "They wouldn't have sent me here without expecting me to act on my own."

It sounded reasonable. Srayan's position did mean he had a little more freedom than most. But as always, Tsana found herself uneasy. What he said and the look in his eye were completely different. He *said* that the valiants would inevitably attack, that they should do what they could to harry their forces before the valiants made war on their homeland.

But the look in his eye wasn't the look of a commander. It was something darker, something that made Tsana's stomach twist in knots.

It made her think about Seri.

If Seri were here, Tsana knew she wouldn't let things stand. But Tsana had always been a coward because she was a child of the Hollows, and her Hollows were not like the People.

She hadn't been lying to Seri. She had lived among the People long enough to see who they were. In some ways, they were grotesque—clothing themselves in the skins of beasts, taking their power, celebrating war and death and greed. But in other ways, in other ways Tsana envied them.

Because among the People, there was no such thing as bloodline. There were only those who were of the People and those who were not, and if a child of the People was abandoned, or if their parents died with no one willing to step in and raise them, they were given to a caretaker. They were raised as full children of the People, and when they became adults, their futures were their own.

It wasn't like that in Astira, or in any of the Hollows.

In the Hollows, to survive one needed either blood or power. And Tsana had neither. Her father had been someone. Once. Someone Srayan had known from childhood. But Srayan had had power and her father hadn't. Srayan rose to ranks Tsana couldn't even dream of while her father descended, down and down into the dirt. Until he died, and there were no caretakers to help Tsana. There was nobody.

A child of the Hollows without blood or without power was a ghost. She ate from midden heaps and drank the moisture that condensed on the cavern walls, and only when she bonded with Asai, *only* when she proved herself in this regard, was she allowed some measure of consideration. But Asai was a runt from the breeding dens, set aside to be culled, and even then, consideration was light. She might have lived the rest of her life working a menial job in one of the lowest, darkest caverns if Srayan hadn't stepped back into her life. If he hadn't claimed he saw potential in her; if he hadn't taken her in as an apprentice.

If she finished her apprenticeship with Srayan without getting dismissed, it would serve as well as blood. It would serve as well as power. Because some measure of Srayan's status would become her own.

Seri wouldn't have allowed it. Seri wouldn't have stood for what Srayan did. But Seri didn't know what it was like to live in the shadow of power. The Conclave was the most powerful entity Tsana could dream of. If Srayan was truly following their will, she had no choice but to follow it, too.

Tsana tossed the skewer into the fire, watching it snap and

crackle as it burned. The sight of the fire tore at her heart. Maybe it wouldn't be traitorous to watch a little. Maybe it wouldn't be wrong to see if Srayan was really telling the truth. If he was truly following the Conclave's will. She could watch, and she could see for herself, and if he wasn't . . .

If he wasn't . . . Tsana didn't know what she would do.

Seri nearly crashed into Navai's back as the group came to a sudden halt. She had been focusing on not falling behind, using the valiant's deep red armor to set her pace. When she stumbled and nearly fell, Navai reached behind him and grabbed her arm, hauling her onto the branch beside him with a grin. All around them, the other members of the valor were stopping as well, filling the trees like a group of brightly colored birds.

"What?" Seri asked Navai. "What's going on?"

"You'll see," Navai said. Seri saw many of the other valiants were looking her way, fighting to hide their smiles. She couldn't see anything special about where they were. It was just another stretch of rainforest, like all the others they had passed, less-managed this far away from a spreading tree. Except . . .

The tree ahead of them had a strip of leather wrapped around one of the branches. A marker, one of those that guided valiants making their way through less-traveled sections of land. She had never seen a marker like this. Where the other markers had been threaded through with multicolored wooden beads, giving direction to valiants using a coded language she had yet to learn, this one only had a single bead. It was red and hung from the tree like a warning.

A faint rustle from behind them signaled the arrival of Eshai and Lavit. The pair landed on the ground in front of the bead, the only two valiants standing on the earth. The whole thing had the air of ceremony, and Seri wondered what she was missing.

Eshai and Lavit exchanged a glance with each other, a question passing unspoken between them. Lavit tilted his head to the side in acknowledgment, and Eshai stepped forward, pulling her spear from her back. She rested the butt of it on the ground.

"Seri of Elaya! Come forward!"

Seri froze. Navai nudged her in the arm as some of the valiants around them laughed.

"Go on. It'll be all right."

Seri glanced around at the valor, feeling apprehensive. They were all watching her with anticipation, but what they were waiting for, she couldn't guess. Bracing herself for whatever sort of hazing ritual this could be, she kicked off the branch and landed on the ground. Her landing was harder than she intended, and she winced as she felt the impact in her knees. The laughter died down. There was none of the usual teasing as she faced Eshai, whose expression was deathly serious. Seri cast a worried glance at her spear. If it wasn't for Lavit's amused smile, she might not have stepped forward.

She did anyway, coming to face Eshai. Facing that marker.

"Before you stands the unknown world," Eshai said, gesturing at the space behind the hanging bead. "The world in which none of the People have walked, the world untouched by human hands . . ." She faltered a little bit at that, and Seri wondered if she was thinking of Tsana's people. But Eshai quickly recovered. "You have a choice, to pass with us into the unknown world, or to remain behind. If you walk past this marker, you choose to leave the world you knew." Her expression softened. "As with every valiant, this is your choice. We can't make it for you."

The unknown world.

Seri looked past Eshai, feeling a shiver. As a child, she had heard stories of the unknown world, some of it brought back by valiants who had been there—although once they returned with information, the world was no longer unknown—and some of it from the distant past, when the whole world had been known to them. It was a place of myth. She had never thought she would ever cross the boundary into it. Never thought she would find herself here, making this choice.

But Tsana was there.

Somewhere on the other side of that boundary, Tsana and her people waited. Her people and, if Tsana was right, Seri's father's people, too. She didn't know if she believed that yet. It was so tangled up in her own memories and her own knowledge and her own dreams. But she knew she wanted to know the truth. She wanted to find out.

She looked back at Eshai, her voice tight when she spoke. "How do I choose?"

In response, Eshai turned aside. Opening the way.

It was silent in the clearing. Seventy odd valiants shouldn't be so silent. It was unnatural. She could feel their eyes on her and wondered what they would do if she decided to stay behind. Probably escort her to the nearest spreading tree and leave her until they came back. If they came back at all. There were so many stories of people venturing into the unknown world and never returning, leaving their knowledge of it with them.

She gathered her courage and stepped forward, approaching the bead.

When she reached it, she paused, her hands curled into fists at her sides. The world didn't look all that different on the other side of the boundary. She saw only rainforest, the same as the world behind her. And yet, it *felt* different. Like there was a power here, an energy she couldn't describe.

She took a step forward, underneath the bead. The ground was springy beneath her feet on the other side.

The farthest any of the People had ever gone. The first feet to touch this ground were her own.

She looked back at Eshai and the others. They were all watching her. Eshai's eyes gleamed with pride.

"You have traveled farther than any of the People," she said. "Tonight, you are no longer Seri of Elaya. You are Seri who has seen the unknown world, and you will be marked for it." She stepped closer, joining Seri. When she spoke next, her words were for Seri alone. "You aren't a valiant. But you've traveled farther than any of the People can claim. Whether you become a valiant or not, no one can ever take that away from you."

Eshai looked back, facing the waiting valiants. As Seri watched, Eshai drew herself up to her full height, pitching her voice to carry. She raised her spear.

"Forward!"

CHAPTER 13

Rain in the unknown world, as it turned out, was the same as rain anywhere.

Seri huddled underneath one of the tarps strung up to protect their supplies, holding her tally board close to herself to protect it from the downpour. All around her, water fell as if the clouds had torn open, the rush drowning out all sound. The tarp bulged alarmingly overhead, making her worry about their rations. She poked at it with one gloved finger, praying the oilcloth fabric held out.

It had been surprisingly uneventful since the crossing, two days ago. If it hadn't been for the attitude of the valiants, subdued and oddly reverent, the explorer's mark that still burned beneath her right shoulder blade, and the increased security measures, Seri might have thought they were still in the known world. It wasn't at all what she expected.

With a sigh, Seri crouched down to examine their supplies. On record, she was still here as Eshai's aide, which meant she had to do her job. And part of her job was to keep the camp organized. Somehow.

She started making an inventory of their rations, counting out boxes of grains, dried fruits, and meats, counting each in a separate category. They had enough food to continue for days yet, particularly if they could augment their supplies by hunting. That relied on there being fewer days like this one, although with the year starting to turn toward the wet season, that seemed less and less likely.

The now-familiar thump of boots on the platform made Seri look up, a retort already on her lips about how she *would* be there for evening training, when she realized it wasn't Eshai but Lavit, rainwater trickling down the length of his armor. He stepped under the tarp, careful to turn his spear away from the fabric, and pulled his helm off his head to shake out his wet hair.

"I feel like I've been swimming. How are things here?"

"Good," Seri said, when what she meant to say was "damp."

Lavit tilted his head away from the dip in the tarp, and reached out with one hand, shoving against it with his palm. There was a loud splash as water fell down the side of the platform, some of it spraying Seri on its way down.

"Taking inventory?" he asked, looking over at the boxes.

Seri shrugged, tucking a lock of damp hair behind her ear. "Someone has to."

Lavit nodded. "Eshai wouldn't. She has a lot of strengths, but organization isn't one of them."

She looked up, surprised, and only then noticed that Lavit carried his own tally board in his free hand, covered in oilcloth to keep it safe from the rain. At her glance, he grinned.

"Believe it or not, this isn't our first expedition together."

Seri blushed, turning away. She knew that, of course. The stories about Lavit's exploits weren't as popular as Eshai's, but she knew that he had been there before Eshai had earned her name.

"I can stop—"

"By all means," Lavit said, waving his hand, "continue. I could use the break." He took a seat, resting his back against one of the crates of supplies. Had he been anyone else, Seri might have asked him to move, afraid he might get them wet, but he was the second commander of this expedition. She held her tongue and went back to work.

Lavit seemed content to sit there, looking out at the rain. She ignored him, focusing on examining the crates for water damage.

"It almost seems normal, doesn't it?" Lavit asked, as she was sifting through packets of dried fruit wrapped in banana leaves.

She looked up. "What does?"

"The unknown world." He made a sweeping gesture at the rain. "I thought so, too, my first expedition. We build it up so much back home, and it's just more rainforest in the end." He grinned. "And more rain."

Seri wasn't sure whether or not she was expected to agree. She settled for a neutral "I suppose."

"You'll see things," Lavit said. "Things that will make you question your idea of reality. But that doesn't mean there won't be a lot of boredom and rain in between. How do our supplies look?"

The shift in subject was so abrupt it had Seri reeling. She glanced down at her tally board. "Er—we have enough to last at least two weeks, even assuming we can't find more."

"Good," Lavit said. "We don't expect them to be more than a week from the border. The council thinks they have to be at least that close."

They. Tsana and her master. The people her father might have come from. She felt a shiver. Lavit looked over at her, and although it was impossible, Seri felt a tightness in her chest. She looked away.

He knows.

"Have you looked at a map lately, Seri?"

"I didn't think it mattered," Seri said, pretending to be engrossed in counting fruit packets.

"It does, if only to know where the nearest border is." Lavit shrugged. "It used to be that the nearest spreading tree was your new settlement, but we've gone south since then. The nearest village is Elaya."

He knows, he knows, he knows. She felt like being sick. But then Lavit smiled, leaning back against the boxes.

"We might be able to stop in when we return. I'm sure there are people you want to see."

Seri let out a breath, nearly dropping the packet of fruit she was holding. She lowered it slowly into the box, making a meaningless scribble on her tally board. Relief threatened to overwhelm her. She managed a smile.

"That would be nice."

Privately, she made a note to speak to Eshai and make sure the valor didn't go anywhere near Elaya.

The sound of a distant horn made them both look up, Seri tensing as it was followed by two more long blasts. The scouts had found something they needed to see. A gleam flashed in Lavit's eyes, an almost predatorlike anticipation. It faded as he reached out, grabbing his spear from where it lay next to him.

"Come on." He jerked his head toward the sound. "It looks like you might get to see something today after all."

※

The beast was old.

That was obvious just by looking at it. It walked slowly along the rainforest floor beneath the trees, one of its eyes completely white, the other threaded through with cataracts. Its movements spoke of a power and grace long gone, its hide falling loosely around its frame. It stopped in its walk to look up at the trees for one terrifying moment, regarding them with its good eye, before it lowered its head and continued walking. Seri had never seen an old beast before, and it was strange to see the weakness in this one. Animals had short lifespans, but she'd heard beasts could live as long as humans, maybe longer. It was rare to hear of a beast surviving to old age. Not in the known world, where there were so many hunters.

The pair trailing along behind it were still very much young and could have been twins, carrying the same coloration as the beast they followed. They were a type Seri hadn't seen before, feline in shape and powerful, nearly twice as large as the *abensit*. Their fur was white instead of dark, threaded through with black and with the peculiar crystals that sprouted from beasts. They were young enough and strong enough to be a threat, but although they made it clear they could see the valiants in the trees, they made no move to attack them.

The whole thing made Seri twitchy. She fingered the shaft of her spear—in this weather, there was no way she would have risked bringing her bow—and watched the scene.

"Why aren't they attacking?"

Lavit, on the branch beside her, said nothing. He watched the beasts with silent intensity, his spear ready. On her other side, closer to the trunk, Eshai looked troubled. From the branch next to theirs, one of Lavit's valiants moved to strike. Eshai raised her open palm, wordlessly halting the attack. The valiant drew up, looking at her in confusion. Lavit turned as well, as if he had just noticed she was there.

"Eshai?" he asked.

"Wait."

They waited. Below them, the beasts continued their silent procession, moving across the mossy ground. Rain fell from the sky, muting all sound. The elder beast passed out of sight first, moving over a tangle of branches and vanishing into the trees. It was followed by its entourage, although the last one, the smaller of the two young beasts, looked back and hissed at them in warning.

The beasts moved on, vanishing from even Seri's sight. Seri looked over at Eshai and realized she wasn't the only one—the other valiants, almost half of their valor—were watching Eshai as well. After a moment of thought, Eshai nodded, jerking her chin in the direction the beasts had gone.

"Follow them."

The valiants complied, letting Eshai and Lavit lead the way. Eshai gripped a strap on the back of Seri's vest, guiding her through the air and helping her soften her landing as they made their way from tree to tree. They caught sight of the beasts soon after, but though the one in the rear growled at them a few more times, they still did not attack, letting the valiants trail behind the procession.

Perhaps Seri was imagining it, but the light was changing up ahead. The sound of the rain had changed as well, the steady crash of falling water against the leaves becoming something else, something more like the roar of a waterfall. And then Eshai pulled her to a stop on one of the branches, and Seri realized why the sound and light had changed.

The rainforest ended.

There was no other word to describe it. The expanse of trees simply stopped, as if a line had been drawn in the earth, like the open ground before a spreading tree. But there was no spreading tree here. Instead, the world opened into a deep valley, bordered on both sides by sheer stone cliffs. She could see outlines of trees at the tops of the cliffs, but the valley commanded all her attention.

The valley where the beasts walked.

The old beast moved forward, picking its way slowly across the earth. And then, as if obeying some signal only it could hear, it stopped, its attendants trailing a few steps behind it. Slowly, it sank to the ground, resting its head on its paws with a weariness that was almost palpable.

It lay there, motionless. The light from the crystals protruding from its skin pulsed slowly, steady waves that continued to dim in radiance. And dim, and dim, until the light was hard to see, all while the attending beasts looked on.

It took her a while to understand. And then her eyes caught on to other shapes strewn across the valley floor, shapes much like this beast—feline, white-furred, where the fur was still visible. Crystals and bones.

The beast had come here to die.

It was hard to focus on anything else after that.

Though the beasts had never attacked, and no battle had been fought, the valor returned to their camp heavyhearted, as if they were returning from war. Seri found herself distracted, too, barely watching where she was stepping as she did her best to follow the valiants' movements. Her mind was still on the graveyard, on the sight of all those dead beasts. On the two younger ones, watching their elder as they passed away. Standing vigil, like any valiant or child of the People might stand vigil over their own elders.

It was a level of emotion she would not have expected from the beasts. That nobody would have expected.

In their mourning, they had seemed almost understandable. Almost human.

She couldn't help but think of Tsana's words. *You murder them, and you wear their skin . . .*

Her armor itched. She wanted to take it off. But she didn't want any of the valiants to see her do it, to know she had spoken to Tsana. That maybe, just maybe, she was starting to think like *them*.

Not that it mattered. Not that any of the valiants cared. As soon as they returned to camp, word of what they had seen spread quickly. The valiants dispersed, those not on watch breaking off into small, somber groups. Individual platforms on miniature spreading trees, separated from each other by the dark of night.

At least it had stopped raining.

Seri chose a spot for herself on one of the more isolated platforms that made up their camp. It was one of the rope platforms that hadn't had the luxury of a tarp, so it was soaked through, with a terrifying drop visible through the netting that Seri had learned to ignore. Somehow, after her fall from the tower and her practice with the valiants, heights had ceased to bother her. She sank back down onto the net, looking out at the world below her.

There was very little privacy in a valor camp, where there were no walls and only a handful of the platforms even had a wood floor. But there were areas of isolation, sleeping perches concealed behind swathes of insect netting, where valiants could go to be alone.

Or to be together.

She watched several pairs of valiants slip away from the main assembly, some sharing flasks of fruit wine or liquor she was sure they were not supposed to have. Seeking solace in each other. Some were friends; some would talk through the night. Others, she suspected, would do more than talk. She tangled her fingers in the rope netting below her and imagined Eshai and Lavit, stealing off into one of those isolated places.

And when she thought of them, she couldn't help but imagine another. A smaller, slighter figure, with gleaming eyes.

She shouldn't want her, she knew, but it felt like the world was pressing down on her. The valor camp was too close, the others too near—even in the highest platform, she couldn't escape them. Seri rolled onto her back and looked up at the sky, but the clouds from the rainstorm still hung overhead, blotting out the stars and making the world feel even more suffocating. Her fingers tangled into the rope netting, gripping it tightly.

She knew she needed to stay in the camp.

But tonight was a night for being reckless.

CHAPTER 14

✤

Eshai looked around at her valiants, watching as they slunk back into the camp.

They were not, technically, her valiants. Her valiants were under Turi's command, fortifying their settlement against a possible invasion. This was Lavit's valor. But it was hard not to think of the valor as hers while she traveled with them. Hard, even when she knew how much Lavit valued his command. It was just another thing that lay between them, this inability of hers to let someone else take charge.

Regardless of whose valor they were, they were acting as if they had returned from war. Eshai couldn't blame them. She was still reeling from the sight. From the way the pair of young beasts had watched, reverent, as their elder lay down. Feline creatures with white fur, one of the breeds the People had left unnamed. She had seen their like before, had fought their like.

Had killed their like, in Ushi's valor, in the unknown world.

She had never questioned killing a beast before, had never felt bad for doing so, except for one time when they were young aspirants and she had accidentally killed a beast meant for Lavit. But the sight of that elder beast waiting for death left a hole in her heart. Maybe Lavit was right. Maybe they were hunters in an age when hunters were no longer needed.

She didn't know where Lavit had gone. If she knew him, he was off somewhere where he could be alone. A part of her wanted to be there with him, but she held that part of herself back. *Someone* had to keep an eye on the camp.

As far as excuses went, that one was particularly terrible. But it was easier to cling to that than to admit she didn't want to be near Lavit just now.

That she, Eshai Unbroken, was afraid.

So, she walked through camp and pretended not to notice the wine and drink valiants always brought on expedition, sanctioned or not. She pretended not to see or care when valiants drifted off to isolated spaces together, pretended not to notice the seemingly random assortment of pairings and triads that drifted off into the trees—lovers, enemies, spouses, friends, people who were known to have lovers or spouses elsewhere. In the morning, her valor would handle whatever consequences arose. They were all adults and most were older than her. They didn't need her meddling or her judgment.

She tried not to think about Lavit seeking his own comfort. Tried not to let herself wonder, as she sometimes did, about those people Lavit may have sought comfort from during the time they had been apart.

It was while she was making her circuit of the camp that she noticed Navai.

It was not hard to notice him, because he was walking. In the unknown world, where danger lurked around any corner, the only valiants that walked the rainforest floor were those that were on duty. Or drunk. Or unable to care whether or not danger found them.

Navai was not on duty, last she remembered. And he was walking so stiffly, his footsteps staggered, that she decided it had to be at least one of the others. *Probably both*, she thought, as she caught sight of his face.

"Something on your mind, Navai?" Eshai asked, breaking the silence.

Navai shrugged, lips curling in a smile. He held a flask in one hand, gripping it tightly by the neck as if he were afraid to drop it. As if it were his spear.

"Nothing," he slurred.

Eshai rolled her eyes. "It isn't *nothing* or you wouldn't be like this. What's the problem?"

Navai took a swig from his flask, his eyes fighting to focus on Eshai. "Beasts can have vigils. I can get drunk. What does it matter anymore?"

"You need to focus," Eshai said. "We're doing this to guard the People."

Navai snorted. "Do you have any idea, Commander, everything I've done for the *People*? Everything I've lost?"

"We've all lost people—"

"Just because it's easy for you, doesn't mean it has to be for me."

"Watch it," Eshai warned, her eyes narrowing. "You're still a valiant in the unknown world, and I'm still your commander."

"Right," Navai said. "The unknown world. I hear we're hunting humans now, Commander. Is *that* true? How many of us do you think are coming back?"

"If we have our way, all of you."

"And how many times have you had your way lately?"

Eshai fell silent. Her mind was racing, but no matter how hard she tried, an answer wouldn't come. Navai stared at her for a long moment, then took another swig from his flask. Her silence was answer enough.

"If I die out here, you think these beasts would stand vigil for me?"

"If you're that worried," Eshai said, "I can send you home. No one is forced to be here. You always have the option to leave."

"Send me home?" Navai let out a broken laugh. "So that, what? I can tell those sons of bitches in Vethaya that I turned tail and ran before even catching up with the enemy? No, thank you, Commander. 'Sides . . ." He took another swig. "You're no better than me."

Eshai went cold. "*Excuse me*?"

"The way I see it, we're both walking the forest floor tonight. Alone."

"It's hardly the same—"

Navai cut her off. "At least I can *admit* I'm scared. What's your excuse?"

"What are you saying, Navai?"

"Do you really think we haven't *noticed*?" Navai asked. "The whole damn valor's noticed this dance between you and Commander Lavit. Hell"—a swig from his flask—"we've had a pool out on it for *years*. If you'd make a move tonight, Commander, you'd make me a rich man."

Eshai gaped at him, floundering for words. The right thing to do would be to scold him, to give him such a dressing down that he wouldn't ever *think* of bringing the subject up again. Instead, she looked up at the canopy, as if she could pick Lavit's form out of all those platforms in the dark.

"You realize you're being insubordinate, don't you?"

"Maybe," Navai said, "but is it helping? *Someone* deserves to be happy tonight."

He raised his flask, about to take another swig. Eshai grabbed his wrist tightly, stopping him. Navai blinked, surprised, and looked up at her.

"Commander?"

She took the flask from him, raising it to her lips and tipping it back. It was fruit wine, not the foul-tasting homebrew valiants usually hid among their belongings during expeditions, thinking their commanders had never been ordinary valiants themselves. It felt like warmth and fire as it traveled down her throat.

Eshai handed the flask back to Navai and wiped her mouth with the back of her glove. Navai looked at her with wide eyes, mouth slightly open. He very much resembled a fish, and Eshai was inwardly pleased with herself for how solidly she was able to break his composure. He gripped the flask with numb fingers. With any luck, he wouldn't remember any of this in the morning.

"You're on duty tomorrow, Navai," she warned. "Don't overdo it."

She left Navai staring in her wake as she kicked off the ground.

Seri leapt from branch to branch, barely pausing for breath. She knew she shouldn't have left camp, knew Eshai would have a fit if she ever found out. But the camp had felt too close after that encounter, as if there were eyes everywhere in the darkness. She couldn't have stayed a second longer.

She would stay close. She was only going out for some air, and she would stay in the trees. What she was doing wasn't *technically* against the rules. *Technically*, valiants were allowed to leave camp if they wanted to, to make their own judgments when they weren't on duty.

Technically, Seri wasn't a valiant, but she felt like that distinction hadn't mattered for a long time.

She just wanted to get some air. To clear her head, so that when she returned to camp, she would be able to think clearly. She knew she shouldn't be dreaming about Tsana. Tsana was an impossible dream, and it was foolish to want her. She knew nothing about her.

Except that Tsana might know about her father. Tsana was part of a people that might understand why Seri had always felt different, like she didn't belong. Tsana would know why the beasts stood vigil in that valley as their elders died.

She wanted to scream with frustration. It wasn't Tsana she wanted, not Tsana she needed. She didn't *know* what she needed, but she knew it wasn't a girl she had only met a handful of times, one of those being when she was organizing an attack on a city of the People.

But . . .

"I wanted to save you . . ."

Only because of her blood. If Seri hadn't been there, if she hadn't rung the alarm, it would have been much worse. So many more people could have died. And Seri *hated* herself for how easy it was to forget that.

Seri had saved those people. *Tsana* had tried to kill them.

It should have been easy, but it wasn't.

Go back, she told herself. *It isn't Tsana you want.*

Something twisted inside her. Seri straightened up, resting her hand on the trunk of the tree. It wasn't that there weren't women in Lavit's valor—there were, and some of them were even close to her age. Some of them were beautiful. She had no doubt that if she went back, if she tried hard enough, she could find somebody.

But just the thought of flitting from platform to platform, looking for companionship from people she didn't even know . . . it was enough to turn her stomach.

She didn't *want* any of them. They weren't Tsana.

She wanted lantern-lit nights and the crowds of Vethaya. She wanted music and wonder and the feeling that she could say anything here, anything, and nothing would change. But had any of that really been Tsana? Or had she just been dreaming?

Did she even know where camp was at this point?

Seri paused, looking behind her at the expanse of rain-soaked trees and shadow that she had left behind. Even with her sharp vision, she couldn't pick out the path she had taken. She felt a chill. If she had lost sight of the camp . . . if she couldn't find her way back—

No. She hadn't gone far. If she turned back and retraced her steps, she was sure she would find it.

Of course, it was equally likely she would stumble across the beasts' valley. Seri looked around, feeling hopeless. And then something caught her eye.

A light.

Her heart leapt as she whirled around, focusing on it. There *was* a light up ahead, waiting just beyond the next tree. It was a faint glimmer, shaded blue, and it didn't have the same steady radiance as the light Tsana had used to signal her on the outskirts of Vethaya.

But it was still a light shining out of the darkness ahead. Like a beacon.

She swallowed, her mouth dry. The rainforest behind her looked dark, forbidding. Even if she started back now, there was no telling how long it would take her to find her way back to camp. And there was no telling if she would even be able to find this place again.

She reached behind her, feeling for her spear. After being caught unaware outside Vethaya, she had made sure not to leave the safety of camp without a weapon. It wasn't as reassuring as her bow, which she had kept safe with their supplies in the event of another downpour, but it was better than nothing.

Making her decision, Seri kicked off from the branch, making her way toward the light.

In two leaps, she ran out of rainforest. The path yawned open ahead of her, as empty and forbidding as the valley had been. But she had been traveling in the wrong direction for this to be the same valley.

The light was ahead of her. It was stronger now, with no trees to conceal it, and she realized what she had thought was a single light source was in fact many lights, all gathered around something in the distance she couldn't see. The lights were tangled together, like a net woven around something *massive*, something with a wide base that dwarfed her even at this distance. They clustered around the base of the structure, traveling upward like moss or vines, thinning out the higher they got until eventually, they vanished entirely. The lights pulsed, as if alive.

Seri looked, but she didn't see any movement around the lights. She listened, but didn't hear anything aside from her own breathing. No growls in the darkness, no shining points of light that would signal beast eyes, or the crystals that protruded from their skin.

Her heart hammered in her chest, but she had come this far. She leapt down from the tree, feeling the squelch of soft, rain-churned earth beneath her boots. Seri tugged her spear free from its straps, holding it in one hand as she made her way toward the structure.

As she drew closer, she could see the light truly was coming from something alive—a mat of glowing plants like the lichen she sometimes saw growing around stone. No, not *like* the lichen. It *was* lichen, which meant the substance it was resting on had to be stone.

But that was impossible.

Her neck craned as she tried to get a sense of the immensity before her. If the lichen were growing on stone, then she had never seen stone this big, all gathered in one place, as high as any spreading tree. As her eyes adjusted to the darkness, she started to get a sense of stones all piled on top of each other, arranged in a deliberate pattern. A wider base, with the next set of stones slightly narrower, and the next set of stones narrower than that, until she could no longer keep track of them. The arrangement was deliberate, not natural, and for one terrifying instant, Seri thought it might have been built by beasts. And then she saw steps leading up to an entrance in the structure, an entrance that looked very much like a *door*, and she realized that beasts hadn't built this. Humans had, somehow. A building made of stone.

Tsana's people? Tsana had said they lived in caves under the ground, but it was also possible that Tsana was lying. Or a third group, living out here in the unknown world, somehow undetected by both of them?

She reached out and touched the stone before her, a signpost at the base of the structure, feeling the roughness of it through the pads of her gloves. There was something carved into the stone, and it wasn't until the tip of Seri's finger traced a familiar curve that she realized they were *words*.

Her words.

This impossible creation was carved with the language of the People.

Lavit was alone.

Eshai didn't realize how relieved that made her until she saw him, sitting at the edge of the platform with his legs hanging over the side. She managed to land softly, barely rattling the platform. He had chosen the command platform for his perch, the highest in the camp. It was one of the few platforms in a moving camp that was made of wood, and the only one that didn't hold supplies or valiants on duty. From up here, with their helm on, a commander could see everything that happened in the camp below.

Lavit did not have his helm on.

It rested on the platform beside him. In the dimness of the lanterns that had been strung up around camp, Eshai could see his profile clearly. How many times had she sought comfort in the sight of him? Since she was a child, dying of fever in the middle of the rainforest, and Lavit had found her and brought her home. The fever had stolen all her memories of her past, her childhood, her parents.

Her first clear memory was of his face.

She reached up, tugging at her own helm. It came free with ease, and as an afterthought, she took the strap that bound her hair with it. Waves of dark hair swept down to the small of her back as Lavit turned around.

She wondered what he saw when he did. Her armor would reflect the lantern light—she knew the songs said she glowed.

It was surprisingly intimate, the two of them without their helms. In the field, valiants rarely removed their armor except to bathe, or to treat an injury, or to be together.

But *this*, at least, was an intimacy they had shared before. So Lavit's eyes swept over her, and though she thought she saw a heat in them, a question, he didn't press her. He slid to the side, offering her room to sit beside him, on this platform overlooking the world.

It was something they had done before, on nights when it seemed as though the entire world had dropped out from under them. They would sit in silence, never speaking, as if afraid that a word, once spoken, would chase the other away. But her mouth still tasted of the wine she had stolen from Navai, and her heart was still pounding in her chest from her decision, an energy crackling beneath her skin.

It wasn't enough. It had *never* been enough, and she was tired of lying to herself.

She reached for the strap of her right glove with her left hand, keeping her eyes on him as she tugged it free. It fell from her fingers, landing on the platform with a soft thump. She took hold of the other strap.

Lavit swung his legs over the side of the platform, getting to his feet. She knew she wasn't imagining the heat in his eyes now as he approached her, cautiously, as if she would vanish at a sudden move. He reached out, his hand closing around hers before she could tug it free of the glove.

He didn't ask her what she was doing, or what her intentions were. Instead, what he asked her made her realize she had waited too long.

"What changed?"

Eshai didn't have an answer. She said the first thing that came to mind instead.

"I'm tired of pretending."

He said nothing, his eyes on hers. His hand tightened its grip around her glove, but he didn't move. He seemed to be watching her, waiting for something. Waiting for her to change her mind.

That irritated her. She wasn't a child. She didn't *need* him to second-guess her, or wait for her, or be gentle with her. She drew herself up to her full height, every inch the commander.

"Help me with my vest," she said.

He kissed her instead, his arms wrapping around her to lift her up and pull her to him. She returned the kiss eagerly.

He did eventually help her with her vest, and the rest of her armor.

CHAPTER 15

❧

There was someone sleeping on the command platform—from her angle of approach, Seri couldn't see if it was Eshai or Lavit. It didn't matter. If it was Lavit, she would apologize profusely and find Eshai. She winced as she landed too hard, the shock of her impact making the platform sway. Another day, she might have been embarrassed, but her mind was still reeling from the structure she had seen in the rainforest.

"Eshai," she said, running over to the sleeping figure. "Eshai, I'm sorry, but I—"

She drew to a stop.

It *was* Eshai, and she was awake, lying on a pallet underneath a thin blanket with a scowl on her face. But she wasn't alone. Beside her, Lavit pushed himself up on one arm, the blanket sliding off his torso and exposing Eshai's shoulders and back to the air as it pooled around his waist. Seri flushed and stepped back, quickly turning around.

"I'm sorry!" she said, her voice coming out as a high-pitched squeak. "I just—"

"It's fine." Eshai let out a tired sigh. Seri heard her get up, clothing rustling as she dressed. "What is it?"

"I—found something in the rainforest," Seri said. "Something you should see."

Silence on the platform. Seri kept her eyes fixed on an

innocuous point in the distance, wishing more and more that she could disappear. After what seemed like forever, Eshai spoke.

"I think my helm might have fallen off when you landed. Could you get it for me? We'll be ready in a minute."

Seri nodded quickly, grateful for the escape. "I'll do that," she said, for the first time not hesitating before leaping off the platform and into the dark.

Eshai's helm *had* fallen off the edge of the platform, along with one of Lavit's gloves. Seri scooped both items up from where they lay, earning her a knowing look from a pair of sentries who had seen the armor fall. She flushed and did her best not to start any more rumors as she hugged the pieces close to herself, making her way back up to the command platform. Inwardly, she promised herself she *was* going to master these boots, if only to avoid causing a scene like this again. She landed on the command platform, softer this time, to find Eshai and Lavit already dressed and wearing the remaining pieces of their armor—Lavit looking bemused as she handed his missing glove to him.

Eshai placed the helm back on her head without much ceremony. Seri wondered why *she* was the one who felt so embarrassed about this whole thing—by all accounts, it should have been Eshai and Lavit. But the two of them were acting as if nothing had happened at all.

"Now," Eshai said, "what was it you wanted to show us?"

Seri cleared her throat, letting out a small cough. "It's—um—a little far from camp."

The pause behind her said a lot, and Seri didn't look back, not wanting to see the reprimand in Eshai's eyes. She was already

mortified enough. Without waiting for a signal, she kicked off
the platform, launching herself into the trees.

※

Tsana. Seri is coming to you.

The image Asai sent her shook Tsana out of sleep. She
opened her eyes, giving them a moment to adjust to the dimly
lit world around her.

She was lying alone at the mouth of a stone hallway, looking up at the night sky through the open archway at the end.
Around her, blue light threaded through veins in the stone,
giving the building a familiar, haunting glow, both like and
unlike their navir crystals. Asai was nowhere to be found, but
Tsana still heard the echo of her voice in her mind. She felt
suddenly cold, chilled down to her bones. She knew what
Srayan would do.

Keep it secret, Asai suggested, and with those thoughts came
the impression of shadows, swirling to cover truth like a blanket. Seri's face disappeared, hidden beneath. *Make him leave.*

Tsana was tempted. Her hands flexed and curled at her sides,
drifting over the hilt of the sword she wore. Asai's urging felt
like pressure in her mind. If she kept this a secret, if she convinced Srayan to leave before they arrived . . .

He would know. He would always know.

Tsana turned, reluctantly, and started walking down the dark
passages, avoiding the traps that had been placed here long ago
by those who had built this place. She passed detailed carvings that spoke of histories she had heard a thousand times
before—histories that made her heart heavy and served only

to remind her of loss—and made her way down to the heart of the temple.

Srayan waited in a room at the temple's center. It was a small room, but with high vaulted ceilings, a raised dais standing in the center. All around the dais, beasts lounged and slept, their presence lending the room an earthy animal scent.

Srayan himself sat on his heels in the middle of the dais, his hands clasped in his lap. His eyes were closed in meditation. As Tsana climbed the steps, she felt the beasts around her stir, heads turning to follow her passage. Although Srayan did not move, by the time Tsana reached the top step, she was sure he knew she was there.

"Master," she said, and the word felt thick in her throat, like she was choking on honey. She waited.

Srayan collected himself much faster than she had, although he was reaching out to many minds and not just Asai. He opened his eyes, shook his head as if to clear it, and then stood up. In front of him was a carving, cut into the stone so that it could be seen by whoever meditated here. It showed a coiling serpent, its eyes flashing in the dim light of the cavern as it drew itself high into the sky to strike. The figures across from it, five armored men and women carrying spears, seemed small and insignificant in comparison.

There were many names for the creature. The sky-serpent, the *anishien*, the king of the beasts. Whoever bonded with one would be *enkana*, the greatest of their people. Tsana knew of only seven, including the one depicted in the stone. She wondered what it said about the *anishien* that in every story she heard about them, a valiant always rose to slay them in the end.

The seventh *enkana* regarded the carved serpent for a long

moment before turning to face her. Tsana watched his eyes, wondering if she would see sorrow there. If she did, she thought this would be easier, but all she saw was rage, tightly controlled. Rage that made her hesitate when Srayan said, "What news, Tsana of Astira?"

Tsana bit back the thought that Astira had never done anything for her, that she was truly Tsana of Nowhere. She felt Asai's pressure on her mind to lie and chased that away as well, drawing in a breath.

"Eshai Unbroken and the other commander are approaching the temple."

Tsana braced herself for him to start shouting, but he never did that. *It would almost be easier*, she thought, *if he did.*

Instead, he said, his voice deadly calm, "How did they find this place?"

"Seri is leading them."

Srayan's eyes flashed, and Tsana wished she could vanish. She could feel the shadows calling her, beckoning sweetly. But Srayan would find her. He always did.

"I told you the girl would be more trouble than she's worth."

Tsana said nothing. Srayan looked around the room at the beasts there. As if sensing his tension, they were starting to rise, shaking off sleep. He scanned the room as if counting heads, then looked back at Tsana.

"How long until they arrive?"

Tsana reached out for Asai, did the calculations. "Not long. Perhaps half an hour."

"Very well. If they seek to defile this place, then this place will be their grave."

Tsana shivered. Behind her, the stone serpent gleamed in the half-light. The First, they all called him, except there had to be others before him. He was the First because he was the First since their histories changed. The ones who had carved him had done so knowing this would be the last temple aboveground. The last holy place before the retreat to the caves.

"This isn't a place for killing," she said, her voice soft in the stone chamber.

"This isn't a place for *enshkai*, either." Srayan walked to the edge of the dais, looking down at the beasts below. In Tsana's eyes, the *anishien* was framed behind him, making him look like part of the carving, like a king out of the stories. He studied the beasts and said, "Tsana, I know what I need to do."

Tsana opened her mouth to ask what, but before she could even get the word out, Srayan reached out his hand and closed it into a fist.

It was rare that Tsana could feel another's influence at work. Her own abilities were so miniscule, a drop in the water compared to Srayan's river. She could barely reach out to Asai. But she *felt* what he did here. She felt it as an ill wind, blowing through the cave, sweeping over the beasts. She heard them roar, and then she felt something in them *snap*. She looked around, but the light was dying from each of their eyes. The cavern filled with the sounds of angry growls, but there was no rhythm to them.

She was moving forward before she realized she was running, grabbing for Srayan's outstretched arm.

"Stop!" she heard herself shout, but the arm swung around, catching her under the chin. The blow knocked her back, and Tsana landed on the ground, tasting blood in her mouth. She opened her eyes and saw Srayan facing her, standing over her.

Tsana wiped the blood from her lip with the back of her hand. "You can't *do* this! What have you done to them?"

"Eshai Unbroken thinks they are monsters? Then let her *see* monsters. They will fight and they will kill, and they will destroy until they die or she does."

Tsana shivered. "You *can't*—"

"I *can*," Srayan said, interrupting her. "I am done waiting, Tsana of Astira. I am done plotting. I am done biding my time. If the Conclave will not avenge the Seventh, then *I* will. The *enshkai* have been thorns in our side for too long. It's time for this to end."

He started walking past her. He turned to look back at her, his steps never wavering. His eyes were fixed on something Tsana couldn't see.

His footsteps echoed behind her, heading down the stairs.

The beasts let him pass.

It was only when he left that they erupted into a frenzy, a roiling mass that streamed from the room.

They were only five minutes out of camp when Eshai drew up on Seri's right side, her own passage nearly noiseless through the trees. There was a rustling sound to her left, and then Lavit was beside her, flanking her on her other side as if cutting off her escape.

"What were you doing this far away from camp?" Eshai asked.

The word 'again' went unsaid. Seri felt her face heat up. She shook her head, pretending to concentrate on finding the path. It wasn't as though she needed to pretend. She had left markers to guide her way back to the structure, marks slashed into the trunks of trees, but even with her eyes, it was difficult to see them in the dark.

A glance at her left told her Lavit was watching her closely, his expression troubled each time she drew up beside one of the slashes to trace the lines with her fingers. She realized she wasn't wearing a helm, didn't own one, and that she may have exposed her secret. But she couldn't bring herself to care.

When they burst out of the trees, revealing the glowing structure that stood on the open ground ahead of them, both Lavit and Eshai drew up short to stare. Seri landed on the ground between them, the force of her landing driving her to her knees. She straightened up, wincing as she rubbed at her legs.

"It's some kind of building," she said. "Made of stone. The lights are lichen."

Lavit nodded. "We see the glowing lichen sometimes on expeditions. It glows after a rain."

If it hadn't rained, would she have missed this entirely? If she hadn't left camp, would she have ever seen this? She felt a shiver at the thought.

"Inside?" Lavit asked.

Seri shook her head. "I didn't go inside. Once I realized what I was looking at, I went to get someone."

"Good," said Eshai, her voice tight. She started walking forward, unhooking her spear from her back. "Stay behind me."

Seri didn't hesitate to comply, but as she followed Eshai, she realized there was something else she had left out. Something Eshai and Lavit needed to know.

"Eshai," she said, "I found carvings. On that signpost, near the steps. They looked like they were made by our People."

Eshai shook her head. "That's impossible. We've never lived in stone."

"They were the same as our writing," Seri said. "Mostly, anyway. There were some slight differences, and there were some words I couldn't read."

"What did they say?" Lavit asked, breaking in.

Seri glanced at him. "I didn't get a chance to read them all, but—they were words of welcome. There were some words I didn't understand, but I think they were saying this was some kind of—of sacred place. Like Lanatha."

Eshai snorted. "This is *nothing* like Lanatha."

"Eshai," said Lavit.

Eshai nodded, drawing in a breath and letting it out. She turned toward Lavit and Seri. "We can discuss this all later. Stay on alert. We're heading in now."

Seri nodded, taking hold of her own spear. Her mouth was dry as she followed Lavit and Eshai up the steps and into the structure.

❧

Inside was quiet and damp, their steps echoing on the stone in a way that set Seri's teeth on edge. Lichen grew on the stone walls and corridors inside the structure, their glow providing enough light to see by as the three of them walked through the entrance hall. Eshai's eyes were fixed straight ahead, looking for enemies, but Lavit's gaze wandered, sweeping over the walls and ceiling.

"They built all this out of stone. Incredible."

"We don't even know who *they* are, Lavit," Eshai said.

"No," said Lavit. "But Seri's right. These carvings are our words, Eshai. I understand some of them."

Eshai paused, the look on her face one of impatience and irritation, but she didn't say anything as Lavit broke away from the group, walking toward the left wall of the corridor. This wall was *covered* in carvings, Seri saw. Some of them were overgrown with lichen, making them hard to see, but the others . . .

She hesitated, glancing at Eshai, then hurried after Lavit. He moved to the side, making space for her as she drew up next to him, leaning closer to see the lines on the wall. They weren't just words. Some of them were pictures, carved into the stone. Illustrations of people and beasts.

They weren't fighting, at least not at first. At first, they lived in harmony, beasts plowing fields and guarding homes and accompanying people on their hunts. But the farther they walked, the more the story changed. A beast killed a man here, another there. A figure in armor spoke at the center of a crowd of listening people, his arms spread in supplication. Then there was war, people killing people. And then the carvings simply *ended*, leaving a blank expanse of empty wall ahead of them.

Someone spoke from behind them. "You shouldn't have come here."

Seri whirled around, but Eshai and Lavit were faster—they had their spears up and ready before she even started moving. Tsana simply *melted* out of the darkness of the hallway behind them, as if the shadows were a cloak she had slipped off and thrown to the ground. The expression on her face wasn't one of anger or hostility. It was fear.

"Tsana—" Seri started. "What—?"

A low growl echoed from the corridor ahead, followed by

another. Seri looked over her shoulder to see beasts, white-furred and with gleaming eyes, pouring into the corridor from up ahead.

"A trap!" Eshai said, turning around to face their enemies. "Lavit!"

Lavit spun to meet the threat, the two of them putting themselves between Seri and the charge. Seri hesitated, seeing Tsana turn to run out of the corner of her eye. She started after her, taking off at a run as Eshai shouted her name.

Tsana turned sharply off the path to the front door, following a narrow side corridor that Seri might not have seen if she hadn't watched Tsana take it. Seri changed direction quickly, grunting in pain as the sudden change forced her to slam into the corridor wall. She pushed off it and hurried to catch Tsana.

Ahead of her, Tsana was just running, head down, arms and legs pumping, no deliberation to her movements. As if she were only trying to get away. Seri tried to keep track of where they were going, but lost count after the last few turns.

"Tsana!" Seri called after her. "Tsana, *wait*! I'm not going to hurt you—!"

Tsana continued to run. Seri pursued her, aware in the back of her mind that she needed to get back to Eshai and Lavit. That the two of them might be even now being overrun by beasts. But Tsana was just up ahead of her, running toward what looked like an open room. Seri picked up speed as Tsana crossed the threshold, slapping something on the wall. There was a groaning sound, stone scraping against stone, and then there were slabs sliding into place, threatening to close off the entrance. Seri closed her eyes, putting on a sudden burst of speed and kicking off the ground. She shot forward like an arrow, sailing through the narrowing gap.

It closed a second behind her, the force of her leap sending her sprawling onto the stone ground. A cloud of dust rose in her wake.

Seri coughed, fighting for breath. She pushed herself up onto her arm, disoriented, and saw that Tsana had backed into the corner of the room, her eyes wide. She had one hand on the hilt of that strange weapon she carried—the long knife—but she hadn't drawn it from its sheath yet.

"Tsana," Seri said, pushing herself to her feet. Her heart was pounding, and she couldn't believe what she had just done. Eshai and Lavit— "Tsana, what is this place? Did your People make it?"

Tsana shook her head, her face pale in the dim light from the lichen. "It was a temple once—a sacred place. You shouldn't have brought them here. This place isn't—it's not for them."

"How did you find us?" Seri asked. When Tsana didn't answer, she felt a thread of cold realization worm its way through her. "Were you following us the entire time?"

Tsana's silence was answer enough. Seri looked around the room, trying to think. They were in what might have once been a storage room, but whatever had been stored here had long since crumbled to dust. The walls were free of carvings, but her mind was still full of the sight of them in that hallway, immeasurably old. Men and beasts living together.

"Did my People make this place?"

"There were no *your* People back then," Tsana said, letting out a breath of exhaustion. "There were no *my* People, either. There was only one People, yours and mine, together."

"What happened?"

"Your People call it the Great Disaster. The event that forced you into the trees. Mine have a different name. In our language, we call it the Great Betrayal."

Tsana's eyes were like beacons in the dark. Seri felt the weight of her words settle on her like a shroud. The Great Betrayal.

In those carvings, the people killing others had been wielding spears. And wearing armor.

The spear in her hand felt wrong, entirely too heavy. She wanted to drop it, but her mind was still on Eshai and Lavit. Eshai and Lavit, in a corridor with beasts.

"I have to get back," she said, turning around to face the stone slabs covering the exit. "I have to help them."

"It's too late," Tsana said, sounding afraid. "The beasts will be everywhere in the temple now. You'll only die."

"Then call off the attack!" Seri said, looking back at Tsana.

"I—" Tsana looked stricken, shaking her head. "I *can't!*"

"What do you mean? You can control beasts! Eshai *saw* you do it."

"I can only control one! And only—"

Tsana paused, looking away in defeat. She stretched her arm out along the wall, making a soft clicking noise under her breath. As Seri watched, a reptilian shape, like an oversized lizard, materialized out of the shadows on the wall, crawling up Tsana's arm and coming to rest on her shoulder. It was impossible to tell the color of its scales in the dim light, but its eyes gleamed, fixing on Seri as Tsana reached out and scratched the top of the creature's head.

The creature's hide was threaded through with crystals, like a beast. But if it *was* a beast, it was the smallest beast Seri had ever seen.

"This is Asai," Tsana said to Seri, drawing herself up to her full height as if challenging Seri to comment on the beast's size. "My bondmate. Most of us can only control one beast at a time, and she is mine. Occasionally, I can calm a tame beast, but . . ." She looked away, shivering. "They're angry, Seri. They're so angry. An unbonded beast takes reason from the mind that touches it, but he isn't *letting* them gain reason. He's feeding their rage. They won't stop for me, or for anyone."

"Then I have to go," Seri said, turning back toward the slabs. "How do I open the door?"

"Seri. You'll die."

If she listened, she could hear growling from the other side of the stone. The fighting would be thickest around Eshai and Lavit. The two of them would be trying to make their way to the front door. They were powerful, but even they could be overwhelmed. And if they *were* overwhelmed, if they died here, they would die while Seri cowered in a room safe, unharmed.

Two more souls on her conscience. Two more lives.

Two more *Ithims.*

When she spoke, she barely recognized her own voice. The real her wasn't nearly this confident, this sure of herself. The real her was scared out of her mind.

But she walked forward, spear in hand, and said, "Tsana. *The door.*"

"Aren't you *listening*?" Tsana asked, frustrated. "You'll *die*! It's better this way, Seri. Just . . . just . . ."

"Just *what*? Just stand here and wait until it's over? What kind of person would I be if I did that?"

"The Unbroken doesn't deserve—" Tsana broke off sharply as Seri whirled to face her.

"*Eshai Unbroken* has been working *tirelessly* to make sure no more of our People die. No more innocents. Tsana, how do I open the door?"

Tsana looked down at the ground, defeated. "It wasn't supposed to be this way," she said, hardly seeming as if she was speaking to Seri at all. "Master Srayan and I were just supposed to watch you. Just *watch*."

"I'm only going to ask you one more time. How do I open the door?"

Tsana's gaze flicked from Seri to the door. One of her hands cradled Asai's head, the beast watching Seri closely. The other worried at the hilt of her weapon.

She sighed. "Right side. There's a switch."

Seri looked and saw something like a lever embedded in the stone. She walked up to it, tracing her fingers over it. So small, to shift so much weight. She wondered how it had been built.

"As soon as you open the door, they'll attack," Tsana said, her voice almost a whisper. "They're under *his* control now. I won't be able to stop them."

Seri considered that for a moment, her expression grim. Then she reached out and pulled the lever up. The room filled with the sound of grating stone.

There was a rasp, and Seri looked back over her shoulder

to see Tsana holding her weapon in her hand, having pulled it from its sheath. The blade gleamed with the same shine as the strange ornaments on Tsana's clothing.

The slabs came apart and the beasts roared in challenge as they poured into the room.

CHAPTER 16

◊

Eshai's spear took one of the charging beasts in the neck. She bent her knees and slipped underneath it, pushing the beast up off the ground. With a deft twist of her hands on the shaft, she flung the beast at the wall, the creature's bones breaking on impact. Without wasting a breath, she stepped in, using the shaft of the spear to block a swiping paw aimed at her face. Its claws skittered ineffectively against beast-bone as she slid in, taking the beast in the throat.

Behind her, she heard the dull thump of Lavit throwing a charging beast aside, the valiant taking a step closer to her. Eshai sucked in a breath through her teeth. The two of them were pushing back toward the exit, Eshai fighting to make a path forward while Lavit kept them safe from behind. The beasts had flooded the corridor almost as soon as Seri and Tsana were gone, trapping them from both sides. The corridor was slick with blood, littered with carcasses. And still, they kept coming.

Eshai stepped forward, sliding across the slick stone. Her spear punched straight through the rib cage of a charging beast. She and Lavit were moving, killing as they went, but each step was hard won, each inch a trial. She tried to remember how far they had left to go and stopped herself—it wasn't worth thinking about.

Either she made it through this, or she didn't. Either they made it past this blockade, or they didn't.

Either she survived or her luck finally ran out.

She let her mind clear, all other thoughts running off her like water. Something knocked into her from behind—Lavit, forced back by a particularly strong beast. She looked over her shoulder to see him grappling with the creature, but she couldn't afford to help him now, not with two others charging her from the front.

Eshai moved, crossing the distance between herself and the first beast with one long stride. She swung around, planting her heel into the side of its neck. Bones crunched beneath her boot, the tip of her spear taking the second beast between the eyes before it had a chance to react. While the prowling creatures farther down the corridor took time to collect themselves, Eshai turned back, signaling Lavit with a sharp whistle. He didn't even pause to look at her, pulling back from the grapple and twisting to the side as Eshai moved in, her spear finding purchase in the beast's heart.

She pulled her spear out and resumed pushing forward, not wanting to waste any time. Lavit turned to guard her back as she crossed the long strides toward the three remaining beasts standing between them and safety.

She wondered where Seri was. If she had escaped, or if she was lying dead on the stone somewhere in this cursed building. The moment of distraction cost her. A beast leapt at her while she was thinking. In response, Eshai dug her heels into the ground and lashed out with the butt of her spear, catching the beast in the side. Muscles groaned in protest beneath her armor as she tossed the beast aside, its claws skittering across her vest.

Her heart pounded with the proximity, the air between them filled with the foul stench of the beast's breath.

That one had been too close.

Distraction was a thing she couldn't afford. She put Seri from her mind and charged again.

There were two beasts in the corridor. Only two. A full valiant, one with Eshai's training, might not see that as a challenge, but Seri's heart was pounding like a rabbit's as one charged her. She rushed forward, remembering Eshai's lessons about beasts. At the last moment, as the beast committed to the initial charge, she threw herself to the side, using the burst of speed granted by her boots.

It wasn't as smooth as a true valiant might have managed. She had to land on one foot, weakening her position. Still, her gloves did their work as she thrust forward with her spear, the bone blade opening a gash along the beast's flank.

It roared in anger and pain, rearing up to strike her. Seri raised the spear in both hands to block, the beast's front paws slamming into the shaft and throwing her to the ground.

The impact took her breath away, and the beast bore down on her, pushing her into the ground with its paws. Seri fought back the urge to panic, summoning all the strength she had in her gloves. She braced her elbows against the ground, shoving back against the beast with all her might. The spear's shaft— ordinary animal bone instead of beastbone—creaked with the weight and Seri felt a flash of alarm.

The spear held. Seri flung the beast off her, throwing it to the side with a shout of effort. It crashed into the wall, roaring, as Seri leapt to her feet.

The second beast entered the room before she could recover, charging at her.

Tsana melted out of the shadows, the tip of her weapon piercing the beast at the base of its neck. The beast jerked once and then went still, its limbs going slack as Tsana pulled the blade free. Blood stained its tip, dulling its gleam. There were tear tracks down her cheeks, but Tsana's eyes were hard as she stepped away, giving the weapon a flick of her wrist to shake off the blood.

The first beast, the one Seri had thrown, was getting back up. Tsana jerked her head toward the door. Seri ran and she followed, slapping at the switch as she crossed the threshold. The beast roared as it charged them, crashing into the stone slabs as they came together to seal off the storage room. They could hear it roaring on the other side of the wall, rage and pain echoing in the corridor.

Tsana held her weapon in one hand, breathing hard, Asai clinging to the wall beside her. At a jerk from Tsana's head, Asai scuttled forward, vanishing in the darkness.

"I can use Asai as another pair of eyes," Tsana explained. "She'll find us a way out." Her gaze drifted to the blood on her weapon and she grimaced, looking away.

"Tsana . . . ," Seri began, but Tsana brushed her off with a wave of her hand, still not looking at her.

"Even my People kill beasts. When they lose all capacity for reason, or when they're bred weak and sickly, or when they're too powerful and won't bond. We don't talk about it, but we do. When I said those things to you in Vethaya, I . . ." She shook her head. "We *should* be the people we say we are. The ones from *our* stories. But we aren't always."

Seri understood. Her People lived on their songs. The songs of valor, of heroes. Maybe they were all lies. Maybe *none* of them were really true, and there were no heroes.

Except there was Eshai.

The songs left out a lot about her. They left out her temper, her disorganization, her penchant for being overly controlling. They left out her uncertainties and her insecurities and her flaws. Eshai wasn't the perfect hero the songs made her out to be. She made a lot of mistakes, and she had more fears than Seri would have imagined.

But Seri had also seen her rise to the occasion, time and time again. Somehow, she fought past all those flaws and all those fears to become something *more*.

Eshai made her believe in heroes. As long as Eshai existed, the songs could never be truly wrong.

She reached out and grabbed Tsana's wrist, startling her and making her look up from her bloodied sword.

"We can be the people from our stories. We can save them, Tsana. *Help me.*"

Tsana stared at her, eyes wide. Beneath her grip, Seri could feel her hand trembling. "It's too late."

"I'm *not* leaving without them." Seri pulled away from Tsana, tightening her grip on her spear. The blade was chipped, cracked along the shaft, but she expected that. Ordinary bone couldn't hope to stand up to a beast for long. Not without a beast-heart at its core.

Despite her bravado, Seri's heart was pounding, her nerves frayed down to their ends. She could still smell the beast's breath. The spear was too close, too personal a weapon. If she had her way, she would be far in the distance, with her bow and nothing else.

But she didn't have her way. And Eshai and Lavit were going to die if she didn't move. They might die anyway, but at least Seri could *try*.

"You look at a situation, and you ask yourself what you can control..."

Eshai's words, from another lifetime.

Seri met Tsana's eyes, daring the other girl to challenge her again. And Tsana, thankfully, didn't. She simply sighed, holding her weapon out to her side.

"Let's hurry. If the entrance gets cut off, none of us will have a chance."

Seri nodded gratefully, running back down the corridor toward the sound of battle. She heard footsteps as Tsana fell into step beside her, her cloak pushed over her shoulder to free her weapon arm. Tsana's eyes passed over her once, moving over her armor.

"Is that supposed to happen?" Tsana asked.

Seri looked back at her. "Is what?"

"Your armor. Is it supposed to change like that?"

In confusion, Seri looked down at her hand, the one not holding her spear. It was hard to tell in the dim light, but she thought there was a spot of lighter color spreading over her fingertips.

A valiant's armor reflects their heart.

Seri breathed deep and put it from her mind, focusing on what was coming.

The side of Eshai's fist slammed into a beast's skull as it rushed at her, knocking it aside. Lavit stepped in, skewering it with his spear. She knocked a second beast out of the way with the butt of her spear, dropping her weight and thrusting her spearpoint straight through the open mouth of a third. Her world blurred as she sank down further, letting out a grunt of effort as she shoved the dying beast aside. Her muscles strained, her breath like fire in her lungs.

So close. They were so close.

She could hear the way the quality of sound changed ahead, could smell the warm, earthy scent of the outside air. Not much farther. A miniscule distance, for a valiant.

By now, she and Lavit had killed most of the white-furred ones. But more had come, sleek, black-furred felines she hadn't seen before. Those were harder. They were smaller, but faster, more vicious. They attacked in packs, two trying to flank Eshai and keep her distracted while a third came in for the kill. It would have been exhausting to keep up with had she been fresh. And she was already so tired, so very tired.

Escape seemed like a dream.

Her shoulders sagged, and Lavit stepped back to her, his back touching hers. The feeling made her stand up a little straighter, grip her spear a little tighter. Her vision cleared, if only for a moment.

This was a cruel ending to their story.

"Eshai . . . ," Lavit said.

Eshai heard the resignation in his voice. She looked out at

the two beasts still pacing in front of her, waiting for a moment of weakness, at the shadows of other beasts gathering behind them.

It was so tempting to give up, to lay down her spear.

She drew herself up straighter instead.

"Lavit," she said. "The first charge of valor?"

Lavit paused, then let out a ragged laugh.

"Be dauntless," he quoted, "for the hopes of the People rest in you."

Eshai nodded, her expression grim. She and Lavit had memorized every line of the charges, over and over again, while they were children in their village. By the time they left for Vethaya, they could recite them by heart. Being valiants was all they had ever wanted, once.

Once, when times were simpler, being in the unknown world had been a dream.

She tightened her hold on her spear once more, leveling the point of it at the beasts.

Then she let out a war cry, charging forward.

Tsana grabbed Seri by the arm as she ran, pulling her back sharply. Seri stumbled, annoyed, and looked back at Tsana, about to protest. Tsana's eyes weren't on Seri, though, but on the patch of stone she had been about to step on. Her expression was so focused that the complaint died in Seri's mouth.

They were running down a side corridor, one Tsana had led Seri through. The main corridor, the one that they had entered, was blocked by beasts, and Tsana claimed there was a secret door that connected them.

"What?" Seri asked. "What is it?"

"Trap. We use similar . . . things where I'm from. Watch."

Before Seri could question her, Tsana leaned forward, tapping the stone with her weapon. She pulled it back quickly, just as a series of spikes erupted from the walls and the ceiling. The spikes thrust through the air from floor to ceiling in a complex, interlocking pattern, blocking the way for just a moment before they pulled apart again. Seri stared in shock at the empty air where the spikes had been, taking a step back.

Tsana nodded in approval, seeming impressed. "Good metal," she said, the word unfamiliar to Seri. "For it to still be sharp after so long. This was likely one of the false paths to the inner sanctum. You didn't come in this way, so you wouldn't have noticed."

"Meh-tal?" Seri asked.

"*Metal*," Tsana repeated, gesturing at her weapon. Her brow furrowed in thought. "It's . . . something you can extract from rocks. It will take too long to explain. We should leap over." She nodded at Seri's boots, still looking uncomfortable at even acknowledging the armor.

The distance over the plate would have been easy, even for someone as inexperienced as Seri. She nodded, about to grab Tsana by the waist, then paused as a thought occurred to her.

"Tsana," she said, looking back at her. "This trap will work if anything steps on it, right?"

Tsana nodded. "It's triggered by pressure. The weight of someone or something stepping down on it. Man, beast, or stone, it doesn't care."

"And there are many of these? On the path we'll be traveling on?"

Tsana nodded, and Seri saw the instant she began to understand. "Do you think . . . ?"

"You'll have to guide me," Seri said, wrapping an arm around Tsana's waist. She tried not to flush at the contact, and almost succeeded. "And we have to hurry."

She focused on the open air ahead of her, adjusting her angle. Her leap carried her off the ground, bringing her and Tsana over the plate and onto the path ahead.

The beast's paw caught her in the side of the head, making her see stars. Eshai stumbled back and away, managing, just barely, to lift her spear to deflect a swipe of another beast's bladed tail. The paw had knocked her helm askew, obscuring her vision. Her head was pounding, and she struggled to bring her spear back up. Lavit quickly stepped into the gap, defending her against a strike, but that left them open from behind. Eshai pushed her helm back into place with one hand, the two of them shifting positions as she swiped at the legs of a beast that moved in too close, Lavit focusing on the path ahead while she turned to the path behind. His back against hers was a reassurance, and she leaned into it.

"Not much farther," Eshai said, gasping out the words under her breath. Breathing had been hard ever since one of the beast's claws had managed to break through her armor's protection, scoring a wound along her side. "Not much farther, Lavit."

Lavit sounded just as out of breath. "Heh. I used to hate—"

He paused to stab a lunging beast in the flank, the effort changing the quality of his voice. "—that about you."

"You hated something about me?" She drove two of the pacing beasts back with another sweep, forcing them to look for another angle of approach.

"When I was younger?" Lavit asked, punctuating the sentence with another stab. "Stupider? I hated a lot of things. Your confidence." A sweep, and a grunt as he threw a beast off the end of his spear. "The way you were always so *sure* of yourself. How hard you worked. And in the end, you always won."

Oh, Lavit... Eshai thought, but she didn't dare say it out loud. *I don't think either of us will be winning here.*

The wall to her right slid open.

Eshai's eyes widened, unable to fully process what she was seeing. The stone simply slid *away*, folding into itself and revealing another passage. And in that passage, a girl in valiant armor waited, out of breath with fresh bruises on her face and shoulders.

"Eshai!" Seri said. "This way! Quick!"

Seri turned and started running back down the corridor. Eshai followed, grabbing hold of Lavit's shoulder and pulling him with her. Lavit turned to follow, sweeping his spear out to drive the beasts away from their escape route.

The path ahead was narrow and dark, but it was free of beasts. In the dim light from the lichen, Eshai saw that Seri wasn't alone. Tsana was with her, running beside her, her weapon out at her side. Without boots, she couldn't hope to run as quickly as a valiant, but Seri had an arm around Tsana's shoulders, helping her keep up with them. The open path let them run faster, but the beasts were closing in from behind. Eshai could hear their growls, could smell their fetid breath. She didn't dare look over her shoulder to see how close they were.

"They'll catch up," she warned Seri.

"Don't worry about that," Seri said, her expression grim. "Just follow my lead!"

They burst out into a wider corridor, the stone walls unadorned. As they ran, Tsana kept her eyes on the ground.

"There!" Tsana said, pointing at something Eshai couldn't see.

"Jump!" Seri called, kicking off the ground and leaping over the space. Eshai did the same, Lavit following close behind her. The four of them sailed through the air, the beasts tight at their heels.

One of the beasts ran across the surface, lunging at her.

Spears thrust themselves out of the floor and the walls of the corridor, skewering through the creature and the two behind it, hiding the others from sight.

CHAPTER 17

❧

The air outside the building was alive with the sound of roars and growls, the clash of a distant battle. Seri drew up short as soon as they reached the tree line, trying to pinpoint the source of the sound. Behind her, Eshai tilted her head up, looking out into the woods.

"The camp. We should hurry."

Eshai sounded out of breath. Seri looked back at her to see a dark spot spreading across her side, staining the white of her armor. Eshai had one hand clamped to it, blood seeping between her fingers.

"You're hurt—"

"I'm fine," Eshai said, drawing in a pained breath. "We need to get back to the camp."

"I'll see if the way ahead is clear," Tsana said, turning toward the trees. A dark shape rushed out from her, only briefly visible as Asai before its scales changed, taking on the coloration of the forest around them. Eshai rounded on Tsana, as if she had only now remembered she was there.

"You—" Eshai said, grabbing Tsana's shoulder with her bloodied hand. Tsana flinched as Eshai spun her around. "You caused this. What have you done?"

"Eshai—!"

Seri started forward but was stopped by an arm thrust in front of her to bar her way. Lavit's. He was watching the scene between Eshai and Tsana, his expression grave, fingers twitching around the shaft of the spear in his other hand. Tsana looked pale, but she met Eshai's eyes.

"It wasn't me," Tsana said. "You have to believe that."

"I don't have a good reason to believe anything you say."

"I helped save your life."

"As far as I'm concerned, *Seri* saved my life," Eshai said. "What are you doing here? Explain." Her grip tightened on Tsana's shoulder, visibly.

Tsana winced but didn't pull away. "We don't have *time* for this. If we stay here, your people will die."

"Then explain quickly."

Tsana took in a deep breath, indecision and hesitation playing across her features before her shoulders slumped in resignation.

"It was my master. He wanted to—he saw this as an opportunity to end you. He—broke the beasts. Set them on you. Turned them feral. Such a thing is . . . it isn't done. I tried to stop him, but I . . ."

Tsana trailed off. There was a mark on the side of her face, Seri realized, now that they had time to think. Barely visible in the dim light, even to Seri's vision, but it was there.

Eshai saw it, too. Her hold on Tsana didn't slacken, but her voice was softer when she spoke.

"Why are you here?"

"He left me behind. It wasn't supposed to be this way. A scouting mission, we were told. Nothing more." She shook her head, seeming to grow more confident as she pressed her lips together. She looked up at Eshai. "This was *wrong*. What we did at your city was wrong. I came to help."

"You came to help *us*?"

Tsana's eyes moved past Eshai, resting on Seri. Seri understood, with a jolt. Tsana hadn't come to help Eshai. Tsana had come to help *her*.

Eshai followed Tsana's gaze, looking at Seri as well. She understood, too. She pushed Tsana back, releasing her.

"The camp," she told Lavit.

"Your wound."

"It will keep until we see what happened to our damned *camp*." Eshai glared at Lavit, grounding out the words. "Let's go." She looked back at Tsana. "Follow us or don't. It's your choice. Seri, with me."

The valiant's tone brooked no argument. Seri hesitated, but leapt into the air after Eshai, following her path into the trees. She looked back as she landed on a branch, down toward Tsana on the ground. The other girl looked back at her, one hand rubbing the shoulder Eshai had grabbed. Seri wanted to ask if Tsana was coming with them, if she would ever see Tsana again or if, this time, it really was goodbye.

The words were frozen in her throat, but they were written on her face.

Tsana held her gaze, slowly nodding. "I'll follow."

Seri wanted to believe her; she really did. But she couldn't forget searching for Tsana in Vethaya, not so easily.

"Seri!" Eshai shouted from ahead of her.

"Go," said Tsana.

Reluctantly, Seri tore her eyes away, leaping to catch up with Eshai.

❧

Even when she was injured, following Eshai through the trees was not easy. The valiant moved like a woman possessed and made no effort to slow down for Seri or to help her along. Seri knew Eshai was still angry, knew she could expect another questioning, at the very least, when this was over.

If this ever ended. The closer she neared to camp, the more her stomach sank, everything inside her coiling with dread.

She could still hear the battle, the sound of growling beasts and voices calling out in pain, but they were growing farther away. Farther than they should have been, if the battle were at the camp.

She didn't like it. She tried to get a glimpse of sky during one of her leaps, to use the position of the moon to track how long they had been inside the stone building, but there were clouds in the sky, and it was hard to say.

The closer they came to camp, the more her heart raced. And then at last, she lost sight of Eshai and Lavit and found them a moment later when she burst out of the trees and into their clearing.

The camp was in complete disarray. Platforms had been torn from the trees, their supplies dumped in a pile on the forest floor along with the tarps and canopies that had kept the rain off them in the night. The trees bore claw marks, and the earth had been churned by the fighting. Here and there, the ground was dotted with dark, broken forms. Beasts mostly, but every now and then, a smaller form that made Seri's breath catch. Eshai was already standing over one of these smaller forms, carefully arranging it into some form of repose. Seri caught sight of a hand, a flash of brown skin, and she felt her heart sink.

The dead valiant was a young woman she had never gotten the chance to know. Would never know, now.

Lavit clearly knew her. Eshai took one look at his face and stepped away from the fallen valiant, her head bowed. He crouched beside the body, gently closing her eyes with his hand, his fingers brushing against the crumbling leather of her helm.

"Peace, Ivasa," he said. "Your journey has ended."

He straightened up, looking back at Seri. His fists were clenched at his sides, as if he were bracing himself for a blow.

"Who else?" he asked.

They made a circuit of the camp, searching for human forms among the fallen. They found only one more, a young man lying crumpled in the roots of one of the trees they had slept in. The battle had clearly caught him by surprise. He barely had his armor on. Eshai and Lavit laid him out beside Ivasa, and only then did they speak to each other.

"The battle's moved on," Eshai said.

Lavit nodded. "They had standing orders. If something like this happened and I wasn't around to say otherwise, they were to head back to the known world." He looked over at Eshai. "It's been our way, ever since . . ."

Eshai didn't answer, but a look of understanding passed between them. Seri wondered if Lavit had meant to say *Naumea*.

"Can we catch up?" Eshai asked.

"Inadvisable." The voice startled Seri—she had almost forgotten about Tsana. She turned to see her materialize out of the darkness, her strange weapon still in her hand. Her *metal* weapon.

Eshai and Lavit swung to face her, spears up. They looked a second away from attacking. Eshai scowled.

"*Do not* scare us like that again."

Tsana looked confused for a moment, then looked down at herself. "I'm sorry. I sometimes forget . . ." She shook her head. "You can't follow them."

"Why not?" Lavit asked.

"They're fleeing." Tsana's expression grew distant, as if she were watching things happen somewhere far away. "Heading toward your territory. The—the feral beasts are chasing them, but they're putting up a considerable fight. But there are too many beasts, and they are between you and the rest of the valor. Sooner or later, the beasts will tire and turn back. Sooner, if they can find more tempting prey. If you try to reach them, the beasts will almost certainly turn on you."

"How can you *possibly* know that?" Eshai asked.

Tsana looked uncomfortable. "I can see through her eyes."

"Whose?"

"My bondmate's. You would call her my beast."

Eshai looked as though she was about to say more, but Lavit cut in. "You're a spy."

Tsana didn't even try to deny it, although she did look ashamed. "Yes." After a moment, she added, "That was why we were sent here—Master Srayan and I. We were meant to observe you. The Conclave was concerned . . . your expansions were drawing too close to our homeland. We studied your language—it's an older form of ours, and the Conclave still remembers it—and then we were sent out. We were supposed to be a reconnaissance party, to see if you could be reasoned with. That was *all* we were supposed to do."

"Let me guess," Eshai said, her tone dangerous. "Your master didn't see it that way."

Tsana shook her head. "Master Srayan said you were all monsters. That you all needed to die."

"What is he planning?"

"Master Srayan is an *enkana*," Tsana said. "It is . . . you would call it a position of honor. He has the talent to bond with many beasts at once. At first, his plan was to attack Vethaya using his army. But when that failed, he decided it wasn't enough.

"Even an *enkana* has limits. Master Srayan can control many beasts, but not enough to single-handedly destroy you. By turning them feral, though, he can make them fight even without his influence. Beasts kill for food or to protect their territory. They have some reason. But the beasts Srayan broke have none. They will continue killing until they themselves are killed." Her hands clenched into fists. "Among our people, bonding with a beast is sacred. From man, the beast gains reason and thought; from the beast, the man gains power. But what he's doing—he's taking their reason and power both. It's more than forbidden. It's *ashkar*—'that which must never occur.' I couldn't stand by and watch."

"But you could stand and watch when this Srayan threatened our people," Eshai said. "When he murdered innocents in the streets."

Tsana opened her mouth as if to retort, but Seri could see how the words struck her. She looked away. Seri wanted to go to her, to speak up for her, but she couldn't. People had still died in Vethaya. Tsana had *still* done that. Willingly or not.

"You have the right to hate me for that," Tsana said. "You don't need to trust me. But let me help make things right."

"No amount of words will change what's been done," Eshai said. "But if that's how you truly feel, let your actions speak for you." She looked over at Lavit, who had remained silent through this exchange, his spear at his side. "You said our valor will eventually shake the beasts. What will they do after that?"

"Feral beasts will . . . will return to where they are most comfortable. They will likely return here."

"So, we're cut off," Lavit said. "That's what you're saying, isn't it?"

Tsana looked uncomfortable but nodded. "We should leave as soon as we can. We shouldn't be here when they return. If they come across us, they will kill us."

"We'll have to head back to the known world another way," said Eshai.

Lavit spoke up. "We can take the southern route. It will take us a few days out of our way, but the four of us alone can travel faster than a valor. We should be able to catch them in the known world."

He looked over at Seri as he spoke, his expression unreadable. Seri understood. She remembered their conversation earlier that day—a lifetime ago.

The southern route.

Elaya.

Eshai nodded, and Seri's blood went cold. "We leave immediately. Take as many supplies as you can carry. If we travel through the night, we can separate ourselves from the pack. When we reach the known world, I'll send a message to Turi. My valor can cut off the beasts and tend to your injured."

"Eshai . . . ," Lavit said, his expression dark. His gaze drifted toward the pair of bodies, lying still on the ground. Seri understood—if they left now, the valiants that had died in the camp would never have a vigil. No one to stand their watch as they passed into the earth, back into the water.

A pained look crossed Eshai's face.

"We can't afford to lose a day, Lavit. I'm so sorry."

"A night, then," Lavit said. "At least a night."

Eshai lowered her gaze to the ground. She hugged her arms close to herself, wincing as she accidentally brushed up against the wound in her side. Lavit noticed the wince and softened his tone.

"You're injured. We need our rest. The valor will stop to rest, too, as soon as they're safe. And these two deserve a vigil. They were mine, Eshai. My first command. Please."

At the word 'please,' Seri knew Lavit had won. Eshai's shoulders slumped, and she looked back at Tsana. "Is there somewhere near here we can stay for the night? Somewhere safe, close to water?"

CHAPTER 18

॰

T sana led them to a spreading tree.

It was smaller than the spreading trees Seri was used to, but it was still unquestionably a spreading tree, towering above the other trees by a wide margin. It was fed by a pond of clear water, one Lavit immediately went to wash in to prepare for the vigil. Eshai went with him as his attendant, leaving Tsana and Seri alone. With most of the night gone, it wouldn't be much of a vigil. Certainly, it wouldn't have the usual rites. But it would be enough to honor what Ivasa and Marim, the other valiant, had been.

Seri was left to set up camp. Tsana helped where she could, but the girl was so clumsy in the trees that after a moment, Seri left her on one of the branches, spreading out the folding platform they had taken from the camp alone. When the platform was secured, the two of them sat in the center of it, Tsana eyeing the drop on the other side of the platform warily.

She was sitting cross-legged, her weapon in one hand, the blade resting across her knees. Seri had learned, while walking here, that it was called a *sword*.

Seri had rescued her bow from the wreckage of the camp and was now restringing it, wanting it close at hand in case the beasts attacked again.

Below them, Lavit sat alone among the roots of the spreading tree, where Ivasa and Marim were laid out. Eshai, after having her wound seen to by Seri, was standing watch. She would soon relieve him. By necessity, the ritual of washing had been shortened.

She didn't bother asking if Eshai and Lavit were planning to sleep tonight. She knew what the answer would be.

"This could be a village someday," Seri said, to break the uncomfortable silence between her and Tsana. Her fingers moved over the sturdy outline of her bow, checking for cracks in the beastbone.

Tsana looked up in alarm. "No. You can't bring them here."

"Why not?"

"This valley is holy. It is a sacred place for the beasts. If you come—" She broke off sharply, looking off to the side. Seri understood. She remembered the beasts in the valley, the ones that had come here to die, and those that had come to attend them. Seri wondered how many of them Srayan had touched, how many were now mindless. Were there any left to stand vigil?

"Srayan couldn't have broken them all," said Tsana. "Others will come, and your People cannot be here when they do."

Seri nodded. "I won't tell a soul." She wasn't sure the same could be said of Eshai and Lavit, but that was a worry for another time.

Tsana looked down at her sword and then carefully slid it back into its sheath. The lantern they had salvaged from the camp cast eerie shadows across its length. "It's so strange."

"What is?"

"Your custom of watching the dead. The dead are already gone—why do they need watchers?"

"Our People say the soul lingers for a night after death. We watch over them to make sure that their souls find their way back to the water, where they can be born again."

Tsana shook her head. "Strange."

"Your People don't do that?"

"A body is only empty flesh. The soul leaves as soon as it dies. One night, two, or three. It doesn't matter."

"What do you do with your dead, then?"

"We take what we can," Tsana said. "Personal effects, anything that can be left behind or inherited. And then we take the bodies outside the caves, before they can rot."

"And bury them?"

"No." Tsana shook her head. "We take them to the trees. And we leave them."

Seri felt a shiver, revulsion running through her as she understood. "You leave them for the beasts."

Tsana shrugged. "The beasts protect us. It's our way." Seri must have made a face, because Tsana looked at her solemnly and said, "You think we're disgusting."

"It's not what we do," Seri said, trying to keep her expression neutral. On the inside, she was imagining Ithim, Ithim's body left out for the beasts. The same beasts that had brought about his death, one way or another. Something in her stomach turned.

Tsana watched her, and Seri knew she wasn't fooling anyone.

"We think the same of you," Tsana said. "You kill the beasts and make armor out of their skin, gaining their strength that way. In the Hollows, that's considered a perversion of the way."

Seri tugged at a strap of her vest, feeling the leather between her fingertips. After so long, it felt as though it was part of her. It had molded itself to her so completely that it was like a second skin.

Because it was. It had once been alive.

She thought of the beast that had killed Ithim. And then the one whose hide she was wearing, the one that had attacked Eshai. She didn't regret killing those beasts. Was that wrong?

She glanced to the side, where Asai lay curled up on the platform, Tsana's cloak resting on top of her. If she killed Asai and turned her into armor, she would probably feel guilt. She would probably feel shame. Because Asai had done nothing wrong. Asai had never tried to harm her or anyone.

"We have no choice," she said, feeling secure in her answer as she looked back at Tsana. "The beasts try to kill us. We have to kill them to survive. Even your People have to kill beasts sometimes. You told me that yourself."

Tsana's hand twitched where it held her sword, and she looked away. Seri remembered that Tsana *had* killed beasts in the temple. To save them. She felt a flash of guilt and opened her mouth to take the statement back, but Tsana spoke before she could.

"They kill you because you've always killed them. To them, you're enemies, with generations' worth of blood on either side. A gap that no one can breach."

The thought made Seri suddenly afraid. "Is that what will happen to us?" She thought of the hatred she had seen in Vethaya, the readiness with which Lavit's valor and the others had responded to going out and finding "the enemy." "Our Peoples?"

Tsana looked away. "It's already happened. Once before, in our history, in the time of the Great Betrayal."

"What happened?" Seri asked. She corrected herself. "What do *your* People say happened?"

"What do yours?" Tsana asked, her gaze lifting to meet Seri's.

Seri looked at her and felt herself drawn into her eyes, as if Tsana's gaze could encompass the whole world.

"The Great Disaster happened before the founding of the known world," Seri said, the childhood stories coming easily to her. Caretaker Nasai had told her the stories, over and over again until Seri could tell them as well as anyone. "Once, we lived somewhere else. A prosperous land. We didn't yet know how to fear the beasts, so we didn't live in the trees. We lived on the ground by our farms. When the beasts came, we were almost destroyed by them. The survivors fled, hiding in the trees, but because they didn't know how to build platforms, their situation was desperate. Beasts would hunt them every time they left the trees to gather food and water. It looked as though the People would soon be devoured.

"That was when Yatari, the First Valiant, discovered armor. By making armor from beastskin and beastbone, with beast-heart at its core, a man could become as strong as a beast. As swift. More than a match for any creature." When she had been younger, Ithim would often play at being valiants. He would always ask to be Yatari. Every little boy wanted to be Yatari. Maybe some of the little girls as well. "Yatari created five sets of armor, one for himself, and four for anyone who would rise up to fight with him. Four youths from the remnant of the People did: two men and two women. With his valor at his side, Yatari beat back the beasts, destroying them so fiercely that for years, they were wary of approaching the People's settlement. That became Vethaya, the Place of Spears. The first spreading tree."

"From there, the expansion," Tsana said.

Seri nodded. "As the People grew, it became clear that Vethaya would no longer be enough. So, the valiants were charged with venturing out into the unknown world, reclaiming spreading trees for the People. And they've been doing so ever since."

She finished the story somewhat uncertainly. There were many more stories about Yatari and his valor, all well-loved and told multiple times among the People. There were stories, too, of the valiants that had come after Yatari. Generations upon generations of songs, only the best of which survived to this day. Songs of which the ballads of Eshai Unbroken were only the last in a long line.

But Tsana probably didn't want to hear those stories. And Seri found she was waiting to hear what Tsana had to say about her own People.

She didn't speak up immediately. She set her sword beside her, resting her hands on her knees. Her expression was pensive, as if she were thinking hard about her words. Translating them, possibly, into words Seri could understand.

"My People have a different accounting of events," she said. "Once upon a time, there were two kinds of humans. There were the *en*, those who could communicate with the beasts, and then there were the *enshkai*, those who could not. The *en* had great powers. Their bonds with the beasts allowed them to draw from each beast's unique traits, taking them on for themselves, and in return, their beasts gained human thought and reason. Because of this, they were warriors and leaders among the community. But the *enshkai*, who could not do such things, were jealous of this. And so, out of the *enshkai* arose Yatari.

"It was Yatari who discovered armor. A perversion of the way. By wearing armor, Yatari discovered he could take on some ability of the *en*, even though he was *enshkai*. At first, he tried to experiment with this. He would take skins and hearts from beasts that had died naturally, of old age or of illness. But he found that that did not work. For armor to be effective, it had to be made from a beast that still had life and power within itself. One that had been killed.

"Yatari assembled his followers," Tsana said, looking off into the dark. "And they killed the beasts, taking their hearts and vanishing into the night. When the *en* found out about this, they were appalled. They ordered Yatari and his followers executed, but by then, Yatari had become a hero among the *enshkai*. So, the *enshkai* protected him."

Tsana bit her lip, and Seri thought back to the carvings they had seen inside the temple, carvings that depicted people killing each other. Some of those people were wearing armor. Some were not.

"What followed was a time of bloodshed and war. *En* turned against *enshkai*, neighbor against neighbor, friend against friend. The world became divided into two camps, *en* and *enshkai*. The *enshkai* were driven into the trees, but from there, they created their own stronghold. They attacked, forcing the *en* to flee. The *en* retreated to our Hollows, our sacred caverns, and there we remained for centuries, separate from the *enshkai*, fearing them and telling these stories for so long the *enshkai* became our demons in the night, things we used to frighten children."

Seri held her breath, trying to think through Tsana's words. She felt the weight of history pressing down on her, untold generations. How was it that two people could have such different stories from the same event? Which was true?

She didn't know. Looking at Tsana now, she wondered if it

mattered. After all, whatever had happened, Yatari and his people were long dead.

"Do you think we're demons?" Seri asked.

"I . . ." Tsana hesitated. "I . . . lived among you for a little while. In Vethaya. I saw monstrous things. But I also saw beautiful things. And above all, I . . . saw us. You're like us. Just people, living their lives." She shook her head. "I don't think you're demons. But I don't like the things that you do."

"That's fair," Seri said. She didn't think she would take back any of her decisions. Given the chance to do it over again, she would have still killed the beast that had threatened Eshai, the one that had taken Ithim. The one in the watchtower that had been trying to kill her. But it would have been nice to live in a world where she didn't have to. Where all beasts were like Asai.

But to live in a world where only some people had power and others did not? Where power was an artifact of birth and not skill? She would have been *enshkai* in that world, like Eshai and Lavit and Ithim and everyone she had ever loved. In that position, would she have done what Yatari did? Would she have supported him?

Something nagged at her memory, and she looked down, her gaze falling on the bow across her lap. A weapon that by all accounts, she should not have been able to aim unaided.

No. She *wasn't* one of them. She wasn't *enshkai*, not truly.

"What am I?" Seri asked, looking up at Tsana. "You said that my . . ." Even *thinking* it was strange. ". . . my father was one of you. Does that make me *en*?"

Tsana paused. She looked hard at Seri, as if she were trying

to see into her soul. "I don't know. There hasn't been someone like you in so long, someone born of both *en* and *enshkai*.
You have our eyes. That should be enough. But the true test is
whether or not you can bond with a beast."

She tilted her head toward Asai, sleeping quietly on the platform. Seri followed her gaze, but she didn't see Asai. In the
back of her mind, she saw the creature that had taken hold of
Ithim. It had tried to control her, but it couldn't get through. It
couldn't break her.

"Tsana, has there ever been a beast that could control minds?
Human minds, I mean?"

Tsana blinked, surprised at the question. "There are some
beasts that can read emotions, others that can touch memories.
But I've never heard of any one *controlling* minds. The ones I
know of are only observers."

"Is it possible . . ." There were thoughts swirling in Seri's
mind, vague notions that felt interconnected. She felt like she
was swimming in a river among them, trying to gather them all
before the current washed them away. ". . . is it possible that a
beast's abilities affect *en* and *enshkai* differently? Like *enshkai*
are more affected somehow?"

"I . . ." Tsana hesitated, biting her lip in thought. "I'm not
sure. It's been so long since we've had contact with the *enshkai*.
I think—there are *stories* that talk about things like that, but—
you know how stories are."

Seri nodded mutely, but in her mind, she was there again.
There with Ithim and there with the beast. *En* and *enshkai*,
another dividing line between them. If she was truly *en*, then
her survival made sense. It wasn't because she was stronger

than Ithim. She felt light-headed, like she wasn't getting enough air. In her mind was the running dream. Was she on all fours in the dream? Had she been dreaming of beasts this whole time?

"I don't think I could ever bond with a beast. I wouldn't even know where to start . . ."

Tsana shrugged. "There is no 'start.' If you are meant to bond with a beast, it will happen. Sooner or later."

Seri barely heard Tsana's words. There was a high-pitched ringing in her mind, as if she were sitting in a cloud of mosquitoes. She was halfway to believing Tsana about being *en*, but the thought of bonding with a beast left her mind in free fall. Without thinking, she rose to her feet, testing the string of her bow. It was taut, the tension satisfactory against the pad of her finger. Her other hand brushed against the quiver strapped to her hip, counting arrows. Her body felt tight with the overwhelming urge to run.

"I—I'm going to see if Eshai needs me to relieve her."

"Seri—"

She was already turning away. "Are you going to be all right up here? I know there isn't much to do, but I could—"

A part of her recognized she was babbling, but she couldn't stop. She might have leapt off the platform entirely, still speaking, if Tsana hadn't reached out and taken her wrist. Gently, ever so gently, but it pulled her back from the precipice she was approaching.

Seri turned to look at Tsana. Her eyes sparked golden in the lantern light, like sunlight warming the earth. They were filled with so . . . much. Understanding and sympathy and acceptance and all the things Seri had always wanted but had never been strong enough to admit to herself. Tsana's touch smoothed away the rough edges, the buzzing noises. Made her feel more grounded, more human.

Seri swallowed and said, "I don't know who I am anymore."

Tsana's grip tightened, just a little. Her eyes flicked toward the shifting blue and violet of Seri's armor. She hadn't spoken, but Seri understood.

A valiant's armor changes with their heart.

"It doesn't *tell* me anything. The colors keep changing. I don't know who I'm supposed to be, or even what this color says about me."

Tsana was staring at her, and at first Seri thought Tsana was coming closer to her, and then she realized she was the one moving, drawing closer to Tsana. Then she realized that both were true, that Tsana was moving toward her just as she was moving toward Tsana, and Eshai and Lavit weren't around to separate them or disapprove and there were no crowds surrounding them and no master hanging over Tsana's head. For the first time in a long time, they were alone, just the two of them, and the thought made her heart race for an entirely different reason.

And then Tsana looked at her, *really* looked at her, their faces *inches* apart, and said, "Maybe change is who you are."

She was so close, after so long. Seri couldn't help but kiss her.

Seri felt two paradoxical things in the kiss—a sweeping light-headed giddiness that felt like lightning sparking across her skin and a sudden wash of calm, as if this was where she had always been meant to be. The combination of both was heady and impossible and frightening and she couldn't get enough of it, so she kissed Tsana again, and a third time, and a fourth, until her fears melted away and she worried she was taking advantage of Tsana and the way Tsana made her feel.

But from the way that Tsana pulled her closer, she didn't seem to mind.

❧

At dawn, when the first rays of sunlight filtered through the canopy, they gathered on the platform to discuss their next step. Eshai and Lavit looked worn from the vigil, but if they were tired, they didn't show it, taking their seats on the platform.

Seri hadn't had much sleep, either. Thoughts and memories and the nearness of Tsana—across the platform, close enough that Seri could hear her breathing but still so damnably far away—kept her up the entire night. She didn't know how they had both decided, without speaking of it, to keep what happened between them to themselves, but neither she nor Tsana said anything to Eshai and Lavit, and they barely looked at each other in the morning. She wanted to look at Tsana, but she was afraid that doing so might give her away, and this thing was so new and fragile that Seri felt like she needed to protect it. From Eshai and whatever harsh words she might have, from everyone.

"I went scouting this morning, just before dawn," Eshai was saying. "The old camp is mostly overrun with beasts, but they haven't strayed too far from the valley. This confirms the information we received from Tsana's beast." She paused to glance distrustfully at Asai. Asai, curled up in Tsana's lap and eating jerky out of her hand, didn't seem to care how Eshai felt about her. "The southern route should be clear. If we can slip past the beasts, we can make it to Elaya."

"We'll have to be careful," Tsana said. "By now, Master Srayan will know that I'm with you. He might be able to predict our movements."

"He'll attack?" Lavit asked Tsana.

"If we're lucky, he'll be occupied with other things. He's acting alone. He might not be able to split his focus. But he'll be aware of us."

"Could you fight him?" Eshai asked, meeting Tsana's eyes. "If he did attack."

"I don't think I would win. Mas—Srayan is a fearsome opponent. And I am not as strong a fighter as the rest of you."

"I didn't ask you if you could *win*. I asked you if you could *fight*. Could you raise a weapon to him if he came for us?"

Seri saw indecision flash across Tsana's face. It vanished quickly, too quickly, her hand going to the hilt of her sword. There was anger in her eyes, but there was also fear. She nodded. Eshai frowned but didn't question her further.

"We're decided on a course of action, then?" Lavit asked. "We're heading back to the known world via the Elaya route."

Seri nodded, although she felt something turn in her stomach at the prospect of returning to Elaya. With Eshai and Lavit and Tsana, and with all those people who thought she had killed Ithim.

"We have to catch up with the others," Seri said, "and spread the word to the outermost settlements that an attack might be coming. Elaya is the closest settlement to us, and it has a valor outpost that can send messages. It's the best way forward." She didn't add that Eshai had made a promise, to Raya, to send a message if they ever needed help. From the grim look on Eshai's face, Seri thought she hadn't forgotten.

"We'll have to move fast," Eshai said. "It would help if we knew where Srayan was, so we could stay a step ahead of them." She looked at Tsana. "That beast of yours. Could it get close to him without him noticing?"

Tsana paused to scratch under Asai's chin, thinking. "He's very skilled at sensing beasts. And he has worked with Asai before. But Asai is quiet, good at remaining unseen. I don't think I would trust her to get too close to him. But from a distance, it might work."

"Can you order her to do that? Track Srayan down and relay information back to you?"

Tsana paused, tilting Asai's head up so she could look the beast in the eye. At first, Seri thought she was merely thinking, but then she noticed that Tsana's lips were moving, making a low crooning sound under her breath. Asai seemed attentive, alert. Seri watched them, fascinated, as she realized they were communicating.

Asai's tail flicked, almost eagerly. She sprang off Tsana's lap, scuttling along the platform. Her scales began to change before she reached the trunk, and by the time she reached the edge of the platform, she was invisible. Tsana looked back up at Eshai and Lavit, who were watching her as if she had grown a second head. "She'll do what she can."

"Then we'll return to the known world." Eshai glanced at Seri as she rose. "Via Elaya."

Seri's stomach dropped, but she nodded, following Eshai to her feet.

CHAPTER 19

֍

The southern route took them away from the valley, through a stretch of rainforest where the tree cover was thinner, exposing sections of blue sky. The thin cover made Seri itch, even though there were plenty of trees to hide in should the worst happen. She wondered if that meant she was starting to think like a valiant, like Eshai and the others. She followed along behind them, tense, focusing on her footing.

Ahead of her, Eshai and Lavit led them toward Elaya, following some method of navigation Seri couldn't quite figure out. Eshai had told her that it had to do with the position of the sun during the day and certain stars at night. Tsana had showed her a device she carried, a small disk with a metal needle inside it that always pointed in the same direction. That confirmed they were heading south and east, as intended. But the time for teaching had passed—none of them could spare the time to show her how they found their way. She could only follow and hope she didn't get lost.

By necessity, Tsana traveled with either Eshai or Lavit. Without boots, she couldn't hope to match the valiants' speed, and Seri could barely carry herself through the trees, let alone herself and another person. At the moment, Tsana clung to Lavit's back, Eshai leading the way.

They were drawing closer to the known world, but they

weren't there yet. They needed to stay on their guard. Anything could happen.

At least there didn't seem to be much danger of Srayan finding them. From Tsana's reports, Srayan wasn't overly concerned with their whereabouts. Instead, he was focused on gathering as many beasts as possible. The effort of holding on to so many minds at once was draining him, at least according to Asai's reports. Eshai, Seri knew, still didn't trust Tsana, and kept them on a strict double-watch schedule regardless. Two people awake at all times, while the other two slept, and never Seri and Tsana alone.

In two days of hard traveling, they had managed to make up about as much ground as the valor had traveled in four, but Seri was starting to feel the strain. Eshai and Lavit had to be tired as well, despite all their efforts not to show it. At this rate, Seri mused, they would be too tired to do anything when they finally made it to Elaya.

Elaya. Home.

She tried not to think too much about where they were going, what people were going to say when they arrived there. There were much more important things to worry about.

Still, as they traveled, leaping from treetop to treetop and steadily heading back to the known world, Seri couldn't help thinking about what she would find there. The home she had left what seemed like forever ago. The home she never thought she would return to.

❦

"I have something to tell all of you," Seri said that night, when they were sitting down to eat. Ever since they had started moving in earnest, Eshai considered it too risky to use a lamp, so they sat in darkness. It didn't matter—Seri and Tsana could still see clearly, and she knew that with their helms, the valiants could do the same.

Eshai and Tsana, Seri noticed, both watched her, their expressions solemn. Lavit's brows rose. Seri knew he had been observing her over the past few days, that he had questions. She didn't know how much Eshai had already told him and didn't really care. If Eshai had told him anything, it would make this easier on her.

She drew in a deep breath, gathering her courage. "Eshai knows part of this story. And Tsana knows the other part. But I don't think I've ever told anyone this story in full. And I think we're well past the time for secrets." She looked over at Tsana, who nodded, her expression grave. She didn't stop Seri from speaking.

So Seri spoke. She told them everything, starting with how she had never known her father, how she had always been different from the other children in the village. How her mother had cautioned her to keep this difference a secret, before the illness that had taken her away. How she had become a caretaker's ward, like Eshai and Lavit, and how she had met Ithim. How they'd fought that one day because of something stupid she said, because of how jealous she was of him. How Ithim had died. How Tsana had come to her later, telling her that her father had been one of her people. An *en*, who could communicate with beasts, and how Seri was starting to believe it. She didn't tell them about her and Tsana—if there was a "her and Tsana." Not yet. That was still hers, one little secret she could keep close to her chest, and Tsana wasn't rushing to reveal it, either. Eshai asked questions; Tsana broke in to explain about the *en* and the *enshkai*.

And then it was done.

Seri sat in silence after, her hands curled into fists in her lap. She felt drained, as if her secrets had been a living thing inside her, and in telling them, she had lost a part of herself. For a while, none of them spoke. Seri looked at Tsana, seeing the girl watch her with new pain. She didn't dare look at Eshai and Lavit.

Lavit spoke first. "Can you do what Tsana can?" he asked. "Bond with a beast?"

"I don't know. I asked Tsana about that, but . . ." She shrugged, looking over at the other girl for help.

"Even among the *en*, it's not something that is guaranteed. A bond forms in an instant. It cannot be taught. In theory, every member of the *en* can do it—whether they actually do depends on whether they meet the right beast. *Enkana* like Srayan are very rare, perhaps one a generation. But some do find more than one bondmate. Some never bond. I don't know what it would be like for Seri. We haven't had anyone like her in recent memory."

"What I want to know about is how Seri's father found our settlements," Eshai said. She looked over at Tsana. "You're *sure* you were the first group to be sent here?"

"By the Conclave, yes," Tsana said, although Seri saw a flicker of doubt cross her expression. "Reasonably sure. But . . . I don't know. I mentioned that your language is . . . an older form of ours, one that we occasionally use for ceremonial purposes, but your language isn't completely identical to our old tongue. That the Conclave knew the difference tells me they may have been watching you. He could have been sent by them. He could have been a wanderer. Or . . ." She hesitated.

"Or?" Seri asked.

"*Khashkai.* Without honor. An exile. For us, exile is usually a death sentence."

Seri said nothing, looking down at her hands. It was one thing to consider her father a member of Tsana's people, but a criminal? She searched her mind, grasping for anything her mother had said, any scrap of information. She couldn't think of anything.

Eshai and Lavit had gone silent, watching her. Seri drew in a deep breath, realizing they expected her to say something.

"It doesn't matter. Whoever he was, he's dead. I never knew him."

Eshai looked Seri in the eye, studying her. Seri held her gaze, trying to keep her own racing heart under control. She hadn't lied, or at least, she didn't think she had.

"We should rest," Eshai said finally, picking up her spear. "I'd like to reach the known world by tomorrow. Seri and Tsana, take first watch."

Seri blinked, surprised.

If Tsana noticed this new arrangement, she made no sign. She only nodded, getting to her feet and making her way carefully to the edge of the platform.

Eshai and Lavit slept in the middle of the platform, their breath evening out within moments of settling down. The two valiants seemed able to fall asleep anywhere, at any time. Seri was glad Eshai had let her take the first watch, because she didn't think she would have been able to do the same. She sat near the edge of the platform with Tsana, her bow in her hand as she scanned the horizon.

It was a quiet night, like all their nights had been. Seri tried not to let that lull her into complacency, but it would have been impossible to relax anyway. This was the first time she and Tsana had been alone since the night they stopped to take vigils. Now that they had been granted this time, Seri felt pressured to *do* something with it.

The problem was that she had no idea what, exactly, she was supposed to do. The first—and last—time they kissed was still on her mind, and it kept coming up at inopportune moments, but while that had been wonderful, it had sort of . . . just *happened*. She wanted it to happen again, but the thought of initiating set her face on fire. Besides, how was she supposed to know that Tsana wanted that, too?

Maybe it had all been a mistake. Maybe Tsana was just waiting for the opportunity to tell her that.

They sat in silence for a while, Tsana's hand on her sword and Seri's on her bow, as Seri tried to work through her nerves.

"It means nothing," Tsana said after a while.

Seri's heart sank until she realized Tsana had no way of hearing her thoughts and was probably *not* talking about the kiss. She looked over at her, frowning.

"Who your father was. At the end of the day, it means nothing. *Khashkai* or not."

"Would your People see it that way?"

Tsana's silence was confirmation enough. Seri thought about her own People. By law, a criminal's family wasn't punished for their actions. But sometimes, especially when people were angry, things happened that could not be controlled by the law.

"It doesn't matter to *me*," Tsana said, her voice soft.

Seri stopped, facing Tsana. The girl wasn't looking at her. Her gaze was fixed on some point far in the distance—keeping watch, which was what they were supposed to be doing. Unbidden, Seri found herself looking down at Tsana's hand.

She wasn't wearing gloves today. The backs of her hands were smooth, not a name-mark in sight. She had never seen hands like that before, completely unmarked.

She wanted to take Tsana's hand. She wanted to so badly that it felt like an itch under her skin, a high-pitched yearning on the inside of her mind. Tentatively, she reached out, her heart pounding.

Her fingertips traced the back of Tsana's hand. She felt Tsana flinch at the contact, turning sharply to face her. Seri flushed and nearly pulled away, feeling like a child that had gotten caught sneaking treats. But something in Tsana's eyes stopped her, holding her there.

Tsana's hand relaxed beneath her own, pressing flat against the board between them. Seri let out a slow breath of air, let her hand relax as well, pressing against Tsana's more firmly.

They sat there for a while like that, in silence. And then Tsana's hand moved, turning so she could lace her fingers through with Seri's. Seri felt as if her heart was going to leap out of her chest, as if every nerve in her skin were alight. She let out a nervous breath—it sounded almost like a laugh.

"What does your name mean?" she asked, looking away from Tsana to hide how nervous she was. She tightened her grip on Tsana's hand.

"It doesn't mean anything," Tsana said. Was Seri imagining it, or were there nerves in Tsana's voice, too? "It means me. Your People are so focused on names. On the meaning of them. You name children after anything."

"Things that exist, mostly. Things that we can see, feel. Things that we want our children to be."

Ithim had been named after moonlight. She'd thought that had been such a pretty name. Lavit, after rain. Eshai, after the stars.

Tsana smiled faintly. "I noticed. But we don't do that. A child is themselves. We don't feel the need to name them after objects, or feelings. A name is something you should be able to grow into. Not something that already exists."

"So, your parents just liked the sound?"

Something dark crossed Tsana's expression, and Seri wondered if she had overstepped her bounds. "Tsana?"

"Nothing," Tsana said, shaking her head. "I haven't thought about my parents in . . . a very long time."

"Do you want to talk about it?"

"There isn't much to say," Tsana said. "My mother, I didn't know. My father . . ." She shrugged, making an airy gesture with her free hand. "Maybe my father would have been *khashkai*, too, if he ever had the courage to *do* anything about his station instead of drinking away his days in silence . . ."

She trailed off, her eyes fixed on the ground far below them. Something in Seri's heart clenched at the sight. She squeezed Tsana's hand, drawing the girl's attention back to her.

"It doesn't matter to me," she said.

Tsana stared at her, and a distant, keening part of Seri's mind pointed out that this might be a good time for kissing. Her heart raced, but she swallowed her fear, leaning forward slowly. Tsana didn't move. When Seri inched forward again, so there could be no mistaking her intent, Tsana still didn't move. Instead, Tsana tilted her head back and upward, the slightest of movements. Accepting. Waiting.

Her eyes were on Seri's, and Seri wasn't breathing. Tsana was. She could feel Tsana's breath against her lips, little puffs of air. She wanted—

Tsana jerked back suddenly, eyes wide. Before Seri had registered what had happened, she was on her feet, her gaze on something in the distance. Seri felt bereft for a moment before she remembered what they were *supposed* to be doing and alarm replaced the disappointment. She grabbed her bow, trying to follow Tsana's line of sight.

"What?" she asked. "Do you see something?"

Tsana shook her head, turning away from Seri. "Nothing. I just—I think I'm getting a message from Asai."

Seri's heart sank like a stone.

"Oh. Is it urgent?"

"I'm not sure," Tsana said, but there was a hush to her voice that told Seri it probably was. Tsana had her back turned to her, one hand to her temple. "I need to concentrate to understand it. I'm sorry."

"It's fine," Seri said, fighting back the voice inside her that wanted to protest. "You can wake Eshai. It's just about time to change shifts."

"All right," Tsana said. "I'll do that." And then, so curtly that it seemed like an afterthought, "Good night."

"Good night," Seri said, but there was no response. The space around her was cold where Tsana had been. She sighed, raising a hand to her mouth.

Well.

She *thought* that meant Tsana was still interested. But who knew when she'd have another chance to find out?

Seri watched the tree line for a few more moments, then shook her head, waiting for Eshai.

❧

Tsana waited until Eshai had gotten up, going over to take her watch with Seri. When she was sure Seri wouldn't be alone, she picked up one of the thin blankets that lay discarded on the platform and found another spot to lie down. Her heart was still pounding, too many emotions at once. It never occurred to her how much excitement could feel like fear until she felt the two of them together. The last thing she wanted to do was lie down, but she found a spot far from the edge of the platform, lying on her side and wrapping the blanket around herself. Her hand was still warm, and her head was still light, and she could feel the urgency of Asai's summons in her mind.

Asai was also afraid. The fear fed into hers, growing stronger because Asai was not given to panic.

As Eshai sat down, striking up a low conversation with Seri, Tsana forced her eyes shut, letting her mind carry her off across the miles, so she could see through the eyes of her bondmate.

Srayan was looking through them, right at her.

Tsana tensed and stifled a whimper. She tried to force the beast's limbs into motion, tried to get her to run away, but Asai remained stuck to the tree she was clinging to, as if by magic. It was Srayan's will against hers, and his was the will of an *enkana*. A drop against a river. It was like trying to move a mountain.

"I know you're listening, Tsana," Srayan said, his voice dangerously soft. "Nod if you can hear me."

She wanted to pull away, but she could feel Asai's breath coming shallowly in her chest, as if something was holding on to her throat. Srayan's power. He could stop Asai's heart as easily as breathing or break their bond and turn her feral. Tsana had never been so afraid. She forced Asai's head into a nod.

"Good," Srayan said, and some of the pressure eased up, Asai taking in a breath of air. Linked to her as she was, Tsana could feel that, too, the sudden rush of life and consciousness. The sweetness of air after being deprived of it. She felt Asai's anger, buried deep down, and somewhere in there, Asai's guilt. She had made a mistake and been caught. Tsana knew her bondmate well enough to know Asai would not forgive herself for that.

"I've decided to forgive you for your actions at the temple. I can see why you would have reservations about this course of action. You *are* still a child, after all."

Tsana didn't move. Asai didn't move. She couldn't have done anything but listen.

"I will offer you a chance to make things right. If I am understanding things correctly, you are in the company of Eshai Unbroken. Is that true?"

She thought about shaking her head, thought about lying. There was no way Srayan could know the truth, was there? But a wave of pain moved across Asai's body, a sensation like having a knife pressed to one's throat.

She forced Asai's head into a nod again, feeling tears prick at the back of her eyelids.

"The girl is with you, too? The one you have an interest in?"

Seri's hand over hers. The warmth of her presence. The way it felt when they kissed.

Asai nodded again.

"Good," Srayan said. "I want you to do something for me. Deliver Eshai Unbroken to me, and I will forget about this . . . incident. I'll even put in a good word for you when we return to the Hollows, so you can leave my service. And I'll spare Seri."

Seri.

It was the first time Srayan had ever said her name. The first time he ever called her anything other than "the girl."

Tsana felt something hot make its way down her face. She pulled her head under the blanket, afraid Eshai or Seri would see her crying.

"I'll let her live. You can do whatever you want with her as long as you do this for me. You only need to follow instructions. Will you do it?"

The pressure on Asai's throat increased. The threat was clear. Srayan wasn't going to let her go unless Tsana did what he asked. He could kill her easily, but he could kill her slowly as well. She could feel Asai's defiance, Asai's bravery.

Asai would gladly die if Tsana wanted to be free.

But out of the two of them, Asai had always been the brave one.

And even if she let Asai die, even if she survived what that separation would do to her, Srayan would still come for them. He would still kill them, and this time, he would spare no one. Even if Eshai and Lavit survived, he would kill Seri just to punish her. That was the kind of person Srayan was, and she knew it without him having to say anything.

If she refused, Seri would die.

Seri could hate her forever as long as she stayed alive.

Tears continued to fall from Tsana's face as Asai nodded one last time.

CHAPTER 20

⟡

After all the ceremony of moving into the unknown world, moving back into the known world was almost anticlimactic. They passed the marker strung across one of the trees that marked the boundary, barely giving it a second glance. Seri wondered if it would be moved after this, if someone would go out and find that strange stone building and the valley of the beasts. Most likely, it wouldn't be anytime soon. After all, they hadn't truly made the world *known*—they hadn't had time to properly survey the area or draft a map. And she had promised Tsana she wouldn't bring the People to the valley.

Seri looked over at Tsana as she leapt, able to do so without losing her footing now. The girl clung to Eshai's back, but her face was turned away from Seri. She had been quiet since last night. Seri worried that she had gone too far, or if something had happened to Asai, but each time she tried to bring the subject up, Tsana brushed it off and said it was nothing. She didn't know whether she should push or give Tsana her space, and in the face of her indecision, their conversation had withered and died.

Seri kicked off a branch, adjusting her angle to better follow Eshai and Lavit. As she moved, she kept an eye out for any familiar landmarks. She knew, because she had seen the map, that they were close, that they would be upon Elaya by tomorrow at the latest. And she'd always known, growing up, that

Elaya was a border town. That was why they had a valor out-post, why they were so small, why beasts were a constant threat.

But somehow, she'd never been able to reconcile the two. The knowledge that Elaya was only a day's hard travel from the unknown world, and the idea that one could cross the unknown world into Elaya.

Was this the same path her father had taken, all those years ago?

Seri glanced down at her hand, taking note of the spot of bright color on her gloves. It had grown since the events at the temple, a splash of orange across a background of twilight. At the moment, it had settled in a pattern that spread from her fingers to her knuckles, orange rays diffusing into the background like the first rays of sunlight at dawn. Eshai had been surprisingly unhelpful in helping her figure out what it meant when Seri asked her.

"It happens," she had said. "Your armor will go through a few colors before it settles. As long as it takes for it to understand who you really are."

But who was she? And what did this color say about who she was becoming?

Just outside of Elaya, the earth split in two, forming a ravine. It was a familiar sight to Seri. Would-be hunters often traveled into the ravine in search of beasts. Eshai and Lavit drew to a stop at the entrance, studying it.

Tsana slid off Eshai's back as the valiant straightened to stretch her shoulders. Seri glanced at her as she caught up with them, but Tsana avoided her eye. She felt a flash of concern, but Eshai spoke before she could say anything about it.

"You know the area best, Seri. How do we get to Elaya?"

"We usually go around the ravine," Seri said. "I've never approached it from this way, but some people come this far out to forage. They avoid heading into the ravine if they can."

"Is there a way through?" Lavit asked.

Seri nodded. "Young hunters use it, when they're looking for beasts." She hesitated, but added, "It's quicker than going around. But there's a part of the ravine where the walls are sheer rock. Nothing to hold on to. It will be hard to get out once we're in."

Eshai nodded. Armored boots could gather and maintain a lot of momentum, but only when given the opportunity to do so. A rock-walled ravine might be even worse for a valiant than open ground would be.

"Are there usually beasts in this valley?"

"One or two. They come in from the unknown world. Sometimes, hunting parties head down into the ravine and don't find anything, though."

Eshai and Lavit exchanged a guarded look. Seri understood. A career valiant, one with a full set of armor, could easily handle one or two beasts, unfavorable terrain or not. Even the beasts they tended to get this close to the border. Under normal circumstances, the pair might not have hesitated to go through the ravine.

But these circumstances were hardly normal.

"How far away is Srayan from the outermost villages?" Eshai asked, looking past Seri at Tsana.

Tsana jerked, as if surprised to have been addressed. "Very

close," she said. "I would be surprised if he wasn't already planning his attack. He is going around the ravine, though. From the other side. If we go through, we may be able to overtake him."

Eshai looked back at Seri. "How much time would we lose by going around?"

"At our speed . . . a few hours? Maybe six?"

"The valor?" Eshai asked Lavit.

"If they kept on the same path, they would have passed Elaya on the other side," Lavit said. "I imagine they'd go to your settlement first—on the route they took into the unknown world; it's the closest spreading tree."

"If they did, then Turi would have sent word to Elaya and the other border villages," Eshai said. "If they aren't out looking for us as we speak." She clenched her hands into fists, eyeing the ravine ahead of them. Seri thought about Raya, Turi, and the others scouring the rainforest looking for them, unknowingly putting themselves between Srayan and the known world. She understood Eshai's urgency. "We can't afford to lose any more time. We're going through. Tsana, travel with Lavit. Seri, with me. You'll have to lead the way."

Tsana nodded, moving past Seri on her way to Lavit. Seri reached out for her as Tsana neared.

"Tsana—" she began.

Tsana's eyes were unusually cold.

"You heard her. We can't afford to lose any more time."

The ravine was quiet, devoid of even the usual sounds of the rainforest. Seri had never been this far and found herself tensing as the walls to either side of them grew taller and taller, the world she knew fading away. Ithim had come out here once, with some of the other hunters. Had he felt this way, too, as if he were isolated, cut off from the world? It was hard to believe they were so close to Elaya.

It might have been easier if they talked, if they did something to shake off the silence, but they did not. Eshai was grim-faced, her eyes on the path ahead of them as she leapt over rocks, seeming frustrated with the pace she had to set on open ground. Lavit followed her, carrying Tsana, and Seri was too out of breath to even *think* about speaking.

That left Seri alone with her thoughts, with the swirling mass on the inside of her head and the heaviness in her heart.

They were a few hours into the ravine when Seri heard the growl.

It came from ahead of them. By now, the ravine was deep and wide, sheer rock walls on either side. There was no way a valiant would be able to gather enough momentum to leap out of it, least of all a novice like Seri. Seri drew to a stop beside Eshai and saw them materialize out of the darkness ahead, a group of beasts blocking the way. She counted six or seven, all different breeds, some of the white-furred felines from the unknown world, but also a pair of the reptilian creatures, and one large, hulking *varrenai*.

She looked behind her. Another group of beasts were closing in. The same mixture of species as the beasts ahead of them, two halves of the same army. Beasts from ahead, and beasts behind. As if they had known where their group would be.

Eshai didn't even look surprised. She reached behind her, freeing her spear from the cords that bound it with a practiced flick of her wrist. Behind them, Lavit paused to let Tsana down, shooting her a glance that made Tsana shrink away from him before he reached up to free his own spear.

Tsana turned away from Lavit, her hands clenched into fists at her sides. Something in her face gave Seri pause. Guilt, she thought. And pain. But not a lot of fear.

Seri had a chilling realization.

That message from Asai . . .

"Tsana . . . ," she began.

Tsana bit her lip and turned away. Her hands were clenched so tightly at her sides that her knuckles had to be white underneath her gloves. She didn't reach for her sword, and Seri's stomach sank like a stone.

If they were feral, Tsana would have fought. If they were Srayan's, she would have fought. That left only the possibility that Tsana had known they would be here. From the beginning.

"Deal with her later," Eshai said, her voice a dangerous murmur at Seri's side. Seri turned toward her, feeling as if her world had been pulled out from under her. She had the lurching feeling there might not *be* a later. "I need you now."

The way Eshai was looking at her, wary, told her that even Eshai wasn't sure what Seri would do from here.

Which side she would choose.

Tsana was standing behind her, and Eshai was standing in front of her, back to her, spear raised to fight. Her memories of Tsana were lantern-lit nights in Vethaya and conversations in the dead of night and a handful of stolen kisses that made her heart jump when she thought of them, but her memories of Eshai were blood and sweat and fire and pain and *heroes*.

She would never have been here if it wasn't for Eshai. She would never have believed that she could protect anything, that she could be *more* than she had been. *Eshai* made her believe that.

She felt a flash of anger toward Tsana for putting her in this situation. For forcing her to make this choice. She felt betrayed and realized that was exactly what she was supposed to feel. Because Tsana had betrayed her, betrayed *them*.

And she realized, as she reached for her bow, that this wasn't a choice.

The first beast charged, one of the white-furred creatures from the valley. As it rushed at Eshai, Seri pulled an arrow from the quiver at her hip, pulling back her bow. She barely paused to take aim, setting the arrow loose.

Seri's arrow caught the beast in the flank, making it stumble to the side. A good blow, but not a killing one, if anyone still cared enough to keep score. Eshai didn't—as far as she was concerned, Seri had earned her armor a thousand times over. Still, she rushed forward as soon as the beast was out of the way, her own spear sweeping upwards to slice its throat.

One down, a dozen or so to go.

She spun around, catching one of the crocodile beasts under the chin with the butt of her spear as it tried to go for her leg. Its jaws clamped on empty air, her spear knocking its head backward. Before it could right itself, Seri's next arrow caught it in the eye, the thrum of her bowstring echoing in the chasm.

Two down.

Eshai swung around, blocking a blow from the great ape with her shaft. The impact was staggering, nearly sending her sprawling, but she spread her legs and bent her knees, redirecting the energy into the ground. She looked back to see Lavit fighting alone, defending them from behind. Tsana had stepped aside. To be out of the way.

Her lip curled in disgust, and she was about to tell Seri to help Lavit when Seri fixed an arrow to her bowstring and pivoted smoothly on her heel. Her shot distracted a beast that was snapping at Lavit's heels long enough for Lavit to dispatch it with a quick turn and a thrust of his spear.

Eshai felt a flash of fierce pride.

Be dauntless.

The phrase echoed in her head as she stepped forward, holding her spear with both hands. She moved her other hand closer to the butt of the spear, blocking high with her shaft and then snapping it up to slash the *varrenai* across the side.

They would fight as long as they had breath in their bodies.

Because *they* were the hope of the People.

Tsana felt ill, watching the scene play out before her. She could do nothing but stare, helplessly, as it all came undone, nothing but watch all while Asai's emotions burned through her like fire. Accusation. Disappointment. Anger.

Asai would have died so Tsana could do what was right. But Tsana couldn't. She had been too weak. She had *always* been weak.

Too weak to make any difference at all.

Her hands closed into fists as she watched the battle. Eshai, Lavit, and Seri moved in harmony, spears and arrows blending into a whirl of motion that kept the beasts at bay. Tsana flinched with each beast that was killed, but she also flinched every time one of the beasts landed a blow.

She couldn't look away. There was a ferocity in the way they fought, a determination to live and hold on for even a moment longer, that was fascinating—compelling. But the ground they were fighting for was getting smaller and smaller, the beasts pressing in from all sides.

They would be overwhelmed.

Tsana's hand reached for her sword before she stopped it, her breath catching in her throat. Her fingers dug into the palm of her hand; she could feel the pressure even through her gloves.

They would be overwhelmed, and Srayan would win.

So many more would die. People and beasts both.

All because of Tsana.

But Seri would live. Seri, at least, would live. It was too much to ask for someone like Tsana to save everyone. She could only save one person. Srayan had promised—

He lies!

A message from Asai, strangled, as if it had caused her pain to force it through Srayan's blockade, but strong nonetheless. Tsana's head snapped up in time to see a beast running at Seri, slinking around Eshai and Lavit's defense to rush her from the side. Lavit noticed it, too, and looked back over his shoulder to give warning. His shout broke off as one of the reptiles, the *kuwai*, leapt onto him and threw him to the ground.

Tsana's sword was free of its sheath before she knew what she was doing. She ran forward, her feet moving of their own accord.

"*Seri!*"

Seri turned and saw the beast at the last moment. It was one of the great cats—white-furred, jagged streaks in black along its sides. A *kuraen*, one of the high beasts. Experienced valiants like Eshai and Lavit would have had trouble defeating it. Seri alone stood no chance.

The *kuraen's* enormous paw took Seri in the side, throwing her off her feet like a rag doll. She made a sound like all the air had been knocked out of her, her arrows clattering to the ground. Tsana drew up short, her eyes wide, her sword useless in her hand. Her heart was pounding with the force of Asai's message.

He lies.

That had been a killing blow.

Srayan had no intention of letting Seri live.

And if he had lied about Seri, then neither of them were safe.

Out of the corner of her eye, Tsana saw one of the reptilian beasts, a *kuwai*, move toward her. She reached for her bond with Asai, concealing herself. As she vanished from sight, she leapt out of the way, dodging the *kuwai's* attack. It looked for her, scenting the air, and Tsana knew she hadn't escaped it for long. It would find her soon.

She looked around and saw Seri struggling to her feet, one arm wrapped around her side. The *kuraen* was moving toward her, although its movements were slow, oddly cautious. As if it was considering how to approach.

That was strange. A beast such as that wouldn't normally be

cautious about someone like Seri. It would have killed her and been done with it.

Except Seri was looking at the beast, too. And there was something like defiance in her eyes, the two of them watching each other.

Eshai surged forward, letting out a loud battle cry as she swept toward the *kuraen*. The great beast leapt back, narrowly avoiding a slash from Eshai's spear. Tsana saw her chance.

She ran forward, grabbing Seri by the hand. As she did so, she let Asai's binding slip so Seri could see her. Seri's mouth fell open in surprise and disbelief.

"Wha—?"

"Come with me!" Tsana said, tightening her hold on Seri's wrist.

She spread Asai's power, letting the veil stretch outward from her to envelop both of them. While Seri protested, Tsana started running, heading back the way they had come. Seri stumbled, and Tsana feared she would try to break free. With her strength, Tsana had no hope of holding her. But Seri fell along beside her, one arm wrapped around her midsection as she gasped for breath.

"Tsana, stop! We can't leave them. Tsana—!"

Tsana ignored her, urging Seri forward.

CHAPTER 21

✤

Eshai looked back as Tsana vanished, dragging Seri into thin air with her. The beast that had been staring Seri down a moment before moved to pursue, but there was nothing Eshai could do about that, not with the *varrenai* charging her again, the force of its blows driving her steadily back. She couldn't think about what it meant that Tsana had pulled Seri away, whether Seri was safe. She couldn't even think of a way to save herself and Lavit.

The walls of the ravine taunted her, sheer rock to either direction. If they hadn't been so high, if they had been rougher, if there had been ledges within a leap's distance—but there weren't.

The *varrenai* roared at her, swiping at her head with its fist. She ducked under the blow and snarled back, thrusting at it with the butt of her spear. Bones broke and snapped under the force and Eshai spun around, thrusting the spearpoint through the chest of one of the crocodile beasts leaping at her from behind. Blood spattered the white of her armor as she pivoted, glancing over her shoulder at Lavit.

The press of the fight had brought them closer together, so that Lavit was now almost an arm's length from her. The ground between them was almost pitifully small. Soon, there would be no space left for either of them to retreat to, and the beasts would overwhelm them.

They were trapped here, and her helplessness galled her. She hadn't survived that mess at the temple just to die here. She *couldn't* die, not a stone's throw from Elaya. Not now.

One of them had to survive, or they would never find Lavit's valor, and the border villages would never know the threat they were facing.

One of them.

Eshai looked back at the wall, the pieces of a terrible calculation fitting together in her mind. Lavit fixed her with a tired smile, understanding, and she hated then how in sync they were.

"I can throw you, I think," he said. "If we both leap, and you kick off me at the last moment, you might be able to get out of here."

"No."

"You have to survive, Eshai. They need you."

"Lavit, *no*."

Eshai practically spat out the word, all of her being rebelling against the thought. Lavit fell silent, focusing on the battle, but she knew that he hadn't given up on the argument. She knew, because she knew him, what Lavit wanted her to do.

She thought of the dead in Vethaya. She thought of Naumea, and her resolve to never let those things happen again. And then she thought of Lavit and the moment they had together in the camp and how she would like for that to happen again. Many, many times. Perhaps for the rest of their lives.

No. She couldn't die here. And she wasn't going to let Lavit throw his life away, either.

In their hurry to return to the known world, they hadn't brought much from camp. Medical supplies. Rations to last until Elaya. Their platform, but Tsana had been carrying that. Rope, to secure the platform to the branches.

Rope.

Her eyes darted across the battlefield, looking for the rope. She found it lying amid the bundle of their camp platform that Tsana had thrown aside. It would be difficult to reach, but with a concentrated push from her and Lavit, it might just be possible. And if she had that rope . . .

"Lavit!"

Lavit looked over at her as Eshai took a step back, narrowly avoiding a claw to the throat. She gestured at the rope with her spear. Lavit's eyes widened, and then he was with her, helping her fight her way toward the bundle.

The beasts—or whoever was commanding them—had not been expecting them to change directions. Together with Lavit, Eshai fought her way through the struggle at an angle, her eyes on the rope. Beasts charged them from all sides, but they pressed forward. Lavit let out a war cry, using both of his hands on the shaft of his spear to throw a leaping beast away. At the same time, Eshai launched herself forward, rolling underneath a beast's leap. With one hand, she reached out, grabbing the end of the coil of rope. It came free from the wreckage of the platform, snapping up like a whip. She quickly pulled it toward her, grabbing it in her spear hand before it could tangle itself in the melee. With her free hand, she reached out for Lavit.

"Now!"

Lavit grabbed hold of her hand, pulling her close to him. She wrapped her arm around his waist and helped him kick up off the ground. Her stomach lurched, and she had the disorienting sensation of the world spinning around her as Lavit directed their leap, high away from the struggle below. The walls of the ravine rose up around them, but the walls were too high.

Even combined, their rise was already slowing. A valiant would never be able to leap out of this chasm alone.

But Eshai and Lavit were not alone.

She felt Lavit's rise slow and twisted out of his hold quickly, pushing herself up. Her boots met his chest, the leather of his armored vest hard beneath her soles. Holding her breath in the hopes that this would work, Eshai *leapt*.

The force of her jump sent Lavit plummeting back into the chasm, but the leap had enough force to send Eshai up. And up, and up, until she crested the top of the ravine and saw the dense canopy of trees that waited.

As she crossed the lip of the cliff, she stabbed her spear down into the soft earth, using the shaft as a pivot to flip herself up over the edge. Eshai landed hard on the ground beside the spear, knees bent and legs spread apart, breath coming hard. But she wasn't done.

She looked back over the edge to see that Lavit had landed on the ground below. He was fending off the beasts alone, his back to the wall. His helm was askew, and it was hard to see him in the knot of battle. He was barely holding his own.

She kept one hand firmly around the shaft of her spear to steady her. With her other hand, she unfurled the rope. Eshai whistled, shrill and clear.

Lavit leapt out of the fray, kicking off the head of one of the beasts and launching himself upward. As his ascent slowed, she felt a rush of dread—the rope was too short. There was no way Lavit would be able to reach it. But then Lavit's hand closed around one end of the rope, and it went taut in her hand, nearly dragging her off the edge of the cliff.

Her feet slid, but her spear held fast. The half-healed wound in her side stung with the effort as Eshai clung to the spear, hooking her arm around it. She grabbed at the rope with both hands, coiling it over one arm in case she was forced to let go.

Lavit began to climb, holding the rope tight and walking himself up the edge of the cliff. Eshai held on until she saw him pulling himself over the edge, his breathing labored. She didn't let go until he collapsed to his knees on the ground, pulling off his helm to take deep breaths of air. Blood matted his scalp, but he didn't seem to notice.

He looked up at her, wonder in his eyes. "We're alive."

Eshai looked down at the seething knot of beasts in the ravine below. "We're alive."

"Seri and Tsana?"

She thought about Tsana dragging Seri away and forced back the initial rush of anger and fear. She had no idea where Seri and Tsana were, and there wasn't enough time to find them. But if Tsana had meant to harm Seri, she wouldn't have saved her. Tsana might let the entire world burn, but she wouldn't willingly harm *Seri*. Eshai could trust that, even if she couldn't trust anything else.

They had no time. Srayan had done his very best to keep them from reaching the known world. And Eshai had to be a step ahead of him.

"Seri knows where we're headed. If she's all right, she'll follow. We need to get to Elaya."

She pulled her spear from the earth, and the two of them leapt into the safety of the trees, heading toward the village. As she moved, Eshai only hoped that she was right.

❧

Tsana released her hold on Seri as soon as they reached the safety of the trees. Asai's veil slipped from her as she collapsed on the ground. She breathed hard, coughing and choking with the effort of her run. Ahead of her, Seri sank to a knee, grimacing. Tsana looked over and saw that the armor on Seri's side was cracked, claw marks marring the blue-violet colors. Seri winced in pain with each breath.

"Are you hurt?" Tsana asked.

She shouldn't have spoken because Seri turned to face her. And Tsana wished she could disappear. The hurt and anger and naked disbelief in Seri's eyes made her look away, her fingers digging into the soft earth beneath her.

If Seri started shouting, screaming at her for what she had done, Tsana thought she might be able to bear it easier. But she didn't.

Her voice was soft, almost pleading when she spoke. "Tsana . . . tell me it wasn't you."

Tsana looked away.

"Tsana!"

"You already know the answer."

She wanted to hide, she wanted to die, she wanted to lie down and let the earth swallow her whole. The last thing she wanted to do was look at Seri, but when Seri didn't speak, Tsana had to.

Seri was staring at her. There were tears in her eyes. The silence between them was painful, each second a knife in her heart, but when Seri spoke, the pain in her voice made Tsana wish for the silence.

"Why?"

Her eyes stung. She hadn't meant to cry, but she couldn't stop herself. Tears fell down her face, landing on the ground below. She tried to speak, but her breath came in hiccuping sobs. Still, she struggled for breath, because she had to say something, even if no words could change this.

"He said he would spare you. I wanted to protect you, Seri. More than anything."

She kept her head down, close to her knees, let her hair fall like a curtain to blot out the light around her. She couldn't look at Seri, couldn't bear to see her face. There was a pause, and she thought she heard Seri moving, whether toward her or away, Tsana couldn't tell.

Something very close to them growled.

Tsana looked up sharply, turning toward the sound. Seri had been standing in front of her, her arm outstretched as if she were reaching for something, but at the sound she turned as well, crouched as if prepared to leap. She shifted, blocking Tsana's view.

A shape appeared out of the shadows of the rainforest, walking softly toward them. The *kuraen*. Tsana's heart sank. The great beast was padding toward them, its golden eyes on Seri.

Tsana's hand was trembling, but she reached for her sword, willing it to be steady. "Seri, get away—!"

Seri wasn't moving. The hand that held her bow had stopped mid-raise, her eyes fixed on the beast's. Her mouth was open, but the emotion on her face wasn't fear.

It was awe. Wonder. Understanding.

The beast watched Seri as well, as if the two of them were the only ones in the world.

Tsana froze.

The *kuraen* lowered its head. And Seri reached out to touch it as if in a trance, her gloved fingers moving through its fur.

❧

It felt like a part of her heart that had been missing had come back to her.

Seri looked into the beast's eyes and felt a rush of emotion. Years of dreams flooded her mind, as clear as if she were experiencing them in an instant. Running through the rainforest, the scent of prey in her nose and the earth warm and soft beneath her feet. Her heart pounding with the thrill of the chase, the hunt. She looked into golden eyes and thought—*it was you. The thing I've been seeing in my dreams.*

The answer came back as a thought, stiff and stilted, as if its owner was still unused to the action. They were thoughts that came with scents and tastes and feelings—longing was bitter and smelled like rain, happiness was sunlight and the taste of clear water.

I think . . . I have been looking for you.

She understood what Tsana meant then, that the bond was something that would either happen or not. It was all or nothing. One moment separation and the next completion, so it was difficult to find the seam where they had been joined. She felt a rush of anxiety—her own, not the beast's. The teachings of the People echoed in her mind—*The beasts prowl the forest paths*—and her own memories swept over her. Valiants dead on the ground, Tarim, Ithim—every beast she had killed.

She felt the *kuraen*'s confusion, interwoven with her own fears. He tilted his head to the side, regarding her.

You are . . . distressed?

Seri opened her mouth, closed it again. She couldn't find the words for what she was feeling—excitement and distress and love and discomfort and the odd, overwhelming sense of guilt that she had just betrayed everything she held dear—but from the way the beast's eyes widened, she thought her message had come across anyway. He stared at her for a long moment, and Seri tensed, waiting.

The response came, still laced with confusion.

You are . . . smaller than I thought you would be.

Seri couldn't help it. She burst out laughing.

I am sorry for hurting you.

The beast nuzzled at her injury, his face warm. His whiskers tickled. Seri could hear his thoughts in her head—not a voice, not exactly. Feelings, some of them hard to put into words. It was an overwhelming sensation, seeing herself through another's eyes. She had to lean on something to stay standing, her back against a tree, one of her hands on the beast's head. A part of her still felt uneasy at having him so close to her, his teeth in range of her flesh, but she could feel the thoughts running through his mind. However things might have started, he had no ill intent toward her, not anymore.

You were only following instructions.

The warlord. The beast projected an image of Srayan into her mind. *He was in my mind, directing me to attack you. He forced many of us. Some of them he destroyed. He'll destroy them all.*

How did you break away?

The beast's answer was to nudge at her hand. He looked up at her with large, golden eyes as she idly scratched the ridge of his forehead.

You woke me. I could feel you calling.

I didn't do anything.

You've always been calling me.

Seri sighed, sinking back against the tree. She looked over at Tsana, who was watching her from across the clearing, hunger and awe in her eyes. Tsana hadn't moved since the *kuraen* had approached Seri. Looking at her, Seri still felt angry. She looked away.

Inevitably, her thoughts turned toward Elaya. Home. Her feelings about Elaya were bittersweet—she never wanted to return, and she wanted to go home and never leave. She didn't know which feeling was the truth, but what she felt when she thought about Srayan and his beasts descending on it was real, visceral fear.

The beast growled, startling her. She felt his anger and nearly jumped back, but she realized the rage inside him was not directed at her. It was at Srayan, and what he had done to the beasts. An image of Elaya entered her mind. It was indistinct, a kaleidoscope of scent and blurred, distant images, but she *knew* it.

You wish to save the tree place? I know where it is. I will take you there.

You would do that for me?

We are bonded, you and I. I would take you anywhere.

Bonded. It was still such an odd thought. Belatedly, Seri realized she didn't even have a name for the beast. She thought she might need one. Asai clearly had a name, after all.

I am called Seri, she said, projecting an image of her namemark, the little flame. *Who are you?*

I have no name.

Seri opened her eyes, looking at Tsana again.

"He says he doesn't have a name."

Tsana's answer came quickly, as if the *kuraen*'s arrival had become the most important thing on her mind. "You have to name him. It's tradition."

Seri frowned, looking over the beast again. She ran her fingers through the soft fur on the side of his face. Her fingers traced over one of his markings, a jagged black line.

"Karai. Lightning."

In her mind, she thought of lightning, streaking across the sky. She felt Karai's approval, a low hum against her thoughts.

It is a good name.

Seri felt a swell of affection, strong enough that she had to look away. Was this how it felt being bonded to a beast? Was this why the *en* thought it barbaric that the People hunted them? She wondered if Karai resented the fact that she wore armor at all. She had barely thought the question when she heard Karai's answer.

You are a hunter. Like me. That is why I chose you.

Seri's fingers traced the cracked armor at her side, feeling the places where it was beginning to come together. Armor healed like skin when it broke, as long as it didn't crumble away entirely.

She looked back at Tsana, about to tell her what Karai had said, and saw that Tsana was looking at the ground, her arms wrapped around her knees. She looked as if she might cry again.

"He has Asai . . . ," Tsana said, her voice so soft it was difficult to hear her. "He caught her, and he'll kill her unless I help him. That's why I had to—" She broke off, her voice catching. "He said he was going to spare you. I shouldn't have believed him, but Asai is all I have. I couldn't let her die . . ."

She looked between Seri and Karai. "Don't you understand?"

Seri rested her hand on Karai's head, looking into the beast's eyes. The bond between them was so new, but even now, even with all her misgivings, when she thought about Karai dying, she felt a sense of grief. Of fear. Karai looked back at her, and she was presented with an image of Asai, clinging to a stone at the edge of Srayan's camp.

I remember the small one. The warlord keeps her close.

A thought occurred to Seri. It was a wild thought. But once the idea had taken root, she found that nothing she could do would dislodge it. Srayan couldn't see through Karai's eyes anymore. He had no idea whether Tsana and Seri had escaped or not. They would have no better opportunity.

How far is Srayan from us? she asked Karai.

Karai's answer carried with it a sense of distance, shorter, much shorter than Seri would have expected. *Close.*

Seri nodded. Tentatively, she opened her mind, sharing the details of her plan with Karai. It wasn't really a plan. Not yet. It was only an idea, a handful of thoughts. But she felt Karai's approval, a growl that seemed to come from the earth beneath her feet.

Bold, he said. *Good.*

"What?" Tsana asked. "What are you saying to each other?"

Seri drew herself up to her full height. "We have an idea to save Asai."

CHAPTER 22

✤

Karai carried them to Srayan's camp, as fast as any valiant in armor. Seri sat astride his back, grabbing hold of the scruff of his neck so she wouldn't fall off. Tsana sat behind her, her hands around Seri's waist to keep her balance. Her grip was tentative, almost too careful of Seri's injury. The armor was healing, and the skin beneath it was whole, if bruised. Nothing seemed broken. That was good. This plan depended a lot on her, and there wouldn't be much she could do with a broken rib.

She felt stronger than she ever had and wondered if that might have been the bond changing her. Tsana said there would be changes—just as Tsana could hide herself using Asai's power, Seri could draw on Karai to bring herself to new heights. Maybe it was Karai that was making her fearless.

Except she wasn't fearless, not really. She wasn't confident. She still felt afraid to touch Karai, to be close to him, even though she knew her plan wouldn't work without it. Even though she understood—because she could feel his feelings as if they were her own—that he wouldn't hurt her.

And she was afraid of Srayan.

Find the things you can control and decide what you're willing to live with.

She remembered what it was like to lose Ithim. If she had her way, no one would ever have to lose anyone precious to them again.

Your color has changed, Karai said.

Seri jumped. It was still strange to feel his thoughts inside her mind, so alien and yet so familiar, but she looked down and saw he was right. The orange marks on her gloves had spread, covering the backs of her hands and creeping up past her wrists, almost all the way up to her elbow. Looking at them, she was struck with the sensation that she was witnessing a sunrise, a rebirth.

The dawn of a new day.

Seri flexed her fingers, relaxing and tightening her grip on Karai.

She turned her thoughts to the path ahead. Karai had helpfully given her a vision of Srayan's camp. He had camped on the ground, in a secluded area guarded by beasts. Asai would be in the center of the camp, near where Srayan himself slept. The beasts would watch her to make sure she could not escape, even when Srayan himself was not watching her.

Will Srayan's beasts stop you, if you try to go through them? she asked Karai. *Will they know you aren't one of them?*

Karai paused to consider this. *The beasts will not*, he said, and Seri felt his disdain in that answer. *They are not intelligent, and the warlord holds their minds. They will not recognize me. The warlord might if he took notice.*

Would he?

Perhaps. His attention is spread thin.

Between so many beasts?

Affirmation. Not a nod, but close. Karai was thinking about this as hard as she was.

Seri spoke next. *If he were distracted?*

He would be focused on the distraction. He would not notice me unless one of the other beasts reported, and as I said, they wouldn't.

Out loud, she said, "Tsana, can Srayan see through your veil, or can he only sense beasts?"

"I'm not sure," Tsana said. "I haven't heard of *en* sensing other *en*, but he's always seemed to know where I am before. I'd rather not test it."

"And beasts?"

"They might be able to smell me. If they knew to look in the first place."

Seri nodded, thinking through her plan one last time. It was mad, completely and entirely. But if it worked, Asai wouldn't have to die.

"All right," she said. "Listen carefully . . ."

Are you certain about this?

Karai's question rang in her mind as they neared Srayan's camp, jostling for space against all her other thoughts. She was cold beneath her armor, her heart feeling like it was about to burst out of her chest. Honestly, she thought she might be sick.

Certain? No. She wasn't certain. This was a plan that would more than likely get her killed, and she had very little confidence in her ability to see it through. But . . .

. . . if she was certain about anything, it was that this was *right*. This was the right thing to do. She felt Karai's assent, felt his fear. He was uncertain, too. Somehow, knowing that made this easier.

Once Srayan realized Tsana and Seri had escaped, he would expect them to come. He'd know Tsana wouldn't leave Asai, that she *couldn't* leave her. Maybe it wouldn't be the first thing he would expect, but he was crafty enough to prepare for it. She wanted to subvert his expectations, to do something unexpected. All she had to do was make Srayan stop and think, distract him for a little while.

As they rode, however, she began to wonder if she was being too predictable after all. They were well within range of Srayan's beasts, and yet none of them had approached her. Nothing had attacked.

It was like Srayan already knew she was here.

This is a good place, Karai said as he came to a stop. *Far from his camp, but not too far. The warlord will see you from here.*

Now or never.

Seri took a deep breath and reached for the arrow she had separated from the rest of her quiver, firing it up into the air. As it soared, a red cloth unfurled from around the head, patterned with black. It caught the sunlight. Among the valiants, such an arrow was usually used to signal position, so those in need of rescue could be found. She didn't know if Srayan understood the full meaning, but she thought it would serve to get his attention. And there were many uses for so obvious a signal.

Tsana waited, camouflaged, in the trees upwind of camp. She didn't dare approach, not yet, not until she had seen Seri's signal. If she tried to come closer, one of Srayan's beasts would sense her, and that would be the end of Asai's last chance.

Asai was, miraculously, still alive. Tsana had cut herself off from Asai in her mind, not wanting to accidentally give anything away to Srayan, but she could feel Asai's presence like she could her own heartbeat.

She wondered what they were doing here. How could they possibly expect to take Asai out safely from the middle of this? Their plan was impossible, and yet . . .

Seri made Tsana believe in the impossible.

Her eyes scanned the canopy, and she held her breath. If Seri failed, she would die, and it would be Tsana's fault. Seri knew that—there was no way she couldn't have known—but Tsana wasn't worth dying for. She didn't understand why Seri would help her, after everything she had done.

But Asai's life hung in the balance.

She still remembered the day Asai had come to her, when she was sitting alone in the tunnels of Astira, dirty, starving, and afraid. Asai had been cast out of the hatchery. A runt, just like Tsana herself. Their eyes had met, and that had changed Tsana's life forever.

Tsana watched the canopy, more afraid than she had ever been. She had just started to give up hope, just started to think that something had gone wrong, that their plot had been discovered and Seri was already dead. And then she saw it. An arrow, piercing through the trees, with a red cloth tied just under the head.

The signal.

Karai alerted her to the change. He growled, the sound vibrating throughout his whole body as he dug his claws into the dirt.

Seri tensed, but she had only a moment to ready herself before Srayan emerged from the rainforest, flanked by two great beasts. One of them was a *varrenai*, its knuckles bloodied from an earlier battle. The other, the one his hand rested on, could have been Karai's twin.

Seri forced herself to sit straighter, keeping the fear from her face as she raised her hands, showing them empty. She stayed on Karai's back and tried not to even think about her arrows. Srayan's gaze moved over Karai for only a moment before meeting hers.

"Seri, is that right?" Srayan asked. "Is my apprentice not with you?"

This was what they had intended, and yet Seri had to fight to keep her voice steady. "Tsana betrayed us. You made her do that."

"And yet you survived. Well done bonding with the *kuraen*. Our children dream of such a feat." He smiled at her. It made Seri's skin crawl. She sank deeper into Karai's fearlessness. It was still alien to her, but compared to Srayan, it was a comfort. "Why have you sought me out?"

Her stomach was in knots, and a part of her wanted to take Karai and run. He *would* run if she asked him to. He would run like lightning and take her anywhere. But she had to buy Tsana enough time.

"Bonding with Karai made me realize some things. About myself . . . and about my People. I . . . I want to know more about where I came from. About my father. Tsana told me once that you might be able to tell me."

Srayan smiled again. It was a thin, predatory smile that reminded Seri very much of a snake. "So, you come to me in the end? Very well. I'll gladly trade one apprentice for another. Follow me back to camp, and I'll give you the answers to your questions."

"You'll give me the answers here," Seri said. "You've tried to kill me twice. I'm not going anywhere with you until I'm sure."

"Really?" Srayan asked. "And are you speaking to me from beyond the grave? Killing you has never been my goal, Seri. I have no quarrel with you."

Keep him talking. She wasn't sure if the thought was hers or Karai's or both, as tangled up as it all was deep inside her.

"You were never going to spare me. You just told Tsana that so she would do whatever you wanted."

"Now you're being unfair. I would have taken you had you joined us when Tsana asked you. It's clear to me now that you would have proven useful. But while Eshai Unbroken and I would have very little to speak about, I suppose we could commiserate on the folly of the young. You never would have joined us then."

"I'm still not sure I'll do so now."

"You might not, but you're beginning to run out of choices. Tell me, do you think your People will accept you, when you return with *him*? Will they open their arms and let you back into the fold as if nothing had changed? Or will they brand you an outcast and a traitor?"

Seri hesitated. The thought of returning to the villages with Karai hadn't really occurred to her. What *would* people say? What would *Eshai* say?

Srayan's smile widened at the change in her expression. Something in his face reminded her of a snake.

"They would kill him. You know that, or you wouldn't hesitate. Do you understand what it feels like, to have your bond broken in such a way? To feel your bondmate's life slipping from your mind. It's like losing a part of your soul."

"Eshai wouldn't—"

"Wouldn't she?" Srayan's gaze was sharp, as if he could see right through her to her core. "Are you *sure*, Seri? Do you want to know what your precious Eshai Unbroken has done?"

Do not be distracted.

It was only when Karai said that that she realized she was, her mind going down twists and turns, imagining Karai dead at the end of Eshai's spear. She steadied herself and said, "We're not talking about Eshai. We're talking about my father."

"I knew your father," Srayan said. "You even resemble him, just a little. Is that what you wanted me to say?"

She was prepared for this, ready to have this conversation, and yet Srayan's words were like cold water pouring over her. Her *father*. A mystery, an unknown, a hole in her life she had always been too afraid to poke at. Longing was an ache inside her, and one she didn't have to fake.

"Come to the camp. I'll tell you everything."

"Tell me now. Or I'm leaving."

"What, so soon? I still think we should have this conversation at camp." He began to turn and then stopped suddenly, shooting her a knowing look over his shoulder. "Unless, of course, there's something in the camp that you don't want me to see."

Her breath caught in her throat.

Srayan turned to face her fully, walking toward her. "Did you think I was a fool?" he asked. "You and my apprentice have been joined at the hip since the first day you saw each other. Did you really expect me to believe you would abandon her now, and come to find *me*?"

Srayan's smile was a knife in her chest.

"Didn't you wonder where my beasts are, Seri?"

Srayan raised his hand. Seri saw it as if in slow motion, felt a flash of fear at what it meant. Before she could react, Karai growled and surged toward Srayan. It was all Seri could do to hold on, curling her fingers into the fur at the scruff of Karai's neck.

Srayan was fast, faster than a man his age or build had any right to be, especially without armor. As Karai charged at him, Srayan spun out of the way, aiming a kick at Karai's flank. The blow hit hard, forcing Karai into a slide and nearly unseating Seri. She gripped Karai's flanks tight with her knees, grimacing at the pain she felt through the bond between them. Karai whirled around to face Srayan, snarling, but Srayan had his hand in the air, fingers closed into a fist. Seri heard the sound of distant growls.

The thought came to both of them at the same time. *Tsana.*

Seri bent low over Karai's back, her stomach lurching as he whipped around, running fast through the trees. As they ran, she heard Srayan laugh, his laughter high and terrible.

"When you're ready to join me in truth," he called after them, "come back!"

Tsana crept into the center of camp, fighting to keep her mind firmly in that space between her and Asai where she could maintain the veil. Seri would draw Srayan out to speak to him. There was no telling how long she could hold him there, or how long before he saw through the ruse. She had to move quickly.

Srayan had placed Asai near the center of camp, in a supply crate repurposed as a cage. Were it not for the bond between them, Tsana might not have been able to find her. She ran toward the crate, knowing they didn't have much time, and shoved aside the stones that rested on the lid, throwing it open. Asai looked up at her from inside. Whole and alive.

She felt the moment of recognition as Asai's eyes met hers, sharp and quick, an echo of the sensation Tsana had felt when they bonded. A feeling like her soul was being laid bare, that Asai knew the whole of who she was and accepted her regardless. And Tsana knew the same.

There was something on Asai, some remnant of Srayan's control that held her frozen in place. She could feel it at the edges of her mind. But not even an *enkana* like Srayan could fully control a bonded beast. Tsana reached for that control, reached out for the force that pressed down on Asai's mind and pushed on it, breathing deep.

Srayan's barrier resisted, but only for a moment. Tsana felt it shatter and crumble around her. Felt Asai's surprise as Tsana reached down to scoop her up in her arms, Asai's anger at the fact that Tsana had betrayed her allies for her in the first place.

And, underneath it all, Asai's *pride* that Tsana had come for her. Asai did not often choose to speak, not in the way that some beasts did, but the thoughts that echoed in Tsana's mind resolved themselves into words.

Yes. I am proud.

Tsana held Asai close to herself, wrapping a veil around them both. It was easy to hold Asai. Easy to hide the tears in her eyes. And wrapped up in Asai's feelings as she was, it was easy to feel the sudden current of alarm that ran through the beast.

Tsana.

Tsana's head jerked up, her blood running cold at the sound of growls. All around her, she saw beasts slinking out of the trees that surrounded the camp, sniffing at the air for her scent. Panic made her throat seize up, and she fought to keep her breathing steady. The veil wavered, but she grabbed at it and forced it still. It wouldn't be enough. She could maintain the veil, but it wouldn't stop scent, and she knew she reeked of fear. They would find her.

Asai's touch on her mind was a sudden, steadying warmth. It was a lifeline, and Tsana grabbed at it to keep herself from spiraling.

Breathe, Asai reminded her. *You're better than this. Breathe.*

Asai's thoughts were a pulse in her mind—expanding and then contracting like a slow breath. It was calm in the center of a raging storm.

There were beasts surrounding them, but they hadn't been found yet. If she could leave the camp—if she could get to Seri—

Run, Asai told her, and Tsana did, holding tight to Asai and bursting into motion. The second she started moving, the beasts charged as well, converging on her location. But Tsana had the head start. She was small, and fast, and she knew how to run. She kept her mind firmly on the goal, the meeting place between her and Seri, and she didn't look back even when all the beasts in the camp were on her heels.

Seri's first thought, when she arrived at the meeting point alone, was that Tsana hadn't made it out, that Srayan had caught her.

The beasts were howling frantically from the camp's direction, hunters in pursuit. She could barely breathe from fear, and she nudged Karai in the sides, about to instruct him to move toward the camp when she felt Karai's touch on her mind.

They are chasing her. She is coming.

No sooner had Karai said that than Seri caught sight of a flash of light out of the corner of her eye. Blue light, sparkling in the shadows of the canopy. She turned her head and saw Tsana emerge from the undergrowth, her veil falling apart around her. In one hand, she held a navir crystal aloft, the same one she had used to signal Seri in Vethaya an age ago. The other arm held Asai firmly to her chest.

She was running at full tilt, breathing hard, a bleeding scratch across her face. Behind her, there were beasts in full pursuit, steadily gaining ground. Karai charged before Seri could even think to tell him to, and it was all Seri could do to stay seated as he ran toward Tsana. She crouched down, holding Karai's fur tight with one hand and reaching the other out to Tsana. Tsana dropped the crystal, grabbing her by the arm. Even with the gloves, Seri felt like her arm was about to be pulled out of its socket, but she clenched her jaw and gripped Karai's sides tightly with her knees, pulling Tsana up.

Tsana leapt up and slung her arm around Seri's waist. She had barely settled behind Seri before Karai turned to flee. Seri's world dissolved into Karai's strides eating up the distance ahead of them, into the sound of growls and snapping jaws and angry roars behind her, until the beasts in pursuit dropped away. She looked behind her and saw them running in the opposite direction, responding to a signal Seri couldn't hear.

"What—?" she began, still breathless from the chase.

"He's started the march," Tsana said, sounding just as winded. "The battle will begin soon."

And the closest settlement, Seri realized, was her hometown. Her Elaya.

"There has to be something we can do."

Tsana shook her head. "There isn't enough time. Even assuming Eshai and Lavit made it there, Srayan's beasts would stop any messenger they send."

Seri clenched her hands into fists, trying to think. Eshai wouldn't give up in this situation. She would continue on. But what could she possibly hope to do?

They were outside Srayan's cordon for now. *They* could be messengers. But it would take too long. Seri didn't relish the prospect of running *away* from the battle, heading who knew where to find help. She wanted to take Karai and chase after Srayan, to help Eshai however she could.

And then a thought occurred to her. She looked at Asai and tried to remember the details from Eshai's map.

They were on the northern side of the village from Elaya. That meant there was only one other settlement nearby. It had taken Seri days to cross that distance in the past, but armored valiants didn't have to pick their way across the rainforest floor.

Srayan did.

Lavit's valor might be there.

It would cut things close, very close. But they might have enough time.

"Tsana," Seri said, "do you think Asai's up to delivering a message?"

CHAPTER 23

⚘

They had just passed the markers informing travelers of their proximity to Elaya when Eshai fell for the first time, her knees buckling under her. She dropped to one knee on the branch she was resting on, Lavit placing an arm around her to keep her from sliding off. Her vision swam, her injuries throbbing. The wound at her side, the one she had sustained in the temple, felt as if it had opened again.

She sucked in a breath through her teeth, cursing Tsana as she pushed herself to her feet.

"Eshai?"

"I'm all right," Eshai said, gulping down air. She rested her back against the tree trunk—wasting valuable seconds—and placed a hand on her head. "I'm . . . all right. Just . . . a dizzy spell. It happens."

Lavit didn't look convinced. Eshai couldn't blame him. She knew what he would have said, had she been one of the recruits under his command. Valiant armor could do a lot of things and could even fend off exhaustion for a while. But just because a valiant didn't *feel* tired, didn't mean they weren't running themselves dry. And eventually, the price had to be paid.

He wasn't doing much better. She could see the makeshift bandage they had tied around his head from underneath his helm, saw that it was stained red. Lavit might still be riding the battle high, but even that would run out. He had to know that, too.

He didn't suggest they rest. Time was too short, their duties too pressing. They had to push forward, to reach Elaya at all costs. But she could tell he wanted to.

"Can you keep going?" he asked her instead.

She heard what he didn't say. *Can you keep going, or do you need me to carry you?* Eshai had no doubt Lavit would if she said that was what she wanted. But that would only tire him out more, and besides, Eshai Unbroken had to enter Elaya under her own power. It was more than just pride. If she had had her way, she would never have gone down in the songs, would continue being nothing more than an ordinary valiant in an ordinary valor, wearing ordinary armor.

But like it or not, she *meant* something now.

Ushi had explained this to her once, when she was still in Vethaya, the night before the ceremony that would make her a valor commander.

People wrote songs, people invented heroes, because they *needed* them. They needed symbols of strength, of will, of resilience. When times were dark, they needed people to point to, people who could fill them with hope. The name they had given her was evidence of what they needed from her, what they saw in her.

Eshai Unbroken.

Dark times were coming to Elaya. Whether she wanted it or not. Elaya would need a symbol. And in absence of anyone better, it would have to be her.

She straightened up with more force than was strictly necessary, nearly stumbling straight off the tree branch. Eshai caught her balance just in time, steadying herself before Lavit could reach a hand out to catch her. She looked off in the direction of Elaya.

"I'll make it," she told Lavit. "Don't worry about me."

Lavit hesitated, and she wondered what he saw when he looked at her. Did he see that same nine-year-old girl delirious with fever that he had rescued from the rainforest? Or the rival he had grown up with, that he had pushed away when they were both younger valiants with too much pride?

Or did he see someone else? Eshai found herself hoping, really and truly hoping, that he looked at her and did *not* see Eshai Unbroken. She didn't think she could be that for him, if she had to be that for everyone else.

Whatever he saw, he tapped his heart over his armor. A valiant salute. And then he reached out, lightly tapping her across the back of the head. A thing they had done as children, to annoy each other.

He smiled. "Onward, then. To Elaya."

Eshai nodded, looking at the path ahead. Lavit kicked off the branch and she followed, fending back the dizziness.

Onward to Elaya.

To Seri's hometown. And to whatever fate awaited them.

Elaya was a small village, a border settlement that boasted a modest twenty-five years of occupation. Seri was a member of the first generation to be born here, one of the few people who could honestly say she was from Elaya.

Arriving in the city's central square, Eshai understood why Seri had been so intent on escaping this place.

It was very neat, very formal. A settlement that had been planned along certain lines, and that had never deviated from them. To Eshai's eye, it was perfectly serviceable, perfectly average.

And perfectly boring.

No valiant had found Elaya and thought this would be a settlement for the histories. There had been no epic battles fought at this site, nothing like Naumea or their own new settlement. Someone had looked at Elaya and thought, *This is a perfect place to build a village,* and then did so. Even the name of the place was bland. Elaya—the Place of Grass. As if there wasn't grass aplenty in the whole known world.

When Eshai and Lavit landed, they caused a stir. People circled them, buzzing like flies, all trying to get a glimpse of the famed Eshai Unbroken. Eshai looked around, trying to imagine this place becoming a battlefield. Some of these people might fight well enough, but she wasn't hopeful. She understood why they hadn't believed Seri's story, despite living so close to the unknown world. Easier to believe Seri was a murderer than to believe the world had changed. To believe they were wrong about what beasts could and could not do.

She thought, as she straightened up and surveyed the crowd, that she was about to ruin a lot of days.

"Who is valor commander here?" Eshai asked, pitching her voice to carry. "I need to speak to them immediately."

❧

The commander, a man by the name of Rukai, at least looked as if he would be a fair hand in a fight. Older than both herself and Lavit and scarred from battle, in some ways, he reminded her of Ushi. It was the way he greeted them both with a grin that belied the fact he knew they couldn't be here for anything good.

"If I'd known I was going to receive Eshai Unbroken and Commander Lavit, I would have set out a feast."

"No feast, thank you," Eshai said, although her stomach growled at the mention of food. She declined Rukai's offer of a chair, fully aware that if she sat down, she might not be able to stand back up. Instead, she focused on keeping her weight centered above her feet so it wouldn't feel so much like the earth was trying to drag her down. "We need to speak with you about a matter of urgency."

Rukai's smile faltered a little, but he nodded. "I expected as much. You two aren't known for being the heralds of good news."

"We have reason to believe that a horde of beasts is about to descend on Elaya and the other outlying villages. These beasts can climb skillfully and coordinate their attacks with intelligence. I need you to send out your scouts immediately, to find the beasts and report on their position. We'll also need to strengthen the village's defenses. And send your fastest valiants as messengers. The other outlying villages will need to be alerted."

Rukai's face fell, and Eshai knew, looking at him, that there would be no more smiles today.

The scouts returned with reports. Srayan's horde had been sighted less than a day from the village. At the speed they were moving, they would descend upon Elaya at dawn. The scouts were pale, terrified of what they had seen. Wherever Seri was, Eshai hoped she had the sense to stay far away.

The villagers were frightened. She could hear them clamoring outside headquarters, demanding to be let in. A pair of valiants kept them out, stone-faced, although Eshai could tell they were just as scared. Fear hung heavy in the air as Eshai and Lavit sat at Rukai's strategy table, looking down at his map of the surrounding area.

"We can mount a defense here," Rukai said, pointing at the entrance to the ravine. "If we do this properly, we can turn the ravine into a killing ground."

"Archers?" Eshai asked.

Rukai nodded. "We have a few handy with a bow. A storm of arrows in the air will take out any but the hardiest beasts." He didn't say what Eshai was thinking—that Srayan *would* have the hardiest beasts among his number. It was what she would do if she were planning an attack on the known world.

"What about village defenses?" Eshai asked. "Ballistae?"

"We have them. But they haven't been used in more than a decade. After the area outside Elaya was explored, we stopped needing them. I don't know what state they're in, but I have a group of my artisans servicing them now."

Eshai ground her teeth. If they survived this, she would ensure every village within three days of the border had working ballistae and a group of people trained in their use. She would do that even if she had to repair the damn things and train their operators herself.

"Are there any among the people who will fight?" Lavit asked. "Any aspirants who might have one or two pieces of armor?"

"There are a few," Rukai said. "Some of them hang around headquarters. There are some hunting parties." He hesitated. "The village has always been peaceful for a border town. I don't know how many will be willing to fight. You might be able to round up volunteers."

Lavit glanced at Eshai for confirmation, and Eshai nodded. He rose to his feet, saluting Rukai politely before heading out the door. Lavit was always better with large groups of people than Eshai was. He would go out into the crowd and ask for volunteers, and within an hour, he would have a militia to drill. Not that there was much they could do, with so little time.

"The beasts will surround the city," she said, looking at the map of Elaya. "They'll likely charge across the plain, where our valiants will have the hardest time fighting them. We can make that route less tempting."

"Caltrops," Rukai said, "I've already sent some of my valor out to ready them."

Eshai nodded. The valor's caltrops were made from sharpened beastbone, three slivers arranged so no matter how they were thrown, one sharp end always pointed upward. Deployed en masse, they could effectively halt a single charge. But they were costly to make and each border settlement only had enough for one or two uses. They would buy them a little bit of time, but that was all.

"Not just those," Eshai said, "traps and pitfalls, too. Anything we can do to slow their charge. We should do as much as we can in the time we have. Conscript some civilians into working if we have to."

This is their home. They should fight for it.

Rukai looked grim, but he nodded. "I'll see to it. What will you do?"

Eshai could feel the exhaustion creeping up on her. She would be useless in a fight in this state. She knew she had to rest, knew this might be the only time she could. But Lavit was out there working—she could hardly afford to falter now.

"I'm spent," she admitted. "I need an hour or so. I also have some messages to write—we've lost contact with Commander Lavit's valor, and it's possible they might have turned up at my settlement. But after that . . ." People needed a hero. A symbol to believe in. "I suppose I should go out and give some sort of speech."

Rukai's worried face relaxed a little. "Good. Hearing from you will boost morale."

Eshai wasn't so sure, but that was the role she had been chosen to play. She sighed and said, "We can only hope."

They sent Asai off at sunset, a roll of parchment tied around her neck with twine, and then at Karai's insistence, they stopped to rest. Seri didn't want to. She wanted to keep moving, to get to Elaya as quickly as possible. She even felt like she could, her veins singing with power and energy. But as soon as she stopped moving, as soon as she and Tsana settled down for an evening meal, she realized Karai had been right. The energy vanished like smoke, and she was exhausted. She ate, her mind filled with thoughts of the battle ahead.

They didn't dare build a fire, so their meal was dried meat

and whatever was left of their rations. And without their supplies, they couldn't make a place for themselves in the trees, so they camped on the ground. It was muddy and uncomfortable, but Seri didn't care. She thought she could fall asleep anywhere.

She was chewing a strip of jerky, her back resting against Karai's side, when she noticed Tsana looking at her. Karai glanced over, saw Tsana watching, and let out a huff of air. He stood up, the movement so quick it nearly sent Seri sprawling onto the ground.

What—? Seri thought, looking back to see Karai walking away. *Where are you going?*

Karai's answer was laced with exasperation and impatience, as if Seri were very dull. *Hunting. I smell game.*

It felt like Karai wasn't being entirely honest, which was odd, but Seri didn't think he meant any harm. She looked back over at Tsana, who was watching the scene with some confusion.

"I don't know," she said. "He says he's hunting."

Tsana shrugged. "Who knows the mind of the *kuraen*?" She continued to watch Seri. Seri finished the last of her meal, slightly uncomfortable under the scrutiny.

"Seri," Tsana said after a long moment. "What you did for me . . . I don't know how to thank you."

Something inside Seri warmed at the praise. She shook her head, feeling embarrassed. "It was nothing—"

"It wasn't nothing," Tsana said. "You risked your life for me." She looked down at the ground, at the sword that lay across her lap. "I don't deserve that sort of kindness. But . . . thank you."

A million things rushed through Seri's mind at once. She settled on the question that came to her mind first, speaking it softly into the air between them. "Why do you think that?"

"I've only caused trouble for you. For everyone. Ever since I was born. Srayan's the only person who's ever paid any attention to me, and I betrayed him, too."

Seri remembered the bruise on the side of Tsana's face from the temple and felt a sudden flash of anger toward Srayan. Her breath caught.

"You deserve every kindness."

Tsana shook her head. "I'm a coward and a traitor. I deserve to die."

"You stood up for me. For us. You might have just saved all our lives. You're better than you think you are."

"How can you possibly think that?" Tsana asked, looking up at Seri. "After everything that's happened. How—?"

"Because I believe in you."

"How can you believe in me?" Tsana was shaking. "How can you believe in me after everything you've seen me do?"

Seri hesitated. Tsana was staring at her, trembling, and she stopped herself from saying something trivial, something meaningless, because Tsana didn't need empty words. Tsana needed the truth. She thought about *why* she trusted Tsana. Why she believed in her. When she opened her mouth, the words came hesitantly at first, then grew more confident.

"I believe in you because . . . because I've seen how hard you *try*. You didn't have to come save us, back at the temple, but you did. You didn't *have* to send Asai to follow Srayan, but you did. You made mistakes, Tsana, but—I understand. If Eshai were like Srayan, I don't know that I wouldn't have done the same thing."

Tsana's eyes were wide, and Seri smiled tentatively. "I see you, Tsana. Srayan isn't the only one. I know it's not worth much, coming from me, but—"

She wasn't expecting Tsana to surge forward, wrapping her arms tightly around Seri before she could finish the sentence. Seri blinked in shock, but her arms went up automatically, wrapping them around Tsana's shoulders. Tsana was crying, her shoulders shaking with sobs even if she was trying to stifle the sound. Seri held her close, stroking her hair, letting her cry.

She felt Tsana shift, pulling her head back slightly so Seri was looking into her eyes. Brown and gold, gleaming in the sunlight. Lavit could keep his beautiful eyes, Seri thought. Tsana's were like the rainforest. Deep, enchanting, a little terrifying, but so very *alive*.

"I see you, too." Tsana's breath fanned across Seri's lips, little puffs of warm air. "You don't need to keep trying to belong. You're not alone anymore."

There was no one interrupting them this time when Seri leaned down to kiss her, deeply, with all the words she had ever thought and all the truths she could never say.

CHAPTER 24

✲

Eshai stood on the platform, surveying the approaching army. There was no other word she could use for them. They waited on the outskirts of the village, hidden beneath the tree line. She couldn't remember ever seeing a force like this, hundreds of eyes gleaming in the predawn light. Valiants stood in their positions all around the village, ready to defend them, but she could feel the tension in the air. One way or another, valiants would die today. Maybe they all would.

The village's creaking ballistae had been brought out to the forefront, those civilians and valiants that were willing given cursory training in their use. Lavit's militia also stood ready, with instructions to keep the beasts from entering the village at all costs, but they would be nothing more than a token resistance against this force.

She pulled her spear from her back, holding it at her side as she waited for the charge.

Her platform rattled as Lavit landed beside her, his expression grim with the look of someone who had done all they could and still wasn't sure it would be enough.

They didn't say a word. They didn't need to.

He drew up beside her, holding his own spear at the ready, and she made space for him.

Sunlight crested the tops of the trees, staining the dark green of the canopy with golden light. She scanned the line of beasts, looking for Srayan. Odd, how just a few weeks ago, she had been thinking about how hard it would be to lift her spear against a human. If Elaya was going to be overrun, Eshai thought, if she was going to die here, and if everything she had ever worked for was going to amount to nothing, she was damned well sure she was going to take Srayan with her.

She could feel eyes on her, valiants and villagers both. They were watching, waiting for her to say something. The weight of their expectations was crushing. She had never been a very good speaker. She hadn't chosen this life because she wanted to lead anyone into battle. She chose this life because she wanted to see the unknown world. To protect the People.

"I'm not going to tell you this is going to be easy." At Lavit's glance, she swallowed, and made her voice louder. She didn't need to shout—with helms on, the valiants would hear her— but for the sake of the villagers, she did anyway. "I won't stand here and tell you that we'll win the day. But I will tell you that this means something.

"What happens here sends a message. To Srayan, to whoever sent him, to anyone who might think like he does. And it sends a message to the people within our borders, to all the valors of all the settlements, to Vethaya, and to every aspirant that's ever dreamed of gaining armor. To all those people, we're saying that we will stand—that the People will not go down without a fight.

"When we become valiants, they tell us to be dauntless. They tell us we are the future of the People. But every single one of you is valiant, whether or not you've gained your armor. Be dauntless, Elaya!"

She wasn't expecting a response. But then from beside her, Lavit raised his spear and cried "Elaya!" and from her other side, Rukai did the same. Others took up the charge, until the air was filled with screams and war cries and Eshai's heart swelled to hear it.

The beasts charged forward, a wave of death that rushed toward Elaya. Battle horns sounded, adding to the cacophony. Entirely unnecessary, given how everyone was watching the charge, but Eshai felt the sound sing in her blood. She let out an answering shout, leaping from the platform and into the fray.

Karai's strides ate the distance between them and Elaya, the scenery flying past as they raced toward the battle. Seri bent over Karai's back with his fur in her hands and Tsana holding tightly to her shoulders. She urged him to move faster, but even then she was filled with the sense that they might be too late. The rainforest was too quiet, the usual sounds of life replaced by a stillness that chilled her blood. If she strained her ears, she thought she could already hear the battle, growls of beasts accompanied by the war cries of valiants.

Elaya, her hometown, the place she loved and hated. The place where she had been born, and where she had killed Ithim and died in her heart.

She looked down at her hands as Karai flew over the distance, as the dawn light broke through the trees. The golden tint had spread across her gloves fully now, shining in the sunlight. It touched the hem of her vest and the edges of her boots, beginning its slow spread across her body. The speed of the transformation had increased since last night. She half-imagined she could feel it moving, taking over her.

A new day was dawning.

Her nearly empty quiver bumped against her hip as they rode, a stark reminder that they were almost out of supplies. She didn't know how she could help in this fight, but she knew she had to try.

As if sensing her thoughts, Tsana's arms tightened around Seri's waist. A show of support. Seri drew in a deep breath, remembering and drawing comfort from last night's warmth. Whatever happened here, at least she wasn't alone.

"We'll stop this," Seri said.

Tsana nodded. Seri could feel that, Tsana's forehead resting against her back.

"We will."

They arrived to a scene of slaughter. Srayan's beasts had started the charge against Elaya, but they had been stopped by a line of traps just on the outskirts of the trees. Beasts howled in pain as they fell into pitfalls or raced over spiked caltrops only to be cut down by valiants. A small party had gone down to the ravine, where Srayan had sent another charge, the air thick with arrows as the defenders rained them down on the beasts' heads. And through it all, Elaya stood in the center of the carnage, the sight of the spreading tree somehow both familiar and jarring. It was smaller than Seri remembered, so small she had no idea how it would stand against this force.

On the battlefield below, beasts howled with pain. Seri felt Tsana tense at each howl, her fingers digging into the leather of Seri's vest. She could *feel* the growl Karai let out at the sound of the battle, a vibration that seemed to come from underground. It rattled her bones.

It was an awful sight. The defenders were holding the beasts back for now, but there were already armored figures lying on the ground. Dead valiants. No more than a handful, a countable number. But there would be more before this was through.

From Karai, she felt anticipation, but Karai was an old warrior. Seri felt sick to her stomach. Karai seemed to think valiants and beasts fought because they were scrabbling for territory, and most of the time that was true, but this wasn't like that. Srayan's beasts hadn't *chosen* this fight. They weren't feral yet— not all of them. Srayan wouldn't want too many uncontrolled elements in this battle, too many feral creatures that might turn on him. But even those that were not feral had still been forced into this fight by Srayan's hand. No matter what happened today, valiants and beasts would die, and there was very little she could do to change that.

Except for one thing.

Srayan was controlling the beasts. If she stopped *him*, things would end.

"There," Tsana said from behind her, her voice tense as she pointed at something in the rainforest, just behind the tree line. "Do you see him? He's there."

Seri looked, squinting. There was a human standing in the shade of the outlying trees, his head turned toward the battle. He hadn't noticed them yet.

Seri scanned the battlefield and saw one valiant rallying the others to herself, running from fight to fight, bellowing orders. She was easy to spot in her bright white armor.

Srayan and Eshai, on opposite sides of the battlefield. Engaged in a war that, if allowed to run unchecked, would destroy both of them.

Tsana slid from Karai's back, one hand on the hilt of her sword. Seri spun around, alarmed, and grabbed her by the shoulder before she could run into the mess.

"What are you doing?" she hissed.

"I have to stop him." Tsana's eyes were wide with fury and pain. "I have to do it. I can't let this go on."

"You can't go alone—"

"He's my master, Seri. I've worked with him. I know him. He might listen to me this time."

Seri looked Tsana in the eye and saw the frayed, desperate hope in them. A part of her wanted nothing more than for this to be finished without further bloodshed, but she knew that was impossible. Even if Tsana did manage to talk Srayan into backing down, Eshai and the rest of the valor wouldn't let Srayan leave alive. And Seri knew Tsana knew that.

But she also saw, looking into Tsana's eyes, that Tsana *needed* this. She needed to try one more time, just as Seri had needed to come back for Eshai and Lavit.

Reluctantly, she let go of Tsana's shoulder.

"Be careful," she told her.

Tsana nodded. Her gaze lingered on Seri for a moment longer, as if she were about to say something more.

"If I don't come back . . . ," Tsana said.

"You will."

"But if I don't—"

Seri cut her off with a quick kiss, a touch of fire that lingered on her skin when she pulled away. "You will. Whatever it is, tell me later."

Tsana held her gaze for a moment longer, then nodded. She turned away. A veil rose up around her before she had taken two steps, concealing her from sight. With a heavy heart, Seri turned Karai's head toward the battlefield, toward that figure in white. Without even needing a signal from her, Karai charged into the fray.

❦

Eshai leapt over one of the lines of caltrops, slashing out at a beast that drew too close. The blade cut through the beast's neck, sending a gout of blood spraying, but Eshai was already moving back before its companions could think about avenging it. She leapt back over the line, looking to the left and right at the valiants that waited on the other side of her.

"Nets at the ready! Don't let them through!"

A meaningless command. The beasts had already pushed through the first of the defensive rings they had constructed around Elaya. They would likely also push their way through this one. But the more they made them fight for it, the longer they held them back, the more of a chance they had.

If they were going to die here—if this was where her luck finally ran out—then they would die fighting. Eshai had promised herself that.

A roar drew her attention, and she looked up to see a great beast running straight for them, one of the white-furred felines from the valley. One of the valiants nearest her let out a volley of curses at the beast's approach, and two more readied nets. Eshai, seeing the figure pressed low against the beast's back, sounded a halt. The great beast leapt straight over the line of startled valiants, stopping in front of Eshai. Seri scrambled off its back, facing her.

Eshai looked her over quickly. She didn't seem injured, although she was clearly out of breath. The change in her armor was unmistakable now, orange-gold light covering her gloves entirely. The sleeves of her vest were tinged with it, and the light had begun to spread up her boots, starting from the soles and climbing past her ankles. She looked different, carried herself differently as she met Eshai's eyes.

Seri looked like a warrior.

"Eshai," she said.

"You've been busy," Eshai remarked, letting the others around her continue the siege. A few valiants cast wary glances at the beast behind their lines, but it clearly wasn't a threat, and there were so many others to worry about. Eshai raised a fist to ward off one of the ballistae, which had swung around to aim at the creature.

Seri glanced over her shoulder at the village, grimacing. She faced Eshai. "His name is Karai. I can tell you more about it later. What's happening?"

"We're holding them back as well as we can, but they're relentless. We managed to send out messengers, but we can't afford to wait for help."

Seri shook her head. "Srayan has scouts in the rainforest to strike messengers down. Tsana and I saw them."

"Tsana?" Eshai asked, frowning. "She's with you?"

Seri's response was to look guiltily at the tree line, where Srayan waited.

"She's gone to talk to him. She didn't want to betray us, Eshai. He captured Asai and forced her to." A look passed in front of Seri's face, confidence, defiance, and pride. Somehow, when she wasn't looking, Seri had grown up. "We got her back. Now, she's trying to talk him down. It won't work, but she had to try."

Eshai left aside the matter of Tsana's betrayal for now. There wasn't enough time, and if they didn't find a way through this, there might never be. She eyed Karai warily. He looked back at her, tilting his head up in challenge. Eshai looked at Seri as all around them, beasts and valiants died.

"What are you going to do?" she asked.

"I want to stop this. Killing the beasts won't help, Eshai—they're only being forced into this. Srayan's the real enemy. If we stop him, the battle will end."

"We can't exactly *stop* fighting," Eshai said. "They'll overrun us the moment we show weakness."

A pained look crossed over Seri's face. She nodded.

"Then we need to go after Srayan. It's the only way."

Eshai looked at the trees, at the valiants that fought around her, awaiting her command. At the bolts that sang through the air, finding their homes in beast-flesh. At Lavit, still fighting, leading the charge. At Elaya, alone and vulnerable in the center of their defenses.

She looked back at Seri and understood how this was going to play out. A few weeks ago, even a few *days* ago, she would never have accepted it. Would never have let it come to this. But this Seri standing in front of her wasn't the same Seri she had taken into the unknown world.

This Seri had known *exactly* how this was going to play out, from the very beginning.

"I can't leave," Eshai said, because the words needed to be said, even if they were just a formality. "I'm needed here, Seri." People needed heroes, needed symbols. "I need to be seen."

Seri kicked off the ground and leapt onto Karai's back in one smooth motion—when had she gotten so good at using her boots? Her gaze fixed on the tree line, where Srayan waited.

"Then," she said, "I'll go."

CHAPTER 25

֍

Karai sprang back over the line of valiants with a roar, Seri clinging to his back. Moving like this, he reminded her of his namesake, a flash of lightning. Even the other beasts made way for him as he ran, too slow to recognize he was no longer one of *them*.

Srayan's command had to be stretched thin. He couldn't give orders to individual beasts, only directions. Elaya would be a test run, the proof of Srayan's method. After this, the beasts would be set free, turned feral with only one directive.

To kill any of the People they came across.

It would be a massacre, and if they let things get that far, there would be nothing they could do to stop it.

Still, she thought, pressing herself down against Karai's back to keep as low of a profile as she could, it was one thing to tell Eshai she would go deal with Srayan herself. It was another thing to do it. She was running low on energy, on supplies, on arrows. She had very little left.

You have me, Karai said, touching her mind and filling her with strength and warmth. *I am stronger than any arrow. And you are strong, too.*

Seri hoped so. She really, truly hoped so. Because she wasn't ignorant of the stakes. If she failed to stop Srayan, then her hometown, the Elaya she sometimes hated and sometimes loved so much her heart ached, would be gone. Wiped off the map, along with herself, and Tsana, and Lavit and Eshai Unbroken, and anyone who would ever remember Ithim.

The light changed as she charged into the tree line, the canopy casting the earth in shadow. Karai didn't slow, didn't falter. Seri could hear Srayan and Tsana now, even over the sounds of battle. They were shouting at each other—or at least Tsana was shouting. She knew her voice, even if she couldn't understand the words she said. And there was another sound, punctuating their argument. An unfamiliar, sharp noise.

It took Seri a moment to place it, but it must have been the sound of their weapons clashing.

Metal on metal.

She supposed that told her how well Tsana's last plea had gone.

Seri spurred Karai onward. The air just inside the tree line was filled with the sound of war. It wasn't just Srayan and Tsana. Here, Seri couldn't ignore the sounds of valiants fighting for their lives. But just up ahead, she could see them.

Tsana and Srayan, dueling in the center of a clearing, surrounded by a ring of Srayan's beasts. They were both wielding swords, the blades drawing together and coming apart in an intricate dance so fast Seri had a hard time keeping up. The narrow blades, so much more maneuverable in close quarters than spears, parried, blocked, and thrusted as if this was what they were meant to do.

Tsana was doing all she could to hold her own, but it was clear she was struggling. Seri remembered the *enkana*'s strength from their earlier encounter and wasn't surprised. Tsana parried his attacks, but she was growing tired. She was being driven back. She wouldn't last much longer.

And then Tsana looked up and saw her.

Seri registered the moment Tsana's gaze met hers. And she saw the moment that inattention cost her.

She opened her mouth to shout a warning, but it was too late. Srayan charged in, blade raised. Tsana's eyes widened, and she turned to meet it, but she turned too late. Srayan's sword caught her in the shoulder, and Tsana let out a gasp of pain, her own sword falling to the ground from nerveless fingers. She staggered back, blood spattering the forest floor.

Seri saw red.

She could smell it—whether because of her bond with Karai or not, she wasn't sure. Coppery and thick. She let out a shout of anger and defiance, and Karai launched himself into the air without her even having to say so, crossing the distance between her and Srayan.

He leapt out of the way and turned to face Seri, the tip of his sword wet with blood. Tsana scrambled back against one of the trees, pressing a hand to her wound. Seri barely glanced at her to make sure she was all right, keeping her gaze focused on Srayan.

Srayan breathed out a sigh, his mouth curving in a grin. He raised his sword, holding it in front of him in a stance Seri thought might have been defensive. The rage in his eyes was on full display—he wasn't even trying to hide it now. With a start, Seri realized where she had seen eyes like this before, why they were so familiar to her.

Ithim's eyes, when he'd been controlled by the beast. When he had advanced on her with the intent to kill her.

The memory was so powerful, Seri almost faltered. She might have, if it hadn't been for a low growl from Karai, bringing her back to the present. That was right. She *wasn't* that same girl anymore—the one who stood back and let people die because of her, let people save her, all because she was too scared to stand out. Too afraid to be seen for who she was.

She wouldn't be that girl ever again.

"Are you here to join me after all, Seri?" Srayan asked. "I'm afraid you'll have to wait. I'm a little busy at the moment."

She thought of the horde attacking Elaya and felt a wave of fury course through her—part of it Karai's, part of it her own. And then she recognized what Srayan was doing—trying to rile her up and make her lose her focus. She loosened her hold on Karai's fur.

"I can see that," she said, fighting to keep her voice calm. "But why are you doing this? If it's because my People hunt beasts, that's because we don't know any better. We'd be willing to listen if you *talked* to us."

"Is that what you really think would happen?" Srayan asked. "How do you think that worked for your father?"

Seri hesitated, caught between the need to end this and the need to know. Srayan's grin widened at the look on her face.

"Oh yes. I wasn't lying about knowing your father. He and I were of the same Hollow. Irkhai of Vima. Do you know what his crime was, Seri? Do you want to?"

Did she?

She had told Tsana she didn't care, but she knew so little about her parents. About either of them.

"Irkhai's crime was that he killed a beast. Even now, it might have been considered justified. After all, the beast had gone mad. It was trying to kill him. But it was a bonded beast, and its death broke its bondmate. And for that, Irkhai was exiled. It was expected he would die out here, but he didn't. At least, not at first. He made his way to *this* little forgotten corner of the world, met your mother, had *you*, and then they killed him anyway."

Seri froze, because as much as she didn't want to listen to Srayan, as much as she didn't want to believe him, his words struck something in her. A memory. The sadness in her mother's eyes whenever she asked about her father, the way that none of the other villagers would so much as speak his name.

"They didn't—"

"You don't think your precious People are capable of murder? Haven't you wondered why they never fully trusted you? Do you know what sort of beast your father had, the one sent out to exile with him? It's the sort of creature Vima Hollow calls a 'soother,' a beast with the ability to read emotions. To touch *minds*. Does that sound familiar to you, Seri?"

Seri's hands shook where she held on to Karai. She remembered that beast, that beast whose heart and hide had become the gloves she was wearing. The beast that had killed Ithim, the one that had been unable to break her.

Her father's beast.

Her gloves itched. She wanted to be sick.

"A beast loses itself when its bondmate is killed," Srayan said, his voice growing oddly soft. Sympathetic. "The same is true in the reverse, and that's something your People will never understand. Your People, who are rewarded for killing beasts without so much as a thought for the lives they end. Your People, who become heroes and legends for slaughter. You don't even know the pain you cause. You can't even comprehend it."

Seri gritted her teeth. She wanted to shout that Srayan wasn't much better, that *he* was the one sending beasts out to die, but looking into his eyes, she could see the depths of grief there. The brokenness.

An *enkana* could bond with many beasts. Maybe so many he could no longer feel each one, was no longer affected when one slipped away from him. But how did one become *enkana*? To realize he had the ability to bond with many, he first had to bond with one, didn't he?

What had happened to Srayan's first beast? The one that was to him what Asai was to Tsana, and what Karai was to her. The question slipped out before she could stop herself.

"Is that what happened to you?"

"You already know the story, Seri. How did your precious Eshai Unbroken come to be?"

Seri's breath caught. Eshai . . .

Everyone knew the story, even in outlying villages as far away as Elaya. New heroes rose up so rarely that when they did, their tales were told everywhere.

Eshai—Eshai had killed a beast. A kind of beast no one had ever seen before, one with the ability to corrode armor. A beast whose size and strength changed with every retelling.

Where else could a strange beast like that come from, if not for the *en*?

"She didn't know . . ."

"Does it *matter*? Do you know how it feels, to lose one's bondmate? Can you even imagine?"

She could. She had, in fact, when she found out Srayan had threatened Asai to keep a hold over Tsana. She had looked at Karai, in the newness of their bond, and tried to imagine, if only for a moment, what it would feel like to lose him.

"They took everything from us, Seri," Srayan said, his eyes

on her. "They took your father from you, and they took my *anishien*, my Rigana, from me. They turned you into a killer. These people don't deserve your love, or your protection. They deserve to die. So stand aside, and I will end this for both of us."

Seri thought of Elaya, thought of the hard eyes and the whispers behind her back when she had returned from the forest bloody, without Ithim. She remembered that beast and the rage that had come over her as she killed it, remembered its blood on her hands. Her father's beast. She felt sick and shaken, and for a second, she was tempted to do it. To stand aside. This wasn't her fight. It had never been her fight.

But then she thought of Eshai and Lavit, and all the people she had left behind at the new settlement. Thought of four valiants, lying broken in the roots of a spreading tree, and the dead they had left in the lower branches of Vethaya. And she thought about the lantern-lit nights and golden days that she and Tsana had spent together in the city. Thought about becoming the people in her stories. About believing in heroes.

Maybe this *wasn't* her fight.

But she was here now.

"No," Seri said, staring at Srayan. She drew herself up straighter on Karai's back, closing her fingers in his fur. "No, you will not."

Srayan let out a roar of anguish, charging at her.

Seri had been expecting the charge. She let Srayan come, then pulled Karai aside at the last moment, when Srayan was in the air, his sword pointed at her throat. Srayan was strong and fast, but not even he could change direction while airborne. As Karai swept past him, Seri gripped the beast's sides with her knees, reaching for one of her arrows. She twisted around in her seat, firing the arrow before he could land.

She wasn't expecting Srayan to swipe his sword upward, cutting the arrow out of the air.

He landed on the ground and had barely touched the ball of his foot to the earth before he was launching himself at her. The full force of his weight crashed into her, knocking her from Karai's back and onto the ground before she could even blink. The blow drove the air from her lungs.

"*Seri!*" Tsana screamed.

Seri gritted her teeth, twisting out of the way as Srayan brought his sword downward. It stabbed into the earth beside her head, and she shifted her weight the way Eshai had taught her, bracing herself on the ground and kicking out with her boots. The movement pushed Srayan back and off her, forcing him to stumble to his feet.

She heard footsteps and looked up to see Tsana rushing at Srayan, her sword in her hand. Tsana made to stab at his face, but Srayan reached up with his left hand, knocking her sword arm aside. As she stumbled, he raised his sword.

Karai launched himself at Srayan with a roar, snapping at Srayan's sword arm. His jaws closed on empty air as Srayan stepped backward. Tsana seized the opportunity to back up, panting, and Seri leapt to her feet. She shot two arrows in quick succession, one at Srayan's feet to force him back, and another at his head.

He danced back and away from the first arrow, tilting his head to the side to avoid the second. It sped past him, nicking his ear before slamming into a tree trunk behind him. The wound bled, but Srayan barely seemed to notice the warmth trickling down his face. He looked at Seri, met her eyes, and smiled.

As he rushed at her, Seri reached for the quiver at her side. Her fingers brushed through the fletching of the arrows she had left—three. She reached for one precious arrow and leapt into the air, aiming the arrow not at Srayan but at the space straight ahead of him, where he would be. She drew it back and fired, her breath catching.

Srayan *disappeared*.

The arrow struck the earth unimpeded. Srayan was gone. Seri had a half-second to look around for him, before she felt his hands on her arms, his knee digging into the small of her back. That was the last thing she knew before they were falling, Srayan driving her into the ground.

She hit face-first, the impact making her see stars. Her arrows scattered as she fell, falling somewhere out of sight. Srayan's knee in her back was a point of pain, and Seri gasped for breath.

He twisted her arm behind her, not far enough to break it, but enough to make Seri aware that he *could*, and leaned down to whisper in her ear. She shifted and squirmed, trying to throw him off her.

"Did you think Tsana was the only one who could do that?" he asked. "Did you think that I wouldn't have learned that trick, too?"

Seri groaned, struggling against his weight. Karai charged him, snarling in rage, and Srayan kicked off her, shoving her farther into the ground with his leap. Seri felt a flash of pain as bright as if it had been her own as Srayan's sword scored Karai's flank, opening a deep gash. She turned her head to face the fight, spitting out a mouthful of dirt and mud.

Karai's white fur had been stained red with blood, and the wound was still bleeding. But he faced off against Srayan, undaunted.

Seri pawed at the ground for her arrows, her muscles protesting the movement. She felt fletching beneath her fingers and quickly pulled the arrow toward her but stopped when she realized it had been broken. Snapped in half like dry tinder.

There was another arrow beside her. Her *last*.

Light flashed behind Srayan. Tsana appeared for an instant, her sword materializing out of the air as she aimed for the back of his neck. Srayan turned with casual grace, drawing his arm through the air. His fist caught the side of Tsana's head. She hit the ground like a rag doll, rolling across the earth. With his sword hand, Srayan blocked Karai's swipe.

Seri pushed up to a knee and fired, but Srayan rolled out of the way. The arrow vanished into the trees. He looked at her, and Seri realized she was out of arrows, out of ideas.

Srayan grinned. "What are you going to do now?"

Her heart pounded, a steady beat. Seri turned to face the rainforest behind her. She kicked off the ground and ran.

CHAPTER 26

⚜

Branches whipped at her face as she leapt through the trees, heading for open ground. Seri could hear her heart pounding, her blood rushing in her ears as she jumped from branch to branch. She acted on instinct, without thought, without planning. All she knew was that she needed to draw Srayan out. To bring him to the killing field, to make him be *seen*, so that Srayan wasn't the one hiding in the shadows anymore. So that everyone would know who he was, what he had done.

If Srayan were being rational, he would have stayed behind to deal with Tsana and Karai first. But she knew the look in his eye. She had seen it before, in the beast that had killed Ithim.

The eyes of a predator.

The eyes of someone who would *chase*.

He would follow her. When she heard someone crashing through the undergrowth behind her, she knew she was right.

Srayan was just as strong and fast as any valiant, but he had none of their training. He was almost as bad as Seri had been, once upon a time. He crossed the distance between them, crashing toward her as if he didn't care about getting hurt, as if the branches and leaves that swiped at him were nothing more than inconveniences. They had to be scratching him, but just like the wound Seri had dealt to his ear, those little injuries didn't matter. It was as if the part of Srayan that cared about such things had died the day Eshai became Eshai Unbroken.

She saw him coming out of the corner of her eye, when she was mid-leap. Seri turned to face him, but couldn't do much more than raise her arms, crossing them in front of her face. He slammed into her with force, propelling her into the air. Seri burst through the tree line and out into bright sunlight, landing hard on the grass at the outskirts of the village. She rolled to a stop and pushed herself up quickly.

She was surrounded by the dead. The line of battle had pushed closer to the village, but there were dead beasts and valiants all around her. Her head spun as she stepped back, and she nearly tripped over a spear. Seri picked it up, holding it out in front of her in a defensive position as Srayan landed on the ground, turning to face her with a calm that belied the storm in his eyes.

When a valiant died, spears were the last of the armor to crumble away. This one was blackened slightly at the butt and at the tip of the blade, but still whole.

It was a borrowed weapon. It wouldn't last long, and it wouldn't be as effective in her hands as in the hands of its owner.

And from the way Srayan was looking at her, Seri knew he understood that, too.

He advanced on her, sword raised.

Seri sank down into a defensive stance, holding up the spear.

Eshai looked up from a particularly hard blow, one that swept her off her feet and sent her falling, to see Seri facing off against

Srayan near the tree line with a spear in her hands. Srayan was rushing at her, relentless. Seri was struggling to hold her own, blocking his strikes with the shaft of her spear. Her movements were swift, more powerful than they had been, but she was still a novice at the spear, and even from this distance, Eshai could see that it was crumbling. Seri wouldn't last very long.

A hand appeared in her field of vision, clad in blue. Lavit. Eshai grabbed it, letting Lavit haul her to her feet.

Her head spun as she stood, a sudden rush making her see stars. Lavit didn't look much better. His armor was stained with blood and dirt, and from the way he was standing, some of it was his own. His expression was grim as he watched the fight between Seri and Srayan, and he didn't release her hand.

All around them, the battle continued. Valiants and beasts died.

"I have to help her," Eshai said under her breath. "She can't do this alone."

Lavit nodded, squeezing her hand. "I'll cover for you. Go."

Eshai breathed in, tightening her grip on her spear. She could feel her attention wavering, the exhaustion she had fought off threatening to overcome her now. The distance between her and Seri, a distance that would have been insignificant any other day, now seemed insurmountable. She was fully aware this could be her end.

The last charge of Eshai Unbroken.

She took a step forward, willing her vision to steady, preparing to launch herself across the gap.

And then she stopped, her eyes wide, her attention fixed on the battle.

Something was happening to Seri.

Tsana wasn't sure how to explain it, how to begin to understand what she was seeing, but *something* was happening. She stood at the edge of the tree line, one hand pressed against the wound on her shoulder, her vision blurring and her sword hanging limply from the other. Karai lingered beside her, his protective warmth shielding her from the battle, but his white fur was matted with blood, and despite all he tried to hide it, he was limping.

She couldn't talk to Karai, not the way Seri could, but when Srayan left to pursue Seri and Karai had approached her, she understood the two of them were going to help. Even if it meant their deaths. They wouldn't let Seri fight alone.

Tsana had come here prepared to fight, prepared to die if it came to that. But now, she found herself standing at the edge of the trees, doing nothing more than looking out at the battlefield.

Because something was happening to Seri.

Srayan was driving her back, his sword moving in patterns and fluid motions Tsana had never seen before. She knew he was skilled, but she had never imagined this. If it wasn't for the frantic motions he was making, the edge of desperation in his attacks, she might have said he was one of the best swordsmen she had ever seen.

But Seri was holding her own.

Not well—not gracefully. She looked as if each strike she blocked might knock her over. She was only barely managing to turn them aside. But she was still blocking them. Even though her spear was beginning to crumble to dust from both ends, even though its once pale green color was beginning to fade, Seri was holding her own. She wielded the crumbling weapon as if it were the most important thing in the world, and despite everything, she refused to back down.

Where had Seri found this strength? Had it always been inside her? Tsana wondered how she had never noticed, and then she realized she had. Of course she had.

She had seen it in Seri from that first night in Vethaya, in the crowds. She'd seen it when Seri had sent a watchtower up in flames rather than retreat, rather than surrender.

It was breathtaking, and as Tsana watched, a change began to take hold of her.

It spread through her armor. The golden orange light that had been gathering at her gloves and boots was spreading visibly now, consuming the bluish violet it had been before like . . . like sunlight.

No. Like more than that.

Like liquid gold.

Like fire itself. Like light itself.

It spread over her armor as if it was flowing across her, until the only remnant of violet was a small streak across her back.

And then, as Tsana watched, the light consumed that, too.

There was a flash, like the world had been made complete. Srayan charged, a snarl on his lips, spittle flying from his mouth. And Seri raised her broken, crumbling spear to block it.

And then the light spread through her hands and into the spear, like a bolt of lightning. Like a flash of molten gold.

Seri didn't know what was happening.

She should have fallen long ago. She could feel the exhaustion in her limbs. Even the strength she had borrowed from Karai was starting to run out. The spear in her hands was starting to feel unsteady, its pale green color washing away. It barely had anything like a blade left, and the shaft felt like brittle bone, like it would crack and crumble if it were struck too hard.

But something kept her going. Something kept pushing her forward.

If she didn't stop Srayan here, it would never end. Even if the valor managed to defend Elaya, even if they managed to defeat the beasts, the slaughter here would be the spark that started a fire, one that would consume all the known world, and all of Tsana's Hollows, too, before it was done.

She couldn't let that happen. She had to stop Srayan.

Thinking that gave her strength. And when Srayan came at her, sword upraised, his face twisted into an ugly grimace as he prepared to deal a killing blow, Seri gritted her teeth, summoning up all that was left of this newfound strength as she raised her spear to meet him.

There was a flash. A bright light, and then it was like lightning, flowing from her hands into the spear she held. As light flowed over the spear, Seri felt something else wash over her as well.

Twin thoughts, twin hearts, so intertwined she barely knew where one began and the other ended. The first was a beast, a lean, thin hunter, like the ones that hunted in packs in the night. It had slain many humans, but it felt no guilt for that, because those humans had killed beasts in their turn. And at the end of its life, it too was slain, by a youth in mismatched armor, a snarl of rage and anger across his face as he stood over the limp form of another of his kind. And she *was* the youth, feeling both triumph and pain as she stabbed her makeshift spear through the hide of the beast. She felt everything that youth was, everything he became as he took what was left of the beast with him, as he grew in strength and power, making the pilgrimage to Vethaya and becoming a valiant. She felt his pride at the induction ceremony, his wonder at crossing into the unknown world, his pain as his comrades died in front of him. She felt his nervousness at being assigned to Elaya, and his regret at being sent to a relatively peaceful village instead of exploring the world like the rest of his compatriots. Love and loss and joy and hate and frustration. Everything a human life had been.

She understood. This was a kind of bond, too. Not the same as the bond of the *en*, not the same as her bond with Karai. But it was still a bond, not between man and beast, but between man and weapon. It was as close to the *en* that the *enshkai* would ever get.

She understood that because both of those pieces were in her. *En* and *enshkai*. Power and exploration. Knowledge and discovery. Stillness and motion. Serenity and *dauntlessness*.

She reached out for that heart, that thing at the center of the spear, at the center of this little world, and she felt it respond to her, felt it open to her the way that Karai had.

She reached for it, twisted it, and changed it.

The spear in her hands glowed with a bright, golden light. As she held it, as she took both of those wills into herself, it changed. Where it was once crumbling, it became strong.

The blade regrew itself from the end of the shaft, becoming a slender, shining thing. And before Seri could even really think about it, before Srayan could understand what she was doing, she pushed forward, slashing at him with a loud battle cry.

There was a sound like a thunderclap.

The spear became solid in her hands, the blade snapping into place. At the same time, the blow struck home. She felt the resistance in the spear as it pierced flesh. The force of her attack threw Srayan back. He fell away from her, collapsing into a heap on the ground.

The light faded. In her hands was a spear, fully formed, with a long, slender blade. The shaft was golden orange, the same color as her gloves. She gripped it to herself, breathing hard in exhaustion. Around her, the battle raged on, beasts charging the lines of valiants and pushing closer to Elaya. A few of the valiants had stopped to watch the scene, but they couldn't be distracted for long. Eshai was—

Eshai was watching her. Eyes on Seri, as if she had never seen anything like her in her life.

Seri felt a twinge of self-consciousness and looked away. She wasn't done, she reminded herself.

She started walking over to Srayan.

"Seri!" Tsana called.

Seri looked up to see Tsana stumbling over to her, still wounded. Karai was with her, and although she could feel his pain, she could also feel his triumph, and his willingness to continue the battle. And his pride. Karai was . . . proud of her.

She let Tsana catch up to her as she reached Srayan, turning him onto his back with the butt of her spear.

His breathing was coming in ragged pants. As strong as he

had been, he wasn't wearing armor. The wound across his chest, the one she had dealt him, bled freely. He might survive if he allowed them to help him. Might.

She stood over him, then leveraged her spear so the blade was pointing at his throat. Srayan's eyes focused on her, and she knew he was still conscious, still driving this battle.

"Call them off," she said.

Srayan's only response was to laugh, throwing his head back. Flecks of blood escaped his mouth, his eyes rolling back to expose the whites. Seri's hands faltered on her spear.

Tsana reached her then, looking down at her former master. She hugged her arm close to herself, saying nothing. Her face might as well have been stone.

"I mean it, Srayan. It's over. Call them off, and we'll help you."

That only made Srayan laugh harder. His laughter was loud and ragged, and he looked back at her, lips pulling back in a bloody grin.

"You think it's *over*, Seri of Elaya? No. No. It's only just begun."

A wave of unease washed over her, something cold settling in the pit of her stomach. Karai growled low in his throat, a warning. All around her, beasts stopped what they were doing, shaking their heads and thrashing like they were fighting battles against themselves.

Tsana realized what was happening first. The color drained from her face.

"No!" she said. "Stop him! He's turning them all!"

Seri's hands moved before her mind caught up. She leaned her weight on the spear, thrusting it forward. It caught Srayan in the throat, freezing his grin on his face as it slid through flesh and bone, slamming into the earth below with a wet thunk.

Srayan's eyes stared up at her, but the light in them was fading. Seri stood there, her weight resting on the shaft of the spear. There was a high-pitched keening sound in her ears, and she heard her heart thudding in her chest. Three words echoed in her mind, again and again as her stomach roiled and she had to fight to keep from retching.

I killed him.

And then Eshai's voice.

You're the kind of person who can do what she has to.

She swallowed back bile and pulled out her spear, trying not to look at Srayan's face, at the spear's bloodied edge. Across from her, Tsana was staring at her in awe, her expression touched with something Seri thought might have been fear. She could still feel the weight of Eshai's gaze on her back as she turned to face the battlefield.

Some of the beasts, the ones at the edge of the fighting, looked like they were waking up. They shook their heads, confusion in their eyes as they looked at the force in front of them and turned tail and ran. These were the ones Srayan hadn't corrupted, the ones he hadn't had time to turn feral. These ones wouldn't fight a losing battle, and they wouldn't fight a battle they hadn't chosen.

Some of them, but not the ones closest to Elaya. Not the ones threatening the city. Those were the ones whose minds were truly gone. They attacked the valiants with new fervor, their reason extinguished. The valiants rallied, but these beasts no longer seemed to care about pain, or their personal safety, no longer seemed to care that they had been fighting for hours. They attacked as if they were fresh from a rest, as if the only thing they wanted to do was kill. The valiants were tired, and there were so few of them left.

Seri looked at them, her heart clenching. They had done so much, she and Tsana and Karai, she had even killed Srayan, and for what?

She didn't have anything left. There was nothing more she could do for the valiants, or for Elaya. She wanted to fall to her knees.

Beside her, Tsana's head jerked up, turning as if she were listening to a sound on the wind. Her eyes brightened, and a smile appeared on her face. Seri looked at her, worried Tsana had snapped, too.

"Tsana?"

Tsana met her eyes, her smile widening into a grin. Seri didn't think she had seen Tsana smile like this before.

Then she heard it, coming from the rainforest. The sharp sound of a valiant's horn, followed by another, and another.

Valiants leapt out of the trees, yelling war cries as they charged the beasts from behind. Seri looked behind her, startled, and realized she recognized them. She saw Navai in his red armor, and the other members of Lavit's valor, but that wasn't all. One of them, a bearded man with dark green armor, ran straight at the beasts attacking Eshai and Lavit.

Turi.

Turi from the settlement.

A valiant in heavy red armor leapt from a nearby tree, letting out a yell of exultation as she landed on one of the beasts. Her spear stabbed through the delicate part at the base of its neck, her weight carrying her forward as she landed on the ground.

She pulled the spear out, spraying blood across the grass, then turned to face Seri and Tsana.

She was grinning. A beast clung to her shoulder, holding on to one of the spikes. Asai.

"Hey!" Raya said, waving her spear at Seri. "Give a girl a warning before you send a message like this! This little thing was almost lunch!"

CHAPTER 27

⚇

The battle for Elaya lasted until the end of the day. The beasts fought hard, harder than any creature she had ever seen. They fought without regard for their lives, as if battle were the only thing they cared about. But there were fewer of them than before, and not even Srayan had been expecting the arrival of two full valors.

What Seri remembered most was exhaustion. She threw herself back into the fight with Tsana and Karai beside her, pushing toward Raya's position. She remembered standing with Raya, the two of them lowering spears to stop a charge of beasts. She remembered Tsana's sword, whirling through the air like the wind itself as she cut down a beast that was trying to take Seri's head off. She remembered the way valiants made space around Karai as he leapt, unafraid, into their midst to fight. She remembered, impossibly, a moment where she was back-to-back with Eshai. She remembered falling. A blow caught her on the back of her vest, not strong enough to do more than bruise, but strong enough to send her to her knees. She remembered the way the world spun when Lavit pulled her to her feet.

He didn't ask her if she was all right. And he didn't try to send her away. She squared her stance the way Eshai had taught her, sinking down so she was closer to the ground. And continued the fight.

The sun reached its zenith and passed it. Tsana disappeared

behind the lines of valiants, whisked off by one of the medics to a tent that had appeared at the base of Elaya's trunk. At some point, Seri glimpsed a pair of nervous physicians suturing the wound on Karai's side. They flinched every time the beast growled in pain, but Karai never struck at them. He understood, because Seri understood, the necessity of what they were doing.

Seri lost track of time. She took a turn sitting at the back of the lines. When Eshai ordered her to rest and all but shoved her behind them, she took some food and water. But as soon as she felt anything close to rested, she came back to the fight. The battle had become important to her, something she needed to see through until the end.

Whatever else it was, this was *her* hometown. Her Elaya.

By dusk, the valor had pushed the beasts back to the tree line.

There were only a handful of beasts left, enough that she could count them on her hands. The battle was now confined to isolated pockets in the rainforest. This last bit had been left to Rukai, the valor commander, a man Seri remembered meeting only once, when she had returned from the rainforest with the heart of the beast that had killed Ithim.

The beast whose heart had become her gloves. Her father's beast.

Her gloves felt warm as she took a seat outside the medic's tent, breathing hard. She wanted to take them off but didn't dare. They had become a part of her, a messy, twisted part of her own life.

A mark for her losses.

Karai sat at a guard position beside her. Eshai had once again forced her off the battlefield, claiming that there was nothing more for her to do. So Seri sat, and drank water, and watched the last of the battles wind down around Elaya.

Her hands were shaking and her muscles were sore from the exertion. When she closed her eyes, she saw Srayan's own staring back at her. The ground was stained in blood, and the cries of valiants and beasts alike echoed in her ears, but the setting sun was starting to color the world, and fighting had slowed to the point that most of the valiants she saw were walking around with the same dazed look that she had.

They had won.

But how much had they lost? The battlefield was covered with the dead. Valiants in crumbling armor. Valiants who had died defending Elaya, and the beasts they had slain. She and Tsana had stopped the battle from spreading beyond Elaya. She had killed Srayan, so something like this would never happen again.

But would it be enough?

Would the valiants who died think it had been enough? Would their families?

Would war come after all?

She heard shy, hesitant footsteps from behind her. Seri glanced at her bondmate out of the corner of her eye. Karai's ears twitched, but he didn't growl. Not a threat. She looked back over her shoulder to see Tsana standing there, a jug of water and a package of rations in her hands. She looked down at them, embarrassed, and then back up at Seri.

"I thought you might be hungry," she said. "And Eshai said . . . She said the valiants are going to start preparing for the vigil, after a short rest."

The vigil. They would need everyone they could get to go

out into the battlefield and gather the dead. She would be surprised if tomorrow was spent doing anything other than burying them.

She would be part of the burial party, she decided, even if Eshai tried to force her off it. Elaya was her home. She had to be there.

"You and Eshai are talking?"

Tsana flushed, looking away. "Not really. She's still angry at me. But she let me apologize to her. I suppose that's progress." Seri noticed Tsana hadn't said Eshai *accepted* her apology.

It would take time. Even understanding why Tsana had done what she had, it was hard for Seri to accept. There was no reason why it should be any easier for Eshai. But they had time now. For everything.

Seri shifted, making space beside her.

"Why don't you sit? We can eat together."

Tsana took the offered seat. She hesitated, then lowered her head to rest on Seri's shoulder. Seri tensed in surprise, feeling heat rise from the point of contact between them.

"Tired," Tsana mumbled, her face turned away from Seri's. "Is this okay?"

Seri breathed out, relaxing. "Yeah. Of course."

She took the food, unfolding the banana leaf to reveal a small square of rice and a few strips of dried meat. Not exactly a hero's feast, but Seri hadn't realized how hungry she was until then. She took one of the strips and a handful of rice, chewing carefully. Tsana's warmth at her side was calming, soothing her fraught nerves. It was like the world around her had faded, dwindling down to just the two of them.

"I'm thinking of asking Rukai about my father, when this is

over," Seri said. "At the end, Srayan said the people of Elaya . . . they killed him. If anyone knows the truth of that, it would be Rukai."

"Are you sure you want to know?"

Irkhai of Vima. Seri thought back to Srayan's words and felt a shiver.

"No. I'm not. But I think I have to."

Tsana nodded. Seri watched as she picked a piece of meat up between her fingers, staring at it dubiously before taking a bite.

"I think I'm going home."

Seri let out the breath she was holding. She hadn't realized until Tsana spoke that she had been bracing for the blow. It didn't make it any easier. She tried to keep the pain out of her voice. "You are?"

Tsana nodded. "The Conclave will need a report. I'll bring Srayan's body back as proof. They need to know what was done here."

"Will they believe you?" Seri asked. She was struck by a vision of Tsana's Conclave thinking the People had murdered Srayan in cold blood. Of returning with an even larger army.

"I'll *make* them believe me. Somehow." Tsana looked down at the food in her lap, hesitating. She touched the corner of the banana leaf, bending it backward and forward between her fingers. "It . . . it would be much easier if you came with me. They might not believe me, but they'll believe anyone who's bonded to a *kuraen*."

Go. With Tsana, to the Hollows. To the place where her father came from.

Seri raised the clump of rice to her mouth, taking a bite. She wondered what Eshai would have to say about that, but more and more, she was starting to realize that while she respected Eshai, she didn't need her to tell her what to do with her life.

"Will they understand me? I can't speak your words."

"It doesn't matter. About half the Conclave speaks your language. I learned it from them."

At some point, she was going to have to ask Tsana to teach her how to speak her language. But they could handle that another day.

She was surprised to find how quickly her decision came to her. There was no hesitation, no uncertainty. This was the only thing that *felt* right. "Will it help prevent war?"

"I can't think of anything else that would help more."

"Then I'll do it," Seri said. "When do we leave?"

Tsana looked out over the battlefield, taking it in. The valiants, sprawled across the blood-soaked grass. An army of the dead.

"The day after tomorrow. After your vigil and a night's rest. I'm sure you want to see your hometown."

Seri thought about Elaya, about the bridges and platforms that had once been the only home she had ever known. Her world was so much bigger now. She didn't want to stay here for much longer. Not among these people who might have killed her father, among her memories of Ithim. The fingers of one hand brushed against the back of her glove as she shook her head. "Let's go tomorrow. I can take care of everything tonight."

Tsana finished off her strip of meat, handing the rest of the food to Seri before getting back to her feet. "I'll start making preparations, then. After everything, it's probably best I don't stay around the village. I'll come find you tomorrow."

Seri nodded, then hesitated, watching Tsana walk away. She

thought about valiants, and how they sometimes paired off out of proximity or necessity. How sometimes, relationships between them boiled down to people stuck in stressful situations who enjoyed each other's company, then drifted apart when they returned to their own lives. Was that all she and Tsana had?

They had never spoken about it, never put a name to their feelings. They hadn't talked about the future. Seri didn't know if Tsana wanted more than what they had.

But *she* did.

"Tsana," she said.

Tsana stopped walking, looking over her shoulder at Seri. Her eyes gleamed gold in the fading sunlight.

"Yes?"

"I really do care about you. I want you to know that. I don't want *this*"—she gestured between the two of them—"to end. I want to stay with you, with your People or wherever, if you'll have me."

Silence. Seri's heart dropped as Tsana stared at her, but then Tsana's lips curved in an answering smile. The smile lit up her face, like the sun coming out from behind the clouds.

"I'd like that," Tsana said. "There's an eatery in Vima. It's the closest settlement to yours, so we'll have to stop there first. It's . . . not the finest place, but it's one of my favorites. We should go there."

A warmth crept into Seri's heart. "You'll have to show me all your favorite places. When we're in Vima, I mean. And when we get to . . . wherever it is your Conclave lives."

The future stretched on ahead of them, warm and golden. There was blood on the grass and dirt on her armor, and Tsana's arm was in a sling, and Seri would be having nightmares about this for a long time, but in that moment, the future was in Tsana's eyes. In Tsana's smile. In the realization that somehow, there *would* be a future. A month, a year, two years, the rest of their lives. As long as they would have each other.

Tsana smiled and said, "I will."

Eshai watched Seri and Tsana from a distance, trying to be discreet. It didn't matter. She could have been standing in front of them, blowing a horn and doing a festival dance, and the way they were, they wouldn't have noticed. It was as if their world had shrunk down to the two of them. She wondered if she and Lavit had ever been like that. If so, it explained why her entire valor had never given her any peace about her relationship with Lavit.

She leaned back against the trunk of Elaya's spreading tree, careful of a sharp pain in her side as she raised a flask of water to her lips. Eshai tried to think about Seri and Tsana together, exploring her feelings on the subject as if she were prodding at sore muscle. She was surprised to find it didn't bother her. Even if Tsana had betrayed them, it was hard to *hate* the girl.

They were just so . . . *young.* They were doing their best.

And the road was only going to get harder from here.

Lavit settled against the trunk beside her, a flask of water in his hand. Eshai shifted to the side, giving him more room. The two of them said nothing, settling into the usual silence that accompanied the end of a battle. A silence that encompassed their thoughts—thoughts of those that had died, of survival, and what survival meant from here.

This time, their survival was nothing short of miraculous. Considering how she, Lavit, and Seri had been caught behind enemy lines, the fact they had made it out alive was incredible.

And not just alive.

Triumphant.

Lavit caught where she was looking and nodded, gesturing at Seri with the hand that held his flask. "They'll make songs about that one. The girl who rode into battle on a beast, with armor shining like the dawn." He grinned. "You have competition, Unbroken."

Eshai's response was to punch him in the side. Lightly. Lavit probably had a few hidden injuries of his own.

"She can have the attention. It's not something I ever wanted, anyway."

Being a hero in the songs had always been Lavit's dream. Eshai had become a valiant for other reasons. To explore the unknown world. To make what was unknown known again.

She leaned back, considering Seri and Tsana. Everything would change after this. An entire group of people, living out in the unknown world? Was the world even truly unknown if there were people living there? And how would the rest of the world take to learning about Tsana's People? After this, there was no way they could stay hidden. They'd have to send . . . messengers or something. Open talks. Stop hunting beasts. Otherwise, there could be *war*.

Eshai's head hurt just thinking about it. She rubbed at her forehead with the heel of her hand.

As if reading her thoughts, Lavit looked over at her.

"So," he said. "What's next for Eshai Unbroken? Heading back to your settlement?"

Eshai shook her head. "Vethaya first. We need to report back to the council, figure out what to do about . . ." She nodded at Tsana. "And then . . ."

"And then?"

Eshai looked past Seri and Tsana, at the group of valiants that huddled together in exhaustion, sprawled out on a cloth that had been laid on the ground. Raya was unmistakable in her spiked armor. She was sitting with Turi, the two of them chatting, but when she noticed Eshai looking, she raised her arm in a wave. Eshai raised her hand in acknowledgment, finding herself smiling.

Raya—taking a message from a beast and following it, rather than killing it outright. Raya and Turi, coming to save the day.

She wouldn't have imagined it. Maybe Raya was right. Maybe she did give her valor too little credit.

"I think they can handle the settlement for some time, don't you? I'm going to ask for a little personal leave. I think I've earned it."

Lavit smiled, tilting his head back. Eshai followed him, the two of them looking up at the sky together.

"You know what?" he said. "I think I'm going to join you."

EPILOGUE

꩜

Vethaya looked different after three years.

The watchtower and the lower platforms, the ones that had been destroyed in Srayan's attack, had been rebuilt, bigger and stronger than before. The lower platforms were sturdier now, built with several layers of wood and fastened to the platforms above them with thick twine. Seri recognized the design, remembered seeing the blueprints when they were handed off to the Conclave's messenger. They would be able to hold larger, heavier buildings than they had before, and looking at the collection of structures that gathered around the outer area of the platform, Seri thought some of those buildings had already been built. No longer the worst parts of the city, the lower branches might end up being one of the more desirable places of Vethaya to live someday. She felt a touch of cynicism at the thought, hoping it wouldn't mean that the people that *had* lived there would be pushed out to live elsewhere, but it was good to be back in Vethaya after so long underground. Good to see spreading trees and feel the open air again.

A patrol of valiants spotted her and waved her through, openly gaping at the beast she was riding. Seri smiled and waved back, expecting the reaction. At least they didn't give her any problems for wearing her armor. It had taken so long for the people in Astira Hollow to stop glaring at her for it. She was fairly certain they still did, but they glared behind her back, rather than to her face.

She leaned down, running a hand through Karai's fur. *You should enjoy this. There's bigger game in the wilds around Vethaya than in Astira.*

Karai snorted.

Giant rats and wildcats. When will you take me to hunt real game again?

Real game. Unbonded beasts, creatures Karai considered worthy to battle the *kuraen*. He would fit in with many of the valiants. Seri scratched behind his ear, distractedly wondering if this was why Tsana's Hollows rarely managed to bond with the *kuraen*.

"What's Karai saying?" Tsana asked from behind her, tightening her grip around Seri's waist.

"The usual. That I never take him anywhere fun."

Tsana snorted. "Barbaric creature," she said, but there was a fondness in the way she said it. Tsana had quickly gotten over her reverence of Karai, which Seri thought was well-deserved. Karai complained too much for anyone worth reverence. Seri wasn't sure he meant it, though.

I mean everything I say. Tell her that if she does not believe me, she is welcome to walk. This saddle chafes.

"He told me to start walking, didn't he?" Tsana asked.

Seri only smiled in response. *Put up with it a little longer*, she told Karai, touching the straps of the leather harness the artisans of Astira had fashioned for them. It really did make traveling long distances much easier, especially while carrying gear. She knew Karai didn't like it, though.

At her insistence, the harness had also come with a strip of leather to tie around Karai's right foreleg, marked with her People's word for lightning. His name-mark, to match hers. That, Karai wore without complaint, and perhaps a measure of pride.

We're almost there.

And after this, the hunt?

Karai's motion jostled the case strapped to the side of their saddle, reminding Seri why they had come here.

Soon, Karai, she said, looking back up at the spreading tree of Vethaya. *Very soon.*

❧

"These nuisances are a threat to our way of life," Sukuna was saying, his voice dominating the council chamber. "We should no longer accept them into the city."

"These *nuisances* have helped us rebuild our city," Anai of the Dancing Waters said, scowling in Sukuna's direction. "They bring new medical and construction techniques. The quality of life for the citizens of Vethaya has increased drastically since opening talks with these people. Only a fool would suggest that their knowledge is not an asset to take advantage of."

"But at what *cost*, Anai?" Sukuna asked. "We have always lived this way. Why should a group of outsiders change that?"

Anai's eyes flashed, and the aged councilwoman leaned forward to offer a rebuttal.

Eshai rolled her eyes from the seat she had taken in the outer ring of the council chambers, high above the space where the Council of Valor debated. She had no idea why she was still coming to these meetings. Day in and day out, it was the same—more arguments about whether envoys from the Hollows should be allowed to teach the People their language, or their medicine, or their manufacturing techniques. No one was *really* talking about what it meant to have a new group of people to talk to, to exchange information and insight with. No one was talking about what it meant for the valors, to know some beasts could be benevolent, even helpful. And no one was talking about what this meant for the second charge of the valor, the one that Eshai had taken to heart.

Go forth and make the unknown world known, for in you is the future of the People.

The future of the People.

For all Sukuna and the other councilmembers liked to throw that phrase around, they hardly seemed willing to talk about it. The longer Eshai stayed here, the more she was convinced that until they were willing to really *talk* about the future, nothing would change. The empty talk and empty promises would continue, until discontent in Vethaya grew and it became too much. Already, there were murmurs of rebellion among the aspirants. The council's moratorium on beast hunting, put in place shortly after the first envoys from the Hollows reached them, was an unpopular gesture. People were claiming the valor was trying to keep power for itself, and it was because of these half-hearted measures—paying lip service to one change while insisting that everything else remain the same—that this rift was forming.

They were like a spreading tree with something rotten inside it. They needed to tear the bark open and cut out the rot, or the whole tree would die.

"I see that look," Ushi said from the seat beside her. "Are you leaving already?"

"I have no idea why you keep asking me to attend these. It's not as if anything important ever gets discussed."

Ushi gave her the same grin that he was fond of giving her when she was a young valiant. The grin that said, *I know something you don't.* It annoyed Eshai then and annoyed her now.

"It's good for you to keep your finger on the pulse of things. Wouldn't want people to think their hero was going soft."

"Who says that?"

After all the travel she had been doing, going from village to village to ensure people knew what to expect before envoys from the Hollows could arrive, Eshai didn't think she was going soft. True, she hadn't fought a great battle or gone on an expedition in a while, but none of the valiants had. Not since the discovery of the Hollows. The last few years had been all talk and very little action.

She didn't miss the battles, but she did miss the exploration. The break was nice, but she hoped this wasn't the new normal.

"No one, of course," Ushi said. "But they might."

Eshai shook her head. "If they say that about me, I wonder what they say about you." She got to her feet, frowning at Ushi's disappointed glance. "I have another appointment. I'm expecting a guest."

"Ah," Ushi said, "our new ambassadors. Of course. Give them my regards."

Eshai nodded, touching her fingers to her heart in salute. She stepped past Ushi, heading out the door. The guards stood aside to let her pass, none of them even looking surprised at the fact she was leaving.

She stepped outside into bright sunshine. A pair of messenger birds chirped at each other from the eaves of the headquarters' main building. Eshai glanced at them. Small with dark plumage, the messengers had been another piece of the reparations made by Tsana's Hollows to Vethaya. At first, the council had distrusted them, but now, a scant two years since their appearance, they had become ubiquitous around headquarters and valor outposts. A few civilians had even taken it upon themselves to breed them for private use.

She understood Sukuna's reservations a little. Things were changing in Vethaya. It had been only three years since the Battle of Elaya, and the world was a different place. She wondered what the world would look like in three more years. One could argue that the point of exploration was to bring about change, but if Sukuna hadn't accepted that argument by now, she doubted she would be able to convince him.

She made her way toward her apartment, lost in thought.

"Eshai!"

Eshai looked up at the voice, catching sight of a flash of golden armor. Even though she was bracing herself, she was surprised. Seri had grown in the past few years. She carried herself with more confidence, less of the shyness that Eshai remembered from the first time she had met her. Her armor had settled into a golden color streaked through with orange, a half-sunburst sigil on her back like dawn cresting over the horizon. Although she still wore her armor, the Hollows' influence was clear in the rest of her clothing, metal buckles standing out sharply against the gold leather. Some sort of long, cylindrical casing was strapped over her back, resting on top of her spear. She had pierced one of her earlobes through with a metal stud, like some of the Hollows' representatives that came through Vethaya.

She looked good. They had exchanged letters over the past few years, but Eshai was surprised at how good it felt to see her in person. Whole, alive, and thriving.

Tsana was with her. She had also changed over the past few years—she no longer shrank away from Eshai's gaze. She wore armor after a fashion—light leather armor made from ordinary hide that would not impede her movements. She was wearing her sword. Asai was draped over her shoulder, drawing some murmurs from the people of Vethaya, although the citizens of the Hollows weren't as uncommon a sight around here anymore. The fact that she was with Seri also seemed to relax them. The People had made songs about her deeds at the Battle of Elaya, calling her Seri of the Dawn.

Eshai smiled, raising her hand in greeting.

"You look well," she said as she reached them. "Should I be calling you Ambassador Seri now?"

Seri cringed, her face flushing. That, at least, hadn't changed. "Please don't. I'm really just a messenger."

"It's an important position. Ambassador to the Hollows. And—" She looked over at Tsana, who was watching her from behind Seri. "The Conclave's Ambassador to the People. You two have been busy." She tried not to sound *too* jealous about that.

"Well, we get by," Seri said with an embarrassed smile.

"Where's your overgrown housecat?"

"Hunting, somewhere. He doesn't like cities—says they smell too much like people. I'll find him after we leave." The two of them clasped arms. "Eshai, it's so good to see you again."

"It's good to see you, too," Eshai said, giving Seri's arm a squeeze. She glanced over at Tsana. "Both of you." She tilted her head down the street, toward her new building. "Come on. Let's head home. I'm sure we have a lot to talk about."

Seri let herself fall behind Eshai as they moved through the city, taking in the surroundings. Even here, the influences of the Hollows were evident. Messenger birds flitted from house to house, tapping on windows and resting on eaves to sing their songs.

Lavit was standing outside the apartment he and Eshai shared. As Seri and Tsana approached, a knowing smile passed between them. Before even greeting her, Lavit glanced over at Eshai.

"Have you told her yet?" he asked.

Eshai sighed. "Not yet. They've only just gotten here."

"Told me what?" Seri asked.

Eshai shot Lavit a long-suffering look and raised her right hand for Seri to see. At first, Seri wasn't sure what she was looking at. Eshai was still wearing her glove. But as Seri watched, she undid the fastenings that held the glove in place, pulling it off.

Seri's eyes widened. Below Eshai's name-mark, she had tied a strip of braided cord—blue and white cloth intertwined into a band. Lavit was beaming, and Seri had no doubt that he wore its twin, underneath his own armor.

"*When?*" Seri asked.

"What is it?" asked Tsana.

"It's—" Seri broke off, glancing at Eshai. The valiant was smiling, but there was a flush on her cheeks. She didn't think it was possible for anything to fluster *Eshai*. "It's an engagement band. A promise to be wed. Eshai, you didn't say anything about this in your letters."

"We wanted to surprise you," Eshai said, replacing her glove.

"And we want you to be there," Lavit added. He smiled. "I don't know if any of this would have happened without you. We were thinking of having the ceremony in a few days, if you're willing to stand witness."

"I—" Seri swallowed, feeling a lump in her throat. To stand witness for a couple was a great honor, usually reserved for family. For Eshai to ask her—"I . . . well, of course. Of course I will."

"Great." Lavit cleared his throat. "I ordered some food and drinks from the market down the road. It's a little too much to carry. Tsana, would you—"

"I'll help," Tsana said, before Lavit could finish. "You two will be all right without us, right?"

"Uh, sure," Seri said. "We'll be catching up."

Eshai's new apartment was bigger than the one she had lived in on Spearwork Branch, with a spare bedroom that had been set up for Seri and Tsana. It had a few more decorative touches than her old apartment had had—Lavit's influence, no doubt. Eshai's old apartment had felt like barracks. It had all the necessities, but it had felt like temporary accommodations, with the air of a place that stood empty for long periods of time before being occupied by strangers. This place, though, this place felt like a *home*.

Eshai leaned against the dining table, turning to face Seri.

"There's something I have to tell you," Eshai said before Seri could start. "Something I learned about during the reconstruction of Elaya. It felt too important to put in a letter."

Seri shifted uncomfortably, fingering the leather strap for the case at her back. Eshai looked so serious. She had a feeling she could guess where this was going.

"Is it about my father?" she asked. "About his bonded beast?"

Eshai's eyes widened in surprise. "You knew?"

Seri nodded. "Srayan . . . told me. At the end. And I asked Rukai about it. He said my father was killed by some of the villagers who suspected him. The valor had nothing to do with it, and the murderers were punished."

Her doubt must have shown on her face, because Eshai asked, "You don't believe that's true?"

"I don't know if it matters anymore," Seri said. She'd made her peace with the beast she had killed. Her time among the Hollows had taught her that bonded beasts often rampaged when their bondmate died, and even in the Hollows, they had to be put down. But the story of her father still tore at her sometimes. Part of her wanted to march to Elaya and demand the truth, to pull the city apart until she had her answers. The rest . . .

The rest never wanted to set foot in Elaya again. But that wasn't why she had come here. And she wasn't going to let Elaya distract her from what she *really* wanted to share with Eshai.

Seri slung the case over her shoulder, letting it fall into her hand. "Let's not talk about Elaya right now. There's something you need to see."

Eshai frowned but said nothing as Seri unscrewed the top of

the case, taking out the scroll inside. She walked over to the dining table, unrolling it and using both hands to keep the edges down. Eshai looked over her shoulder, and Seri heard her faint gasp.

"Is this . . ."

Seri nodded, looking down at her creation. "It's a map. I've been working on this for the past few years. It combines our known world with the maps made by the Hollows. This is the entirety of the world we know now. The new known world."

It was more than twice as big as the map they had had three years ago. Eshai ran her fingers reverently across the scroll, tracing lines of ink, her fingers passing over the divide, the scant distance between Elaya and Vima Hollow. And then she paused, looking off at the edge of the map.

"What are those?" she asked, pointing at a set of raised ridges that bordered the map.

"They're called mountains," Seri said. "You can see them from some of the westward settlements. *Enormous* hills, Eshai, stretching up to the sky, higher than any of the spreading trees. They completely cover the horizon. Tsana's people mine the base of them for ores."

"What's beyond them?" Eshai asked, resting her hand on the far side of the scroll, where there was empty space.

"That's the thing, Eshai. No one knows. Tsana's people have never been explorers. They'll go to the base of the mountains for resources, but they've never tried to go beyond them."

Eshai paused, her hand pressing the scroll flat to the table. She looked up at Seri, and Seri saw the expression in her eyes. Curiosity. And wonder.

"It's going to take me a while to convince the Conclave that we should plan an expedition," Seri said. "And the mountains *are* treacherous—we're probably going to need to assemble some equipment from the Hollows to get all the way over them. And I don't want to drag you out of Vethaya right after your wedding. But, when all that is done, Eshai, I think *someone* is going to have to go. I can't think of any group better than the valiants for leading an expedition. So, Commander . . ." Seri grinned.

"Do you want to come along?"

ACKNOWLEDGMENTS

It takes a lot of people to get a book from idea to publication. I'd like to thank my editor, Rachel Diebel, for helping me get this book from its messy beginnings to the version you now hold in your hands. Thank you also to everyone at Swoon Reads who worked on the publication of this book, especially Jean Feiwel, the publisher, Dawn Ryan, the production editor, Mallory Grigg, the designer, and Sarah Gonzales, the illustrator who helped bring the world of *Dauntless* to life in the cover art. I also want to thank Lauren Scobell for the life-changing email that started me on this publishing journey, and all the Swoon readers who read the initial manuscript and decided it needed to be out in the world.

I'd also like to thank the Swoon Squad for their indomitable support, and my debut group, the 22Debuts, for joining me on this strange journey. I would especially like to thank Caris Avendaño Cruz for letting me talk her ear off about the cover, the title change, and everything that I couldn't share in public just yet; Sam Taylor for checking in on me during the publication process; and Aiden Thomas for their mentorship and advice. You all are the best author buddies I could have asked for.

To the Filipino book community, including Kate Heceta and too many others to name, who spread the word about *Dauntless* when it was still called *Brave*, I hope this book lives up to your expectations.

Dauntless was written during the last year of my PhD, so I would like to thank my grad school cohort at the University of Washington, who might not have read the book but who knew that I was writing and thought that was cool. I would especially like to thank Marta Wolfshorndl and Hilary Palevsky, who didn't say anything about me writing in our office in between working on my research, and Theresa Whorley, who talked me out of quitting this book halfway through the first draft, in a small conversation that means more to me than she might know. National Novel Writing Month, founded by Chris Baty, also deserves special mention, because *Dauntless* was finished during NaNoWriMo.

But before the first word of *Dauntless* was even written down, there are people who supported my writing and my dream. I'll try to list them all here, but there are so many that I'll undoubtedly miss a few. My mom, who read my first ever story when I was eight years old, and who has always believed that I would get a book published someday. My sister, Isa, who stayed up with me on many nights to help me plot out my stories. The role-players of Hyakuji High School/Shin Hyakuji High School/Shinya Academy, who grew up with me while we wrote together (including Rob, who I took home). The readers of my four (yes, *four*!) Fanfiction.net and AO3 accounts who were my first critics and my first fans. My teachers who believed in me and encouraged me to write; and my classmates, who read the first stories I ever wrote. Thank you for your help and support. It's been twenty-two years, but I finally did it.

To Rob, for being locked in with me during our first two years in Germany and still cheering me on through all of it, for doing chores when I had deadlines and listening to me whine and cry and complain about publishing and life, thank you. I could not have gotten through it without you.

To everyone who grew up wanting to see themselves in a book and see themselves in this, this one is for you. Be dauntless.